To Calery,

Rancid

Fight with love,

[signature]

Vicki V. Lucas

Rancid

By Vicki V. Lucas

©2013 Vicki V. Lucas

Published by Fiction on Fire
http://vickivlucas.com//fictiononfire

ISBN-13: 978-0615893945
ISBN-10: 0615893945
Also available in eBook publication

PRINTED IN THE UNITED STATES OF AMERICA

$16.99

Acknowledgments

For Cassidy

You came into my life during the writing of this book. You have brought more joy, love, and wonder than I could ever have dreamed possible.

I love you so much, baby girl.

And...

For Cade

You are my best friend, an amazing husband, and an extremely awesome Dad. Thanks for your help, encouragement, praise, feedback, and everything else you do.

I love you with all my heart.

CONTENTS

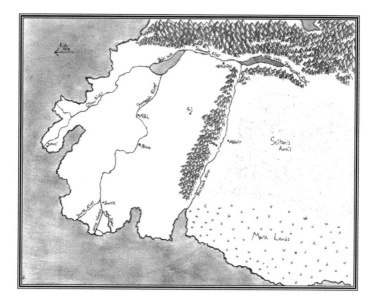

AWAKENINGS

*"The words we hear while sleeping resound
within us when we are awake."*
~STRACHAN DALYEL

A jolt shot through the earth directly below
Northbridge. Jehun groaned. He had just examined
the area underneath the city beside the Razor
Mountains thoroughly. It was his habit to do so
before the annual horse races ever since Adoyni had
given him the responsibility to ensure the safety of
the humans on top of the soil, and Jehun took his
duty very seriously.

He knew from experience that whenever large
gatherings of people occurred, they broke everything
in their paths as they tromped around, never
thinking about what was under their feet.

What were they doing now to cause him more
pain and work?

He forced himself to ignore the new problem
and look at the damage caused by the poison in the
water. He was horrified as he rolled through the
loam. He had worked endlessly to get the soil soft
and enriched with nourishment for the seeds to
grow, but the poison from the water had seeped into
the dirt and stripped the ground of life.

It almost made him sick to look at it. His hard work was ruined, completely wasted because of one heartless person's actions. And who would clean it up? Of course, it would be left to him to fix. It always was.

The poison spread through almost all Eltiria, stretching as far south as the city of Souchrie. Every creek, stream, and river was saturated. Vile toxin had soaked through the soil, killing every root in its path.

He only explored for a short time before the ruin was more than he could handle. Everything he did was always messed up. Couldn't people for once respect his work and take care of things on their own?

He dove deep down to the walls of the inner core to look for leaks of lava. He loved it there because it was impossible to hear the humans over the roar of molten rock.

Halfway through his underground inspection, he spotted scorching liquid metal flowing out of the walls. The earth searched for something to block the flow while he fretted about the mess it was making.

It was another thing for him to clean up, but if he didn't, the molten metal would escape to the surface and destroy the humans in its path, not to mention that it took forever to clean up hardened lava.

As he worked, he wondered if they realized that he wasn't an ordinary caretaker. He saw a boulder and pushed angrily on it but jerked back when he heard a voice.

"Take the magic from my heart."

He never heard anyone here, other than Adoyni. Besides, this voice was too deep and harsh to be Him. Jehun ignored the words and shoved the large rock with all his might, but the boulder refused to move.

He just wanted to be left alone. People were always hollering for help. He was constantly doing one thing after another like moving rocks, breaking up the top soil, and diverting poisonous gases.

It wasn't that he minded helping. He liked lending a hand when he had the time, but he had so much to do. Spring was almost gone, and he still wanted to divert that underground river into a waterfall in the mantle.

Jehun felt bad for the people. He really did. But he was busy. He was doing his best to make sure the toxin didn't spread further into the earth.

So, he had to sacrifice what he wanted to do, once again, and clean up another problem that wasn't even his in the first place.

He knew Adoyni kept calling, and the farmers were giving up hope of crops, but he didn't have time to answer. He'd help them when he had time. They would have to wait.

The strange voice came again.

"Tear Northbridge apart."

Northbridge? Jehun stopped pushing. A tremor of pain directly under the city followed the words. As he rushed from the inner core to the north, he wondered who would have the authority to speak into the deep parts of the earth.

As he entered the mantle where the pain was the strongest, he was rocked back by a force of power. The layer of rocks directly underneath Northbridge was trembling as a thin line appeared out of nowhere and shot straight north under the city.

The humans were a short distance up through the mantle. The annual horse racing was in full swing. Thousands of people had descended upon the city to test their horses in all sort of races. Others gathered to sell their goods, gamble, entertain the crowds at night, or steal from others' gain.

If the crack grew any bigger, the rocks would split and create a chasm in the center of Northbridge, killing hundreds of people.

Jehun threw himself into action. He scrambled to find rocks, clay, or loose gravel to fill the gap. But the rift grew faster, as if a large axe was slicing through the rocks without any effort. He worked feverishly, trying to ignore the increasing pain, but the space continued to enlarge.

Adoyni, I need your help! Jehun called over and over, but to no avail. It didn't seem possible for him to stop the destruction. Everything he tried was demolished before he could finish, but Jehun persisted in his fight. Where was Adoyni?

In his frantic struggle, there was another bolt of pain. This time it was sudden and fast like lightning.

He gasped, unable to move in the agony. But as he examined the damage, the gap expanded into a wide breach in the mantle.

Jehun shook off the pain and shoved more dirt at the split, but before he could do much, the crevice extended so large there was no hope of saving the city.

Buildings began to tumble in the south end of Northbridge. The sound of lumber crashing and screams grew louder as the poorer section of the city vanished into the crack that had sprung out of nowhere.

Some people tried to get to safety, although they didn't know which way to run. Some stood still, either frozen with fear or uncertain of what was happening.

Jehun was paralyzed. He could only watch as those he was supposed to protect were lost into the earth and swallowed up to their death as the crevice continued to grow through the city.

As he watched, he knew this wasn't normal. Earthquakes never left a gaping hole in the soil. He writhed in agony, and he felt the cold chill of fear. Someone, other than Adoyni, had enough power to tear the foundations of the world apart.

The last temple of Adoyni broke into pieces before tumbling into the abyss. The air was filled with the rumbling sound of buildings crashing against each other. Carts and wagons slipped into the gap as the horses whinnied in their fright and frantically tried to get to safety. People shrieked as they clung to each other in their homes, only to scream in horror as entire houses tumbled into the earth.

When the shaking finished, Jehun was filled with shock which numbed the pain for a brief time. A large canyon stretched from north to south for miles, splitting Northbridge in two.

The Temple of All had survived, but the center of the large city was gone. He wondered if it was possible to count the number of humans who had died in the quake.

Only Jehun could hear the cries of the fallen people. Trapped by rubble and debris, they screamed in pain and terror. But he knew they were too far down to be rescued. The walls of the chasm were steep and treacherous. Any rescuer would risk certain death by trying to descend.

Jehun shuddered and deep sorrow welled up in his heart. Never had he known such pain existed. Despair joined the suffering, and he forgot about the small leak of liquid metal as it began to pour out of the inner core.

CHAPTER ONE

Stoned

The first time Kai heard the noise, he dismissed it as his imagination. But when it happened for the fifth time, he couldn't ignore it anymore. He stopped walking, every inch of him praying that he was wrong about what he had heard.

He wasn't. The sound floated down the dark stone hallway to him again. It reminded him of a leather shoe scuffing against a rock or a pelt scraping against a tree, whispering through the silence.

It was so quiet he would've missed it if it wasn't the first sound he'd heard in a while. Although he should have been overjoyed to hear anything, the eerie sound started his heart racing, for he knew one thing. He was not alone.

The smoke from the smoldering torches on the walls made his eyes sting as he peered down the gloomy hallway. Hollowed out of sheer black rock, the weak light revealed very little to encourage him.

Stretching ahead, the corridor continued for fifty paces and then turned to the left. The way behind Kai was not much better. It was roughly ten paces until it twisted to the right.

But looking forward or behind was better than looking down. The floor was littered with skulls and bones of humans. Every so often he'd have to step over the skeletons that blocked his path.

When his foot hit them, it caused a grating sound that sent shivers down his body. *Am I going to end up like them?* He stepped over a bone that looked like a human leg and curled his lip in disgust.

Where am I? How'd I get here? Kai's head almost grazed the ceiling as he turned in a circle, and he hunched slightly without thinking about it.

As he studied each direction, he fingered the hilt of the sword hanging off his belt as if he was waiting to draw it. His fingers tightened around the hilt, finding comfort in the smooth feel of the metal.

He wanted out. Now. There was a feeling about this place like something really bad was going to happen. A sort of eerie silence hung in the air as if no one else in the world existed. The stillness only allowed the questions to build up in his head louder with each passing moment.

He racked his brains for an answer to explain what had happened, but there was nothing to give him any clues.

The last thing he could remember was standing in the courtyard and watching Eladar, the large Archippi, fall dead to the ground. The memory of the white horse lying in the dirt with his powerful wings motionless filled him with grief and anger.

He shook his head. There wasn't time for this. He had to get home and find a way to cure

Rhiana. Then he had to find Shona before something bad happened to her. He'd deal with Belial after that.

Before he could do all that, he had to find out where he was and what was happening to him. *Should I go forward or back? Which way leads out?* He took two steps forward, but indecision filled him, and he stopped. He'd been dreaming the last time something this weird had happened to him. Perhaps this was a nightmare.

"Wake up," he whispered. His voice bounced against the walls and fell to the floor. He cringed at the volume of his words.

There was no change. *This has to be a dream! I just can't wake up.* There had to be a way to jolt himself back to the real world. He spied a small rock lying beside the wall of the passageway and picked it up. *If this works, then it won't hurt at all. If it doesn't work, then I'm an idiot.*

Gritting his teeth, he slammed the rock into his left hand. "Stallion stalls!" Kai dropped the rock and gripped his fingers, feeling the warm blood. He poked gingerly at the wound. It stung to the touch. He remembered Taryn yelling at him for dumb swear words. *He's right, too. But I'll never tell him! What would he say? Stars above?*

With a groan of frustration, he returned to where he'd been standing before. Pausing for a brief moment, he strode down the passageway in the opposite direction. His steps slowed to a stop as he glanced back the way he had come.

Whichever way I choose, it will be the wrong way. Then I'll have to come back all this way. Even though he felt that a wrong action was still better than inaction, he couldn't make a decision.

The silence was broken by that sound again. His pulse quickened as his fingers subconsciously tightened further on the hilt. It came again. A bit closer this time.

"Taryn?" he whispered. He suddenly felt stupid. It was probably either Taryn or Lizzy coming back from scouting out which way to go. But why did he send them and not go himself? "Lizzy? Is that you?"

The only answer was silence. He held as quiet as he could and wished to still his loud heartbeats. The strange shuffle started again. Then over the steps came a low rumble like a bear's growl turning into a roar. Goosebumps ran down Kai's back. It wasn't a bear. It was human.

Kai drew his sword and glanced at the blade in the dim light. Etched into silver was the word *Failure.* That wasn't right. *The word should be...should be...* He couldn't remember what the word used to be. Maybe he dreamed it was something different. *But failure?*

He wasn't a failure. He had purified the water and saved Eltiria. *Didn't I?* All he could recall was Eladar lying dead in the dirt. *Did we fail at cleansing the water?* He fingered the edge of the sword carefully like it was going to disintegrate any second.

The sound was closer. Kai decided he'd figure out what was wrong with the blade and what happened to him later. He turned and ran quietly away from whoever was coming down the hallway.

He dashed through the twists and turns of the corridor, but when his breath started to come in gasps, he paused to listen. Over his panting, he heard the same noise as before. A slow shuffle. It was still behind him.

Running wasn't doing any good. He turned one more corner, planning to spring a trap on whatever was behind him. The torches on the wall made his eyes water as he squinted to see a door halfway down the hallway.

He trotted to it, hope surging through him. The door knob was a rock crudely fashioned into a handle. He pulled. The heavy door slowly opened like it was reluctant to reveal what was behind it. He tugged on it just far enough to slip through. It was difficult to shut it, so he left it ajar and slipped into the shadows until he heard voices.

CHAPTER TWO

Not a Mouse

Kai slipped through the door and hid behind a pile of rocks while his eyesight adjusted to the brighter light. When he could see, he peered around the boulders. He was in a large room hollowed out of the stone like the hallway. On the far end of the room was a large opening. He gasped.

There was clear blue sky. He must have been in some sort of cave, but now he was out! He could already feel the soft breeze and the sun on his face. He barely stopped himself from running to the opening when he remembered the two voices he'd heard.

His muscles cramped, and as he shifted, he caught sight of two tall shadows that filled him with dread. He knew those shadows. They were Seekers.

He studied the creatures, readjusting his grip on his sword. He'd beaten them once with Taryn and Lizzy. Why couldn't he do it again? *But two against one?* He swallowed. *Every time I need Taryn, he runs off, leaving me to handle things.*

The Seekers wore dark cloaks that seemed to radiate evil. On their belts, they each had an axe.

The one farther away wore a sword down its back. Since their hoods were down, Kai could see their faces. Although they bore a resemblance to humans, their faces were too wide to look at comfortably. The skin was pale white and looked like it could crumble off in chunks.

Yet Kai was drawn to their amber eyes. Void of any emotion, they pulled him in and made him feel like a mouse waiting for the hawk to descend on it. He tore his gaze away and tightened his grip on the hilt. He was no mouse. Not anymore.

"Are you sure this human will come, Volundr?" The first one asked with a touch of impatience.

"The Master said he will." Volundr fingered his axe as if he was eager to use it.

"I still can't believe our Master would trust someone like that. I won't trust him. I don't care what the Master says. Besides, with Adoyni..."

"Adoyni!" Volundr snorted. "What can He do? He hasn't been around Eltiria for years. I'll have no problems handling this human. And, once he is broken, he'll be a useful slave. You have nothing to fear from Adoyni." The last word came out like an insult.

"The Master said to make sure he turns. We can't let him die."

"Do you think I'm stupid?" Volundr yelled as he drew the sword off his back. "Do you think that I wouldn't remember the Master's orders, Torleik?"

"No," Torleik cowered. "It's just that...that... the Master was very angry. If we mess this up, it will be our heads."

"That's why he put me in charge." The voice was as sharp as the blade of his sword. "Because I won't ruin this. I have plans. Plans only the Master can help me achieve once the rotten Archippi are taken care of. All of it hinges on this human, both for me and the Master."

Kai took a deep breath, unaware that he had held it so long. *Who were they waiting for?* His leg cramped and he shifted impatiently. But his foot protested at the sudden movement, and he lost his balance.

Scrambling to keep from falling, he grabbed a rock. It pulled free from the pile as he recovered. A pebble rolled off the edge and clattered away. He froze as a small avalanche tumbled to the ground.

The Seekers whirled around to the door. "Where did you come from?" Volundr growled. "You shouldn't be here."

Kai leaped to his feet and charged them. He stumbled as he started to dash across the cave. Volundr snarled and shoved Torleik aside. He met Kai's attack calmly, smoothly blocking Kai's blade in midair with his sword as he stepped in Kai's path.

Kai yelled and feinted left. The Seeker didn't take the bait. Kai struck at the monster's legs, only to be blocked again. He had to get past them and get out of there.

He rained as many blows on Volundr as quickly as he could and pressed forward, but there was no budging. It was like getting a boulder to move.

Volundr laughed. The cold mirthless sound echoed off the walls. "A few more steps, little one, and you'd be free. Enjoy that blue sky, if you can see it." The monster moved forward.

Kai did all he could to stand his ground, but he couldn't hold it. He backed up a step and continued pressing his attack. The Seeker met every blow with skill and ease.

"I'll hack you to pieces," Kai yelled.

Volundr laughed in response. Kai grew angrier. *Doesn't it know what I can do? I killed one before. I can do it again.* He attacked with all the strength he had.

The Seeker blocked it again and smoothly pushed Kai back another step. *Two more steps and I'll be back in the hallway!*

He struck again, hoping for the speed of his sword to come like it did when he sparred with Alyn. But it never came. *I did it before, why won't it happen now?*

The Seeker lunged at Kai. Caught up in his thoughts, he forgot about the cave entrance and leaped away from the blade. Volundr quickly followed as Kai was pushed off balance.

"Too easy," Volundr said with a touch of regret. "They always are." With that, he deflected Kai's sword and used his massive arm to shove Kai through the door.

Kai tripped and fell onto his back. His sword clattered to the ground a few feet away as Volundr spat on him. He rolled aside to dodge the Seeker's attack and sprang to his feet, trembling with rage.

He heard a noise that sounded like a door slamming shut.

When he turned around, his fury was replaced with confusion and frustration. The door was completely gone. All that was left was the same cramped hallway with the endless stone walls.

He could no longer suppress a yell. "Where am I? Get me out!" The words echoed repeatedly through the hallway and slowly faded away with no response. He groaned, stumbled down the stone corridor a few steps and then screamed as loudly as he could.

"GET ME OUT!"

CHAPTER THREE

Drugged and Dying

A scream sharper than a shrill high note of a song pierced through the darkness. Lizzy jerked awake as her heart quickened. *Seekers!* Fear washed over her like a sudden flood, but her eyes refused to stay open.

She struggled to wake up and force herself to move. Yet her arms and legs wouldn't budge. Panic gripped her as she imagined what unseen horror was causing the shriek.

For a minute, she thought she was still with her parents. The yell sounded like a cougar she once saw trapped in a tree by dogs. But somehow she knew this screech was human. She could hear the terror as the cry echoed around her.

It was the sound of something cornered but not yet ready to give up. She fought to keep her eyes open and tried to see something, anything, that would tell her what was attacking.

She glimpsed a small light off in the distance growing close. *Eladar!* She almost smiled. The white Archippos would chase away whatever evil was close. Her eyes closed as she remembered how the winged horse had fallen to the ground covered with blood. Tears she couldn't wipe away streamed down her cheeks as she recalled the instant he took his last breath.

She pried her eyes open again, trying to clear her head. *Why can't I wake up?* The light blinded her as it grew from the size of a small candle to a large torch. Huge shadows reminded her of Seekers. Her weariness disappeared with horror, and her scream joined the other in an eerie harmony.

The other scream changed to shouted words filled with a tinge of panic and hysteria. "Where am I? Get me out!" It repeated, each time growing stronger with terror.

Lizzy stopped screaming. The voice, although strained with fright, was strangely familiar. The name and face that belonged to the voice drifted away before she could grasp it as her eyes began to close again. She struggled to stay awake.

"GET ME OUT!"

The words shot through her, and her eyes snapped open with realization. Kai! It was Kai screaming! *What's happening?*

During their travels, while fighting Unwanteds and Seekers, and battling Belial, she'd never once heard such panic and fear in his voice.

She struggled to get to her feet, but her body wouldn't respond. The blanket around her acted like ropes holding her down no matter how hard she thrashed. Kai stopped speaking and returned to his unearthly shouting which made her even more petrified.

She grimaced as light shone brightly in her eyes. Through the shadows, she saw Kai covered in a blanket. He jerked in convulsions. Someone on the far side held his arms down as the other person reached for a flask.

Kai fought as they forced the liquid down his throat. He choked and demanded to be let out. Lizzy watched helplessly, fighting the urge to sleep, as the red liquid spilled out and slid down his face to his throat.

The screaming ceased and turned into moans. His spasms subsided and soon he was quiet. Lizzy could hear shallow breathing in the stillness. *They drugged him.* She shook her head. *I bet they drugged me, too. That's why I can't wake up.*

"It's not working." A girl's voice broke the silence. Although spoken softly, the words echoed through the shadows. "Nothing works. And we don't have much time left."

Lizzy heard a deep sigh. She hoped it was Taryn, but as soon as the voice spoke, she knew it wasn't. She recognized the voice but couldn't remember why. As he began talking, she strained to remember who he was.

"But now that we are here, away from the Archippi, we can try other things." The deep voice was filled with despair. "You know what we have to do if we lose him."

"I can't do it." The girl responded with a tremble in her voice. "We're trying to heal him. We're not..." Silence filled the room until Lizzy started to drift off, but she jerked awake when the girl continued. "We're not...*that.*"

"We promised." The second voice was laced with anger.

Lizzy caught her breath. *That's Aric! He was here when we arrived at Merrihaven.*

He continued talking. "The Archippi were already going to do it."

The girl's voice shook like she was close to crying. "I wish that we'd never agreed to it. It's horrible, trying to cure him, and then...then... What kind of people does that make us?"

"Stop!" The word snapped like a whip. "We had to try." The words were filled with regret. "We have to face the fact that we might fail him, even after all the fighting he's done."

"How much time does he have?"

No one spoke for a long time. Lizzy opened her eyes to see the girl washing the red liquid away from Kai's face.

Aric cleared his throat. "I don't know. Maybe one or two days."

Lizzy gasped and sat up. Pain shot through her head as waves of dizziness threatened to overtake her. She groaned and lay down, pressing her hands to her forehead. Strong arms pulled her arms away, and a cup was placed on her lips.

"Just a sip," the girl said.

She struggled, but she was too weak to do anything. Liquid poured into her mouth while she tried to say that she didn't want it. The sweet medicine gagged her as she choked it down.

There was a shuffling to her right. "Where do you want this?" The voice sounded like it belonged to a young boy.

Aric turned away from Lizzy. "Right there. And that pack of blankets can go down to the tents.

Why did you demand we bring that stupid tub, anyway?"

"I don't know. It seemed like the right thing to do at the time. Maybe we'll need a bath before this is over," the girl said. She turned back to Lizzy. "There now. It's not that bad, is it? One more time."

The cup was placed back on her lips, and this time she was too tired to protest. She swallowed obediently as her eyes closed, too heavy to lift again.

"Sleep now," the girl whispered

Lizzy fought to stay awake. This wasn't the time to rest. She had to find out what they were talking about and save Kai, but she couldn't keep the sleep from sweeping over her. She drifted off while Aric and the girl continued talking.

"He has a high fever again," the girl said.

Aric spoke up. "He's losing this battle. He's got to fight harder."

"He may be fighting as hard as he can. It's just not enough."

CHAPTER FOUR

Take a Breath

Lizzy couldn't move as a large Seeker swung at her with a bloody axe. She screamed as the scene shifted. Rica, her older brother, stumbled away from her, covered with blood. She couldn't remember why, but she knew she had wounded him. He never looked back.

She winced as a large white horse flew with wings outstretched past her. His neck blossomed into red blood, and he fell to the ground dead.

"Eladar!" She sat straight up and groaned as the movement made her head spin. She carefully lay back down before she passed out.

Opening her eyes slowly, she stared at the scene around her. Soft light from the sun on the horizon filtered in and lit up the cave around her.

A thick woolen blanket underneath her was spread over a carpet of thick sand. To her right, the yellow stone walls of the cave opened wider to reveal blue sky and tips of trees.

All she remembered was arriving at Merrihaven before collapsing. She peeked under the red blanket covering her. She was dressed in a white cotton nightgown that was wrinkled and dirty. *How'd I get into this?* She groaned softly. *Oh, no.*

I'll die if he changed my clothes. He acted like a healer, but still he's... She couldn't finish the thought. She was blushing just thinking about it.

She glanced around to take her mind off *that*. The sun was low, but she didn't know what direction she was facing. She sat up slowly, feeling the blood pound through her as she moved.

Everything looked exactly the same as the first time she woke up, but it felt like she'd slept a long time. Kai was quiet and pale in the bed beside her. *What is wrong with him? Why's he so pale?*

Aric and the girl were out of sight. *I'm going to scream until they come back and tell me what is going on. Maybe Taryn knows what's...Where* is Taryn? She glanced around the cave. *Surely he didn't die!*

She remembered him holding his arm funny, but she'd been too consumed with Eladar's death and Kai's injuries to notice Taryn. *I didn't even get to say goodbye.* Tears rose as she swallowed. *What if Kai dies, too? Eladar said not to trust the Archippi, but surely they didn't kill Taryn. Did they?*

She threw off her blankets. Even if she had to crawl, she was going to find someone to tell her what was going on.

But first she was going to check on Kai. She stood up and adjusted the white nightgown to hang straight. The sand was cold under her bare feet.

She took a small step. Her legs trembled as she hobbled closer to Kai. The three steps to reach

Kai's bed took more out of her than the whole trip through Seiten's Anvil, that horrible black desert.

She sank gratefully onto his blanket, smashing his hand as she sat down. She forced herself up and moved his arm over his stomach.

"Kai? Are you awake?" she whispered. Maybe he was playing a joke on her. He never moved.

His face was bleached white, erasing the tan and sunburn. There were cuts and scratches over his arms and hands, and a large bruise below his eye.

She put a hand on his chest. *If he wakes up now, I'll scream from fright, and he'll never let me forget it.* She waited for his reaction, but he didn't even moan.

She started to want him to scare her. His breathing was shallow, and there was a long pause in between, like he was forgetting to inhale. She resisted the urge to pound on his chest.

"What is going on, Kai?" she asked. Her voice was shaky like she hadn't used it for a while. She cleared her throat. "You were wounded when we got here, but there's no reason for you to be like this. Wake up. Please."

She blinked back tears. All she wanted was for him to wake up and call her Lizard-Breath again or yell at Taryn about something dumb.

I did so much to purify the water, and now Dad's probably dead from the earthquake. Eladar died, I don't know where Taryn is, and Kai's going to die, too. She wiped away the tears, but two more replaced every one she dashed away.

She took her hand off of Kai's chest and used the sleeve to dry her face. When the tears were gone, she glanced back at Kai. *Is he breathing?*

She shook her head. Of course he was. She was imagining it. She put her hand back on his chest for reassurance and waited. Kai never moved. She leaned closer and tried to feel the slightest movement. Nothing happened. She heard herself screaming as she realized he really wasn't breathing anymore.

CHAPTER FIVE

Screams of Salvation

The dark-haired girl rushed into the cave with Aric on her heels. Lizzy jumped and stopped screaming as they raced to her. Fear was on their faces as they sped to Kai.

"He's not breathing!" she said, panicking.

Aric scooped her up and placed her gently on her blanket. "You're freezing." He pulled the covers up and patted her arm reassuringly, but the look in his blue eyes chilled her more.

He doesn't think they can save Kai. She huddled under the red blanket as she watched the girl kneel down in the sand and try to find Kai's pulse.

The girl's black hair fell over her face as she felt for a beat. She pulled back impatiently and twisted her hair back into a bun. She glanced at Aric, shaking her head slightly. Her large dark eyes were serious.

Aric didn't say a word as he began to press on Kai's chest, trying to make the heart beat once again. Aric paused, and the girl pressed her fingers against Kai's throat for a few seconds and then shook her head again.

Breathe, you idiot! Lizzy pleaded silently as she watched Kai. *If you die, I'll beat you senseless!* She counted with Aric's compressions. *One, two, three, four. When will they say there's no way he'll come back? Seven, eight, nine, ten. Oh, please don't die!*

Aric stopped to rest. He was breathing heavily like he'd run a mile. The girl felt Kai's throat again as Lizzy bit her lip. *Please don't die. Please don't die.*

The girl held still for longer this time. After what seemed like an eternity, she sighed with a slight smile and nodded.

"I feel a pulse. It's gaining. I think he's coming back." She moved her hand to his nose. "I feel him breathing, too." She sat back with a deep breath. "He sure is a fighter."

Aric rubbed his forehead. "He needs to be, if he's going to survive…"

The girl shook her head quickly and glanced at Lizzy. "Looks like someone's awake."

Aric turned and smiled, his dark brown hair falling into his blue eyes. "Thanks to your warning, we got here in time."

She pulled her hair back. "What's happening to him? And where's Taryn? He's not…he's not…" She couldn't let herself to say the word, but it hung in the air. *Oh, Adoyni, please don't let him be dead.*

The girl chuckled, her serious eyes starting to twinkle. "No, he's not dead. Although he probably wishes he was."

Lizzy nodded. She wasn't going to trust her voice not to break or shake as relief poured through her. *But why haven't they answered my questions about Kai?*

"Why don't we head outside so Kai can get some rest?" Aric asked and grabbed a cloak that was thrown over a large metal tub.

She cautiously got to her feet with the girl's help and saw soft tan shoes by her bed. The sand on her feet refused to come off, so she gave up and slipped them on. She awkwardly slid into the forest green cloak Aric held for her and took a small step forward.

"I can carry you," Aric offered.

Lizzy's face grew hot. *Oh, I couldn't bear it if he carried me!* "I can walk."

A smile flashed over his face, and his blue eyes twinkled. "Don't you remember when you arrived here? You walked to the gates of the hospital and then collapsed. When I came to pick you up, you kept saying that you could walk. It was the last thing you said before you passed out."

She slightly smiled. "Where are we now? How'd we get here? And what about Kai? Will he be okay?"

"I'll watch him," the girl hovered over Kai. "I don't feel comfortable leaving him alone right now. You can talk without disturbing him out there. " She took out a silver flask and leaned over to pour it down Kai's mouth.

"What is that?" Lizzy asked, suddenly suspicious of what they were giving him.

"Something to help him sleep. He's been pretty violent, and we hope that by keeping him resting, we can help his body fight what is wrong with him. Thanks for watching him, Rev." Aric offered Lizzy his arm.

Lizzy decided leaning on him was far better than being carried, so she accepted. She hobbled through the sand past the metal tub and packs on the far side of the cave. She saw the tips of her norsaq and darts poking out one of the canvas bags. There was Kai's sword, but Taryn's shield seemed to be missing.

She slowly made it out of the cave and crumpled onto the nearest large rock. Her legs were as weak as soft noodles, and her heart was racing like she had run from an army of Unwanteds. That was a feeling she was all too familiar with.

They were camped in a cave on the side of a mountain as high as an eagle flies. The mountains flowed down to the hills and prairies far below them, only to rise on the far side again. She had a hard time deciding where the far mountains ended and the sky began. *Isn't this most girls' dream, being stuck somewhere with Aric?* But all she wanted was to know what was wrong with Kai and where Taryn was.

As Aric brought a blanket and put it around her, she smoothed down her hair. *I must look a mess! If Mother knew who I was with, she'd die a thousand deaths!*

Lizzy giggled when she pictured the look on Mother's face if she ever got a chance to tell her. Aric sat down on the ground next to her, stretched out his long legs, and raised his eyebrows. She sobered. *Not sharing that thought with him!*

Lizzy nodded. "Are we still in Merrihaven?"

"Yes, we are." Aric turned back to her. "I don't know how much you know of it, but there's a number of islands up here. We are on Bitha. You got here four days ago. It's now the morning of the fifth day." He gestured off in the distance.

The sun rays, pink around the clouds, broke over the tall mountains. The meadows were filled with all kind of flowers surrounded by a lush forest. Along the mountains to her left, a breathtakingly waterfall tumbled down the cliffs and flowed through the meadows.

"It's gorgeous," she whispered. But the picturesque scene couldn't drive away the questions. "What's wrong with Kai? Is he going to get better?"

Aric stared at the sunrise like he never heard her. "First, let me tell you how I got here. Then I'll answer your questions. Are you warm enough?"

His tone left no room for argument, and she didn't feel comfortable arguing with him. Something was wrong – terribly, awfully wrong.

And for some reason, Aric wasn't telling her everything that was happening. Aric waited until she nodded and then started speaking.

CHAPTER SIX

Charming Traits

I guess it's fairly common knowledge what my life was like while growing up in Medora. So, let me just say that while I had everything I ever wanted, I wasn't happy.

Now I know what I really wanted and needed wasn't more things, it was time with my parents that I desired more than anything. And I rarely got time with either of them.

I say all that to let you know I was a very unhappy child even though whatever I said was instantly obeyed and whatever I wanted was mine by the end of the day.

So, naturally, at seventeen years old, I was heading straight to destruction. I was proud, stubborn, and used to getting my way. I didn't know the value of work and rarely thought of the feelings of people around me. All of those charming traits almost killed me.

But my story begins one morning almost like today two years ago. When I woke up, I went to the window in my bedchamber. My father's castle sat on a hill high above Medora, and I saw the sun peeking over the forests and fields around the city. Father had made it very clear last night that I was

supposed to meet Patrin at the practice ring, and I
didn't want to.

It wasn't that I hated practice. It was fun when I
was a kid, and Patrin would take the time to show
me a trick with the blade, but ever since I was
fourteen, Father ordered me to have regular
training sessions, and that killed all the fun of it.
Nothing I said changed his mind.

I groaned in frustration and turned back to my
room. I had already made a pass through my
bedchambers, the small dining room, and the
sitting room and not seen my sword.

Of course, it could be anywhere under the
stacks of books and stuff I had thrown around. I
walked through the rooms again and randomly
kicked aside piles.

The last time I'd seen the sword was the week
before when it was propped up in the corner of my
closet. Father would be furious if I lost it. He'd had
it made for me, as he had received one from his
father.

The tradition of giving their heirs a specially
crafted sword stemmed back for hundreds of years.
And I'm pretty sure no one had ever misplaced
theirs. Until now.

Father was going to kill me.

I gave up the search and quickly ate the
breakfast the servants brought. If I escaped before
Father made an appearance, maybe he'd forget
about it. All I had to do was make it down the
stone hallway and stairs, and my escape was secure.

I pushed my door shut and turned to see
Father storming towards me from his rooms. He

was wearing a blue cloak lined with white jaguars over brown breeches and a white shirt. I could tell he was angry by the look in his dark eyes. Even the yellow eyes of the jaguars on his cloak seemed to glare at me.

There was a sword in his hands. My heart sank.

"Ah, son," he said as he raised the sword in his right hand, apparently not noticing my annoyance. "The person I was looking for!"

I glanced around for a way to escape, but the stone hallways were empty except for the expensive tapestries hanging on the walls and the gold and blue rug on the floor. There was no one to distract Father. "Can we do this another time?"

"You can't sneak away forever," Father snapped, his voice cold.

"We both know there aren't any enemies to fight anymore," I snapped back.

"Aric, we aren't going to start this again." Father's weary tone surprised me. He was always full of gusto. "Go get your sword."

"He can't get it because he doesn't have it." The voice called from the stairs.

Belial came up at a leisurely pace. His jet black hair was smoothed back, and he was wearing black robes that made him appear paler. One of his hands was behind his back. He bowed slightly at Father.

"I found this in the Great Hall a week ago." He pulled out my sword in its scabbard from behind his back. "I haven't had time to return it yet. I'm glad I caught you this morning." Belial held the sword out to me.

I stared at it, caught off guard. The scabbard had white gold jaguars on each side with eyes of dark yellow sapphires. They were posed to bite the hilt with their fangs showing. The hilt had one large yellow sapphire stone in it. There was no way I'd ever leave it in the Great Hall for some servant to find and have to deal with another of Father's lectures about responsibility – his favorite subject.

Belial shook the sword, taunting me to take it. The sight of it in his hands irritated me more than I already was. There was something about Belial that I didn't like even though I'd tried. His smile was a bit faked, his laughter sounded forced. I couldn't pin anything down because he was always doing the perfect thing.

I snatched the sword from him and regarded it for a second. I was positive it had been in my room. How had he gotten it? Only servants and those we invited were allowed on our floor.

Belial raised his eyebrows at my actions. "You'd do well not to leave it lying around where someone may steal it."

"I didn't leave it in the Great Hall, Father! He must have stolen it from my room!" I pointed at Belial. "He's trying to..."

Belial didn't let me finish. He broke in with a laugh as if I had said the funniest thing he'd ever heard. Father joined but not as strongly. When Belial finished, he wiped his eyes.

"From what I've heard from the gossip that flies around this place, even if I went into your rooms, I'd never find it!" Belial chuckled again. "They say

it's a wreck in there! They say that they can barely find your table to put your food on!"

"Is it now?" Father said quietly. "I hadn't heard that. But let's go. You still aren't as proficient as I would like you to be with a blade." Father raised his sword slightly. "Which is why we are going to the practice grounds now. It's a beautiful day. Not to be wasted."

"I'm not wasting it," I growled. His words put me in a foul mood. Normally, I might have heeded my words in fear of his explosive, habitual rage, but this morning I didn't care. "I'm leaving here for some peace."

"Peace?" Father's voice echoed back and forth through the empty hallway. "After I'm gone, if you don't grow up and stop acting like a spoiled child, you'll never have peace."

"I don't want to," I yelled back. "And you can't make me."

"There are few people in this world who can tell you what to do." He said in a quiet tone, but I knew from the past that it was far more dangerous than the cold steel in his hands. "I am one of them. You will practice today. You're just lucky that I'm not making you enjoy it, too."

He stalked down the hallway, not waiting to see if I followed.

CHAPTER SEVEN

A Steely Dance

Of course I followed him. When he issued a command, everyone jumped, even me. I trailed behind Father at a distance certain to irritate him and show my reluctance.

He never looked back to see the glare I was throwing at the back of his head. The fact that we looked alike made me even more livid. The only thing physically that separated us was that I got my blue eyes from Mother. Yet inside, where it really counted, we were totally different, something I was incredibly happy about.

My only hope was the Great Hall and the courtyard. There was a good chance that Father would be stopped with a problem only he could solve. Then I could slip away for the day. It had happened many times before.

As we marched through the hallways and down the many stairs, I realized Belial trailed behind me, far enough away that it was awkward to talk to him, but close enough to make his presence felt.

Had Father commanded him to come with us? I wanted to ask but wasn't about to do anything that might remind Father I was behind him.

We paraded through the Great Hall. No one had the courage to approach Father as we stormed past the long tables, even though he typically encouraged anyone to come near if they had an issue.

The courtyard was empty. Normally it bustled with life, but it was deserted. My hopes of flight died. Father waited until he was halfway across before he turned and gave me a malicious smile. He knew exactly what I was thinking.

I burned with anger that I didn't have the nerve to let loose. I made faces at his back as we entered the practice grounds. I ignored Belial behind me, certain he'd have a smug look on his face that would irritate me even more.

Patrin, the captain of the guard, was waiting for us by the ring. I could tell the sight of us with our tempers in full eruption made him nervous as we approached because his hand reached for his sword hilt even though he wasn't wearing it.

In our current moods, we must have been as frightening as any of the monsters he said he'd hunted in the Razors.

"It's your turn, Patrin," Father commanded. "Teach him a thing or two."

Patrin nodded, his gray hair falling into his brown eyes. "As you wish. But no one equals you with a sword."

Father smiled, but his eyes remained angry. "You taught me everything I know, old friend. Besides, if I got in the ring with him, I'd probably kill him."

Patrin laughed politely with a hint of edginess at Father's tone and selected a wooden practice sword. He slipped through the ropes as Father chose a wooden blade and slapped it into my hand. I refused to let it show that it stung as I closed my hand around the hilt.

Father pointed to the ring. "Go. Before I throw you in."

I rolled my eyes as I climbed through the ropes. Father walked past one of the racks that held steel swords and lounged against the fence that circled the outside of the ring. Belial moved close to him and stood as straight as an arrow beside Father's seemingly relaxed stance.

I moved to the center, wondering once again why it was called a ring. It was as square as you could make it. Yet everyone persisted in calling it a ring. It was one more reason for me to escape the insanity around here before I caught the strange disease that made everyone want to grab a sword, swing it around wildly, and stick it into someone.

I didn't really have a chance against either of them. Father often bragged that his great-grandfather was one of the Slayers and that he had inherited the Slayer's skill with the sword. I shifted my feet. That may not be boasting.

Patrin watched me approach, his brown eyes as hard as the steel in a sword. A scar across his left eyebrow gave him a fierce look that most people misinterpreted. The man had the speed and strength of a lion and the cunning of a snake. Practice times with the two of them made me feel like a practice dummy.

I wiped my hand on my pants and gripped the wooden sword tightly. Patrin's blows often rattled my teeth. But today was different.

I was so angry that I was ready to strike down a Seeker with one blow, if they existed. I decided that if I was going to be forced to do this, I'd do everything in my power to get it over with quickly.

Belial's presence made me nervous, too, as if he was judging my abilities. I tried to ignore him and swung as hard and fast as I could at Patrin.

He blocked it easily with a move that knocked it from my hand. I shook my stinging hand and went to pick up the wooden blade.

"What was that?" Patrin asked. "That was a beginner's move."

I ignored him and attacked with the sword again. In my rush, I left my left side wide open. Patrin ducked the blade and whacked me on the ribs with the flat of his blade.

"Ouch!" I complained.

"Well, stop being dumb," Patrin grinned. "I haven't seen you like this since you were seven. Slow down. Use your brain and fight smarter."

I didn't want to go slower. I wanted this to be over. Before I could gather myself, Patrin came at me hard and fast. His brown eyes widened with surprise as I whacked his wooden blade aside and rained blows on him.

He stepped back quickly before his astonishment disappeared. Regaining his composure, he waited until one of my strikes flew off target and, darting his sword under my arm, twisted his blade so that my weapon went flinging across the ring.

I gripped my throbbing hand and glared at him. "I hate these wooden things. They always leave splitters. Why don't we fight with steel?"

Patrin drew back and shook his head. "Not a chance. I won't risk your life that way."

"You know that's against protocol, Aric," Father growled at me. "I've seen you better than this when you want to be. Think about what your opponent is doing. Watch his hands and feet for a clue of his next movement. You can tell if you only look."

I wanted to roll my eyes, but I'd seen Father predict the movements of two soldiers dueling as we watched from the sidelines. The position of a foot, the way the sword was held, was all Father needed to know what was going to happen. He tried to teach me, but I was always too slow to see it coming.

"Why not, Your Majesty?" Belial drawled as he got my sword and handed it to me. "If the boy wants to play with men, you should encourage him. I know he's not good enough to come close to touching Patrin."

I studied Father. If he thought I was any good, then he'd never listen to Belial. He'd tell us not to use real swords because it was too dangerous.

Father paused and considered me for a minute. He opened his mouth as if he was going to order me not to take the sword, and then his brown eyes clouded like he wasn't really seeing me at all, and he shrugged.

"I guess it would be alright this time," he said quietly. He sagged back against the fence as if exhausted.

I didn't have to guess any more about what Father thought of my skill with a sword. But why did it matter so much what he thought? I didn't like dueling at all, but hearing Father say that,

I knew I was a disappointment to him. I couldn't measure up to what he wanted me to do. What else was he dissatisfied about in me? Did he wish for another son? One that had his ability with a blade?

Belial stretched through the ropes with my sword. I scowled at him as I snatched the hilt out of his hand. A brief temptation came over me to challenge him since Father favored him so much. Maybe then Father would see that Belial was worse than I was and not care about my ability. Before I could form the words, Patrin spoke again.

"It's against protocol," he protested one more time.

"I make the protocol." Father snapped. "It will be okay."

Patrin obeyed reluctantly. As he faced me again, I could see he wasn't pleased. I felt a brief wave of hope, thinking he was worried about my skill. Then I remembered how many times he said novices were the most dangerous of all.

I didn't want to hurt him. He was like an uncle to me. He helped me walk when I was a baby, rode beside me when I was figuring out how to stay on a horse, shared the best stories with me, and taught me how to fight. But I knew Belial was watching. I

ran the sword through the air, listening to the
sound of it, and poised to fight.

Patrin moved with far less pomp. Always one to
conserve movement and strength until needed, he
stood quietly. I lunged, knowing that the first to
attack always leaves an opening, but not caring.

I was sick of Father always being disappointed
in me. It was time he found something to be proud
of in me. Patrin parried my attack with a simple
block, but instead of retaliating, he stepped back.

He didn't think I was any good, either! Rage
swept through me. Why were they so blind when
they looked at me?

I followed Patrin and struck at him high. The
swords rang in the air as I pushed against him,
determined to overpower him. He responded for a
few minutes, then ducked and twirled away. I
growled as he stood waiting for me to make the
next move.

I closed the distance and went through a series
of thrusts Patrin had taught me when I was still
learning to walk. Patrin blocked easily, knocking
my sword sideways. I no longer saw him. All I was
focused on was breaking that guard.

Our swords clashed, ringing loudly through the
air, as neither gave nor gained ground. My arm
began to protest, telling me to rest as sweat stung
my eyes, but I wasn't stopping until I disarmed
him.

And then the opportunity that Father and
Patrin always said to watch for happened. A gap
where the sword could slip in and twist the blade
out of Patrin's hand. Out of the corner of my eyes,

I saw Belial's hand flash in a cutting motion across his stomach.

Before I comprehend what he was doing, my hand with the sword lurched forward. The blade seemed to pull my hand and my strength behind it. I yelled as Patrin moved too slowly, and the sword slashed past his guard.

The sword slashed Patrin's stomach from side to side. Patrin dropped his sword with a groan. I stepped back, confused by his reaction. I had smacked him with the flat of my blade.

But he grasped his stomach with his hands and fell to his knees. I watched in horror as blood crept down his shirt, and he collapsed to the ground.

CHAPTER EIGHT

Gently But Firmly

Father cleared the ropes before I could move. He knelt down beside Patrin as he took off his favorite cloak lined with white jaguars. He shouted for help from the soldiers nearby while he carefully put pressure on the wound. The blood was dripping faster now. Belial stayed where he was, watching motionlessly.

I stood with my sword down, unable to move, as men rushed to the ring and took Patrin away. He was groaning as they picked him up and carried him off quickly. One of the men stayed behind for a moment.

"A cut to each side in the stomach area, Sire," the man said. "Looks deep."

"Find the best healer in the land," Father commanded. "And if they don't want to come, make them. Don't let anything stop you."

"I'll take care of it," Belial spoke up. Father nodded as he followed the guards on their way to the hospital.

When they were gone, Father turned to me. "What in all of Adoyni's green earth were you trying to do?"

As I looked at the sword in my hand, I saw blood on it. I closed my eyes, unable to think of what I had done. Had I done it?

It felt like someone else had taken control of my body and done what they wanted. I stared at the red on the silver. Patrin's blood. My hands shook and the blade trembled in my hand. "I...I don't know what happened. Someone..."

"If he dies, I'll take it out of your hide." Father put a finger in my face. His eyes were hard with anger. "What were you thinking? You knew you were using real swords."

"I...I don't..." I stuttered, not able to get the words out. I couldn't think. All I could think of was the blood dripping down my sword and into the dirt. I had done that. I suddenly wanted to vomit. But Father's hand grabbed my chin and forced me to look into his eyes.

"That's right. You don't. You don't fight. You don't think. You don't do any of the things that you should do!" Father pushed me away. "And now you may have killed a great man! From now on, you're doing what I say."

I glared at him as my fright for Patrin's life slowly turned into a hot rage and my fingers tightened around the hilt of my sword. "If you would listen to me for once," I broke in, interrupting him, something he greatly hated. "Instead of always walking over me, then..."

Father roared over my words. "All you ever talk about is nonsense. I'm trying to prepare you to rule so everything I've built won't fall when I'm gone. But you won't have anything to do with it.

You won't train with the sword or learn battle
tactics. You won't study law. How are you going to
lead soldiers into battle? Or defend a city?
Everything will crumble."

"That's all you care about," I shouted back.
"You've never cared about me. You just think
about all of this!" I waved my hand to encompass
the castle and the land beyond.

"If this falls after I'm gone, you'll have even
more problems," Father roared back. "It's for your
well-being that I've worked so hard to bring
prosperity. I'm trying to train you because I care
about you."

I stood there with my mouth hanging open. I'd
never thought of Father's incessant demands and
pestering that way. Could he really be thinking of
my future?

Father didn't notice my confusion. "You've
never known hunger, cold, or despair. You've
never worked all day in the hot sun to plow a field,
only to watch the crops die. You've never known
the agony of watching a loved one die because you
don't have the money for a healer. You've never
suffered."

I tried to protest. I had suffered from wanting a
Dad who loved me as I was or a Mom who liked it
when I came to see her. I suffered being watched
by hundreds of people. But he never listened on a
good day. And today was a very bad day.

"There's a price." He faced me, making it
difficult to keep my feelings to myself. "That price,
my son, is responsibility. You will meet me in the
Council Hall every day to hear grievances. In the

afternoons, a tutor will teach you law and battle tactics. After dinner, you will train with Straton, Patrin's second. Is this clear?"

I stared at him, words tumbling in my brain, but unable to say anything. This was far, far worse than anything before. What was Father thinking? I'd rather spend thirty days in the dungeon than this! This was a death sentence, not punishment!

"I won't do it, Father," I declared. "I won't study things that I don't like, and I won't spend all afternoon with some bore." I was yelling by the time I was finished.

"You don't have a choice," Father slammed the nearest post. It shook from the blow. "I'm your father, and you will obey me. I've taken all I can of you. Guards!" Father roared off into the distance. He turned to the four soldiers trotting up. "Escort the Crown Prince to his apartments and do not let him leave."

I felt the guards take my arms gently but firmly, not daring to look at me. They pulled me out of the ring, but my feet didn't seem to want to work. I tripped along between them, half walking and half held up by them.

CHAPTER NINE

Lion's Food

I paced my rooms. My loop took me through the sitting room filled with books scattered on comfortable green velvet furniture, through the small dining room with the cherry wood table and chairs where I often ate alone, and into my bedroom decorated with blue and gold blankets. I kicked the clothes on the floor aside as I completed my circle.

Every time Father messed around in my life, it got worse. I had no idea why he couldn't let me be, instead of always pushing me to be what he wanted.

I considered praying for a brief second, but I didn't think Adoyni would do anything. I'd spent my childhood praying for various things and never got them.

I was in the dining room eating an apple when I realized I had one ally who could speak to Father. I trotted to my bedroom and picked up some of my nicer clothes – black breeches and a purple tunic lined with gold. As I slipped them on, I smiled. For certain battles, one wears different kinds of armor. And these clothes would help me win a very important battle.

I stopped in front of my mirror and ran my hands through my hair to calm it down. Did I look like a prince? I gazed at myself for a minute.

Dark hair that was always messed up fell into blue eyes most of the time. I was as tall as Father but not as thick. I sighed. No. I didn't look like a prince or a king.

Stories from Adoyni's word told of princes like Daniyel who was faultless in all he did. Not even his enemies found anything they could complain about to the king because he was so perfect. Did he ever throw his shirt on the floor or go for a ride to clear his head? Probably not.

That was the kind of son Father wanted. Faultless, perfect. Not one who liked his rooms in a mess, or needed time alone to think, or who wanted to do something that wasn't duty.

No, Father wanted Daniyel, and I could never live up to such a perfect prince.

I spun away from the mirror, not wanting to think about Daniyel anymore, and stomped to the door. I flung it open and burst out into the hallway. A soldier snapped to attention. I almost slammed my door in disgust that they'd chosen a boy not even fifteen to guard me.

"My servants didn't bring me any water," I barked. "Go fetch me some."

"Your Highness," he protested. "The King's orders were to stand guard."

"Is a little water too much to ask for, or is your Royal Prince in the dungeon?" When the young soldier cringed at my tone, I knew he was intimidated by who I was.

"No...I...I mean..." The boy cleared his throat. "My orders were..."

"Your orders are to get me water. Hot water. And plenty of it."

I slammed the door shut and grinned. After a minute passed, I checked and the hallway was empty. I trotted to the apartment at the far end of the hall and tapped on the door before I entered.

Maids squealed. Sewing projects fell to the floor as they leaped to their feet and curtsied. One maid with dark hair kept her eyes on me. I gave her a wink which caused her to blush.

"Rise, ladies," I said. "You know that I don't require such formalities." They rose at my words, and I gave them a big smile.

The dark-haired girl spoke up. "It's been so long, Your Highness, that we've forgotten."

"That's true." I quickly counted heads. "But now I see...ten reasons to visit more often."

Every one of them from fifteen to fifty had red faces. I couldn't figure out women. Either a smile or a wink seems to drive every thought out of their heads, or they were cold and distant, ignoring me. All I wanted was to talk to someone about life or about nothing. Like friends do.

"What are you doing here uninvited?" A woman's voice came from the dining room. I jumped, certain I was in trouble. Cordelia always made me feel that way. It didn't help that she'd raised me from my first breath.

"Uninvited?" I asked, anger churning in me. "Since when do I need...?"

"Girls!" Cordelia interrupted, not even caring that she did. "Under no circumstances are you to leave your handiwork lying around!"

The maids began to gather up the sewing projects on the floor, but the dark haired girl stayed on her feet. "We were greeting the Prince."

"You will address me with the proper title." Cordelia snapped. "If I have to remind you of this again, you'll be scrubbing dishes until the skin on your hands withers away."

The girl stood defiant. "We were addressing the Prince in the proper way, Ma'am." The last word was drawn out a little too much. "The others were too excited to hold onto their work."

I realized the girl was holding her tapestry in her hands. Cordelia stepped out of the doorway. I was impressed that the maid stood her ground. Watching Cordelia bear down on you with her wrath was like waiting for a...well...a charging bear to eat you. The girl had courage.

"You're fairly new here, so I'll give you some advice." Cordelia was one foot away from the girl with her finger almost touching the girl's nose.

I realized that the way to the bedroom was clear. Was this the girl's plan? I'd have to thank her someday. I rushed through the dining room and the sitting room. The door to the bedroom was closed. I hesitated. Taking a deep breath, I knocked on the door. It sounded hollow and weak.

"Come."

I entered. The only color in the room was the warm sunshine on the floor like a rich rug. The only furniture, other than the bed, was a plain table with two chairs around it.

A tall slender woman in a white silk dress sat at the table with a book open in front of her. Her reddish blonde hair was pulled into a simple braid that hung to her waist.

'"I told Cordelia to tell you that I have a headache."

"But you don't, do you?" I said as I flopped onto the bed covered with a white blanket.

"Aric, whether I do or not is no consequence to you. Don't you have something you should be doing?" She put down her quill. Her blue eyes held no warmth. "Besides, you know that Adoyni's priests teach that bodily training is good, but godliness has value in every way, both for our present and future life."

"Mother, I need you to help me!" I snapped. "I know you don't have a headache. You use that as an excuse so that you don't have to see anyone you don't want to."

Mother slammed her book shut. It made me jump. She was never rough on her books. "I don't see everyone who comes to my door. Studying Adoyni's word is far more important than anything else. Is the thing that you had wanted more important than that?"

I wanted to say it was. I wanted to tell her that she needed to help make Patrin better. That she needed to help me with Father because he never listened.

But the words wouldn't come. Before I could say anything, there was another knock on her door.

"See what you've done?" she sighed. "You've brought the whole world in." She sat up straighter. "Come in."

The door slowly opened to reveal Belial. He bowed low. "My Queen," he said. "My humblest apologies for bothering you."

"Yes, yes," Mother replied coldly. "Rise and state your business, Belial."

Belial stood. He was older than me, but only recently had entered the court life. Now Father thought he was the greatest thing to ever enter to the court. I thought he was a bore.

"The King is looking for the Prince, my lady," Belial said.

Mother waved a hand. "Go, Aric. Your father needs you."

"To punish me! For something he made me do!" I jumped to my feet as my voice grew louder. "That's why I wanted to talk to you. You need to talk to Father and…"

"Aric!" Mother interrupted. There was a look in her blue eyes that I dared not cross. "That is between your Father and you. I will not be dragged into it. Belial, take him to his father." Mother turned back to her book.

I gave up. Mother didn't care. Belial led the way as we passed through the rooms. As I stormed into the hallway, Belial waited for me with his usual irritating calm.

"I know you stole my sword," I snapped.

His eyebrows rose. "Stole? That's a serious accusation."

"Serious enough to get you kicked out of here," I retorted. "I know you took it. When I'm king, you'll be gone. I won't stand for thieves around here."

Belial laughed shortly. "Well, we'll see when the time comes."

Was that a veiled threat? Belial strode past me. I followed, abruptly remembering that I had bigger issues in front of me.

I tried to appear nonchalant, but I couldn't calm my nerves. It took a brave man to confront a king who was angry. And I'd seen something in his eyes I'd never seen before. There was always disappointment and disdain. I was accustomed to his anger. But this was different.

I took a deep breath to still my heart when we arrived. I wasn't going to let him see I was scared. I pushed open the door a bit too hard and stomped into Father's rooms, ready to shrug off whatever he had in mind.

But my bravado only lasted until I saw his face. They say some animals eat their young. I was facing a lion ready to eat its cub.

CHAPTER TEN

Mucking Stalls

Father stood in front of the large stone fireplace with his hands behind his back. The difference between Father's and Mother's bedchambers struck me.

Where Mother's was sparse and bare, Father's was vibrant with rich colors and red oak furniture. He had a massive desk with many papers and parchments spread across it. There was an overstuffed chair with a footrest by the fireplace. The walls were adorned with tapestry, and there was a red and gold blanket on his bed.

Everything about Mother's apartment showed her frugality. Everything here screamed that you were in the chambers of a king. One with great power. I cleared my throat, determined not to be intimidated.

I noticed with irritation that Belial followed me into the room. He strode confidently to the table and poured two goblets of wine. When Father wasn't watching, he took a small vial out of his robes and slipped it into a goblet.

He swirled it around for a minute and handed it to Father with a slight bow. Taking the second, he stood beside the table.

I opened my mouth to question what was in the vial. "Father, do you know..."

"Thank you, Belial." Father took the goblet. There was a look of triumph on Belial's face when Father took a sip. "What would I do without you?"

Belial smiled briefly, but it didn't reach his eyes.

"Aric." Father leapt out of his chair and paced towards me. "First of all, you should know Belial has told me that Patrin has been stabilized. It remains to be seen if he will survive."

I exhaled deeply. I couldn't imagine my life without Patrin. Then I remembered that Belial was still in the room. "Why does Belial have to be here?"

"I'll decide who is in the room and who isn't!" Father's voice cracked like a whip. I tried not to wince, but I couldn't stop it. "Since I've met him, he's shown far more responsibility and maturity than you. And you'll have to get used to him being around because Belial volunteered to be your tutor, and I couldn't have been more pleased."

A commoner? Teaching me? And Father agreed with this? I was stunned. For the second time that day, I found myself at a loss for words.

"Well, Belial," Father drawled. "He's speechless. That's something you don't see too often. Perhaps he's too excited to say anything."

Belial calmly inclined his head as he regarded me. "Perhaps, my lord."

I saw a glint of satisfaction in his eyes. I wanted to punch him and wipe that self-control off his face.

Turning to me, Father continued in a quieter tone, but I could still see the rage in his eyes. "Your apartments are filthy. Since the day is still full, you will clean up the rooms without the help of the servants. Belial will inspect your rooms when he escorts you to dinner. They'd better be spotless, or you'll be mucking out stalls tomorrow!" He turned to the door. "Guards!"

The door banged open. Three guards entered and snapped to attention. "You will keep the Royal Prince in his rooms. You answer to me alone. Do not obey any of his commands. Do not leave his door. Do not allow him to leave his apartments. Is this understood?"

"Yes, sire!" The three soldiers clipped out their answer loudly.

I wanted to tell Father how much I wanted him to listen to me. All I wanted was to sit down and talk about how badly I felt about Patrin, that I didn't mean to hurt him, that something made my sword move in that killing strike, that I needed Father to be interested in me. But he turned away from me before I could even start.

As the soldiers began to lead me, I heard Belial speaking to Father. "My King, the young guard at the Prince's door should be punished."

"For what?" Father's voice was softer, mostly weaker, as if he was confused about something. "He obeyed the orders of his Prince."

"What matters is that he disobeyed **my** orders!" Belial snapped. "I told him not to leave, but he forgot all about that when another person comes along with a suggestion to do something else. That is not what soldiers are trained to do. You must order that he be punished!"

I pulled back. That wasn't fair. I was the Prince, with more power than Bèlial. The soldier followed the proper chain of command by obeying my orders.

There was nothing he should be punished for. The guards tightened their grips and forced me closer to the door.

Father sighed. "Do what you think is best, Belial. I don't feel like dealing with it."

I gasped and stopped dead in my tracks. Father never backed out of dealing with matters of the kingdom. I'd seen him miss dinner, skip out on sleep even when he was exhausted, and leave even his birthday parties because he felt that something needed his attention. He never once left anything to someone else.

"Gormal!" Belial said sharply.

The soldier on my right let go of my arm and pivoted. "Yes, sir!"

"Find the soldier who disobeyed my orders. The King orders twenty lashes of the whip! See that it is done before the sun sets," Belial ordered.

"As you command," Gormal bowed. He turned back and resumed his hold on my arm.

"Father!" I protested and tried to shake Gormal off.

As I fought against the soldiers, I caught a glimpse of Father sinking into the chair by the desk and putting his hands on his head. Belial picked up the goblet of wine that Father had forgotten about.

"Here, Your Majesty," he said silkily. "Some wine will help. It will make everything better."

Father nodded and took a drink. I saw Belial grinning as I was whisked from the room and led the way to my apartments.

I left them in the hallway as I slammed the door to my apartments and sagged against the dining room table, trembling with loneliness, rage and frustration.

AWARENESS

---

*"To survive, to know the ultimate value of life,
one must be aware and alert."*
~STRACHAN DALYEL

Jehun woke up as urgent cries grew louder. The pain was still throbbing. It had grown during his sleep, and now it was more than he could bear. His anguish was overshadowed by a wave of anger. Couldn't anyone see that he was in pain?

But no one seemed to care. He heard people stomping around. They were tramping through the fields and forests. The men were frustrated as plants refused to mature, and they watched their futures wither away. Women searched for food with small children following behind them. The children cried as hunger ate at their bellies. But there was nothing to eat.

Jehun knew he should do something. Over the pleas of the people, he heard the gentle calling of Adoyni, asking him to work as he was created to do. In the past, he had always answered Adoyni's call with joy. But now he grew more furious every second the torment continued.

No one noticed his pain. And if they did, they did not care enough to help him. After all he had done for the people, they would not bother themselves to do anything for him. Their selfishness shocked him. If that was how they felt about him, why should he do anything more for them? In fact, maybe it would teach them to love him if he stayed away. Maybe then they would realize how much they needed him.

He had never ignored his Master, for Adoyni had always been loving and gentle. But it hurt. It still hurt even though it was days after the earthquake. Adoyni hadn't done anything to help. He hadn't healed the rift. He hadn't taken an ounce of the pain away. He wasn't even there.

Jehun fumed as he rolled through the loam. He seethed for some time about the heartless requests from the people. As his anger slowly cooled into resentment, he settled on a plan.

The people couldn't help him. Adoyni was gone. There was only one with the power to rid him of this agony. He needed to find whoever it was that tore the topsoil apart. One with that kind of strength could surely help him.

Jehun set out on his quest. He journeyed to the north, far up into the Razors where the Sentinels hid from the rest of the world and found nothing. He journeyed far south where the ships brought in fish from the sea. But the man was not there. He went east where swamps were stagnant. No one was there that was capable of ripping the earth in two.

Where do men of great power go? The answer came to him in a flash. In the center of Eltiria, there was a town where people gathered and lived together. On the top of the large hill that overlooked the village was a large castle made out of light gray stone. The King of the people lived there.

He made his way to Medora. On the outskirts of the town was a large palace that matched the white stone of the castle. Inside was the man of power. Jehun could feel it radiating around him like the heat from the sun although this man wasn't the king. He was even more powerful.

"The other people don't care about you," the man said.

Jehun agreed, but he wasn't about to say anything yet. This man said he could do mighty things, but Jehun noticed that one sleeve was empty. Was the man born that way, or did he have strong enemies?

"Even Adoyni ignores you in your pain. How selfish of all of them. After all you've done for them. And now when you need a little hope, they turn their back on you and think only of themselves."

Jehun listened closely. Whoever this voice was, he knew exactly how Jehun was feeling. He stopped worrying about how the man had lost his arm.

"I wouldn't treat you so poorly. I am wise enough to know how much I need you to be happy, and I would do anything to keep you happy."

That caught Jehun's attention. He thought he was all alone, but here was someone who understood and cared for him. And this man had the power to help him. He leaned in closer.

"I think it's awful how you are in pain, and no one even cares. If you followed me, I would care for you because you are special, not because of what you do for me. I would help you when you were hurt. All you have to do is swear allegiance."

Jehun hesitated. Should he turn his back on Adoyni after all these years? But it hurt so badly, and there was so much to do. Not only did he have all the projects he wanted done, everyone was expecting him to do so much. And now he had the earthquake to clean up. He couldn't wait for Adoyni. He'd have to take care of it himself. Things were always left for him to fix after someone else wrecked them.

After he promised his loyalty, the pain seemed to ease a bit. He knew he had made the right decision. After a little time had passed, his new master ordered that Jehun make the soil acidic. Jehun remembered the leak at the inner core and knew that lava was starting to ooze farther out and spill closer to the surface, but he ignored it for now and left to do as Belial requested.

CHAPTER ELEVEN

Old Friends

Kai stopped his screaming when his voice grew hoarse. It seemed that there was no one to hear him, not even Adoyni. He thought of the times when Eladar came to the rescue or Alyn appeared to save them. In the past, Adoyni had always brought someone to help him.

He wanted to hear Lizzy's continuous singing even though it had bothered him before. Even her strumming quietly on her guitar, lost to all the troubles in the world as she picked out a pleasant tune, would be wonderful to hear.

Taryn's mumbling as he read and the way that he burst into conversation with random information that was never helpful would be even more welcome. He'd probably know what kind of rock the hallway was made out of. Maybe he'd even know how deep into the earth Kai was.

They weren't there, and Kai didn't know anything except that he was alone. *That's because I failed. Even Adoyni probably doesn't want anything to do with me because I'm worthless.* He sheathed his sword and started walking again.

Once before he was taking care of his family and solving his problems alone. He could do it again.

When he held his breath, he heard the shuffling of feet behind him a, but this time he ignored it. Everything around him looked the same, and he was tired. All he wanted to do was to eat and sleep. He held back the words as his rage began to boil like a pot of water over a fire.

Kai trudged around several more corners not knowing if he was going in circles until he saw a door. He smiled. *Maybe I'm getting somewhere!* It was made out of rough boards. A rusty old handle was nailed sloppily onto it. It was the best door he'd ever seen.

He jogged to it, holding onto the hilt of the sword, and grinned. A way out of here! As he approached the wooden door, two shadows moved from the walls and blocked the door. He leapt back, his heart beating faster.

The one shadow came closer and laughed. Kai knew he had heard it somewhere before. Somewhere before all this trouble had started.

The laugh broke off suddenly. "Look at him, Bowen, he's speechless." The laughter picked up again. This time it was joined by another laugh that sounded more like a cough.

Kai blinked through the smoky haze from the torches and tried to see. A guy his age was standing before him. He was tall and muscular like someone who had worked hard all day. His dirty blonde hair and dark eyes reminded Kai of someone, but he couldn't remember who.

"Maybe he doesn't recognize us, Bowen," the one continued. The words were slurred like it was hard to speak. He crossed his arms across his bare chest, emphasizing his muscles.

Kai glanced over at Bowen. He looked almost identical as the speaker, with his tattered brown breeches with no shirt and well-developed muscles. Only Bowen had red hair and had a sneer on his face. *Bowen. Bowen. Why did that sound familiar?*

Then he remembered. Bowen and Yorath. Two of Destin's favorite cohorts. He couldn't count the number of times in Shalock Stables when they held him down while Destin took his time at beating Kai to a pulp.

"What are you guys doing here?" Kai didn't want to admit it, but seeing them again alarmed him.

In the back corners of the barns and tracks of Shalock Stables, they used their strength to thrash him. They were never content with Destin's job. When he was finished, they got in their own kicks and punches. *What would they do here where no one can see?*

The laughter started again. "Waiting for you!" Bowen's skin looked orange in the torch light, but Kai could see the veins running up and down the arms. His eyes were green back at Shalock Stables, but now they were brown. Revulsion swept through Kai as he realized they were Unwanteds.

Yorath spoke for the first time and crossed his arms so that they looked like a mirror image. The freckles were gone on his face and arms, leaving behind smooth white skin. "It's been a while since we saw you. There haven't been too many people to torment lately."

Hearing their voices brought back old feelings of rage and fear. He hated them to the core, and he wasn't going to be beaten again. *I could run back the way I came.*

But there was no need to run. He didn't desperately need that job at the stables. He wasn't that same guy. He had killed Unwanteds and Seekers. There was a sword on his hip that worked quite well. He laughed.

"You do realize that you can't beat me up, right?" Kai scoffed. "Even two against one, I can take you down. Get out of my way."

The other two laughed at him. He wasn't going to admit it, but the hollow peals of laughter made his skin crawl.

"We were hoping you would say that," Bowen grinned. Broken teeth lined his mouth. Kai couldn't remember him missing teeth back at the stables. "We always did enjoy beating you up. You fought back so hard. Remember that one time on the backside of the track? We must have given you three broken ribs and a concussion, but you kept swinging at us."

Yorath burst out laughing. "I remember that. You could barely stand. But you kept trying to punch us. Every time you swung, you'd fall over. It was hilarious!"

Kai ground his teeth. "I don't want to hurt you. Let me through that door."

They leaned against the stone wall and laughed harder. Kai's face grew hot. *Why can't they see who I am?* He drew his sword with a flourish and dropped into a fighting stance.

Their laughter died away as they pushed themselves off the wall and stood on each side of him. Hate was etched into their eyes and faces as they approached.

"Put that away," Bowen ordered. His voice was low and flat. "If you thought getting beat up before was bad, we'll beat you to a pulp that you can't imagine now."

"I know what you are, and I've faced creatures like you before and won. I'm not scared. Get out of my way." Kai inched closer.

"Not down here you haven't," Yorath warned. "Down here we have more power and strength than up where the sun is. This is where we rule. You don't have a chance."

"Get out of my way!" Kai roared.

Bowen grinned as evilly as Yorath. "This is going to be fun."

They launched themselves straight at Kai. He yelled as they swiftly closed the gap. This time they wouldn't win or beat him up like they used to. He'd stop at nothing to teach them a lesson. Maybe he'd even do a beating of his own.

But as they rushed him, he realized that they were right. As Unwanteds, they were much quicker than before. Bowen slipped past his guard and punched him in the jaw. Kai flew back and slammed into the wall behind him.

With two of them, he was in trouble. Black spots appeared before his eyes when he slammed into the rock, and he felt the warmth from the blood streaming down his face.

The only sound he heard was their laughter as he sank to the cold floor.

CHAPTER TWELVE

Sweet Revenge

Kai lay on the stones and prayed for the blows to stop. His sword slipped out of his hand and clattered away. He didn't see where it had gone as he rolled into a ball. He knew from experience that if he didn't protect his head, Bowen and Yorath would kick it as hard as they could. He kept his arms around his face and tried to squirm away.

He tried not to cry out in pain, but when Yorath replaced Bowen and kicked him in the stomach with lethal force, he screamed in agony as the boot slammed into his rib cage and smashed several ribs.

Yorath laughed maliciously, his eyes cruel. "He's as easy to beat up as before. I thought the Master said he could defend himself now."

Kai saw Bowen shrug as he kicked at Kai's head. He rolled away as Bowen's foot smashed into his arms. He squirmed farther to the left to get away from their reach.

"Who knows what the Master meant?" Bowen replied. "He relies on magic more than physical strength. I can't imagine this piece of garbage putting up much of a fight."

Kai stopped rolling and tried to catch his breath. He was already aching from his fight earlier, and his side was bleeding again.

He found it hard to think with the new pain coursing through his body as the old feelings of helplessness flooded him.

He wasn't able to fight the two of them. They were too strong. He shifted slightly as Bowen and Yorath talked about the days at the stables and their favorite times of beating him up.

His hand brushed something that didn't feel like stone. He moved slowly so he wouldn't draw attention. His fingers traced the cool metal. *My sword!* He almost laughed.

He gripped the hilt and leapt to his feet with a yell. Bowen and Yorath jumped back at his attack, surprised that he wasn't cowed anymore. He didn't give them a chance to recover. He forgot about the pain that laced his body. All he could feel was pure rage. He was going to teach them a lesson they'd never forget.

Bowen recovered faster and spun around to run down the hallway. Kai let him go. He'd deal with him in a second. Yorath was in front of Kai, too shocked to run or react.

Kai didn't even bother to think about it. He swung in a wide arc. There was a small voice in his head telling him to stop, but he didn't listen. He was too infuriated to care about what he was doing. He had suffered through countless beatings from these two. Now he was powerful enough to stand up to them and show them what pain felt like.

He let his sword fall through the air, and before he could think, Yorath was on the ground. Kai laughed, sounding like the mirthless laugh the others were making, as he realized that Yorath would never move again.

He raced after Bowen as he continued to laugh. Bowen hadn't made it terribly far. He kept tripping over his feet in his panic. Kai caught up with him.

"Please, don't." Bowen fell to his knees. "I'm sorry. I didn't know..."

Kai didn't even listen as he kicked Bowen in the stomach with all his might. Bowen screamed in pain and grabbed his midriff as he fell to the ground.

"Maybe this will teach you not to pick on people," Kai yelled.

Bowen didn't protect his head, so Kai kicked him as hard as he could and laughed when Bowen yelled. He crawled along the hallway in an attempt to escape.

Kai let him go for a few feet before following him and kicking him to the ground. In one smooth motion, he leaned down, flipped Bowen over, and punched him in the face with all the rage he had coursing through him.

Deep inside, Kai knew what he was doing was wrong. It felt wrong to be the bully and use his strength to kill. He knew he was wrong to give into his rage. But something violent and evil was controlling him. Something that delighted in the pain of others. Whatever it was made him laugh so

loudly that he couldn't hear the small voice giving
a warning anymore.

He stood over Bowen for a minute as the peals
of manic laughter swept over him. Then he cut
Bowen down as quickly as he had Yorath. He stood
over the body and stopped laughing. All he was
aware of was blood. His sword was covered with it,
and his leg was soaked from his wound on his side.

The hallway fell silent as he became conscious
of what he had done. He stared in horror at the
two bodies. They were Unwanteds, but they were
also people. He'd seen them laugh and he'd
talked to them. And now they were dead. Because
of the rage inside of him.

What came over me? Kai ran a trembling hand
over his face. His stomach lurched as he stood in
shock. His sword clattered to the floor, and he
caught a glimpse of the word *Failure.* He winced.

That was what he was. He was a failure. He
couldn't remember purifying the water, so he
must have botched that. He wasn't worthy of
carrying a sword. If Alyn or Eladar saw him now,
they'd never understand or be able to forgive him.
And he wouldn't blame them.

He knew only Adoyni could save him. "Help
me," he cried.

As he stood and let his thoughts weigh him
down into deeper anguish, the hallway was filled
with the sound of laughter. Although it sounded
like it was pleased, there was no joy in the laugh.
Kai looked around but saw no one.

"I've been waiting for you." The laugh turned
into words. Kai's heart dropped as he realized that

it was Belial speaking. He snatched up his sword and poised ready to fight.

The laughter picked up again. "Oh, you can't see me. But I can see you. And you did very well. Very well, indeed."

"Where are you?" Kai shouted. "Come on out, and I'll cut your other arm off."

The laughter broke off suddenly. "Oh, no, you won't. By the time you reach me, you'll be my slave. And judging from your recent activity with Yorath and Bowen, you'll be perfect for what I have planned for you." A laugh of triumph reverberated through the hallway.

Kai felt fear course through him, and before he could think any further, he flung open the wooden door and ran through it into the sunlight.

CHAPTER THIRTEEN

Trapped

Rhiana was aware of the pain before she opened her eyes. All she wanted was to slip back to sleep where she could forget the aches all over her body.

She rolled to her side, hoping that a new position would relieve the aches, but the new position made it worse. She wondered when her bed had gotten so hard.

It felt like she was lying on stones, like the time they had gone camping before Dad's accident. And she was cold. She reached for her blanket without opening her eyes, but it must have fallen to the floor.

"Mom?" Her voice sounded like she hadn't used it for a long time. She waited for a minute, but there was no answer.

"Mom? I'm cold." Again she waited, but Mom didn't come. Rhiana rolled toward the door and opened her eyes.

She gasped. The room stayed black. *Am I blind?* She sat up, the hurt now forgotten as panic grew. She waved her hand in front of her face, but she couldn't see anything.

"Mom?" She called louder, but there was no response. "Dad?"

Carefully, she felt for the edge of her bed, but instead of soft blankets, it was cold and hard like stone. The fabric of her clothes rubbed against her arm as she moved, and she patted her clothes. She was not in her night clothes. Whatever she was wearing was scratchy and stiff.

She sat still for a moment, trying to understand what was happening. *Where am I? Where's Mom?* The last thing she could remember was strange, mean men coming to the house. She was on the couch reading her favorite book, *The Amazing Adventures of Cathen.* A lot of the stories about the leader of the Slayers were too scary and confusing, but that book was Kai's favorite, so she tried to read it when she missed him.

The men hadn't even knocked. They forced the door open and went into the kitchen where Mom was. They dragged her into the living room while Dad shouted at them as he wheeled himself after her.

She could recall all of that perfectly. Dad was yelling something that she couldn't understand as Mom screamed for help. The men said nothing. The smell of their sweat mingled with the scent of the roast cooking in the oven.

Then there was a strange noise like thunder, but coming from underneath her. She stared at the floor until she heard Mom's picture of a pansy shaking against the wall. It crashed to the floor as the walls began to sway. She knew she was crying, but she couldn't hear anything over the roar.

After that, she remembered nothing. And now there was only blackness.

She crawled forward, cautiously putting one hand in front of her as she crept forward to find a way out of there. In a few seconds, her hand smashed into something hard. Yelping, she sucked on it and investigated farther with her good hand.

The stone face of the wall rose straight up as far she could reach. She got to her feet slowly and waited for the waves of dizziness to stop. Standing on her toes, she reached up and found that the wall went higher than she could touch.

Turning to her left, she took cautious steps with her hand on the wall. Every few feet, she stopped and checked to see if she could feel the top, but she never did. She made a slow circuit as her bare feet grew frigid.

The wall turned once, twice, and then a third time. On the third wall, there was a change. She felt a crack, but it wasn't a doorway or window because she couldn't feel any air coming through it. Another step, and she found an opening.

There was a gap in the wall about four inches high and six inches long. She poked her fingers through the hole and felt a piece of metal on the other side. It moved when she pressed on it.

"Mom?" she called. "Where are you? Mom? Dad?"

There was no answer.

She started yelling. "Is there anyone there? I need help! Hello?"

The only answer was silence. She fought back tears as she explored the rest of the space. She was so thirsty, and her stomach rumbling with hunger, that she forgot to walk carefully, and she tripped over a coarse blanket that was riddled with holes. When she picked it up, it smelled like it had never been washed. She held it close, trying to breathe through her mouth, as shivers ran up and down her body.

When the small space was thoroughly explored, she sat down close to the hole in the wall. She realized two things at once. She was completely trapped, and she was totally alone.

That was when she started screaming.

CHAPTER FOURTEEN

Not Them

Lizzy shifted on her rock to stretch her stiff muscles. Aric's story had taken her mind off the current troubles, but now she was wondering what the purpose was. Was he trying to entertain her while Kai died? Were they waiting for that?

"It's called a Carachadh Spell."

Lizzy jumped as the voice was beside her, but she never heard anyone approach. She whipped around as recognition set in.

"Taryn!" She launched herself of the rock, stumbled, and gave him an awkward hug. He stiffly returned the embrace with one arm, his smile not reaching his hazel eyes. Black spots appeared in her eyes as she tried to find her balance.

As she pulled back, she noticed a young boy with hair so blonde it was almost white and sea green eyes standing next to Taryn. He was dressed in plain tan trousers and his blue shirt was untucked.

Taryn noticed her stare. "This is Griffen. He was rescued from Eltiria, too."

Lizzy smiled at Griffen before Taryn started talking again.

"How's Kai?" He collapsed on the closest rock. He was dressed in loose tan breeches with a black shirt untucked. His left arm was wrapped in a bandage, and she noticed that he favored it.

"Aric says Kai will be fine." She didn't sound convincing, even to herself. "What did you say about a spell?"

"Yes, they say that, don't they?" His words about Kai's condition were sarcastic. She could tell he was mad by the tightening of his hazel eyes and the wrinkles in his forehead. He fiddled with the bandage on his arm like it hurt as he continued.

"A Carachadh Spell. It's an extremely difficult one, but I've read about it. If you can acquire a possession of someone, then you can place a spell on it, controlling it no matter who holds it. Quite useful when you want a will signed in your favor. Relax, Prince, you didn't injure Patrin. It was Belial."

Aric nodded but his face didn't show much expression. "I wondered if Belial was behind that stroke somehow. Certainly it was in his favor to take out the captain of the guard."

Taryn didn't seem to pay attention as he changed the subject. "What's the plan, Aric? You said there are at least five hundred people here who came when the Archippi left Eltiria many years ago or who have been rescued like us. But you manage to get us on an island that has absolutely no one on it. I tell you, Lizzy, it's awfully good to see you up. Someone to talk to. Someone who's not *them*."

Taryn pulled off his backpack and drew out the wordless book. Lizzy felt a wave of sadness as she remembered the peaceful meadow with the altar where they found the book. She needed that serenity now.

"What are you talking about?" Lizzy asked. He was afraid of something, or mad at something, and a cold hand of fear squeezed her heart.

"The Prince and his girl here decided to kidnap us. They and some *friendly* Archippi whisked us off to this deserted island where there's nothing to eat. But the Archippi left, and we've used up almost all the food. Who knows if they'll ever return? After the way they treated Kai, I wouldn't be surprised if they left us all to die." He leaned closer to Lizzy and whispered, "We should've listened to Eladar when he said not to trust them, especially their leader. They're not like Eladar. I don't know how we're going to…"

"They'll be back!" Rev stepped out of the cave. "They're probably not able to get away without being noticed."

"Faelon, their leader, the tall gray you saw when you first got here, is afraid of what could be wrong with Kai." Aric shook his head. "They don't bring many people up here, so they are paranoid about us contaminating their world. How's Kai?"

Rev shook her head. "His fever is starting to build again."

Aric stood and brushed off his clothes. "Griff, want to come with me to our tent? I want to get the book we brought with us."

"Race you!" Griffen's green eyes lit up as he spun on his heel and bounded down the hill. Aric followed at a trot.

Rev shook her head. "He'll never slow down. When he came here, his legs were broken in multiple places and cut extremely deep with whips. Now he won't stop running!" She smiled at Lizzy. "I'm going to my tent. Would you like to come clean up?"

"But what about Kai?" Lizzy found it hard to resist the chance to get dressed, but there was no way she was leaving Kai alone. "Who will watch him?"

Rev turned to Taryn. "Could you sit by his bed? If there's a problem, Aric will hear your call." Her words were a polite question, but there was a firmness behind the request.

Taryn shifted in his seat. "I guess…I don't know what to do."

"He might hear your voice, and it might help him fight back the…" Her words dropped off sharply. She cleared her throat. "…the injury. Just call if there's any problem. We're not giving him the sleeping draught anymore, now that Lizzy is awake."

Lizzy followed Taryn back to the mouth of the cave where he sat on the sand and opened the book. She saw the pack again with her norsaq in it. She didn't know why, but she wanted it with her. She loosened the pack, and the long darts tangled as she drew them out. Now Kai's sword was the only thing in the bag.

"Taryn, where's your...?" She glanced at him and saw what she was looking for.

The shield was behind Taryn within arm's reach. He looked up from his bed and smiled slightly. "Strange, isn't it? No enemies in sight, but it feels better to have it close."

She tried to smile back, but it was too hard with Kai so deathly quiet. She nodded. Rev waited and then led the way to the tents. Lizzy wanted to ask her questions, but Rev never gave her a chance as she chattered about everything. Everything but Kai.

The tents were set up in a meadow covered with a carpet of grass dotted with small pink flowers. A small crystal clear brook trickled down the mountain on the far side. Lizzy almost smiled at the sight. Almost. Then she remembered Kai.

Rev led Lizzy to the large tent on the right and pulled the flap aside. There was enough space for two bedrolls. Between the blankets was a bulky bag with clothes neatly folded inside. Rev pulled out a green shirt and some breeches.

Rev's constant talking began to irritate Lizzy. She was babbling about everything. Well, not quite. She didn't mention Kai, how they got where they were, or anything Lizzy really wanted to know. *What about the earthquake in Northbridge? Is Dad okay? What about Rica? Did he make it home?*

Lizzy broke in. "Don't you ever want to go back?"

Rev's face changed slightly, like a wall had come up. "Oh, there's so many things here that need to be done. I'm too busy to think about those things." She began sorting clothes in a pack.

She's lying! I know it! Lizzy had seen pain in Rev's eyes when she spoke. Lizzy went along with the chitchat as she slipped on the green shirt and the breeches. *It was a simple question. Why did she lie?* All the unanswered questions were giving her a big headache.

Lizzy tried one more time. "Rev, what's wrong with Kai?"

Rev paused with her hand on the tent flap. "I think it's best if you ask Aric." Pity filled her dark eyes. "We are doing everything we can for him. I know that doesn't sound like much, but we're quite stubborn. It seems that Kai, too, is stubborn. We may have a chance…"

Again, the words died off. Hope given, but then taken away as desperation took over her words and face. "He'll be fine."

The words were as empty as their water flasks in the desert of Seiten's Anvil.

CHAPTER FIFTEEN

Crystal Clear

Taryn watched Lizzy carefully pick her way down the hill and follow Rev into the girls' tent. It was good to have someone around on his side. But was she?

He hadn't missed those adoring eyes she kept making at Aric. He noticed how she was hanging on his every word and was acting all proper around him.

He snorted. Lizzy. Proper! Those weren't words he'd use describing her. She wasn't that bad, but she had a temper and was quite bossy.

He studied Kai. His breathing was so shallow Taryn couldn't understand how he was getting enough air. He hadn't moved in a while.

Aric was relying on traditional medicine, trying different remedies that the Archippi suggested. But it wasn't doing a thing. Taryn knew exactly what would help although no one had asked.

He glanced at the cave entrance. He was alone with Kai for the first time since they arrived in Merrihaven. No one up here, except maybe Lizzy, would cooperate with him on this healing. Lizzy was too addled with Aric for him to ask her. This was his time.

He leaped to his feet and paced to the entrance. There was no one in sight. He dashed for his pack, the one he had with him since the coach was attacked by Seekers so long ago. He'd never completely gone through it after Eladar whisked them off, but he thought he had packed at least one.

He dumped the contents out of the pack on the sand. *Where is it?* His fingers trembled in his hurry. *If they see this, Aric will explode and Kai's only chance will be gone.* He threw aside the few clothes he had and the books. *Where is it?*

There! He caught a glimpse of the small blue velvet case in one of the pockets of his shirts. He could feel the rock in the case as he snatched it up.

He glanced down the hill to make sure no one was coming, and rushed to Kai. His hands shook as he opened the case and dumped the small white crystal in his hand.

He stared at it for a minute. He knew magic was wrong. Belial was murdering people and using it to poison the water, and all with the Goddess' blessing and magic.

But this was a rock. It was something from the earth. It didn't have anything to do with the evil surrounding the poison. In fact, if it healed like people said, then it must come from Adoyni.

But would Kai mind? Of all the things they talked about, they never discussed using crystals. It didn't matter what Kai thought. It was the only way to heal him. Kai would thank him later, when he was better. Taryn took the crystal, said a blessing from the Goddess over it, and lifted Kai's shirt. He placed the white stone on Kai's chest and used a bandage to hold it in place.

He smoothed down his shirt and replaced the blankets so it didn't look like he'd been disturbed. Taryn took a deep breath as he settled down with the wordless book, marveling that now he could see the words. It was easier to read now that he knew Kai would get better.

***

Kai trotted through the open door. He was escaping the dreaded hallway. All he had to do was figure out where he was and then get back to the others. He almost laughed as he felt the sun hit his face. *I'll be okay.*

A sharp pain in his chest took his breath away. He bent over and fell to his knees as the pain grew hotter. Taking short breaths, he pulled up his shirt and saw a burn mark appear over his heart. It was no bigger than his thumb, but the burn radiated down to his heart and through his body.

He lay on the ground, panting, and prayed for relief. *What's happening to me?* But the question was lost in his screams.

CHAPTER SIXTEEN

Show Off

Lizzy picked up her norsaq and followed Rev out of the tent. The warm sunshine felt good, and she felt some strength returning to her. She fingered the norsaq and pulled a dart out from its sheath. Across the meadow was a tall pine tree with a small pinecone dangling from a branch at the top.

Could I hit it? Alyn said that she must clear her mind and think of only the target. She placed the dart on the norsaq and drew back before the doubt clouded her mind. She hurtled the dart at the pinecone as hard as she could.

But as it left her hand, she gasped. She'd never seen it fly as fast as it was now. The dart flew up higher and higher into the sun before arcing and falling back to the earth. She watched, holding her breath. *I released too soon. I always do that.* But then the dart plunged down and smashed through the pinecone. Pieces of it fluttered down as the dart buried itself into the dirt.

"Wow!" Aric said behind her. "Great shot! Where'd you get this weapon?" He examined a dart.

"From Alyn, a Sentinel," Lizzy said, strangely reluctant to say more.

"A Sentinel! No one's ever seen them!" Aric exclaimed. "And this looks like the weapon one of the Slayers had," Aric said quietly.

Lizzy started to tell more about Alyn, but the look on Aric's face chilled her.

"Taryn has a shield, doesn't he?" he asked without acknowledging her words. "Did he get it from a Sentinel, too? What does it do?"

"You'll have to ask him." She didn't know why, but she didn't want to answer these questions.

Aric's eyes narrowed. "Griff, why don't you run up and send Taryn down with his shield?" It was phrased as a question, but it came out like a command.

"Who will watch Kai?" Griffen asked.

"You can for a few minutes," Aric responded as he surveyed the norsaq.

"But then I won't see..."

"Griffen!" Aric barked. "Just go!"

The young boy took off running, but Lizzy saw the disappointment in his eyes. He was only in the cave a few minutes before Taryn came out with his shield. No one spoke as he stumbled down the hill.

Aric studied the shield like he hadn't ever seen it before. "Lizzy was showing us how her norsaq worked. We were curious to see what your shield did."

"And how do you suggest I show you what the shield does?" Taryn had a sullen expression on his face. "It blocks attacks. And it's invisible so you won't see a thing."

Aric hesitated. "Hold on," he commanded and whirled around to his tent. He returned with his sword in his hand.

Lizzy stared at the sword. The scabbard had white gold jaguars streaking toward the hilt with yellow sapphires for eyes. The jaguars' mouths were open so that it looked like they were about to bite the hilt where one large yellow sapphire stone was. She knew that the stone alone was worth more than most people made in a lifetime.

Aric drew the blade. "Do your thing," he ordered. "I'll see if it works."

Rev gasped. "Aric, you can't do that. You know what's..."

"If Taryn's shield works as well as Lizzy's norsaq, there will be no problems," Aric snapped.

Taryn raised the shield and closed his eyes for a breath. *Was he praying?* Lizzy watched. She hadn't really seen him do anything with his shield, although she'd caught glimpses during their battle in the courtyard of the castle.

Aric swung as hard as he could. The blade whipped through the air and sliced down a breath away from Taryn. Taryn yelled and leaped away, tumbling to the ground.

"What are you doing?" he shouted at Aric as he got to his feet. "You almost killed me!"

"I thought you said it was a shield!" Aric roared back. "Aren't you supposed to stop me?"

"I wasn't ready!" Taryn snapped.

"Obviously," Aric retorted. "Get ready or you'll be sorry!"

Taryn glared at Aric, clearly too mad to find any words to say. He spun the shield around a couple of times and held it in front of him with a nasty look. Aric swung again.

Lizzy couldn't help the shriek that escaped her lips as the sword flew through the air. There was no chance of it missing him this time. If the shield didn't work, the sword was going to land on his neck. She grabbed Rev's arm, not wanting to watch but not able to look away.

The sword dropped closer to Taryn. Lizzy screamed when it was a hand's space from Taryn. But as quickly as the sword was falling, the blade stopped not far from Taryn's neck. It jerked to a stop and then ricocheted back through the air at Aric.

Aric yelled as the sword whipped back at him. He let go of the blade inches away from his face and dropped to the ground. It spun through the air before it landed thirty paces across the meadow. Aric sat up and glared at Taryn.

"What was that?" he demanded as he slowly picked himself up. "I thought you said it only blocks things. You didn't say anything about it using the weapon against the attacker! I wouldn't have done that if I'd known!"

"Why were you swinging so close to me?" Taryn yelled. "Besides, I've never seen it do anything like that before!"

"Maybe up here we're better," Lizzy broke in before the two guys really started fighting. "Back on Eltiria, I couldn't have made those shots. But here it was as easy as breathing. Eladar said he couldn't heal down there, maybe we are affected in ways we don't realize."

Aric got his sword and put it back in his scabbard. "And you say a Sentinel gave them to you?" he asked once again. Lizzy nodded and wondered about the stern look on his face. "And this Sentinel gave Kai his sword?"

Lizzy nodded again. Aric evaluated them for a minute and then turned to go back up the hill to the cave. Rev followed behind. As he passed Lizzy, she heard him mutter under his breath.

"The gifts of the Slayers. Why did *they* get the weapons? They're not royalty."

They hiked up to the cave without a word. Aric's mumbling bothered Lizzy more than she thought it would.

Does he think that we don't deserve the weapons? Or that the Slayers aren't our ancestors? Why would he even care? She remembered that the King had to be a descendant of the Slayers to rule. *Did that mean that we're related, if Alyn and Eladar were right about us being descendants? Did Aric think they were going to try to take the throne?*

Rev scooted Griffen away from Kai and checked his breathing. Rev was efficient, but Lizzy could tell she cared about Kai in the careful way she worked. Aric sat in the sand next to Lizzy, and Griffen stayed as close to Aric as he could like a living shadow.

They looked up when Taryn stormed into the cave and didn't sit. "You've been saying you'll tell me what's going on when Lizzy woke up. Well, she's awake. So what's going on?"

Aric ran his hand through his hair and scratched his head. It made him look very different from the prince she'd seen from a distance at one of Mother's performances in Albia. The cave filled with Kai's labored breathing, but no one took their eyes off Aric.

"I was hoping it wouldn't come to this." His voice was quiet but firm. "I was hoping that we caught it soon enough. Or a miracle would happen. I know that none of this makes sense to you." He studied Lizzy and Taryn.

His face and voice grew firm, and Lizzy knew that she was seeing the Prince now. One who wouldn't take arguments. One who was accustomed to speaking and having his words followed without question. She swallowed. Taryn shifted in his seat, but he stayed silent.

"Taryn, you've heard most of what I've already told Lizzy, so I will continue my tale where we stopped." His chin lifted, causing his hair to fall away from his face. His blue eyes held a challenge for them to question his authority. The charm he had when he offered her his arm was gone. The healer slipped away while the prince came forth.

Kai groaned softly in his sleep and twitched. Rev smoothed down his blankets and felt his forehead with a concerned look.

"You'd better tell the story quickly," Taryn said. He was watching Kai and didn't notice the flash of anger in Aric's eyes. "Kai can't wait much longer."

Aric glanced at Lizzy. She longed to see some reassurance, some hope, in his blue eyes, but they were cold. She pulled the blanket up closer to her chin, chilled with the thought that he and Rev weren't what they seemed. Aric began talking as she wondered who he really was. A compassionate healer or an arrogant prince?

CHAPTER SEVENTEEN

The Circle of Chairs

The next day was horrible. In fact, horrible doesn't even come close to describing it. I suffered through Belial's inspection of my apartment, and it took all the self-control I had not to punch him as he poked around. I endured the morning with Father, listening to commoners come for justice.

I heard more about cows on the wrong property and old horses being sold as young ones. Father listened to each grievance thoroughly, probably to irritate me. I couldn't help wondering if this was all a King did? Couldn't a judge take care of these problems to give the King a chance to focus on more important matters?

But it only got worse when Belial led me to the library and set me down at an oak table set between rows of tall bookshelves. As a child, I had hidden many times in the library, lost in the tales of heroes. Now we were in the law section. I stifled a groan.

Belial motioned for me to take a seat on the plush red velvet chairs while he placed his hands on the table and leaned toward me. As I plopped into a chair at the far end, I thought I saw him

*sneer when he looked at me. But it was gone
before I could be certain.*

"Your assignment is to write down each case we
heard. Then find the actual laws the King drew
from. You'll record the number of each law, copy
the exact wording of it and four other similar cases
with their verdicts. I will expect to see your report
at dinner."

My eyes traveled over the multitude of books.
How was I ever supposed to find all the
information he wanted? "That's too much," I
protested. "It will take weeks!"

"Try that area, Prince." Belial waved to his left.
"I suggest you get started now."

I glared at him, but he only regarded me with
disdain. What could I do to disturb that uncanny
calm? "I need something to eat and drink." I
turned away from him, but from the corner of my
eyes, I saw him flush.

"Yes, Your Highness," he said shortly with a
bow. He stomped out of the room.

It was a small victory, but I celebrated by
stretching out for a nap. I must have fallen asleep
because the next thing I heard a tray being set
down on the table and a soft voice murmuring,
"Your Highness."

I leaped up, certain it was Belial, my heart
thudding hard in my chest. On the table was a tray
filled with meats, cheeses, and sweets and a pitcher
of grape juice. Lord Fariel stood before me,
holding his slight bow. I settled back in my chair as
he poured a goblet of juice for me.

"I saw Belial in the hall and offered to bring this to you," he said. I knew the lines around his eyes were from age not laughter, for I'd never seen him even smile.

"Thank you, Lord Fariel." I accepted it with a tone of dismissal. The hint wasn't taken.

"I was wondering if I could talk to you for a minute." He regarded me with such a stern gaze that I knew I didn't have a choice in the matter.

"I am very busy," I drawled.

"I could see that, Your Highness, when I approached," he replied.

I glanced up to see if he was joking, but his blue eyes were serious. I repressed my sigh. When had a noble sought me out to talk? Curiosity grew as I motioned to a chair, and he sat down. I was surprised to see him looking old. As far as I knew, he was the same age as Father, but the years hadn't been kind. His short hair was thin and the light blonde was already gray.

"Thank you," he began. "What I have to say needs to stay between the two of us as I'm not certain who can be trusted. I'm afraid evil is at work here in the palace."

Well, he had my attention. As far as I was concerned, this whole day had been evil. I leaned forward eagerly.

He saw my interest and continued. "As you know, there are five provinces in Eltiria and each province is governed by one noble. This noble is responsible for the well-being of all the people in the province and is honored to advise the king on matters of state."

I sat back in my chair, trying to keep the disappointment off my face. He wasn't concerned about my plight at all. He was talking about the Circle of Chairs, the five nobles who served as a council to Father for a sizable income. Lord Fariel was an extremely wealthy man, due to this honor.

"Your Royal Father, the king, removed three of the nobles from the Circle last night." He leaned forward with his hand on the table. "I was one of them."

Now it became clear. He wanted me to go to Father and ask him to reinstate Fariel. How greedy could one get? Surely he had enough wealth for six lifetimes of easy living. I chuckled. This was the worst time to ask Father for a favor. "Lord Fariel, you know the King can appoint new Chairs any time he deems fit. Surely you have served long enough."

"I was in the Circle before you were born." His voice grew sharp. "And I have no intention of quitting. That's not my point. No other king has removed three at once. Some kings removed one or two, but three new Chairs at once puts your Father at risk for unsound advice."

I opened my mouth to reply but found myself thinking over Lord Fariel's comments. I could not see any greed behind it. "Perhaps some fresh advice, not tainted by the old traditions, is what is needed."

"A valid argument, my lord," Lord Fariel smiled slightly, his blue eyes warming. "I might consider it, but the rumors are saying that Belial is trying to take over the throne."

I couldn't stop the whistle of surprise. Belial wasn't even a Noble. How in all of Adoyni's world did he rise so quickly in Father's favor? I shook my head.

The most outrageous rumors always made their way from the servants' quarters to the royal apartments. Once Mother had tripped on a step, and the rumor circulated that Father had laughed at her and called her handicapped.

"I don't know what you want me to do, Fariel," I said. "I'm sure you've heard through the rumors that I'm not on the best of terms with Father."

"I don't know." Fariel admitted. "I hope that it isn't true, but with the removal of three Chairs, I'm terrified for Eltiria." He looked around and leaned forward to whisper. "Your Grace, some fear Belial is a bad influence."

I couldn't agree more. Maybe Fariel was the ally I needed to get Belial out of my life. "I doubt Father would make that big of a change. He's too traditional to do that. However, I'll do what I can to get back into Father's good graces. Perhaps then I can help you."

You would've thought I'd offered to give him the moon and all the stars by the way Lord Fariel beamed. He suddenly didn't look old as his eyes filled with hope. "Thank you, Your Highness. I knew you would help." He bowed and then whispered. "I'll meet with you again when it's safe." He left before I could say anything more.

Here was the help I needed. I'd play Father's games to get back into favor with him and then oust Belial out of the castle. Patrin would heal, and all would be well.

With my plan in place, the work seemed to fly by, and I finished with enough time to visit Patrin before I had my required sword training.

I flew out of the library, shoved the parchments under Belial's door, and ran to the hospital. A healer let me into his room, but seeing Patrin lying on the bed at the edge of death killed all hope I had.

CHAPTER EIGHTEEN

Fight Alone

I hadn't seen Patrin since they carried him away from the ring, and the change chilled me. His skin, normally tanned from hours in the sun, was as gray as his hair. His cheeks were sunken in as he took shallow breaths. Large bandages were wrapped around his stomach.

"Patrin?" I whispered from the door. He didn't move. I desperately needed him to open his eyes, to get up, to laugh, to be alive. Not this. Not lying in bed, a shadow of a man.

"You can go in."

I jumped and whirled around, furious at being frightened. A man stood behind me. His blond hair seemed to blend into his pale skin. His hands, smooth like one who'd never done menial work, held a tray of ointments and bandages. His light blue eyes slid over me and to Patrin. He briefly nodded as he went to the bed.

He placed the tray on a small table beside the bed. "It would do him some good to hear a familiar voice."

"But he's asleep," I protested. Regrets of what I had done ebbed away as panic doused me. I needed out. This wasn't the place for me. I didn't

know what to do or what to say. This place was as alien to me as a kitchen.

"That's what your father said," the healer grinned slightly as he pulled back the covers. "In fact, he had that very same expression on his face, too. Pull up that stool. Patients have reported they heard people talking when they were unconscious. Patrin might hear us, he might not, but we lose nothing by trying."

I obeyed, but it was like stepping into another world where I didn't know the rules. I could only watch. And hope. My fingers itched to do something, anything, to fix this catastrophe, but I knew nothing about healing.

"Who are you?" I asked quietly.

"Kahil Tawse, sire." He undid the wraps around Patrin's stomach.

I watched as the bandages slowly changed from white to a deep red. My stomach heaved. To distract myself, I tried to focus on the conversation.

"Kahil Tawse? The Physician?" Few healers were privileged to call themselves a physician, since the title belonged to those who completed years of study and had seen success in their work in every kind of ailment.

Kahil briefly looked up at me. "Yes, I studied the sciences under Professor Wallick. In fact, he suggested that I change my field to Medicine. He was an incredible teacher. I followed his advice, and after studying a few weeks, I knew Professor Wallick was right."

I shifted on the stool as the bandages were now soaked with dark red blood. His face showed no concern. I'd never heard of those people he mentioned, but I did know that Kahil Tawse, the youngest physician ever, was considered the greatest healer of the age. I took a deep breath. Maybe Patrin would be all right.

Kahil took off the last bandage and placed it with the rest in a basin on the floor. His face was serious with concentration.

I risked a glance at the wound. It was as wide as several fingers, suggesting that I'd driven the sword in deep as I'd pulled it across his stomach. I grimaced with disgust. Why hadn't Father left me alone? If he had, this would've never happened.

My stomach rolled as I looked. As Kahil washed the wound, I could see that the skin was red around the wound while blood still oozed. Kahil glanced at me and back to his work.

He had noted my repulsion. "If your stomach can't handle this, I understand. The staff will thank you for not making a mess on the floor."

"I'll be fine." I wasn't backing down. I'd watch as my own personal punishment. Father didn't know that seeing this hurt far more than his punishment. "How does it look to you?"

A sickly sweet smell filled the room as he opened the bottle of ointment for the wound. The aroma made my stomach turn even more, but I was too intent on his answer to leave.

"It's fine. A normal wound." The words seemed a bit too loud. He shifted so that his back was to the door. He continued in a whisper. "Belial commanded me to say nothing but positive comments about the wound, but there's something strange about it. Patrin's never gained consciousness, and the wound continues to seep. If it was a wound in battle, I'd think that the blade was poisoned. See how the skin is red around the wound and spreading up his chest?" He began to wrap new bandages around Patrin. "I can't shake the feeling that poison is blocking the healing."

"It's not the disease that the commoners are saying that's in the water, is it?" I tried to keep the panic out of my voice, but I couldn't imagine watching Patrin turn ghastly white, becoming violent, and then slipping into death.

Kahil shook his head. "No. That's different. Look at how red his skin is above the wound. I don't know what it is, but this is not that disease." He bowed slightly and turned to go. As he reached the door, he paused. "Stay if you like. It does good to have someone nearby. No one likes to fight alone."

I moved closer to Patrin and sat down. His slow breathing was the only sound I heard. I hated seeing Patrin like this.

Fighting alone was the worst thing I could think of doing. Unless it was sitting by the bed of the man dying, a man who loved you, and you were the one who had caused it.

I was used to being alone, even though I was surrounded by people. But there were three people I always counted on when life got bad. Father, Mother, and Patrin.

Father clearly didn't need me or like me now that Belial was around. Mother didn't want anything to do with me or life outside her books. And Patrin was dying in front of me.

I had no one to talk to, no one to help me. No one who was glad to see me because we were friends, not because I was the Prince.

Father was wrong. I didn't want to run from responsibility, not the kind that was real. I may not have seen why I had to be present at all the banquets and celebrations wrapped up in my finest clothes with my crown on my head. I didn't get the reasoning for the pageantry that surrounded royalty or the games we played. I didn't see why the power of a king was wasted on trivial disputes.

Patrin was responsibility. Whether or not I was right in my assumption that Belial had controlled my sword, it was my job to make sure Patrin was healed and justice was done for whoever had caused it.

Nothing was going to stop me finding out the truth if Belial could possibly have controlled my sword. And when I found the truth, Belial would answer for it.

CHAPTER NINETEEN

Washing Dishes

I didn't realize it was dinnertime until one of the healers brought me some soup and bread. I tried it, but my stomach was in knots as I watched Patrin. I couldn't eat while I watched him fight death. I willed him to open his eyes. But he never did.

My mind kept going back to what Kahil said. Did Belial really command him not to talk about the wound? Did Father know? Was Father trying to protect me by not telling people it was my sword?

A memory flashed of Father and me riding in the countryside. I couldn't have been more than six, but he set me up on his horse and let me take the reins. I remembered laughing with him. Why didn't we laugh now? Tears threatened to come again, so I decided to leave and meet Straton.

He was in the ring warming up without a shirt on as he went through a series of forms I had never seen. I was surprised at the skill he used as he went through a new set of moves.

I could see no flaw in his ability. He moved like he was one with the blade, like the sword was another limb on his body. Patrin had experience and knowledge over him, but Straton had sheer

talent. I was impressed, even though I was trying
not to be.

When he finished, he didn't acknowledge me.
He climbed out of the ropes and placed the sword
on the rack. Then he put on his shirt and chose
two wooden swords.

"Your Highness." He turned to hand one to
me.

He didn't even bow. I paused, wondering if I
should command him to show me respect. He was
my age, but he came to my shoulders. He looked
like he was from the plains with his tan skin and
dark eyes and his black hair that was pulled back
in a ponytail. Wherever he was from, he was as
lithe and quick as a blade. His eyes held reproach
and dislike. I decided against the reprimand. He'd
probably laugh at me.

I accepted the sword. We never said a word
after that. We faced each other in the middle of
the ring. The disdain in his black eyes turned to
pure dislike. My palm felt moist. I shifted my feet.

Straton took my movement as his opportunity
to strike. As he came at me high, I stepped back to
block the wooden blade. He moved to the left and
attacked low with a quick jabbing motion. I barely
saw it coming, but I felt the sting on my thigh as
the flat of his sword hit me.

I jumped with a yelp. He paused with a look of
triumph which quickly disappeared as he began to
circle me, looking for an opening. I refused to give
him one as I studied him.

We exchanged a series of blows in an effort to feel each other out. Straton responded to my every attack with a speed faster than Patrin.

It was like he could see my thoughts and responded to them before I even started to move. The thuds of the sword grew louder as we both sought for an opening.

And then I saw it. His grip shifted. Whether he was nervous, sweaty, tired, I didn't know and didn't care. I wasn't going to miss it. I brought my sword down on his blade with all the force I had. His blade twisted and swung through the air, clattering to a stop outside the ropes. Straton grabbed his hand from the sting of the hit and froze. I kept the sword ready to strike as a message to him.

"Well done, Your Highness," he said simply without any praise in his voice.

I lowered the sword. "Thank you." I didn't know what else to say. He was saying all the right things, but there was coldness in his manner. I couldn't reprimand him for that. Yet. And, besides, I needed the chance to catch my breath.

Straton jumped out of the ring to retrieve his sword. I ignored the sweat rolling down my face and turned towards him again. In his eyes was a fresh determination that made me very nervous. He didn't like to get beaten.

His wooden blade flashed again, and I blocked at the last moment. How in the world was I supposed to see that coming? I stepped back to give me more time to know what was happening, *but he followed with two quick steps, pushing me back to the ropes.*

I knew what he was doing, but I was too busy blocking to figure out a way to stop him. I missed one of his strikes, my sword swinging back, as he attacked. He restrained the force of the blow as the blade struck me below the ribs.

I dropped my sword and yelled. "Watch it! Don't you know who I am?" Wiping my hands on my pants, I picked up the wooden blade.

"I know who you are," Straton said. His voice was now filled with contempt. "You are the one who killed Patrin."

"He's not dead yet, in case you didn't know," I yelled. "And it was an accident. I didn't do it on purpose." Through my rage, I wondered why I was lowering myself to explain my actions to a commoner.

Straton swung before I was ready. I ducked as it cut through the air where my face had been. I pushed him away with my hands and trotted to the middle of the ring.

"There are no accidents here," he lectured. "What is done is a conscious action. A thought translated into action. You alone are responsible for what your blade does, for if one can't control the blade, one cannot fight."

He was instructing me on responsibility? Father would love that. "I reacted. There was no translating going on."

"Then you'll never be a master of the sword. The sword will be the master of you." He grinned

maliciously. "That is the difference between you and me."

I roared in response as I charged. I wanted to say that the difference between us was that I was born a prince, and he was born a nobody. But I couldn't. The words were lost in my rage.

I flew across the ring at him. His eyes grew wide with surprise as I swung at his head. He blocked my strikes. I didn't even hear the sound of the blades connecting. All I could think about was how he had dared to instruct me.

I pushed him back against the ropes, gaining inch by inch. He tried to swing away, but I blocked his move with a strike to his leg. He jumped back with a cry of pain and held the leg off the ground. I refused to give him any time to recover. Pressing my advantage, I pushed him against the ropes. I had him trapped! Now to disarm him!

But before I could, he stood on his injured leg and after avoiding one of my strikes, whipped his sword past my guard. The blade whacked me on my thigh and stung. I yelped and jumped backwards. My leg throbbed, and I knew there'd be a bruise there later.

I limped back another step. The little thug tricked me. He wanted me to believe that he was hurt and get cocky. And it worked. Before I could grasp what was going on, Straton leaped away from the ropes and circled me.

I blocked his strikes, still reeling from what had happened. He smacked me in the side with the flat of the blade. I bit back the yell I wanted to let loose and backed up to give myself a second to *think, but I felt the ropes of the ring in my back. I wasn't going to give him more satisfaction. He was already getting too much. I could tell by the grin on his face.*

He was playing with me. He was choosing his hits. Both sides now stung from his blade, and my other leg ached below my knee. For every strike I blocked, I missed three. He never missed.

I realized I could drop the stupid wooden blade, and the duel would be over. But I wasn't going to admit defeat until I had to. I clumsily attacked. He blocked effortlessly and then twisted the blade out of my hand. It clattered to the ground. Now I had to admit I was defeated.

"There's always tomorrow," Straton called out. I ignored him as I eased through the ropes and limped away. After a pause, he continued with great scorn. "Your Highness."

I stormed up to my rooms as the sun was beginning to set. What a horrible day. And I had to wake up and do it all over again tomorrow. I punched a tapestry as I reached my door. Waiting for me was one of Father's guards. He snapped to attention as I approached.

"Sire, Your Royal Father the King requests your presence. I am ordered to wait until you are cleaned up and then lead you to him."

I snarled at him and slammed the door. Great. More fun with Father. Had he heard that I talked to Lord Fariel? Or was he watching my time with Straton?

Maybe he had more fun planned for me like washing dishes.

CHAPTER TWENTY

Good Knight

I followed the guard to the Throne Room that was filled with nobles. They huddled in small groups whispering in the shadows. I ignored their bows as I swept past the tapestries of white jaguars and banners of past victories. As I sat down in my chair on the right side of the throne, the whispering resumed.

Golden candelabras with golden candles lit the room. Around the throne was Father's standard of the white jaguar. Far in the background was Lord Fariel with the two other lords who had been removed from the Circle.

Father rarely gathered all nobles together. What was he doing? I smiled as I realized his plans. Father was atoning for his unfair punishment and was rewarding me with knighthood! This was the day when I would become a knight, taking the next step toward the crown.

Father strode through the door, dressed in his finest apparel. His golden crown sat firmly on his head, and he carried the royal scepter. Whatever he had planned, he was using everything he had to show his power as king.

All conversation ceased. As he made his way to his throne, the men bowed. I rose from my chair, feeling the aches from Straton.

My anticipation died as I saw Belial following Father. As Father took the throne, Belial remained standing on his left, just behind the throne.

Normally Father held every eye. But tonight every eye was on Belial who was dressed in black robes without any gold or finery. I couldn't tell if everyone was staring at him because of his choice of clothes or his choice of position.

No one dared stand behind or beside Father when he was on the throne. Even my chair was set down a step and to the side. Yet Belial had taken a position behind him.

I waited for Father to scold him, but it never happened. Silence filled the room. I heard his words but couldn't take my eyes off Belial. He looked like he had won a great victory, for there was triumph in his eyes. I shifted, suddenly nervous.

Father continued. "I removed three nobles from the Circle of Chairs. This has produced many rumors and speculation about whom I will choose next. Tonight I shall end these rumors."

Lord Fariel pushed through the nobles to the front of the room and bowed on one knee. In the candlelight, I thought he looked older than before as worry bore down on him. "My Liege, who are the men that will fill the empty chairs?"

"Worried, are you, Lord Fariel? About the realm or about your purse?" Father scoffed. I gasped. Father never treated the nobles without

respect. I had never heard him even raise his voice
to one of them – something he never hesitated to
do with me.

"Of course the realm, My King, and the crown,"
Lord Fariel shifted.

"None of those things are your concern!"
Father leaped out of the throne as he yelled. Lord
Fariel shrank back in the face of Father's fury.
Father sat back down as Lord Fariel took the
chance to retreat into the crowd of nobles.

"There will be no men to fill the empty chairs,"
Father said, his voice again calm. "I've decided
that this tradition is useless. I am dissolving the
Circle."

Gasps rose from the crowd. I searched for Lord
Fariel. He ignored my glance and stared with fury,
not at Father, but at Belial. I followed his gaze and
saw the victory in Belial's eyes grow stronger.

Belial orchestrated this! These were his words
coming out of Father's mouth. I moved to argue
with Father, but I saw Lord Fariel shake his head. I
settled back with confusion.

"From now on, there will be only one advisor.
He will receive all the compensations that the
former Chairs held, including but not limited to
the full salary, the housings with all their
possessions in each province, the use of the royal
stables, and the honor accorded to the king."

Cries rose up as most of the nobles protested. I
noted that some of the younger nobles gazed
elatedly at Belial. Father allowed for a few
moments and then held up his hand. The room
fell to complete silence.

"As you may already have guessed, there is only one man worthy of such position and honor." Father spoke in a loud tone that held full authority. "My new advisor is Belial."

There was an uproar as the nobles could not contain their reactions. This time the talking continued for a minute after he ordered them to stop.

Father held up his hand. "I will not listen to anyone about this issue. The legal documents have been signed. They are on the table for those who wish to read them. There is no more discussion."

With that, he stood up and left the room. Belial followed in his wake.

The minute they were gone, the nobles fell into great confusion. Some rushed to the document to read the legal terms. Many argued with each other.

I got up, completely forgotten about, and made my way to Lord Fariel. He was standing in the back of the room with a glass of wine. When he saw me approach, he quickly slipped out of the room.

I followed him, but when I reached the hall, he had vanished. Why didn't he want to see me? Was he no longer fighting against Belial? I returned to my rooms, confused and feeling very alone.

CHAPTER TWENTY-ONE

Left the Battlefield

When I woke the next morning, the papers I had given Belial were under my door with large red circles around most of the work. Belial had written *THIS IS WRONG* many times. At the bottom, he left a note.

"Prince Aric, I find most of your work sloppy and incorrect. Work must be neat <u>and</u> correct. Revise your answers. You have until nightfall to finish this correctly. Your Father has been updated with your situation. Belial."

I crumpled the paper into a ball and threw it across the room. Who did he think he was? He couldn't tell me what to do. I watched as the paper bounced across the table and fell to the floor. But he could. Father had given him that power.

I made my way to the Council Room where the petitions had already started. Father glared as I took my place. It was one of those looks that told me I was in trouble. Again. Belial gave me an unreadable expression, and I scowled back.

In the afternoon, Belial didn't reference the paper with mistakes on it, but I knew he'd tell Father if I didn't do as he said. The library fell quiet as I perused dusty old law books. By dinner time, I'd had more than I could take. I stormed out of the library to eat.

The Great Hall was lit with hundreds of dancing candles. Long tables covered with red and gold cloth were groaning with turkeys, lamb and venison surrounded by a variety of green and yellow vegetables. Servants and nobles, clad in bright cheery clothes, dodged out of my way as they bowed. I brushed past them without a glance.

Father and Mother were already on the dais. I tripped over white and gold roses that circled our table and considered kicking them down the steps but flopped into my chair instead. Mother had on a purple gown that accented her reddish-blonde hair. Her golden crown, with blue and white jewels, sat delicately on her hair. Father sat stiffly in his chair, wearing his formal blue and gold. The golden chain around his neck matched the crown on his brow.

Belial sat on his left, dressed in black. If his desire was to look unobtrusive, he failed miserably. He didn't need a crown to possess dignity or power. It flowed through him freely and without reserve. A shiver ran through my spine.

Father and Belial gave each other a long look as I sprawled in my seat. I knew they'd been talking about me. A dark haired maid I vaguely remembered filled my goblet and smiled at me. Her boldness only added to my anger.

"I won't do it anymore." I half turned to Father. "Not with him. Pick anyone else, and I'll do it. But I won't do anything else he tells me to do."

Mother jumped. "Aric, not here. Not now. The nobles are watching."

"I don't care!" My voice rose. "And I won't stop talking about it until Father says I don't have to spend my time with him." I pointed at Belial.

"Aric! It's rude to point!" Mother scolded, her blue eyes giving me a warning.

"Your mother is right," Father responded without looking at me. "This is not the time or the place for this discussion. Leave it be for now."

I stabbed the steak in front of me and cut it ferociously. "Why him, Father?" I asked around a bite. "He's a commoner. Why can't I study with the nobles?" This would convince Father. He always talked about the virtues of the nobles.

Father faced me, his blue eyes flashing with rage. "Belial shows more initiative than any noble. You could learn many things from him, like ambition and responsibility."

"Your Majesty," Belial broke in. "This conflict is between the Prince and me. We will handle it tomorrow when we meet. Do not concern yourself with it."

"This is between my father and me," I yelled at Belial. "Stay out of it. That's an order!"

"Aric!" Mother gasped.

"Enough!" Father roared. The room fell quiet. "You don't give commands. You obey mine. Do you understand me?"

Oh, I understood perfectly. I understood he wasn't going to listen to me. I understood he valued Belial more than me and that everything I did wasn't good enough. I glanced around the

Great Hall at the nobles. Some studied their plates intently. Others stared with their mouths hanging open. The maid stood with a plate of cake covered with strawberries. Her face turned white as she listened to our shouts.

I tried my last resource. "Mother?"

She put down her fork. She was always desperate to regain the lie that we never had any troubles, and tonight that lie was being shattered. "Your education is up to your father, Aric."

I knew it was over. Mother used to take my side. Now I knew that she wasn't only withdrawn from my problems and the world around her; she wasn't even on the battlefield anymore. I snatched the cake from the maid's hand.

"I understand more than you think," I stood up and made my voice as sarcastic as I could. "I'll be in my room if you have any other orders."

No one said a word. As I crossed the threshold to the corridor, I heard Belial's voice, too quiet for me to catch the words. Father and Mother responded with a loud laugh.

Conversation started up again among the servants and nobles. It was like no one cared that I had left.

CHAPTER TWENTY-TWO

A Royal Gift

The cake I'd taken from the Great Hall sat on the table in my rooms beside the papers Belial returned to me. My stomach rumbled suggestively every time I walked by, but I refused to eat it, like I refused to bow to Belial's wishes.

I wondered if I was being irrational. He had come from nowhere with a plea to build a house for healers on the south side of town, the poor side where no one wanted to go. And from that day forward, he was always around.

I ran a hand through my hair. There was something about him that made my skin crawl. He was too good, too perfect. Could a bad person, acting as good, still feel foul? Could you really sense a person's intent?

I resumed my circuit around my rooms. On the third loop, I heard a slight rustling at my door. When I approached, I saw a paper lying on the floor. Leaping to the door, I flung it open.

The hallway was empty. I closed the door slowly and picked up the note. Inside was neat handwriting, although I got the impression that it had been written quickly.

"Prince Aric, due to circumstances, I have to leave quicker than I planned. There was no time to reach you. However, I must warn you. Belial's influence reaches deeper than I thought and his intent is evil. Be careful when dealing with him. I've had word of his past and go in search of proof of his wickedness. Do nothing until I see you again. Take special care not to let them know of your suspicions. The kingdom may depend on this."

It was signed by Lord Fariel.

I kicked a pile of clothes that had piled up since I cleaned my rooms as I continued my route. It occurred to me that I had two choices.

I could capitulate and redo the assignment, or I could refuse. There was no way I was going to give into Belial. I grinned. There was no way to prove I didn't do it if the paper couldn't be found.

"Watch this, Belial."

Taking both pieces of paper, I shredded them into pieces and threw them into the fire. I watched it burn to ash as I grinned.

Belial couldn't prove I skimped on the work, and it was now his word against mine that I didn't redo it. All I had to say was that I returned it under his door. He either lost it, or he was lying.

Why didn't I think of that before? I glanced out the window. Dark already. I needed to get out of the castle to think of a way to fix all the problems that had cropped up recently.

I dressed in the plainest clothes I could find and slipped out my door. My footsteps echoed through the Great Hall as I trotted for the main door. The courtyard was quiet. I stayed in the shadows, so close to freedom I could almost taste it. I headed to the left as the smell of hay and horses filled my senses. Once I got my horse, I would be free.

The stables were blazing with light. Men's laughter rolled out of the building as a horse stomped. I skirted the entrance. As my eyes adjusted, I peered through the doorway.

One of the newest stallions Father had purchased from the south was standing in the aisle. The tall black horse pranced and pawed as he shook his mane. Father and Belial stood to the side as a groom tried unsuccessfully to hold the steed still.

"I know you are interested in racing," Father said. "What do you think of this stallion?"

"To be honest, I've never seen his equal," Belial didn't take his eyes off the beast. "He could race the wind and beat it without trying. You've made a great purchase."

"I think so," Father chuckled. "His name is Kedar. Son of Horlicks, bred to Chaya. He cost a fortune! Enough to make my accountants almost fall over dead. With a little training, and I think Timo's the man for the job, he'll fly to the finish line like those fabled Archippi."

I studied the horse. Horlicks broke every record, and Chaya was the fastest mare ever raced. By the looks of Kedar, he would be as fast as his parents. You could see it in the way he moved. Fierce, fast, and strong. And a desire to fight. To be free. I knew exactly what he was feeling. I grinned. So this was how Father was going to make up to me.

Father put a hand on Belial's shoulder. "That's why he's yours."

I almost fell into the light, but I caught myself at the last moment.

Father continued. "I know it's been a hard few days with Aric. It's going to get worse. You volunteered for a very difficult job of molding Aric into what we want him to be, and I'm grateful to you. Take this gift as a reminder of my favor and a way to find some enjoyment while you mentor Aric."

"S…Sire…I couldn't," Belial protested.

I wanted to strangle him. He wanted that horse as much as I did. I saw it in the way he stared at Kedar hungrily, like he was looking at a million Flames, the new currency Belial had just put into place. All he was doing was playing a game to make Father feel good.

"Belial, I don't care what you say," Father laughed, obviously pleased. The jealousy that rose up in my throat almost choked me. "He's yours. With my pleasure."

I couldn't take it anymore. I glanced back one more time. They stood close to Kedar and chatted like old friends. Why wasn't Father like that with me? I left them behind as I stumbled away.

The shadows, once a comfort, filled me with one thought as dark as they were. I was alone.

I stumbled through the gates without another backward glance.

CHAPTER TWENTY-THREE

A Noble Steed

I passed through Medora without stopping. No one recognized me with my hood up. I needed to get out and away from people. I couldn't stand one more conversation, one more fake smile.

I wandered the countryside, following the roads as they became smaller. The lights faded away as small farms replaced the city. Soon, even the farms were in the distance.

I wished I'd waited until Father and Belial left so I could've got my horse. My feet were already aching. I pushed on as I felt for my money.

I groaned when I realized that I'd forgotten it. I wasn't going back until Father realized how badly he was acting and apologized. But would that take forever? And what would I do for money until then? What did people do to get money?

My stomach rumbled as I realized the dawn was getting close. In the east through the trees, I could see the faintest glow. I'd better figure out how to get some Flames and a horse fairly soon.

Once they found out I was gone, they would be searching for me. Walking was not getting me anywhere very fast.

A stick popped in front of me, and I froze. There was someone here, and I was unarmed. What if it was the monsters, the Seekers Patrin always spoke about to frighten little children? I hadn't thought to bring anything. No sword, no knife, no Flames.

Another snap rent the air. I crept forward quietly, watching the shadows for someone that might leap out at me. All I could hear was the pounding of my heart in my ears. I pleaded with it to slow down, beat quietly, but it only thumped louder.

I peered through the branches. Trees hugged the road. Through a small gap, there was a flash of light. I sneaked up to a thicket of small trees, trying not to make any noise. Tall grass lined the side of the road and whispered as I passed. I slowly pushed a branch aside.

On the other side of the brush was a small fire. It licked the last piece of wood in the small ring of stones. That was what I heard snapping. Not monsters.

Relief flooded me as my heart returned to normal. The growing light showed a small pack of supplies which I would bet my last Flame meant food. Beside the pack was someone sleeping under a heap of blankets.

The grass rustled to my left. I jumped and let go of the branch. It slapped against the other trees as it flew out of my hand. The person under the blankets groaned and shifted. I held my breath as the rhythmic breathing started again.

I grinned when I saw a horse tied to one of the trees. And not any horse. This tall bay, though not as grand as Kedar, was well-bred. He pricked up his ears as he studied me intently with his dark eyes. A small snippet of white hid behind his long black forelock.

We stared at each other. I was taking in his strong neck covered with a dark mane that looked like it had been braided and then released from its bonds. Some of Mother's maids would've killed for hair like that. But what caught my eye was his large chest and long legs. I could eat up the ground with him.

I pulled up some of the grass at my feet. It was no different from what surrounded him, but I hoped that the fact he didn't have to work to get it would convince him I was a friend. I whispered soothing words as I crept toward him. He shifted once, but watched quietly.

As I drew closer, he lowered his head and snorted loudly. The person behind me didn't move. When I was close enough for the horse to take the grass, he sniffed it once and regarded me with what seemed like disdain, as if he were the prince and I was the servant.

I held back my impatience. Rushing this would only cause him to make noise. I fiddled with the grass in my hand, hoping to tempt him, and forced myself to wait. Something that I hated to do. The horse stood as still as a statue. Then he stretched his head forward and sniffed the grass.

"It's much better over there," I whispered. The horse flicked an ear. "You'll like it."

As if he understood, he lipped one blade of grass and pulled it free. He pulled back and chewed the grass like it was a test to see if I was telling the truth.

I felt a flash of humor through the frustration. What a snob this horse was! I waved the grass slowly in front of the horse.

"Come on," I hissed. "Take a bite."

The horse responded. I felt a surge of triumph as it took a small bite. Not hungry but ready to be friends. I brought my other hand up for him to sniff as he chewed.

He investigated with his mouth and returned to his grass. I grinned as I stepped closer and petted his smooth soft neck. I ran my hand to his back. He didn't even flinch. I was accepted.

There was a saddle and bridle by the trees. The rich leather creaked as I picked it up. The metal on the straps clinked. I glanced at the blankets on the other side of the fire. No movement. My hands trembled with excitement. A few more minutes.

He stood quietly as I gently placed the saddle on his back and cinched it up. I petted his neck as I got the bridle and removed his halter.

He placed his head into the leather, taking the bit as smoothly as anything I'd ever seen. I exhaled with relief, growing more attached to him. This horse was finely trained. Someday I'd have to find this peasant and royally thank him for this horse, for I didn't see myself parting with this steed.

I paused in buckling the bridle strap. Was I stealing? The morals of the situation hadn't come to mind, just the necessity of escaping. But I was

the Crown Prince. And that meant Eltiria was mine
when Father died. So this wasn't stealing. This
horse was mine like the trees and the fields of
grain. And I'd find a way to compensate the owner
for the beast when I could.

I slid the reins over the horse's head and
pulled my hood up to hide my face. I tightened
the left rein to point the horse to the road and put
my foot in the stirrup. It was going to be a
beautiful day.

The sun was rising in the east as the birds
began to wake up and sing. I would ride as far as I
could, stopping only for a bit of food at some farm
along the way.

My troubles from the recent days would fly
away as we ate up the road, and when I felt like
returning, Father and Mother would welcome me
with open arms and cries of forgiveness. Father
would forget about punishing me, and Mother
would realize how much she missed me.

I almost laughed as I put a foot in the stirrup,
my hunger and aches gone. This was going to be
perfect. Then a sound broke through the silence,
shattering my dream.

"What are you doing?"

CHAPTER TWENTY-FOUR

Guilty

I was too shocked to think clearly. I should have mounted and raced out of that meadow as fast as the horse could carry me, but I couldn't. The voice I heard made me forget every rational thought.

It was a girl.

What was a girl doing out here in the middle of nowhere? Like some gypsy? I thought all girls hated dirt and were frightened of the dark. Didn't they always ask me to escort them home for that reason?

And the only time I'd ever seen one on a horse was when some guy asked them to ride with him. But then they had their frilly lacy skirts and forced everyone to ride at a walk since they were sidesaddle. I got so hung up on figuring it out that I forgot to run.

"You're stealing my horse!" the girl said. Now she was almost yelling.

I tried to look as innocent as possible, but it didn't help that my hands were holding the reins and my foot was in the stirrup.

The bay stepped toward her. There were noises behind me like she was getting out of her blankets, but I was too busy trying to hop with the horse to look. I had to get on, but the obedient horse was quickly disappearing. His nostrils flared as I tried to rein him in, and he danced sideways.

"What kind of lowlife are you?" The girl yelled, now at full volume.

The horse continued to prance. "Easy, boy," I said quietly. It was then that I felt a sudden and sharp pain in my back. "Ow!"

The horse jumped, four feet spread apart, ready to flee any direction. I swore and hopped closer with my foot still in its stirrup. "Easy now."

"Get away from him, you slimy, no-good, idiotic, worthless piece of dung!"

Something slammed into the back of my head, causing me to shift my weight in the stirrup.

"Stop that!" I roared as I was pelted in my back and legs. "I ORDER YOU TO STOP!"

One of her throws landed on my shoulder and bounced between me and the horse. I saw it was a pinecone. She was hurtling pinecones at The Royal Prince like I was a dog. Rage flooded through me. I roared, "STOP NOW!"

The horse had enough. He bolted forward. I was thrown onto the ground and landed with a hard thud. Pinecones fell on me like giant raindrops. One hit my face and I tasted blood on my lips while the girl continued her stream of insults.

I sat up, holding an arm over my face, and yelped at every hit. "I said to stop it!" I lowered my arm and gave her my fiercest and most royal glare.

A pinecone whipped at me, faster than I could duck, and struck me in the arm. I groaned. A second one hit me in the stomach, making me wince. Then they stopped.

"Who are you? Why do you look familiar?" the girl paused.

I looked up at her to see a girl about my age scowling at me with an armful of pinecones. Her long black hair fell over her shoulders in a messy straggly way, and her dark eyes held a fury certain to scorch me to death if her pinecones didn't kill me first. But it was her clothes that stopped my tongue. She was wearing brown breeches and a blue shirt like a man. I'd never seen a girl dressed like that.

"Uh…" Words died before they were even formed.

"So, all you can do is give orders," she snapped and stood ready to pitch another pinecone at me. "When a lady asks you a question, you're speechless. What kind of man are you? Stealing from a lady? And why do I think I know you?"

I wasn't sure which question to answer first, but I knew without a doubt, that if I didn't start speaking soon, she was going to pelt me again. The horse stopped on the other side of the meadow, a safe distance away from two noisy humans.

I couldn't even remember which question she started with. And then it hit me. She called herself a lady. And so I did the worst thing possible.

I burst out laughing. She stared at me for a minute and then hurled a pinecone at my head.

The piercing pain jolted me back to the moment. I swallowed my mirth.

"What's so funny?" she asked without a trace of humor in her voice.

I couldn't suppress another wave of laughter. I choked on my words. "You…you called yourself a…a lady!" Laughter burst out uncontrollably again.

She lobbed another pinecone at me. This one smacked my shoulder and ricocheted to my face. My humor disappeared. As amusing as this was, I was losing time, and she was treating me without respect. It was time to stop this. I got to my feet.

"To answer your questions, lady." I drew out my words for the most sarcasm possible. "I don't think you are helpless if you have pinecones or anything else you can chuck at people. You will address me as 'Your Highness' or 'Sire' as I am Aric, your liege lord, The Crown Prince of Eltiria, son of The Royal King Adric, descendant of one of the Three Slayers who defeated Seiten with the noble Archippi, sent him Elba Isle, and saved this world. I will rule as my Father, my Grandfather, and Great-Grandfather ruled, according to the wishes of Adoyni Himself. You will give me the respect I deserve."

She dropped the pinecone she held in her hand as I spoke. I wanted her to fling them all away and fall to her knees, but she held onto the ones in her arms and stared at me, jaw open, while I crossed my arms over my chest and waited for her response.

"I…you…" Her voice trailed off.

"The correct response would be 'As you command, Your Highness,'" I snapped. "I know you didn't recognize me. It happens with country folks all the time. Now if you tell me where you live, I'll make sure to send you a token of my royal favor when I return." I strode to the horse.

"You can't have my horse," she whispered. She hadn't bowed as custom, but she didn't dare look at me either. Studying her feet, she continued. "He's mine."

I whipped around. The horse stood patiently behind me. "The complexity of the situation has clearly gone over your head. I am your future king." My voice rose to a yell. She didn't flinch, but her face grew red as she glared at me. "I claim this horse. If I had to explain myself to you, which I don't, I'd tell you that my errand is more important than yours. The horse is mine."

I saw her hand twitch to a pinecone while she glanced at her bundle of supplies by her blankets. "Take everything else I have," she offered. "Not my horse. Please."

The angry spark in her eyes had ebbed, leaving behind something I didn't recognize. Was it fear? Was it panic? I didn't know. I glanced briefly at the bedroll and supplies. "You have nothing else that I want. You will be compensated. My word is my honor."

"Honor!" She snapped, the anger back in full blaze. "What do you know of…?"

Her words disappeared into the sound of hooves on the road. Someone was coming fast. I lunged for the horse on the edge of the meadow, knowing who was coming without seeing them. I swore as he pranced away. I chased him, desperate for my last chance of escape. Men's voices filled the air as I lunged at the horse.

But it was too late. The voices fell silent, the horses stopped. I turned around to see the girl on her knees, bowing to my Father and Belial sitting on their horses not too far away. The pinecones were scattered around her like flower petals.

I groaned. So close and then this dumb girl slowed me down. Her horse stood still, as if he too was awed by Father's presence. Why didn't one thing ever go right for me?

"Like I said, Your Majesty," Belial grinned. It was all I could do to hold myself back from pounding that sickening smile off his face. "I can find him anywhere he goes."

"Aric, get on your horse." Father ordered. A soldier pushed forward with one of the horses I liked to ride.

"Father, I don't…"

"NOW!" Father roared.

I flinched and glared at him. As I passed the girl, I heard her sigh. She thought she was almost free. I wasn't about to let her go her merry way. I paused in front of Father.

"This girl is guilty of crimes against the Crown." I pointed back to her. Her head snapped up as she began to protest. I talked over her. "She should be punished."

"Your Majesty, I have done nothing but protect…" The girl stepped forward with her argument but stopped when Father raised his hand.

"Enough!" His voice was with power. "I will not discuss this here. Bring her as well."

"Please, Your Majesty," she pleaded. "Please let me go my way."

Father paused for a second. I held my breath. If I pushed it too hard, he'd leave her here just to spite me. Father turned his white horse back to the road. "Let her collect her things," he ordered. "But bring her. I'll deal with both of them at the castle."

CHAPTER TWENTY-FIVE

A Simple Wink

I followed behind Father to the castle. I didn't look back, but I knew the guards had made certain the girl was with us. Every part of me hurt from the blasted pinecones, and there was blood on my face.

There was no way I was going to feel sorry for her. She brought this on herself by not letting me have her horse. It was her fault they found me so quickly.

We trotted back to the city and through the streets. Father never looked back or spoke, but I knew he was still furious by the way he rode. Once we entered the castle gates and were in the courtyard, Father dismounted.

"Guards, bring the Prince and the girl to my apartment." He began to march off without even paying me any attention.

"Father, the only thing we need to talk about is what this peasant did to me," I protested.

Father spun around. I took a step backwards. I thought he'd been angry before, but the fire in his brown eyes burned hotter than I'd ever seen before. He regarded me without a word before

*continuing on his way. The guards hesitated for a
minute.*

*Belial threw the reins at a nearby stable boy.
"Didn't you receive an order from your King?" His
voice was sharp as a whip. "Obey him." He didn't
look back to see if his orders were being followed
as he hurried after Father. He didn't have to.*

*Once on the ground, the girl hesitated, reins in
her hand, reluctant to give up the horse. I
smirked. Let the stable boys separate those two! It
was like separating the ocean from the beach.*

*A stable boy pushed through the guards. I
recognized him, for he was around my age, and his
bright red hair stood out from the other stable
boys. But his name eluded me.*

*"My name's Olwydd, m'lady." He took his cap
off. His red curly hair sprung up like it had a life of
its own and bounced in every direction.*

*Olwydd! No wonder I couldn't remember it! I
could hardly believe his own Mother hadn't
forgotten it. Then what he said struck me.*

*Did he really call her a lady? Who'd ever think
this farm girl was a lady? Her hair looked a fright,
tangled and stringy. What skin I could see was
covered with dirt and her clothes were stained with
mud and grime. I snorted.*

*"I can take your horse, Ma'am," Olwydd
continued. "You needn't worry about him. I know
it's hard to trust strangers with a horse like that."
Olwydd didn't seem to notice her frown as he let
the horse sniff his hand. The big bay sniffed once
and then lowered his head for a scratch. "He's a
good one. As good as anything we have here.*

And," he winked at her. "If I get to take care of him, then I have a better chance of seeing you again."

The girl blushed and smiled. "I believe you're the most charming man I've met today." She glanced pointedly at me and laid a hand on the horse's neck. "His name is Kaspar."

She handed the reins over to Olwydd as she stepped toward me waiting at the bottom of the stairs to the Great Hall. "He's a pig. Don't let him have a lot of grain."

I gasped. That's what it took to get her to turn over the reins? A smile and a wink? Some silly words? I could've done that. I shook my head with disbelief.

"I won't. Don't worry, m'lady." Olwydd stroked Kaspar's neck.

"And it will be a pleasure to see you again, Olwydd," the girl smiled. This time the smile lit up her face, and her eyes twinkled.

Olwydd returned the grin with another wink. He bowed slightly and turned to lead Kaspar away.

As the massive doors to the Great Hall swung open, I realized the girl was as nervous as I was. She paused in the doorway and took in the large banquet hall with the rich blue tablecloths draped over the many tables and the elaborate tapestries hanging on the walls.

She stared at the dais where the royal table and chairs sat. The golden goblets and plates sparkled in the light. She regarded me with serious eyes for a moment, and I felt a chill from her glance.

"Your Highness." A guard motioned forward. "Your Father is waiting."

I bit back my angry words. Who was he to remind me? I could have him kicked out of the castle forever. But right now I had very little power. That made me furious.

The guard led us through the labyrinth of hallways, staircases, and rooms. The girl beside me gasped at the sights, sometimes stopping to study a painting or a room filled with rich furniture.

We stopped when we reached Father's door. The girl smoothed down her shirt and tried to brush away one of the stains. I almost laughed at her until I realized I was doing the same thing to myself. I stopped instantly.

But I couldn't fool myself. This wasn't going to go well. I glanced over at the girl. She had her eyes closed with a grimace, like this was her worst nightmare. Well, maybe it was. I wanted to say something to reassure her, but what could I say? This was **my** worst nightmare. I strode forward, ready for battle. I heard the girl follow behind me. Father was waiting with Mother sitting in a chair beside the fireplace.

But what really got me mad was Belial standing beside Father, as if that was his rightful place. It wasn't his place. It was mine, and he had stolen it from me. Well, he'd find out that I wasn't going away without a fight.

CHAPTER TWENTY-SIX

Two Girls

I decided as I crossed the room that I was going on the offensive. This time I was going to tell Father exactly what needed to change. The girl sank into a deep bow as soon as she saw Mother and Father. I ignored her. The first thing was to make Belial leave. I wasn't going to have him hear Father addressing me like a little child.

"I will not have this discussion with him here!" I pointed my finger at Belial.

"You are not in the position to order me," Belial snapped. "After all I've…"

Father laid a hand on his arm, and I envied the look of understanding they shared. "Aric," Father moved slowly to where Mother sat. "Your Mother and I tried to give you the very best life possible."

I resisted the urge to laugh. They were never there. I had a string of nurses and tutors. Mother and Father didn't know a thing about my childhood.

"Yet you are spoiled, and it's clear that you don't care about the kingdom." His voice was empty of the rage. The blankness scared me more than his anger. If he raged, I could yell back. I didn't know how to answer this calm.

Mother refused to meet my eyes, staring at the thick rug under her feet. I wondered how much she cared of what was going on. I blinked back tears, determined not to let them know how much Father's words stung.

"Your recent desertion has led us to take serious action. You clearly did not respect our instructions before," Father paused. He glanced at Belial, who nodded slightly at him.

I gasped. Was he looking to Belial for approval? Father never let anyone, not even Mother, give him commands. Advice? Of course. It was always weighed and rarely taken.

But what I had seen looked like he was asking Belial for permission. I glanced at Mother to see if she noticed, but of course she didn't. Belial raised his eyebrows at me when I sneaked a look at him. Triumph filled his eyes.

Father took a deep breath, reached into the pocket of his tunic, and pulled out a piece of paper. It was burnt along the edges, but the words "This is wrong!" was clearly written across it.

I gasped and took the paper from him. There was no shadow of doubt this was the paper I had burned to ashes. How had Belial retrieved it? My hands ran over the sheet to feel if there were seams, but there were none.

Father continued his lecture. "You will continue your schedule as before, except now the evenings will be with Belial. This time will be spent with him and other tutors he sees fit to round out your education in any other aspects you are missing."

I thought the previous chastisement was a sentence of death. Was I wrong! Father didn't notice my discomfort. Silence filled the room as I stumbled to find something to say.

"Oh, yes," Father spoke up again. "To discourage any more attempts like today, a guard will be with you day and night. Cedrik will be in your rooms at night. He will ensure that you do not try anything like last night until you have proven you can be trusted. And that may be a very long time, so get used to it."

Belial glared at Father. Was this not part of the plan? It was the first time I had ever seen Belial lose control of his emotions so completely.

"But, Father, I was getting out of the castle to think about how to fix all the problems like Patrin, and..." I started to protest and tell him of the poison.

"You are the problem!" Father roared. "And until you realize that, then you will be treated like a child!"

I stepped back in his fury. I didn't know what to say as the words cut me deeper than I thought possible. I blinked back the sting of tears while I tried to find a way to say that I had changed.

I might have been apathetic before, but seeing Patrin on his deathbed changed everything. Before I could find the words, Father turned away from me.

Father regarded the girl and then spoke. "Rise, girl."

I turned slightly to see the girl still on her knees behind me.

"What are we going to do with you?" Father asked in the same stern tone.

"Your Majesty, all I want is to get my horse and be on my way," she said quietly. She still hadn't looked up.

"Where are you going, child?" Mother showed more interest in her than in my fate. "Where are your parents?"

"To Albia, Your Majesty." The girl glanced at Mother. "And my parents are...they're...gone."

Mother gasped, compassion filling her eyes. "An orphan! What do you expect to do when you get there? How will you take care of yourself?"

"Your Majesty, I'm not...I mean...I..." Her voice trailed off. "I don't know."

Were there two girls? One as fierce as a tiger, and the other as mild as a lamb? That was the only way to explain the change from the fierce cat to this docile girl.

"Child, you do not need to fear anymore." Mother approached the girl. I smirked. With her pinecones, she didn't need to fear anyone. "Adoyni commands us to look after the widows and orphans. What's your name, child?"

"Your Majesty. My name is... I... My name is Mali."

Mother gently took one of the girl's hands. "Mali, your parents are gone, but you will never want for anything, if you prove yourself honorable as a child of Adoyni."

Mali's face grew white. But I couldn't tell if it was from fright or anger.

"Adoyni brought you into our lives. You'll be my handmaid. This is a position of honor, so do not take it lightly. Now, present yourself to Cordelia." Mother glanced briefly at Mali's hair and clothes. "She'll show you where you can bathe and get some suitable clothes."

Mali's face fell. She looked more like she was sentenced to the gallows than saved from a life as a penniless orphan.

Mother patted Mali's shoulder. "Do well, and your troubles will be over."

Father snapped his fingers, and the guards stepped forward to escort us away. She bumped into me as she rose from her bow. As soon as our backs were turned, she leaned closer.

"You may not have stolen my horse, but you stole my life," she hissed. "I will find a way to get my revenge."

"Watch yourself," I snapped. "Any threat to me is a threat to the crown, and that is punished with death. Want to guess who'd get your horse then?"

She must not have wanted to guess because she stared straight ahead, her face now flushed, her lips pressed together in a straight line. At the door, she headed left while I went right. I'd probably never see her again in the gaggle of handmaids Mother kept. As the guards led the way to my room, I was quite happy to never have to deal with that girl ever again.

CHAPTER TWENTY-SEVEN

Wounded

Weeks later, I lay in bed watching the sunrise through my window. Cedrik snored louder, making me lose my thoughts. The old warrior found a way to fill my ear with something.

At night, he rambled on about his days in the Razors with Patrin. I learned more of which plants stopped diarrhea, caused constipation, or took away pain, or that were good for stopping bleeding than I ever wanted. He talked of fabled animals like Seekers that they supposedly fought.

The rest of the time was a mind-numbing blur. Belial forced me to spend hours studying, and Father dragged me out to practice with Straton.

The first couple of times, Father climbed in the ring with me, but after I disarmed him without even trying, he sat down on the benches outside the ring, looking subdued and pale.

I thought that strange. I'd never seen Father weak or shaky. His soldiers complained that he had the energy of three men. But recently, he had slowed down. In fact, the great event today, which was making me feel even more reluctant to get out of bed, was a banquet in honor of Belial's new

*position. It had been postponed twice in the last
week because Father was sick.*

*A loud pounding on my door caused us to
jump. Cedrik lay back on his bed with a groan and
pulled the blankets over his face.*

*"Stop making such a racket!" I yelled out. "I
can hear you. The whole world up to Merrihaven
can hear you. Give me a second to get to the
door."*

*The thudding stopped abruptly. I ran my
hands through my hair and opened the door. Mali
stood there with her arms crossed. She wore in a
green dress with plenty of lace and ruffles. Her
dark hair was curled into ringlets hanging around
her face while a matching green ribbon circled her
head. I blinked, surprised to see her, surprised to
see her looking pretty.*

*She wasn't thinking the same of me. Her
eyebrows rose as she took in my wrinkled sleeping
clothes, bare feet, and messy hair. There was no
friendship in her eyes. Obviously she still hadn't
forgiven me for whatever misfortune she believed I
caused her.*

*She reached into a pocket of her dress. "The
Queen, Your Royal Mother, requested that I bring
this to you." She held out an envelope of Mother's
stationary.*

*I didn't take it, just to keep Mali waiting for a
moment longer. She lost all patience and started
waving the envelope in front of my nose.*

*"Are you going to take it, or should I chuck it
into your rooms?" she snapped.*

I snatched it out of her hand. "You have a lot to learn if you are going to survive around here. Like how to be respectful."

Her eyes flashed with rage. "And I suppose you would be the one to teach me! In case you hadn't noticed, I don't enjoy doing needlework all day, and I had things to do before you wrecked it. The first chance I get, I'm out of here."

"Good," I teased. "You make a horrible handmaiden."

Her face went beet red as she fought to keep back angry words. I grinned as I leaned against the door frame and crossed my arms. "Why do you hate me so much?" I asked. To be honest, she intrigued me. I think she was the only person who had ever openly despised me. Belial coldly disdained me, but Mali radiated scorn like a fire spreading its heat.

She didn't even pause to think. "Because you take no responsibility for your position. Because you don't care for the people under you. You don't know a thing about your land, and yet you expect honor. All you care about is...is...when you're getting dinner!"

Her words stung. But I wasn't about to admit it. "And what does an orphan know about ruling?" I unfolded my arms and straightened.

"You don't know who I am!" She bit her lip like she was trying to stop herself from saying more. "I'm just delivering that message from your Mother." She started to stomp away.

"Wait!" My voice cracked like a whip. "Don't you know the penalty for not paying respect to royalty is death?"

Mali's face was now pale with anger and her eyes sparked, but she kept her voice low. She said something that I didn't catch. I was sure it wasn't a nice word. It was nice to see someone having a worse time than I was. She gave me an acceptable curtsey and swished away.

Closing the door, I shuffled back to my bed and flopped down while I opened the envelope and pulled out the note. "Cedrik, you'll never believe this. Mother wrote that all activities except the banquet have been cancelled!" I hooted with excitement.

Cedrik propped up on an elbow, his grey hair disheveled and his green eyes serious. "Did she say why?"

"Father isn't feeling well, and they want to make sure he'll make it through the banquet. I'm free!" I jumped to my feet. "Want to go for a ride? I could use a break from this place."

"The King's never sick," Cedrik said quietly. "I've known him since he was younger than you are, and I've seen him sick only twice. Even after nights in the frigid cold, even after all the men around us came down with sickness, your Father stayed healthy. Why is he sick now?"

"Well, he's old," I started.

"He's younger than I am," Cedrik snapped.

"Well, I guess that makes you really old then," I laughed.

Cedrik threw a pillow at me, which I easily ducked, but then he consented to go for a ride. I noticed that Mali's horse, Kaspar, was in the stalls, but Kedar was gone. I wondered if Belial had sent him to Northbridge.

When we returned from our ride, Cedrik opted to go to the library while I visited Patrin.

The hospital was quiet as I entered. I passed by the first couple of rooms when I saw the familiar green skirts dash into a room on the left. I followed, curious to see what Mali was doing. When I entered the room, she was standing in front of the bookcase with her back to me. She was stretching up on her tiptoes to reach a book on a high shelf.

"What are you doing?" I asked.

She shrieked and jumped. "Nothing. I...I..." She stopped talking and started for the door.

"Who are you?" I demanded. "With a horse like that, you aren't some forlorn orphan. Unless you stole the horse."

"It's not important," she protested. "And I didn't steal Kaspar!"

"I think you keep forgetting who I am. Don't forget I'm the Crown Prince of Eltiria. Someday I'll be king, and you will have to answer to me. I'm more powerful than you think."

"And I'm not as low as you think." Mali fled the room.

Curiosity drove me to the bookshelf. What was she trying to reach? I searched the line of books. Every single one was about poison. Was she trying

to poison someone? Is she in league with Belial? I
turned to go to Patrin's room in deep thought.

Patrin's door was open, so I gently knocked
and entered. He was lying on the bed. His cheeks
were beginning to sink in, and there were bags
under his eyes. I stared for a minute, shocked at
how someone so strong and alive could be
reduced to nothing in a few short weeks.

A hand squeezed my shoulder, and I stifled my
yelp, jolted from my lonely thoughts. Kahil
motioned me to be quiet and tiptoed away from
Patrin's room. I followed as quietly as I could.

"I didn't want you to disturb him, Your
Highness," Kahil said. His voice was tired, and he
looked a lot less confident than before. "He gets so
little sleep that I hate to wake him."

I nodded. "How's he doing?"

Kahil shook his head. "It's the oddest wound
I've ever seen. It oozes blood continuously. We
should've seen some improvement by now. That's
not the only odd thing. He's not sleeping. He
tosses and turns, moaning and groaning in his
sleep. When he wakes, he speaks of monsters. Like
I said, if it was a battle wound, I'd swear he's been
poisoned, but who would poison a blade here?"

My good mood from the ride was gone. "Is
there anything I can do for him?"

"You could sit with him a while," Kahil
suggested. "He seems to rest better when someone
is in the room."

I padded back and took the chair by his bed. I
didn't really want to be there. But I was the one
who did this to him. I'd do what I could to help

him. I watched him breathe laboriously and thought about what Kahil said. Who would've poisoned Patrin? Everyone loved the grizzly old warrior.

The minutes turned to hours as I stayed in the chair. Behind me, I could hear the quiet rustle of the hospital. I became increasing frustrated by the task I was given. Was it true that the only thing I could do was to sit here?

I thought about praying to Adoyni, for the priests always said that the prayers of faith will save the one who is sick. I had prayed my way through stuffy noses, upset stomachs, and various bumps and bruises with no dramatic change. But it couldn't hurt to give it a try for Patrin.

"Adoyni," I whispered. "We don't know what's wrong with Patrin, but I think he's going to die, and it's all my fault. Could you please heal him? We need You to work in his life. Thank you."

I opened my eyes and waited for Patrin to turn a healthy pink and leap out of his chair with a cry of joy. But it never happened. I grew more frustrated the longer I waited.

Finally, I couldn't sit anymore. I jumped up from the chair and left the hospital without a word. My mind was tumbling with thoughts on how to help Patrin. If the greatest physician in the world only knew to sit beside him, who else could we ask for help?

I meandered through the kitchens, snatching a bite or two of the delicacies the cooks were preparing. As always, my snacking was treated with a gentle reprimand. When I winked at one of the cooks scolding me, she grinned and slipped me another chocolate delight.

I munched on the snacks as I made my way to my rooms. When I got there, I saw that Cedric was gone. With my mind still churning, I circled through the rooms.

On the fifth pass through the sitting room, I caught a glimpse of my sword. It was leaning on a bookcase. I stuffed the rest of my meat pie in my mouth and drew it from its scabbard. The setting sun shone on the silver colored blade. I was thinking of what Kahil said of poison.

I whipped off my shirt and put the blade to my upper arm close to my shoulder. It was impossible for someone to poison Patrin after he got to the hospital. He had to be poisoned before he got there. He was fine when we started dueling. That left only one possibility.

I pressed the blade into my arm and hissed as a sharp pain responded, but I kept pushing, determined to put an end to this question. I cut until I saw a thin line of red streak my skin. The blood oozed as my arm continued to throb.

Would I see the poison working? I was mesmerized as the red grew larger and began to drip down to my elbow. The cut was as normal as any other cut in the world, expect for the fact that I, an idiot, had done it to myself.

I punched the table in frustration and groaned as my fist reverberated through my shoulder. I was so sure the sword was my answer. If it had been poisoned, it would have answered Patrin's

problems. But, instead I had injured myself
without cause.

I shuffled to a nearby cabinet, trying not to
groan, and searched for the box of medical
supplies one of my many nurses had left behind.
Dripping blood on the floor, I went back to the
table and dressed it.

There was no way I was going to tell anyone,
especially Cedrik, what I had done. They'd laugh
at me for my foolishness.

In a foul mood, I cleaned up my mess,
returned the sword to where it was, and dressed
for the feast. My mood blackened every time my
arm twinged. Watching Belial be honored with a
banquet was going to be even more painful.

CHAPTER TWENTY-EIGHT

Dragons Dance

The Great Hall was prepared like I'd never seen. The candelabras were pure gold, and the candles dyed blue, the color of our house. The usual tapestries had been replaced with ones lined with gold and silver threads.

As I tread carefully not to step on Mother's golden train or Father's blue cloak lined with fur, I noticed that each table was set with goblets and plates that twinkled with blue, red, and green gems.

Fruits, breads, and cheeses were carved into jaguars and placed on the tables. Alongside them, I saw similar decorations of a red dragon in flight on a bright yellow background. The wings were spread and the feet dangled in the air revealing sharp talons.

Was that what Belial chose to symbolize his house? I tried to remember what the tales said about the animals, but I hadn't read those stories since I was a kid.

What I found even more interesting was that the decorations of the fabled Archippi were gone. It was traditional to have some mention of the

*winged horses in every royal proceeding. Why swap
one legendary figure for another?*

I caught myself before I stepped on Mother's
train and stumbled slightly. Cursing myself for not
paying attention, I watched as a servant pulled out
Father's chair, and he lowered himself in his chair
at the royal table with exaggerated care. His face
was white and shone with sweat from the walk. His
eyes were dull, as if he was no longer interested in
the world.

I was so focused on Father that I didn't realize
the servants had made a mistake. They pulled out
Mother's chair at Father's left hand, but then slid
out a chair next to Mother for me.

I glanced at Father to see if he had noticed the
error, but he was taking a drink of his wine. My
place as Crown Prince was at the right hand of
Father. No one ever took my chair. I started to
protest when Mother shook her head and subtly
nodded to the seat beside her.

I balked. But the look in Mother's eyes stopped
my words. Her bright blue eyes pleaded with me to
comply. They were filled with worry and misery. I
sat beside her as she reached out and softly patted
my hand. The nobles took their seats.

Once the hall fell silent, Father began to speak
slowly like it was taking a great effort. "Nobles and
honored guests, we are here tonight to celebrate
the accomplishments of one man."

I almost gagged but kept my face straight. This
was going to be a long night.

"Due to his wisdom, I have appointed him as
my advisor over Eltiria. We gather tonight to

honor him in his new position. Please rise to greet your new chancellor, Chancellor Belial."

The nobles rose as trumpets played. Belial strode into the Great Hall far more majestically than Father had. He was dressed in his habitual black robes. On his arm was a woman with copper hair that flowed freely down her back. Her gown of forest green satin was tied with a gold belt with one golden key. A headband of silver leaves dotted with green gems was the only ornament she wore. They approached Father and bowed.

Father smiled. "Rise, Chancellor Belial and Lady Nephesus. Please sup at my table. Let the feast begin."

Servants appeared carrying massive trays of food. They wove in and out of tables, delivering the delicacies. The musicians in the far corner began a soft tune. I saw Mali bring goblets our direction and groaned.

"What's wrong now?" Mother asked.

"Nothing," I lied. "Just went for a ride today, and I guess I'm sore." I held my breath to see if she would believe me. She must have because she changed the subject.

"What do you think of Nighthawk? Isn't she lovely?"

"Is that the woman with Belial?"

"It's Chancellor Belial now, Aric," Mother corrected with a stern tone. "And, yes, that is Nighthawk Nephesus."

Mali plopped my plate of food down in front of me. I scowled at her, but she was listening intently to Mother. I cleared my throat pointedly at her and motioned to Mother. Mali gave a little squeak and turned to get Mother's plate.

I decided the only way to survive this night was to not talk to anyone. I was still eating when the servants cleared the Hall of the tables and prepared for dancing.

Father acknowledged me for the first time. "Aric, I will not lead the first dance as tradition. You will do it for me. Now."

I pushed back my chair as the musicians took their places. Glancing around, I carefully schooled my face although I wanted to roll my eyes. The Hall was filled with the nobles' daughters decked out in their finest. They watched me like dogs waiting for the rabbit to run. Surveying them made me want to run like that rabbit. There was no one here I wanted to dance with.

Mali stepped up to remove Mother's plate. She was dressed in a beautiful gown of red. Her hair was in ringlets that hung to her waist. She wore a gold headband and around her neck was red gem set in gold. I remembered those pinecones she had flung. It was payback time.

"Mali," I said.

Mali reached for Mother's plate without looking at me. Was she really ignoring me? She still didn't respond.

Mother glanced up at her. "The Prince is calling for you."

She jumped and turned to me.

"You will dance with me. Now." I held out a hand.

Her eyes had the look of a young fawn that didn't know if it should run. She shook her head. I held out my hand with my eyebrows raised. No one said no to me. She swallowed and took my hand, but her eyes held a flash of anger as I led out to the floor.

When we reached the center of the room, I bowed to Mali. She responded with a deep curtsey that made me raise my eyebrows. So she did know how to do it properly. The musicians began the song as we started to dance.

"I'm going to make you regret this," she growled as she twirled. "You keep dragging me into your life, when all I want is to live mine without you!"

"Don't forget the proper terms when addressing royalty," I scolded. "Cordelia would tan your hide if she heard you. Since we're on the subject of names, what's your real name?"

Mali took a few wrong steps. "What are you talking about?"

"Come on." I rolled my eyes as I spun her around. "I'm no idiot. You had to think like mad to come up with a name in Father's chambers, and now when I tried to get your attention, you acted like you'd never heard someone call you Mali before. Who are you?"

We danced several paces while she glowered over my shoulder. If the daughters of the nobles were jealous of her, they had no concern. She clearly hated every minute spent with me.

A shadow of sadness passed over her face. I suddenly wanted her to be the girl in the meadow with the pinecones.

She sighed. "I might as well tell you. After this little stunt you are pulling, it won't take much for the nobles to realize who I am." She took a deep breath and closed her eyes for a second like she was leaping off a tall cliff. "My name is Reveka Turow."

She waited for my reaction, but while the name seemed oddly familiar, I didn't know why I should know who she was.

"Oh, of all the stars above, you are so self-absorbed!" She seemed to stomp with frustration instead of gliding across the floor. "My father is Melchior Turow, Lord of Shiel. You and your parents came to visit our manor on Shiel Lake about ten years ago. Remember?"

It was coming back to me. It was one of the few times Father and Mother had taken some time out of their schedules. I could remember the beautiful manor. While there, we rode over the gentle hills surrounding the lake and boated together. I think Father and I even fished. Just like a real family.

"Your parents loved it there," Reveka continued.

A memory that was almost gone came back with such force that it punched me hard enough to make my teeth rattle. There was a girl at Shiel who knew everything about the province. Father had been captivated listening to her. They had discussed tenant issues and how some laws inhibited the motivated tenants from rising above their position.

I groaned. Father loved Shiel. He couldn't claim it since it was owned by a noble. So, instead, he found the next best thing. The agreements were already signed and sealed. When I was married, Father could enjoy the manor all he wanted.

"No one cares whether I want this or not, but I'll tell you," Reveka continued. "I don't want to be trapped here. I have far more important things to do at Shiel. I left on an urgent errand, and this is slowing me down. It may even be too late, and besides I don't want to marry you!"

I said the first thing that came to mind. "I don't want to marry you, either!"

Judging by the angry flash in her dark eyes, that might not have been the wisest thing to say. But what did the girl think? That the way to get a guy to fall in love with her was to beat him up with pinecones?

I ignored her and continued. "I'm trying to figure out a way to deal with Belial."

"The dance is almost over," Reveka said. "I was in the room with your parents when Belial came with Nighthawk. I saw her slip something into the king's drink. He was sicker after he drank it. And tomorrow morning, they are traveling to a grove of trees for his healing."

If I found some sort of evidence of treachery, I could use it as proof. "I'm going to sneak into his palace and find something to prove what you said," I said. "Come with me."

"No!" Reveka protested. She spun around. "I'm taking my chance to leave while your Mother is gone. My duties are in Shiel, and I have to get back. Please let me go home."

The music stopped. "Meet me behind the stables after they leave. If you're not there, I'll send the guards after you and drag you back to the castle."

Her face grew red with anger. She started to protest, but all eyes were on us. She nodded briefly as she dropped a curtsey. I returned a slight bow and selected another dance partner. But I couldn't stop thinking about Mali. I escaped as soon as I could to my room.

I took off my shirt, hissing as my arm stung with the movement. Deliberately wounding myself for nothing! I grabbed the bandage and growled as it tore off the hair on my arm.

But my anger turned to shock when I saw the wound. The inch long cut was redder than normal, and pus had soaked the wrapping.

I sniffed it cautiously and a gagging odor of death filled my lungs. It was then that I realized the truth. Someone had poisoned my blade. And now the venom was in my blood.

CHAPTER TWENTY-NINE

The Last and First

I woke up the next morning early, thanks to Cedrik's snoring. My biggest problem was how to get away from him. He was the most loyal soldier Father had, and he was smart.

Not only that, I was willing to gamble that he could track my footsteps across stone. But try as I might, I couldn't think of one way to lose him.

Cedrik woke up as we got ready for the day in a quiet fashion. It seemed that someone had a little too much fun last night because he moaned and groaned as he dressed. I hid a grin.

A servant knocked on my door and handed me a note from Father that requested I come to his rooms with Cedrik. We entered his rooms, only to find Father still in bed.

I couldn't keep back the gasp of surprise when I saw him. His face was white, his hands trembled. But what shocked me more than anything was his dull eyes.

His eyes usually sparked with anger, twinkled with laughter, or danced when sharing a joke. Now it looked like life itself was sucked out and all that was left was a dry husk.

"Aric," Father spoke, his voice hoarse and weak.

I knelt beside his bed, suddenly terrified that he was dying. I wasn't ready for the throne. I didn't want it. I didn't want to watch him leave forever. Father took my hand, his palm cold and clammy in mine.

"All the things that I said were your faults are your greatest strengths. I was wrong to try to make you into something you're not. You are not filled with mistakes and errors. You have a fierce love when you choose to love and never give up when you believe you are right."

He took a shaky breath. "I pray you will love Eltiria and do what is best for her. You will be a great king, and I'm sorry that I didn't give you more time to grow into it. I'm sorry we didn't spend more time together. That is my deepest regret."

"Father, what are you talking about?" I squeezed his hand tighter.

Cedrik shifted behind me and caught Father's eye. Father tried to sit up as Cedrik bowed. "You have served well, Cedrik. I never thanked you enough for that or for your friendship. Return to your life. I no longer need you to watch Aric, for he is relieved of all punishment."

"Your Majesty, it has always been my honor to serve." Cedrik bowed low again and retreated out of sight.

"Father, don't go," I pleaded. "Stay here. Trees can't help you. You know that. Let me help you. I'm sorry I haven't been the son you wanted, but

let me try to fix all these problems before you go
to the grove. Please. I can do better. I know I can
fix it!"

Father nodded and started to say something,
but Belial strode into the room. His voice carried
over what Father was saying.

"The King desires to go to the grove for
healing. It may be the only way to save him." Belial
regarded me with a dark expression. "You do want
him to get better, don't you?"

"Of course I do," I stuttered, surprised at the
question.

Belial raised his eyebrows as he looked away. "It
seems strange when the one who would gain the
most tries to keep the King away from what clearly
will help him."

"Are you saying...?"

"Men, bring the litter. We are running out of
the time." Belial snapped his fingers as the men
serving Father jumped at Belial's commands and
began preparing for the outing.

"Aric," Father called as they lifted him onto the
litter.

I drew closer.

"I love you." Tears streaked his cheek.

I stared. Never had I seen him cry. Not even
when his own father or mother died. He said many
times when I was growing up that tears were for
the weak, not something for a warrior or king.

I blinked back the tears that threatened and
said the only thing I could.

"I love you, too."

Belial nodded, and the men picked up the stretcher. Within seconds, the room was empty, and I was alone.

Tears slipped down my face as Father's words echoed in my head.

It was the first time he had ever said that he loved me.

Was it going to be the last time I ever saw him?

TREPIDATION

'When the ruler is filled with trepidation,
fear increases within the realm."
~DOLAG

When Jehun reached Northbridge, he saw the horrors the quake had brought. Even on the outskirts of town, there were demolished houses. People covered in dirt and blood worked in their tattered clothes desperately trying to find family and friends still trapped in the rubble. He saw one older lady sitting on a pile of lumber that used to be a house. The woman wept, but no one consoled her.

He hurried past them to the center of town. The damage was worse than he thought it would be. Jehun paused and examined the tear in the soil with a morbid fascination.

In the past, quakes had come and caused pain to both Jehun and the people living in the area. The tremors caused small cracks in the soil, but with time, the cracks and pain faded.

This quake made one enormous crevice from the north side of town and formed a straight line to the south. It shot through the heavily populated areas – the market, the streets with the inns filled with people waiting for the races, the poorest areas of town. The hole that was left from the quake was as wide as the deepest canyons Jehun knew of and deeper than the subterranean fissures of the ocean.

Angry at whatever had caused this to happen, Jehun whirled away to go to the Temple of All as Belial had ordered.

Before he left, a cry sounded from the rubble, and men ran in answer. With great teamwork, they began to clear away the rubble.

One man in a wheelchair made his way through the woods and debris scattered on the ground. Although the path was littered with obstacles, he barely seemed to notice.

He stared at the men working with an intensity Jehun had never seen before. The man only stopped when it was too dangerous to get closer. Jehun was close enough to hear him whisper a prayer.

"Please, Adoyni, please let it be Rhiana this time. Let her be okay. Please."

The men shouted to stop. Everyone peered down at the hole they had created in the fallen house. There was a time of silence as all held their breath. Jehun didn't even notice the pain as he waited to see who was rescued and if they were still alive.

"She's alive!" The shout echoed up from the hole.

The rescuers yelled in triumph. Some of the men clapped each other on the shoulder. But throughout the joy, there was a hush among those waiting and watching.

Jehun could see their questions as clearly as he could see the weariness on their faces. Who is it? Is it one of my family? Will I be the one who gets to hold my loved one once again and cry tears of joy? Or will I have to be happy for another while my heart breaks again?

The man in the wheelchair gripped the armrests until his knuckles were white. He strained to see over the heads of the other people as the men carefully brought the trapped person to freedom.

"Who is it?" One woman yelled out, unable to bear the waiting any longer.

Silence fell as they all struggled to see the face. The men parted. A young girl lay on a stretcher made out of strong cloth and supported by wooden poles. Her brown hair, soaked with mud and blood, dangled to the ground.

A man in the back of the crowd yelled "Lethia!" He shoved his way past the others. Some stumbled out of the way, but most stood in dumb shock as they realized the girl was not the one they were waiting for.

The man reached the stretcher as the bearers put it gently on the ground. A healer raced up with a bag of medicine while the man collapsed beside the girl. He scooped her up in a hug as he promised to never let go. Tears of joy flooded down his face.

Jehun felt cheered by the happy ending until he saw the man in the wheelchair. The other people turned away and began to search again as soon as they recovered from their disappointment.

But this man watched the scene at the stretcher. Tears flowed down his face with the same intensity as the father who had found his daughter. Only the man in the wheelchair was not crying from joy.

"Where are you?" he asked. "Will I ever see any of you again?"

No one was there to answer his questions.

Jehun turned away from the tears before he was overcome by the raw grief. As he made his way to the Temple of All, he couldn't help but think that it was all Adoyni's fault.

That family had been torn apart, and Adoyni had done nothing to stop it. What kind of love was that? His grief and pain grew into anger as he left the dirty streets and entered the Temple of All.

CHAPTER THIRTY

Snobs

Kai opened his eyes as the pain in his chest receded to a burning throb that allowed him to breathe slower. He took several deep breaths and rubbed his chest.

As he sat up, black spots appeared in his eyes, and he winced. When he peered under his shirt again, he saw the burn mark over his heart. He poked it and gasped as it flamed up in an angry response.

People didn't get burned suddenly. Was it related to killing Bowen and Yorath? But he'd killed Unwanteds before, and this had never happened.

He took another deep breath. At least he was out of the hallway. The sunlight and soft breeze never felt so good.

He stood up slowly and looked around. He was on the top of a hill surrounded by a large city with tall walls. Trees that were beginning to get their leaves covered the gentle hills that lay outside the gates. He didn't recognize anything. Wherever he was, it wasn't home.

He stood on a wide street paved with cobblestones. There were huge houses spread apart by large manicured lawns with flowers decorating them.

A striking black horse pulling a carriage trotted down the cobblestone road to Kai. The man sitting in the back was dressed in fine clothes and a rich red cloak. He gripped his black and golden cane tight as they passed Kai.

"Can you believe that, Edan," he sniffed to the driver. "Now they're coming up here! Why can't they stay down with all the other trash?"

Kai didn't hear the reply of the driver as the man slapped the reins on the horse's rump, and the carriage jerked forward with a sudden burst of speed. As they turned around the corner, the driver peered back at Kai like he was afraid Kai might follow.

Kai almost did. It would've been fun to terrorize someone so rude. What had he done to give such a bad impression? Was it because he wasn't rich?

But before he could do anything, he heard another carriage coming down the road. He fingered the hilt of his sword, contemplating drawing it and scaring the next snob that came his way.

Perhaps it would be better to figure out where he was first. He huddled behind some bushes and peered through the branches.

The other carriage pulled by a sorrel down the road. There were two people in the back. The closer man was older and dressed modestly despite the wealth displayed with the carriage and the horse.

The other person in the back was slightly older than Kai. He wore torn and dirty clothes that were soaked in blood around his waist. He looked hungry, tired, and pale. His black hair was messy and unkempt.

"It's so amazing you made it back alive, Rica," the older gentleman said. "These stagecoach robbers are getting out of control. Surely Chancellor Belial will take some action since it has now struck so close to home."

"I certainly hope so," Rica replied. His voice was low and weak. "Thank you for stopping and giving me a ride."

"Anytime, my young friend," the older man slapped Rica on the back.

The carriage pulled through the driveway where Kai was hiding, and Rica climbed out. He moved stiffly and gingerly like every muscle hurt.

Something about him made Kai think that he knew Rica. But from where? The name even sounded familiar.

Rica made his way up the stairs of the large white house to the large oak door. But before he could open the door, it flung open, and a woman with black hair flew out and ran to Rica.

She swept him up in a tight embrace. Kai saw tears streak down her face as she repeated Rica's name as she squeezed him.

Rica broke away with a laugh. "You don't know how good it is to see you, Mother. How good it is to be home."

Rica's mother laughed and cried at the same time. "I've been beside myself with worry. We received word that the coach was robbed." She broke off, pushed him out to arm's length, and gasped. "Are you hurt?"

"No. Well, yes," Rica laughed shortly. "It's almost healed. I'm sorry for your worry, Mother. They kidnapped us, and it took a while to get away and get back. But it's over now."

"Don't tell me." The woman let go of Rica and stumbled back against a large white column that lined the front of the house. "Don't tell me Lizzy is dead."

Rica! That's right! Kai about smacked himself for being so slow. Lizzy was always going on about her brother Rica. This was her house and family. He'd gotten the impression she and her mother weren't close.

But if he was at her house, that meant that he was in Albia, not that far from Northbridge! He glanced to the northeast to see if the Razors were in the distance, even though he knew they wouldn't be visible. His heart still dropped when the horizon was empty.

"She's not here?" Rica asked. His words were filled with concern. "Where did she go? I waited and waited for her."

"That girl's as flighty as her father," Lizzy's Mom responded shortly. "And of all the times I don't need a scandal! You don't know yet!" She held up her left hand. "I'm engaged!"

Rica didn't respond for a minute. "What about Dad?"

"What about him?" she snapped. Then she waved her hand again. "Look at the ring."

Rica inspected her ring but didn't smile. "Wow! That's a rock! The guy must be rich."

"Oh, he is, and soon he'll be even richer," she grinned. "Come in. I'll tell you how it all happened. We'll spread the word that Lizzy's with her father. I'll have to send someone to find her, but it will have to be quiet. Isn't that just like her finding some way to always draw attention to herself and never think of anyone else?"

Kai heard about all he could take. He knew Lizzy thought of everyone else in Eltiria instead of herself and had sacrificed a lot to purify the water. He knew that she longed for her Mother to love her instead of being so harsh. And he knew that she wanted for her parents to get back together again.

He jumped up, ignoring the throbbing pain, and started through the small copse of trees that ringed the house. But before he broke free from the trees, a shadow ahead of him moved. Volundr, the Seeker from the stone labyrinth, stood in his way.

"Where do you think you are going?" he asked. His axe was still on his belt, but he held a long sword in his four-fingered hand.

CHAPTER THIRTY-ONE

Flying Maggot

Kai didn't even bother to talk with the Seeker. He was going to tell Lizzy's Mom exactly what he thought of her, and then he was going home. No sorcerer, no Archippos, and certainly no Seeker was going to stop him this time.

He whipped his sword out of the scabbard and lunged at the Seeker. Volundr didn't wait for him but met him halfway where the trees were farthest apart. Their blades met in the air over Kai's head.

The force caused him to stumble back. He felt weak. Tired. The constant pain was sapping his strength.

He knew there was more that was wrong, like something was missing. Volundr closed the gap and attacked again. Kai responded, although he knew he was moving too slowly, and blocked the strike before it sliced his stomach.

As the two swords met again, he realized what it was. The sound was gone. There was no clash, no banging. There was no noise of their struggle. No one would hear them and come running to help. He was alone with the monster.

"Belial won't win," Kai panted.

"He already has," Volundr laughed. His teeth were long and sharp like a large cat.

As the Seeker struck again, Kai noticed that he was being pushed back to two trees that stood apart from the rest. Something about them seemed wrong. They didn't quite match the other trees. It seemed like they'd been planted after all the others, like someone purposely planted them beside each other.

He tried to sidestep away from Volundr, but the Seeker casually beat him back. He lost another foot of ground and knew the monster was trying to force him to the trees.

"He lost, remember? I got the salt into the water and purified it." Kai tried to taunt the Seeker into a mistake. He focused on the sword instead of the hideous face or the size of his foe.

Volundr laughed, but it sounded more like coughing. "Ah, yes. The noble quest the Archippos sent you on to save the world from being poisoned."

The Seeker struck at Kai's side. He tried to block it, but it twisted and slipped past his guard to clout him in the ribs.

He thought he heard ribs breaking as he bent over and gasped. He backed up to give himself a little room to recover. The Seeker followed him.

"Did the white maggot tell you that you were the only one, blessed with special abilities from Adoyni, to stop the poison? Ah, I can see from your face he did, and you believed him." Volundr laughed again. "And where are all these special abilities now?"

The Seeker lunged forward, his sword whipping out at Kai's feet. Kai leaped backwards, stumbled over his feet, and landed on the ground. His palm was too sweaty to hold the hilt anymore, and his sword fell out of his reach.

"The poison created thousands of Unwanteds that the Master turned into soldiers, but he didn't care about it. He let you cure it so he'd have the pleasure of killing that flying pest."

Kai didn't want to listen, but he couldn't help wondering if the Seeker was right. Looking back over their journey, it did seem a bit easy. He rolled over and grabbed his sword. Volundr didn't even try to stop him. He got to his feet, using the blade like a crutch.

"That's not true," he protested. He attacked, but his strike was slow. Volundr batted it away like he as a small child with a stick. "You're just saying that."

"Am I?" Volundr stepped closer, looming over Kai. "We tracked you for days. Do you think we couldn't catch up with you over the mountains? Do you really think a stable boy from Northbridge could beat a sorcerer? You're nothing. All you know how to do is shovel manure! And the other two? A bookworm and a girl? You had no chance against Belial. He let you win."

Kai didn't want to back up, but he couldn't stand the Seeker being so close to him. He stepped back, his sword dangling in his hand. "No. No. I won't believe that."

"Yes, you will." Volundr sneered. "It's the truth, and you know it." He swung.

Kai knew he was too weak to match it. He brushed against the branches of one of the trees he was trying to avoid. Volundr roared. Kai flinched back.

Volundr lowered his sword and punched with his other hand.

Kai saw it coming but couldn't react fast enough. The fist slammed into the side of his head, causing tears to spring up in his eyes. Blood dripped out of his nose. He wiped it with his sleeve. Volundr stepped closer, and Kai stumbled back before he could think and stepped between the two trees.

The sunlight and the cool breeze disappeared as he stared into darkness. The last thing he saw was Volundr slamming the doorway to Albia shut, and he was trapped in the hallway again. He slumped to the ground in despair.

CHAPTER THIRTY-TWO

Foul Drink

Rhiana screamed until her throat hurt and her voice was hoarse. No one answered. Then she sobbed until her tears ran dry.

Unable to do anything else, she curled up in the stinky, scratchy blanket and fell asleep, hoping that maybe things would be better when she woke up.

But when she woke up, her throat still hurt and her face felt stiff from her tears. To make matters worse, she was sore from sleeping on the floor that felt like rocks, and she was even colder than when she fell asleep.

As she shifted to get warmer, her stomach growled. She wondered what time it was, but it had to be past dinner.

Am I trapped in the earth? She remembered the walls of the house beginning to topple. The idea of being stuck deep in the earth where no one could get her was terrifying, so she tried not to think about it like Mom always said to do.

Besides, what earthquake would change my clothes? She knew whatever scratchy thing she had on was not her soft nightclothes she was wearing before. *Kai will find me. I just have to wait.*

But Kai was long gone. It'd been forever since he left. She fought back the doubts. *He'll hear about the earthquake, and he'll come and find me.* But she knew he'd never make it in time.

Tears began to flow again until she heard something. She sat straight up and caught her breath, listening as hard as she could.

There was nothing. She let out her breath and slumped back down. But then she heard it again.

Voices were coming closer! She took a breath. There were two voices she could pick out. The deeper one spoke only a little, while the softer woman's voice kept up the conversation. She waited until they were louder and started screaming.

"Help me!" she yelled. "I'm in here, and I can't get out! Help!" She stopped to listen. There was no response. Only quiet. The voices were gone.

Did I imagine them? What if they left her here? She couldn't stay here alone anymore. She'd die if someone didn't help her.

She started to scream when she heard a sound like metal scraping on metal. There was a loud click and the sound of stone sliding across stone.

Light shone in, blinding her. She jumped back and put her right arm over her eyes to shield them. No one said anything, but she could hear the sound of footsteps coming closer. Someone was close by!

"So, this is the little runt," the woman said. Her voice, soft and beautiful, didn't seem to match the cruel words. "The only reason I got stuck with this chore is because I'm a woman."

Rhiana peeked around her arm, her eyes slowly getting used to the sudden brightness. In front of her was a large man with thick arms. Beside him was a woman with long hair in a dress with a key tied to her belt.

"He said to look after her until *he* comes back." She never said who *he* was, but Rhiana could tell it was someone the lady didn't like. "I got to thinking that it's a shame to have her down here wasting away when she could be of some use. At least she would be good for a little sport."

Rhiana dropped her arm and stared up at the woman from the floor. "Wh...what do you mean?" Her words broke as her throat throbbed.

The lady ignored her and bent down. Her long red hair swished around her face. The woman took Rhiana's arm and pulled her to her feet.

"Mistress Nighthawk," the man spoke. "We should go."

"Yes, we should," Nighthawk said. "But I'm not having a sick child throwing up on my things or slowing me down." She reached to her belt and took off a flask.

Before Rhiana knew what was happening, Nighthawk grabbed her chin and forced her head back. The cool metal of the flask touched her lips and a smelly, awful-tasting liquid flowed into her mouth.

She tried to spit it out, but Nighthawk kept pouring. She choked as the drink went down her throat. The stench made it hard to breathe as she fought to get away, but Nighthawk held her tight.

The gunk overflowed and spilled over her face. She swallowed far more than she wanted. Finally, Nighthawk stopped pouring and let go. Rhiana coughed as she tried to catch her breath. Nighthawk watched without care.

"Soon you'll thank me for that drink, for it saved your life," she said. "But, by the time I get done, you'll be thanking me for everything. And when your dear brother comes to rescue you, he'll be heartbroken to see that you don't want to be rescued. In fact, you may even fight to stay with me because I plan to make you love me."

Nighthawk left the cell as the man grabbed her arm and pulled Rhiana behind him. She struggled, but the man's fingers pinched her arm in an agonizing grip. She tripped along, trying to stop the tears that began to flow again.

CHAPTER THIRTY-THREE

Cave Wars

Lizzy jumped as Taryn leaped up from beside Kai with a yell. He snatched up a bandage from the pile near the blankets and rushed back to him. Taryn ignored the questions everyone asked as he knelt down beside and pressed the cloth against Kai's face.

"How'd this happen?" Taryn held up the bandage. "Blood! And there's a bruise on his cheek! We were sitting right here! Nothing touched him."

Aric quickly joined Taryn while Rev gathered a basin of clean water and some bandages. No one said a word as Aric carefully cleaned up the blood. Griffen returned from the creek with a bucket of fresh water for them to wash in.

Rev looked worried, but Aric's face was a mask. Taryn was an open book. She could see the anger in his face, his eyes.

"I've heard stories where people can use dolls and poke them with pins to hurt them. Maybe that's what's happening with Kai," she ventured.

Taryn shook his head impatiently, disregarding her idea. Aric checked Kai one more time before settling down with an expressionless look still on his face.

"Are you insane?" Taryn erupted and leaped to his feet. "A frivolous story of a poor little mistreated prince while Kai lays here bleeding from wounds that just appear! Are you trying to entertain us because there's no hope, or are you so conceited to think we care more about your life than his?"

"Taryn," Aric began. It was a quiet tone filled with a warning, and the red that started to creep up his face was the only sign of anger.

"I've had enough!" Taryn snapped. "I don't care about anything you're talking about!"

"Taryn!" Lizzy gasped.

"I'm sorry." But nothing in his tone led Lizzy to believe that he was. "Kai's dying, and we're swapping useless stories. I don't see how it has to do with what's happening now."

"If you give me time, you'll understand..." Aric said, his tone now dangerously low.

"He doesn't have time!" Taryn shouted as he whirled from his pacing and glared at Aric. "I've never heard of wounds that suddenly appear. He's getting worse, and all you're doing is watching him. If you can't help us, I'll take him to someone else who can!"

"How are you going to do that?" Aric shot back, his blue eyes hard. "Where would you go? Even if you can figure that out, how are you going to get him there? You know we were forced to swear to those conditions."

Conditions? What are they talking about? Lizzy opened her mouth to ask, but Taryn didn't allow anyone else to talk.

Taryn's hazel eyes were hard with anger. "We're running out of time. Why can't we try something different? We tried your path, and it's not working. Why not try something else?"

Although Aric's expression didn't change, anger seemed to radiate off him like a blazing fire. "You're talking about magic, aren't you?" The words were so soft Lizzy barely heard them.

"I'm talking about doing something to help him! I don't care if it comes from Adoyni or Zoria." Taryn spoke a bit quieter, but there was desperation in his voice. "It doesn't matter how."

"Haven't you learned that nothing from Zoria is good?" The quiet rage now blazed at full force as Aric jumped to his feet. "She's evil. Why would you even think that was an option?"

"Because I'm willing to do anything it takes to cure Kai!" Taryn yelled back.

"It's better for him to die than become a slave to evil. No magic! We trust Adoyni will show us what to do." Aric's tone was final.

Taryn began pacing again. "What if He's too late? What if He doesn't do anything?" No one answered. He stopped by a small pile of bags and turned back to Aric. "Then tell me what's in that book. You keep studying it, and you won't let anyone see it. Let me do something." His voice cracked on the last words, worry filling them.

Aric shook his head. "It won't help you until you hear the story."

Taryn glared at Aric for what seemed a long time. He stalked over to where he was sitting and flopped down. "Fine. But if he dies..." He avoided their eyes and stared at the ground, not able to finish his sentence.

Aric started to say something but stopped and sat down again. Lizzy saw an angry flash in his blue eyes. Taryn was oozing frustration and impatience. She wanted to ask what they were talking about. What were these conditions? What promises had Taryn, Rev, and Aric made without her? She didn't want another fight to start, so she kept quiet.

"I know you don't understand, but I plan on getting back to Eltiria," Aric finally said. "Belial will answer for what he's done. He and his magic has made everything he touches rotten, and I plan on stopping him when I return. You need to hear the whole story. From the beginning." Aric said the last words like he was thinking about something else.

Taryn flopped down beside Kai and nodded. As Aric began again, even Rev refused to meet anyone's eyes. Taryn glared at the sand, only looking up to check on Kai periodically. Lizzy pulled up her covers and began to pray for Kai as she listened. She didn't want Taryn to use magic, but she didn't want Kai to die, either.

Aric had better get to his point quickly, or else there was going to be a war.

CHAPTER THIRTY-FOUR

Old Nag

I stormed through the castle. The grief that filled my heart after Father left had disappeared. Father wouldn't have gone to that stupid grove if Belial hadn't taken charge.

There had to be something in his palace that would prove his intentions were treasonous. I wasn't thinking about where I was going until I almost ran over Kahil in the hospital.

"I want to see Patrin. Is he better?" I asked.

Kahil led me into a room I'd never been in before. The stone floor was covered with thick rugs, and the walls were lined with fat, old books. There was a large oak desk in the center of the room covered with books and papers.

On top of the mess was a thick book with its title facing me. "Poisons: Ingredients, Remedies, and Little Known Cures." I caught my breath. That's what I needed in order to find out what was wrong with my arm and Patrin. Before I could pick it up, Kahil shut the door and began talking.

"Patrin has taken a turn for the worse. It's not looking good for him. The wound oozes and refuses to heal. The redness of the skin is

spreading over his body. I'm afraid it won't be long now." Kahil avoided my eyes.

Was he upset about Patrin? "You said that you thought it was poison and needed to know where it came from to help him. Well, I know..."

"It's not poison," Kahil interrupted. His tone left no room for an argument.

There was nothing worse than interrupting the crown prince. "But you said..."

"I was wrong."

He interrupted again! I glared at him, considering the repercussions of throttling him.

He shuffled some of the papers aimlessly. "Look, I thought it was poison. But recent events have shown me otherwise, and now no one is allowed to see him."

"By whose order?" I snapped.

"Belial's, Your Highness." Kahil was now whispering. "I can't disobey."

I didn't even bother to respond. I left. Belial was taking control faster than I realized, and I was not going to stand by and let him. Why wasn't Adoyni doing anything? I had prayed, but there wasn't an answer.

I stormed behind the stables to see Reveka pacing. When she saw me, I could see she was angry. Probably at me. Why was she so wonderful to everyone else? And so continually angry at me?

"Where've you been?" She stopped her pacing and glared at me. "You know I want to go home."

"I'm not reporting to you," I snapped. "Come on. I've had it with Belial."

Reveka kept silent for once. We hurried into the stables to get our horses. Kaspar nickered softly as Reveka approached. A smile lit her face as she kissed his nose.

I ordered the nearest groom to saddle one of the royal horses, Aleta, for me as Reveka slipped into the stall and began grooming Kaspar.

A stable boy popped out from the tack room. As he approached and bowed, I struggled again to remember his name. O...I rolled my eyes...O why did these people have such hard names? Before I could remember, he saw Reveka and hurried to Kaspar's stall.

"My lady," he protested. "I'd be honored to do that for you."

Reveka stopped to grin at him. "But I love to, Olwydd. I'm sure you know what I mean."

That's what his name was! But how in the world did she remember? I watched as they chattered about horses and had to marvel at the friendly side of Reveka.

She'd never once chatted with me. All my life people had catered to me and fawned over me. Reveka clearly preferred this stable boy over me. Why couldn't I have friends? I wanted to join them but was too afraid they'd spurn me.

I stuffed down my irritation as my groom brought out Aleta. He was a tall black with a finely chiseled head, delicate neck, but wide shoulders, a long back with a thick flowing mane and tail that caught the eye of any horse lover. But the way he pranced and the fire in his eyes made everyone fall in love with him.

We mounted, and I grinned as I felt the energy coursing through Aleta. I loosened the reins a little, and he took off at a barely controlled lope. I didn't even bother to see if Reveka was following.

Aleta's hooves clattered on the cobblestone streets as people dove out of the way. They swore until they saw who I was and then called out, "Your Highness!" I laughed as we sped by the colorful shops and the marketplace.

The city gave way to the fields and forest surrounding Medora. I could feel my anger slip away with every step Aleta took. I leaned forward and let the reins loose.

Aleta responded with a burst of speed that rocked me back into the saddle. I leaned forward with a yell, urging him faster, as if I could outrun every problem I had. We flew over the road until I saw a small path that I knew. Turning quickly, we shot through the trees and into an open field.

As we ran through the long grass, I caught a movement beside me. Kaspar was coming up on my right! I leaned closer to Aleta's neck. There was no way she was going to beat me.

We raced side by side across the length of the field until Reveka laughed as Kaspar took the lead. She rode like she was part of him and slowed at the edge of the field where the trees grew thick. Her long hair had tumbled from its braid and her cheeks were flushed with excitement.

"He's an amazing horse." I shook my head. "Very few can outrun Aleta."

"I know," she grinned. "And you still can't have him." She leaned down and petted his neck as he sidestepped, eager to keep running.

A smile? I was shocked. As far as I could remember, it was the first time she had smiled at me. Maybe she was starting to realize I wasn't an ogre.

I sighed. "Yes, I know. I'll try to be content on this old nag."

Reveka laughed. "I'd give anything to breed your nag there to some of my mares at home! Where are we? I thought we were going to Belial's palace."

"That's where we are." I dismounted and held my breath until the pain in my arm stopped hurting so badly. "You didn't expect to waltz in the front door, did you? How fast would his servants tell him who visited? We're going to sneak in." I tied Aleta up to a tree, started to loosen the cinch, and stopped. "Don't loosen Kaspar's cinch. We may need to leave here fast."

Her face grew serious as she tied up Kaspar and followed me. Our conversation died as we entered the trees.

Through the trees, there was a part of the palace close to the woods. We could slip through a window and find what we needed. My heart began to pound as the branches parted.

Belial's mansion was in front of us.

CHAPTER THIRTY-FIVE

All Black

I scanned Belial's palace for a way to get in, but I didn't know what I was looking for. I was a Prince, not a burglar.

Reveka huddled beside me in the bushes. The look on her face said that she was much more interested in tearing off to Shiel, not helping me. I didn't even know why I felt it necessary to bring her. Maybe I needed someone beside me so I could pretend I had a friend to help me.

Although the walls of the palace were made of a gray rock found in east Eltiria, all I saw were three floors of windows. A servant could look out and see us run across the lawn. In front of us was a window with a red drape hanging out. I inspected the windows again and didn't see anyone.

Figuring now was as good a time as any, I dashed out across the lawn. I heard Reveka gasp, and then she was beside me. I reached the wall, put my hands on the window and vaulted through it.

Waves of pain shrieked along my arm. I groaned as I reached through the window and pulled Reveka into the palace.

She came through the window, scrambling like there was an angry monster out there trying to kill her. As I caught my breath, I looked around with a grin. We were in the formal dining room.

I crept toward the door. Reveka followed like she was stalking prey. Her feet made no sound on the floor. I put my ear to the door but heard nothing. Easing the door open slowly, I peered out, but the hallway was empty.

I chose to go right, deeper into the palace. The hallway was red fir lined with tapestries of all sorts of dragons. There were black, green, and yellow ones. They were flying, perched on stone cliffs, swooping down to kill a deer. A man sat astride one large red dragon.

The floor was covered with a thick green rug, but it creaked as we tiptoed down the large hallway. We jumped each time it did. We passed numerous doors and almost made it to where the hallway turned when we heard a noise.

I put out my arm to signal Reveka to stop. We heard it again. **Creak.** My heart pounded like a drum. I heard the noise again, louder. **Squeak.** Someone was coming our way.

I glanced at Reveka. She nodded to the door closer to me. **Creak.** It was louder this time. I pushed Reveka to the door on her side.

She fumbled with the knob, making too much noise, and pushed it open. I shoved her into the room and closed the door with a soft bang in my hurry.

The creaking grew closer. I peered through the key hole to see what was happening in the hallway.

A man shuffled in front of the door. His skin was pasty white, so pale that I could see veins lacing his skin. He dragged his right leg and held a lethal looking axe. He paused for a minute outside the door and moved on. We waited for a long time as silence settled on the house once more. Once I decided it was clear, I let out the breath I had been holding.

"That was close," I laughed softly.

"Too close," Reveka whispered. "I thought my heart was going to beat out of my chest. Aric, what is this room?"

She called me by my first name? No one took that liberty. I started to rebuke her when I looked around the room. Everything was black – the walls, the ceiling, the drapes, the floor. Large bookcases filled the walls. There was one great desk in the middle of the room. It was covered with neat piles of books and papers as well as writing instruments.

The only decoration was a tapestry of a large red dragon in flight with its talons overstretched, like his standard at the banquet last night. Was he so obsessed with them that he actually thought they existed?

I strode over to the desk. Reveka browsed through the books while I sat down on the chair and searched the drawers. The papers and books were mostly about law and policies. I scanned them, but there didn't seem to be anything useful.

"I'm not sure if we're going to find what we need here," she whispered. "Let's go before someone comes. Those books are just about government stuff. Boring."

I nodded, not really listening as I examined the first drawer. I heard a huff and then she moved to the other side of the room.

Nothing in the drawer but writing equipment, a few notes, and random supplies. I slid the drawer closed. Maybe Reveka was right. I glanced over at her and decided I didn't want to admit defeat yet.

The second drawer was also disappointing. It was filled with reports of Belial's possessions and estates. As I scanned lists of what he owned, I realized that most of his wealth had come from Father. Something I planned to rectify as soon as I could.

Reveka paused at the end of the bookshelves, pulled out a few books, and flipped through them. I pulled open the last drawer. It looked as unpromising as the first two. A stack of papers lay in the drawer. I picked them up and felt soft leather underneath them. Placing the papers on the desk, I saw that there was a small journal bound in leather at the bottom of the drawer.

Reveka took a couple steps closer to me, still engrossed in the book. "Look at this..." Her voice died off as she stopped and kept reading silently.

I flipped open the journal and read under my breath.

"Tomorrow I shall embark on my journey. My pretense of being Adoyni's priest in Vesmir has finally raked in enough money to pay for boats and sailors. Although I had reasons prepared, they trusted me so blindly that they didn't question the fees I imposed. I shall travel to Zolari and head to the island from there."

"You're not going to believe this." Reveka interrupted my reading. "All these books are about the Goddess, Zoria. It's that new religion people are starting, but it's stupid. It's about trees, the earth and rocks healing people. He has a ton on it, like how to do it – what herbs to use, what kind of crystals heal, and what candles to burn."

I flipped through the journal to the next few entries, barely listening to her as I read under my breath.

"The only way I was able to hire a crew was to find a captain who was willing to sail before knowing where I was going. Once we were out in sea, I told him. He refused. I cut his throat and threatened the others with the same treatment if they did not obey me. They obeyed. We should be at the island in three months."

What island? And he murdered someone? That alone would be enough evidence to prove he wasn't worthy to serve the king. I tried to remember my geography. What was west of Zolari?

"Are you listening, Aric? I think he's involved with this new religion."

"I heard," I retorted. "He could have those books for many reasons."

The journal fell off the desk and landed on the floor. I scooped it up, afraid the pages were bent, and a piece of paper floated out and landed under the desk. I reached down and felt another twinge in my shoulder. Returning to my seat, I opened the paper and saw with horror that Belial knew exactly what I was doing.

CHAPTER THIRTY-SIX

Hidden Treasure

The paper was wrinkled and torn, and the edges were black like they had burned by fire. I knew that it had. Lord Fariel's writing still looked rushed and tense. I skimmed the words even though I knew was they said.

"Prince Aric, due to circumstances, I have to leave quicker than I thought. There was no time to reach you. However, I must warn you. Belial's influence reaches deeper than I thought and his intent is evil. Be careful when dealing with him. I have had word of his past and go in search of proof of his wickedness. Do nothing until I see you again. Take special care not to let them know of your suspicions. The kingdom may depend on this."

I groaned. Somehow Belial had found this letter and restored it like the assignment I burned.

But how was he doing it? How did he get into my room? How did he even know I had burned them? Was he using magic to put them back together? I snorted. Magic didn't exist.

But one question was even more important. How much more did Belial know?

I spoke with reluctance. I didn't even want to admit it to myself. "Reveka. Belial knows. He knows what Fariel and I have been planning."

I glanced at her, certain she'd be listening with great enthusiasm over my find. I saw that was not the case.

She was standing with her back to me as she browsed the books. Something must have prompted her to respond to me although she wasn't paying any attention.

"Wow," she said. The word was spoken without any feeling. I slammed the drawer shut in frustration. She didn't notice.

"This one is a certificate from the Temple of All. You know, that new temple they built in Northbridge, that one they dedicated to Zoria without asking your Father. This says that the Temple of All certified Belial as one of their priests. It says that he has shown exceptional dedication and the Goddess has blessed him with an unheard of amount of power. It's dated five years ago." She paused, picked up another book and continued talking.

"And look at this book," she continued to say. "It's called 'Spells and Hexes.' It's the second one he has..."

She never finished. As she pulled the book from the shelf, there was a quiet click. The book came out about two inches before it stopped.

She tugged on it in confusion, but the whole shelf moved with the book. She swung it out to reveal stairs that led down to a passageway.

She turned to me with her jaw hanging open and her eyes large. "Where do you think it goes?" she whispered.

"I don't know," I shoved the paper in my pocket. "But I'm finding out." I didn't bother to see if she was coming but plunged down the staircase. The hallway walls lined with walnut were barely wide enough for me.

The walls seemed to close in on me, and I had trouble breathing as I squeezed down the steep stairs. Rev followed on my heels. She tripped once and slammed into me. I fought for balance as she regained her feet.

We reached the bottom where a torch on the wall lit the passageway, but darkness seemed to overwhelm me. I shook my head. My imagination was tricking me. There was nothing evil down here.

The torch showed a small room lined with the same walnut wood. At the back was a door latched with a chain and lock. There was a nail beside the door. An unadorned key hung on the nail.

I hesitated. I didn't want to know what was behind the door. All I wanted to do was to run up the stairs and out of this palace because there was something about it that felt wrong. Rev stood beside me, staring at the key like she was feeling the same thing.

"We could go back?" Rev made it sound more like a question than a statement.

That was the excuse I was looking for. I wasn't being wimpy by turning back. I was being considerate of her feelings. I started to leave.

But I couldn't. I needed something to show Father. The books on magic weren't enough to prove he was up to no good. There was no law in the land that said you had to worship Adoyni.

I took the key from the nail and stared at the lock for a minute. "I have to know. It could be wine or gold down here. But I can't leave without something to prove his guilt."

She nodded and didn't say a word.

I took a deep breath and unlocked the door.

CHAPTER THIRTY-SEVEN

Monsters

The lock turned smoothly like it was used often. I pulled the chain free and dropped it to the ground, trying hard not to wince at every sound.

Before I turned the doorknob, I glanced over at Reveka. She gave me a quick nod without even looking at me.

I pulled the door open, blinking suddenly as bright light flooded out of the room. Torches two feet apart flamed from their brackets on the walls of the large room.

I found it odd that they didn't put off smoke and flicker much, but I forgot about it when I saw the rest of the room.

The room was as big as the kitchens in the castle. We stepped in, unable to comprehend what we were seeing. In front of us was an area that looked similar to the study above us, except this room was messy. Books lined the far wall behind the desk. The desk was covered with open volumes and papers lined with messy handwriting that looked like it had been scrawled in a hurry. A large chair was shoved back from the desk like someone had been rushed when he left. There was a thick gray rug on the floor.

After that, the resemblance ended. The floor was a roughhewn oak that was covered with mysterious stains. Along the walls were shelves filled with vials. Liquids of various colors lined the shelves. In the center of the room were two large tables.

"What's that?" Rev whispered. She was staying behind me, letting me go first.

On the table to the left, there was something that resembled a human body stretched out on it. Straps held down the naked limbs. But it was too white to be human.

I jumped when Reveka grabbed my hand and squeezed it tight. Her eyes were enormous as she glanced at me quickly before staring at the table again.

"Let's go, Aric," she whispered. Even at such a low volume, her voice was filled with fear. "I don't want to know what it is. I want to go home. Please."

I shook off her hand. I didn't care what she wanted. I needed to find something to prove Belial was evil. This place scared me in ways I'd never dreamed possible, but I wasn't going to back down. Belial was maneuvering for my crown, and I wasn't going to let him have it.

I slowly approached the table. The thing on the table never moved or made a sound. I got within five feet of it when I saw that it was an older man chained to the table. He was completely naked and was whiter than the purest snow. Over his entire body were bruises and wounds.

"Is he dead?" Rev spoke quietly behind me.

I jumped, startled. I glared at her and then whispered back, "I think so."

"If he's dead, why is he chained down? Is he breathing?" She stepped forward to examine him closer.

As she was moving toward the man on the table, he jolted and yanked against the chains. Reveka screamed and jumped back to where I was. The man began to moan.

We watched in terror as he whipped his head back and forth, banging it on the table. Then, without warning, his eyes snapped open and he saw us. Panic filled his dark eyes.

"Help me!" He pleaded. "Let me go! Please, please help me! Before he comes back!"

We froze, unable to know what to do, much less say.

The man begged. "Help me! He's trying to make an army! I've heard him talk. And I'm not the only one. He keeps experimenting on us. He's turning us into...monsters. Why won't you do something? Why won't you help me?"

Reveka grabbed my arm and clung to it. I didn't know if she was urging me to leave or to free the man.

The man stopped fighting. His eyes lost focus, as if he was listening to something far away. "He's coming! Oh, sweet Adoyni, save me, he's coming!"

The man turned back to us. "Run! Before he gets you, before he finds out you were here. Run! Run for your life!"

CHAPTER THIRTY-EIGHT

Pure Gold

Reveka bolted to the door. I was on her heels, pushing her to move faster, but as we sped past the desk, I hesitated for a moment. No one was going to believe me when I told them. Even I didn't believe what I'd seen.

I snatched up the first book I saw and raced through the door, slamming it shut. Reveka was already halfway up the stairs. I bounded up after her, and she pushed the bookcase back into place with trembling hands.

There was no way I was lingering in this place any longer. I raced to the window of the office. It looked over the grass toward the horses. Quickly I shoved the glass open.

Reveka didn't have to be told what to do. She leaped through the window as nimble as a cat. I briefly wondered if I knew any other girl who would be as capable at leaping out windows.

I tucked the book into my jacket and went through the window. The jolt when I landed made my shoulder throb more, but I ignored it in my panic to get away. What was that man talking about? Who was coming that he was so afraid of?

My breath grew shallow as we sprinted into the trees. We were halfway back to the horses when Reveka stopped suddenly. I crashed into her and almost bowled her over. As we regained our balance, Reveka grabbed my arm.

"Did you see that?" Her eyes were wide with panic. "Right there! Did you see that horse?"

"What are you talking about?" I asked urgently. "Come on. We've got to get out of here!" I pulled on her arm.

She shook me off. "No, listen! I saw a horse. A big black. It was gorgeous. And it had...it had..." She paused as she stared into the woods.

An eerie silence fell over us. All I wanted was to get far away.

Reveka took a deep breath and whispered, "It had wings."

I stared at her. I wanted to laugh. I wanted to mock her, but after the strange human I had seen in Belial's hallway and the man on the table, I wasn't sure what was going on anymore.

"We're getting out of here." I pushed her down the path to Aleta and Kaspar.

She looked back over her shoulder. "Do you think that horse with wings was what the man in the hidden room was talking about?"

I shoved her on. "You didn't see wings. It was a horse. And I think he meant Belial, who is going to be coming after us. Get moving!"

Despite my words, I couldn't resist looking back to Belial's palace. Was there really an Archippos here? I peered at the cold stone. To my far left, where the lawn curved to the front door, I saw a shimmer in the air. Before I could say anything, there was a flash of bright light.

When the light faded, a large golden door stood in the grass. The door opened, and Belial marched out.

He paused and stared into the woods where I was hidden. Did the trees offer enough cover? I wanted to run, but I was afraid that the movement would catch his attention. I held my breath and prayed that I blended into the trees.

He abruptly resumed his way into the palace. In a few minutes, he'd know someone was there. He'd see that open window in his study and know. We had to get out of there before he sent his soldiers looking for us.

I rushed to catch up with Reveka. Kaspar and Aleta jerked back as we burst through the foliage. Trying to slow my heart and breathe, I forced myself to walk although everything in me screamed to run. She mounted as quickly as I did. I turned Aleta toward Medora and let him run as fast as he could.

As we bolted through the trees, I kept one hand on the pocket where I had stuffed Belial's book. When we reached the main road, I eased Aleta to a slow lope despite his protests.

Reveka moved up to run beside me. We kept the pace until the city walls of Medora came into view. I pulled back on the reins, and Aleta snorted and reared, clearly not spent of his energy although his coat was soaked with sweat. Kaspar pranced in place for a minute before standing still.

"What was going on there?" Reveka asked, her
cheeks flushed.

"I don't know. But it's enough to kick Belial
out of the castle. Maybe even put him in the
dungeon." I couldn't keep the triumph out of my
voice and grinned. "We'll go back to the palace
and tell Father. That will be the end of Belial when
the soldiers investigate."

"Did you put the chain back on?"

I pulled Aleta up again. "What are you talking
about?"

"The chain," Reveka snapped back. "That was
on the door at the bottom of the stairs. That's what
took you so long to get up the stairs, right? You
were putting the chain back."

I groaned and winced. I'd forgotten all about
it.

"He'll know!" Rev gasped, not waiting for me to
say anything. Kaspar pranced again as he felt
Reveka's shock. She laid a hand on his neck and
spoke to him quietly. When he calmed, she turned
back to me. "He'll know we were there. And
he'll...he'll...I don't know what he'll do!"

"Calm down, Reveka," I ordered. "I don't
believe in all this magic. I don't know what he was
doing down there, but he doesn't have any
mystical powers. This will all be over tonight. He
won't have a chance to do anything!"

I remembered the golden door as I was talking.
That had to be magic, but this wasn't that the time
for sharing that with Reveka. It was time that
everyone stopped seeing me as the bad prince who

was irresponsible. Suddenly I realized that it was late in the afternoon. "Let's go!"

When we reached the stables, I saw that the stalls were full. A groom informed me that Father had returned from the grove. I grinned at Reveka as we trotted into the Great Hall.

One of Mother's maids scurried to us. She smoothed her long hair as she approached and curtsied. Then she turned to Reveka. "Mali, the queen has been asking for you. You are wanted right now."

Reveka shot me a worried glance.

I nodded. "She probably wants you to serve dinner."

The girl curtsied to me. Reveka whirled around without a word and started across the hall, but the maid gasped. No one left the presence of royalty without the proper rituals.

With a sigh, Reveka turned and gave me the smallest curtsy I'd ever seen. I laughed as I saw the anger in her eyes. They darted up the stairs to Mother's chambers.

Victory was starting to taste sweet.

CHAPTER THIRTY-NINE

Rug Stains

I paused only long enough to rush to my chambers to change. In my rooms, there was a note for me on my table.

I recognized Mother's delicate handwriting as soon as I saw it. All it said was to meet her and Father in her rooms for supper.

I splashed water on my face and groaned as my shoulder protested. Pulling off my shirt, I saw that the bandage on my arm was soaked with pus and blood. The skin around it was red.

Mother hadn't said Belial was going to be there. This would be a perfect time to tell them what I had found. I shoved the book I had snatched from Belial under my formal cloak.

But when I entered Mother's dining room, I saw Belial and Nighthawk Nephesus sitting at the table. How had he made it here so fast? I flopped down beside Mother.

Reveka came out with a platter of food. She wore a formal dress with her hair neatly combed. She caught my eye once, looking worried, maybe even nervous, but she ducked out of the room before I could say anything.

Father was at the head of the table with Belial
on his left and Mother on his right. His face
looked whiter than before. His hands shook so
badly he could barely get a fork to his mouth.
Although the steak was tender, Mother had to slice
it for him.

I couldn't shake the unease I felt. Sitting this
close to Belial, knowing what I did, unnerved me. I
found myself avoiding his gaze, but I couldn't wait
to reveal him for what he truly was.

"Do you expect good results?" Mother's voice
was tense and her blue eyes worried.

Belial shrugged. "Sometimes we have to work
with the energies to get them to line up right,
especially if there is anyone around with negative
energy." He gave me a cold look.

Was this magic stuff real? Everyone was acting
like it was. What if crystals and the earth possessed
energies that had power to heal? It seemed weird,
but was it wrong?

Reveka entered the room with a pitcher. I
shook my head. My glass was full, and I didn't want
her whispering secret messages that would raise
suspicion.

She shot me a glance that probably would've
killed me on the spot if I had been paying her
more attention. I wasn't, because Belial's next
words took all my self-control to not react.

Belial continued talking. "I will take more
soldiers from the castle guards. There were
burglars in my palace while we were gone."

Reveka gasped and tripped. I cringed, knowing
she'd give us away.

"Careful, child," Mother rebuked. "That's a very expensive rug."

"Sorry, Your Majesty," Reveka blushed. She moved to Belial and reached for his cup as he resumed what he was saying.

"As far as I can tell at this point, there are only two things missing."

Reveka began to pour a red liquid that looked like wine into his cup.

Belial glanced at me. "It's rather strange. All they took was a letter from a disgruntled noble and a worthless book. I shall recover them soon, for I know exactly where they are."

Reveka's hands trembled as she stared at me. The wine continued to pour until the cup was full. She didn't notice as it poured over the brim and onto Belial's lap. He yelped and leapt to his feet as she was jerked back to what she was doing.

Frightened by his reaction, she screamed. The cup and the pitcher went flying through the air, spilling all over her, Belial, and Mother's precious rug.

Reveka's scream ceased. The cup and pitcher thudded to the floor. The room was silent. No one moved.

The silence was broken by Belial. With a look at his soaked garments, he slapped Reveka hard. She stumbled back as she put a hand on her cheek.

His hand left an angry red stain. Tears sprang up in her eyes. The sound of the slap reverberated throughout the room.

I had enough. I was sick of him, and although Reveka drove me mad, I wasn't going to let anyone hit her for some stupid accident.

"How dare you!" I yelled and jumped to my feet. My chair crashed to the floor. "I don't care who you are, but you will never treat anyone that way. That was an accident."

Belial whipped around to me. I almost flinched, thinking that he was going to slap me as well, but I held my ground. Fury burned in his dark eyes and his face was twisted into a snarl.

"You keep out of this!" he snapped. "This is none of your concern."

"How you treat the servants in the palace is my concern!" I shouted. "Father, tell him he can't abuse the servants and he can't speak to me that way."

Father was the only one untouched by the drama. Mother sat frozen, her face in shock at the yelling. Nighthawk was slightly flushed as if the fighting had been thrilling to her. Reveka still had a hand over her cheek but hadn't moved, her fright more powerful than her anger. Father sat, staring straight ahead with a blank look. I wasn't even sure if he heard me.

"Leave Belial alone," he finally said in a low tone. He spoke as if his thoughts were a long ways off. "He knows what is best."

"Father," I protested.

Belial smirked at me and then snapped his fingers. "Guards!"

Four of Father's soldiers tumbled through the door at his command and bowed, although I couldn't tell if it was to Father or Belial.

Belial watched me as he gave his order. "Take this servant girl to the dungeon until I can deal with her properly."

Reveka gasped and looked at me in a silent appeal. Two men seized her arms forcefully. She pulled from them and tried to shake them off, but they gripped her harder.

"Dungeon!" I yelled. "For a spilled goblet? Father!"

Belial settled back into his chair, not giving Reveka a second glance. "I'm sure I can find something else to charge her with. Servants are always stealing things, you know. Jewels, clothes, why, sometimes even useless papers." He took Nighthawk's goblet. "I'd hate to see you involved with such a girl." The look he gave me over the gold glass was one of warning.

I bit my lip and glanced at Father. He hadn't even noticed the commotion. I thought about appealing to Mother, but her face was ashen. She grasped her hands together tightly on her lap like she was trying to get them to stop shaking.

I heard Reveka still protesting and resisting. Then a door closed, and she was gone.

Belial and Nighthawk began a quiet chatter as another servant replaced Belial's goblet and gave him extra napkins in case he needed them. Their laughter filled the room as they began eating again.

I sank to my chair, suddenly frightened. Belial knew our plans, so he used events to put Reveka in the dungeon. Now he was threatening me, and I was powerless against him.

Mother reached for her goblet, her hand shaking. I gazed at her and Father and actually saw them for the first time in years.

Mother was terrified, and Father's body was present, but he was not with us anymore. Belial had us all trapped.

All he had to do was seize the throne, and the kingdom was his.

CHAPTER FORTY

Worst Mistake

Supper seemed like it was never going to end. Belial and Nighthawk continued to chat, but Mother and I had nothing to say. When it was finally over, Belial told Mother to be ready early in the morning and left.

The soldiers carried Father back to his room. I went back to my rooms, but I paced, gingerly poking my arm that was throbbing.

All I saw was Reveka's face when she was dragged from the room. She was expecting me to save her, and all I'd done was stand there.

Father always said it was our job to protect the citizens of Eltiria and defend them when wrongly accused. I'd done nothing. All she wanted was to...

Well, I didn't know what she wanted, but she didn't deserve to be in the dungeon. What could I do? Mother was too terrified to do anything. I needed Father with his decisions and actions. Patrin was too sick.

I was alone.

But I wasn't. There was Lord Fariel. What had he said? "Some of us fear Belial is a bad influence. Maybe he's the evil that's poisoning this place." What if I went to him? We'd use the evidence I had to prove Belial unworthy. I'd kick him out, make Kahil heal both Patrin and Father, and everything would be normal.

Darkness fell as the castle grew quiet. I sprung into action and packed two bags of supplies. I didn't want to admit it, but my arm felt stiff.

I checked to make sure I had everything I needed. Then I hoisted the bags on my shoulder, wincing at the sharp pain, and blew out the candles.

I arrived at the courtyard unseen and placed the bags in a corner. As I entered the dungeons, the guards snapped to attention. I shivered from the chill in the air.

"I need the girl," I ordered, trying to look very put out. "The maid, the one that was brought in earlier," I snapped.

"Your Highness, Chancellor Belial gave orders she be released only to him." The guard shifted on his feet.

The annoyance on my face was no longer an act. What else did Belial control? "I'm here on orders of the Queen. Not that I have to explain to you, but my Mother the Queen has a headache, and she sent me to get the girl. The only thing that soothes her is the servant's voice."

I had no idea if Reveka could sing. For all I knew, she sounded like a rooster with a sore throat. The guard glanced at the two others. They shrugged.

"I believe the order of a queen is more powerful than a chancellor. Once the headache is gone, the Queen will send her right back. Do you want to disobey the Queen's orders?" I crossed my hands over my chest and raised my eyebrows.

That killed all indecision. The first guard grabbed the keys and a torch by the door. He motioned for me to follow him.

As we descended into the dungeon, the air grew colder. I wrapped my cloak around me tightly as we started down steep stairs that were barely wide enough for me to fit through.

There was an old musty rope to grasp, but it looked like any weight would break it. I had been over every inch of the castle, but I'd never been here. I didn't even realize these dungeons existed.

As we passed the first cells, I saw people behind the iron bars. Each cell was barely large enough to stretch out in with a small bed on one wall. On the floor was old straw that stank. I couldn't see any blankets.

The people were dressed in the same way. A straight white tan dress for the women and the same cloth of pants and a shirt for the men, but the clothes seemed too large for them. They didn't have shoes on their feet. They stared at me with blank eyes.

The farther we went, the worse the reek became. The air was rank with disease and fear. The guard didn't seem to notice. He never bothered to look at the people.

We reached the end of the corridor, and I saw another set of stairs leading farther down.

"Are there more people down there?" I asked, my voice sounding weak.

The guard looked at me, surprised. *"Of course, Your Highness."*

"Who?"

"I don't ask. I only keep them in." The guard pulled out his keys.

I glanced to the cell on my right and saw Reveka staring at me through the bars. She was dressed in the same prison clothes as the others with no shoes and her hair hanging loose over her shoulders.

I shook my head over the guard's shoulder to tell her to act like she didn't know me.

As the guard fumbled with the lock on the cell, I couldn't believe the change in Reveka. She was huddled on the bed as far from the bars and the filthy straw as she could get.

Even from the corridor in the weak torch light, I could see her shivering. Her eyes were red, and there were tear stains down her cheeks. I swore to myself that I'd never tell her I knew she'd been crying.

The lock finally opened, and the guard rattled the chain free. He left the door ajar and stepped back. *"Come. The Queen has need of you."*

Reveka slowly got up like she was stiff. When she entered the hall, the guard gripped her arm tightly and pushed her back the way we had come.

She winced. I almost punched the guy but controlled myself to keep the part I had to play. Justice would come after I got rid of Belial.

When we got to the door, the guard released Reveka to me. I grabbed her arm the same way he had and pushed her through the guardroom and into the courtyard. As soon as the door closed, I released her arm. She stumbled once and then stopped.

"We're leaving. And going to get help." I led the way to the bags. The fresh night air seemed to revive her a bit. I trotted toward the gates.

"Wait," Reveka called. I motioned her to be quiet. She came closer and lowered her voice. "I'm not leaving Kaspar here."

"What's with that horse?" I caught from yelling before it was too late. She was going to blow all our chances because of a stupid horse. "We'll get some horses once we get out of here. I won't take the risk."

"I won't take the risk of Belial putting his creepy hands on Kaspar!" Reveka's voice rose. "You got both of us into this, and you'll get both of us out!"

"Do you even realize who you're talking to?" I responded with fury. "You don't order me around! And you do not speak to me like that!"

"This is not about you!" Reveka jabbed a finger in my chest. "This is about **my** horse! I will **not** leave Kaspar. So you can either follow and saddle a horse for yourself or walk. I'm not giving you a ride, and I'm not waiting for you." With a huff, she spun around to the stable and stalked away.

I growled in frustration as she slipped into the dimly lit stable. She was going to get us caught, and I wasn't going to get her out of the dungeon a second time.

I followed her into the stables. Reveka didn't even bother to look in my direction, but I could

see that she was mad. I ignored her and scanned
the horses. I couldn't take Aleta. He'd attract too
much attention. I needed a fast horse that wasn't
terribly exceptional.

In the back of the stable, I saw a sorrel horse
named Wonder. No one rode her, for there was
nothing flashy about her.

She was a well-built horse with a wide chest and
four stockings that reached her fetlocks. Father
bought her for Mother, but Mother never went
anywhere. People joked that it was a wonder that
she was in the stable.

I'd seen her run once. She was released into a
pasture and was racing to catch up with the other
horses. She was fast.

I grabbed my saddle off the rack and started
for her. Wonder stretched her head with its
slender blaze down her face towards me and
nickered softly as she pricked up her ears.

Her whole demeanor screamed that she was
tired of life here, that she was tired of being
trapped! Exactly how I was feeling.

I saddled up as fast as my fingers would let me,
but they refused to move much. Still expecting to
hear the sound of the guards' footsteps on the
wooden floor, I joined Reveka at the door.

Her eyebrows rose when she saw my choice.
"Well, did you actually choose something based on
its value instead of its looks?"

I ignored her comment and led Wonder
through the door, stopping to check if the way was
clear.

The pack felt too heavy to lift with my arm, but I managed to get it on the back of Wonder and mounted. Reveka was right behind. I moved Wonder closer to Kaspar.

"Go slowly and quietly through the gates and through the streets of Medora. Once we are clear, we'll go west as fast as we can until the sun comes up. Understand?"

She nodded and gathered her reins. The horses seemed to sense our need for silence, for they restrained from the usual prancing.

We walked toward the gate, and I cringed at every hoof beat. No one stirred. Inside the castle walls, horses' hoof beats would be unusual. In Medora, people were used to hearing the noise of horses. I pulled up the hood of my cloak to cover my face and kept going.

The town was quiet. Only a few lights flickered from windows. Even the inns had closed down for the night. Kaspar's and Wonder's hooves clattered on the cobblestones, echoing through the city.

It wasn't until I saw the city walls with the open gate that I took a deep breath of relief. We had done it.

We passed through the gates. I paused for one minute to look back. The city sloped up to the castle, which was lit by torches around the walls. My home. My family. My life. Everything was inside those walls.

I suddenly got a premonition that I'd never see it again. As I took in a final glance, it seemed like a black shadow came from nowhere and hovered over the castle.

I shivered before I could stop myself. But though I tried to rationalize the feeling away, nothing reassured me.

I turned Wonder away from the sight. Reveka sat quietly on Kaspar as if she understood what I was feeling. I passed her without a word and waited until the cobblestones ended and the dirt began. Then I let Wonder run.

It was not until later that I realized leaving that night was the worst mistake of my life.

MUDDLED

'Are you miserable?
Is your vision muddled?
Then it is you that must grow up."
~Liusasidh

Jehun hesitated on the road at the entrance of the Temple of All. He knew he had to pass through the cedar archways covered with ivy to meet with Belial. Beyond the gates, fountains shot sparkling water high up into the sunlight.

There was no logical explanation for his reluctance. The Temple was a place of great beauty. Flower gardens added color to the cedar, and wide stretches of carefully tended grass and walkways were lined with hedges that gave a sense of being alone in flawless nature.

He sighed and left the road behind. He only wished he could leave his pain behind as easily as he had stepped off the dirt track. The smell of incense in the main entrance hall was strong, even at the threshold.

He sped by many rooms that were set up in similar fashion to facilitate worship. Not able to hold back his curiosity, he entered one of the rooms. It was large enough to hold a circle of stones at least nine feet across. The room was lined with rich warm colors and comfortable cushions.

On the north side of the room, three lines were drawn in a spiral to symbolize fertility. To mark intelligence and spirituality, a vase with incense and flowers was on the eastern wall. An oil lamp was placed on the south side to show health and success. On the west side of the room was a bowl filled with water to represent psychic powers and healing. The altar in the center of the room had a statue of Zoria, a chalice, incense, a water bowl, and a bell.

Jehun viewed the sacred knife lying by the wand on the altar with disdain. He'd never been in the Temple of All while he worshiped Adoyni. These new practices were weird and eerie to him. He backed out of the room.

Ignoring the rest of the rooms, he hurried on, determined to get his message and leave as quickly as possible. He entered the final room on his right. The room was the same as the others he had passed. He cautiously made his way through the room.

A hidden door in the back of the room was concealed under drapes of cloth and surrounded by pillows and low seats. Jehun slipped into a steep flight of steep stairs. The glow from the torches at the bottom of the stairs lit his way.

The hallway led past many rooms. The first was a library with deep red velvet stuffed chairs, desks, and a large fireplace. The next room was a formal dining room with a long cherry wood table big enough to seat thirty people. He passed luxurious bedrooms and sitting rooms. At the end of the hallway was a small plain door that blended into the wall.

He descended another flight of stairs. This time he was in a poorly lit hallway hewn out of rock. Cells lined each side with bars from floor to ceiling. The people imprisoned were almost naked and looked like they were starving. He continued down the hallway and tried not to look at the prisoners. Although the hallway branched into many other corridors, he went straight to the end.

At the end was a steep circular staircase carved out of gray stone. As the steps wound up, the windows revealed the gash left from the earthquake in the soil. The line ripped back and forth through Northbridge as if the hand that caused it was shaking. The poorer section, and the last remaining temple of Adoyni in the city, was completely gone. Jehun stared in horror. While he hoped to be relieved of the continual pain, there was no way he could fix the damage.

"Jehun, you may enter." Belial's voice echoed down the stairs.

He entered a large room. The floor was the same gray stone in the corridor, but the far wall was sheer glass. Jehun stared at the rolling countryside stretching out as far as he could see. On the other side, the Razors, the huge mountain range that stretched north of Northbridge, still had snow on the peaks.

Belial stood at the far window, one hand against the glass, gazing out over Northbridge to the country beyond the city. Belial's face was taut like he was angry.

Jehun felt a flash of worry that this meeting might not go well. As he turned from the windows, he realized that Belial was not alone.

A woman sat at the table covered by old books and parchments scattered around chaotically. The woman's long copper hair was pulled back in a tight braid, and her hands and face were dusty from the books and paper. Behind her was a large door made out of pure gold.

"He didn't tell me, Nighthawk," Belial said. He slammed his fist on the window. "He had it all planned all along as he listened to my pleas for his power. He was going to use me until I released him, and then he'd take his armies, so long hidden that everyone has forgotten them, wipe me out, and take over my world. It's due to my own luck that I found the parchment that mentions the army."

"You don't know if that's true," Nighthawk protested. "Would he betray you like that?"

Belial let out a sharp laugh. "Seiten is the king of betrayal! I have no doubt of it. I vowed to follow him, but I have no wish to let him out of the prison the Archippi put him in. That's the only good thing those wretched horses did."

"Don't the Sentinels search for that army? Claiming there is still an enemy to fight?" Nighthawk asked. "Perhaps they know something. We could ask them."

Jehun had heard of those strange people called the Sentinels. They kept to the wild places of Eltiria, far from the cities and towns. While they recognized the rule of the King, they regarded their leaders and Adoyni's law as more important. They were said to possess incredible abilities and skills from Adoyni, but Jehun had always regarded the stories as children's tales. Were they true? Were there really people who stood watch for an attack, who trained for war although the war was over?

Belial's voice drew Jehun's attention back to the conversation. "Even if we found a Sentinel and managed to get any information out of him, we wouldn't learn anything. If they knew where it was, they would have already annihilated it. The fact that the Sentinels still search for it, that they even remain, proves they've never found the army."

"What are we going to do then?" Nighthawk sounded worried. "We can't let Seiten out if he'll destroy us. And with the Unwanteds so unstable, we won't have enough soldiers if it comes to a battle."

"I know." Belial lowered himself into a chair with a trace of weariness. "I lost another company last week. Five hundred Unwanteds just turned on each other, and before the Seekers could do anything, almost all of them were dead. It won't take much time for our armies to be gone. I have fewer fighters now than I did a year ago. We need an army like this." He pointed to the parchment. "Real soldiers, hardened by battle, trained to obey every command without thinking, and ready to die for their commander. We need this army."

Silence filled the room as Belial tapped the paper with his finger. Jehun fidgeted. Why was he called to hear this discussion? Belial picked up the parchment and studied it for a while. The room remained silent. Then he threw the paper back onto the table and turned to Jehun.

"Jehun, you will go to Seiten."

Jehun gasped. Yes, it was quite possible for him to reach Elba Isle, for the ocean had earth far underneath it, but he avoided that area ever since the Archippi had imprisoned Seiten there. He could feel the vile leak from Seiten even when he was far away.

"You will tell him that the enemy is not defeated. To completely annihilate them, I must have command of his hidden army. Jehun, you will receive from him the location of the army and any commands I need to control this army."

Jehun hesitated. The lava was quickly flowing out of the inner core and filling up the outer core. He couldn't leave. It wouldn't be too long until it made its way to the mantle. And he was still in pain from the earthquake. Maybe Belial would heal him now.

Belial shot to his feet. "What are you waiting for? Didn't I give you a command? Now get to Elba Isle and hustle back with the answer!" His sharp tone dropped off suddenly. "If you do this for me, I will reward you greatly. The pain you feel? It can disappear. It can also increase if you disobey."

Belial seemed to know exactly what Jehun was thinking. "If you really think I'd heal you first, you are foolish. Seiten is not the only one to be suspicious of betrayal. Go before I lose my patience." The last words were harsher.

Jehun fled before he heard something he didn't want to. He wished he'd never listened to Belial. And he really wished that everyone would leave him alone.

CHAPTER FORTY-ONE

Strange Doorways

Kai trudged through the stone hallway. The despair of being back in the labyrinth ebbed as his feet ached and his legs protested at taking another step. He tried as hard as he could, but he could no longer ignore the growing hunger. A pounding headache was growing, and he felt like he had run a long time.

He glared at the corner of the hallway ahead of him. Every corner used to bring a surge of hope that he would escape. Now he was starting to think the maze would never end.

The slow shuffle stayed behind him, no matter how fast or slow he went. He considered waiting to see what was behind him, but he wanted food. He jogged around the next turn to see the maze before him lined with torches that gave off more smoke than light.

He knew he was going to turn a corner and see Taryn reading by one of the dim torches. Taryn would complain that he needed more time to study and that he was hungry. If he didn't run into Taryn, then it would be Lizzy plucking away at her guitar.

He shook his head. There was a distant memory of burying her precious instrument under some statue. Lizzy cried and talked about her Dad as he and Taryn dug a deep hole for it. Was that a dream?

He plodded around the corner and continued his way the next section of the hallway. Halfway down on the right a stone on the wall caught his eye. It was the same kind of stone as the rest of the hallway, but it seemed out of place as it stuck out at a weird angle. He fiddled with it for a minute and then pushed it.

The rock glided smoothly back with the pressure and sank into the wall. He watched the stone disappear into the wall. With a groan, the wall began to swing back. When it stopped, a small doorway was in front of him. *An exit!* Kai grinned and slipped through the opening. The hilt of his sword caught on the wall. He freed it as he squirmed to the other side.

He was in a meadow surrounded by thick woods. The grass was dead instead of the lush green it should have been this time of the year. The sun was beginning its descent to the west, and he automatically scanned the north to find the Razors. The clouds hovered close to the line on the horizon, making it impossible to see anything. He sighed and sank to the ground.

What am I supposed to do? He couldn't keep going like this. He'd failed at everything. He'd tried so hard, but he couldn't even make it back to where Mom, Dad, and Rhiana were. Did they think of him? Did they think he'd left them because he

didn't care? And what had happened to Shona?
Was she still a prisoner of the disease?

He rubbed his face and ran his hands through
his hair. He glanced to the north again. The
clouds lay low, so close to the land that it seemed
they were touching. *Is that a mountain above the
clouds?* He sat straighter.

Above the clouds, there was a stretch of
mountain peaks, so far they almost blended into
the blue sky. Almost. He could still see the form of
the ridgeline. He laughed. It was the Razors. There
was no doubt at all. He knew each dip and rise as
well as his hand.

He leaped to his feet and trotted to the center
of the meadow. It felt vaguely familiar for some
strange reason, but he didn't care. He was going
home. The word sent shivers through him. He
could taste Mom's roast beef with gravy and
potatoes piled high next to it. The smell of fresh
bread wafted through the air. Dad's merry voice as
he told a funny story to make them laugh.
Rhiana's giggle as she listened. Everything would
be alright. He just had to get there.

Before he could continue, he heard the noise
of horses and harnesses jingling. A stagecoach with
six large horses trotted into the meadow and
lurched to a stop. A ride! He wouldn't have to walk
to Northbridge. He grinned.

But the driver didn't notice Kai as he pulled
the horses to a stop at the edge of the meadow. He
wrapped the reins around the brake and jumped
to the ground.

He flung open the door. "Lunchtime! We'll stop 'ere for a bit, but stay close."

People tripped down the steps one at a time, holding baskets and blankets. The last man who came out hesitated before starting down the steps. He was dressed in thick wool with a black hat on his head. He surveyed the meadow but didn't seem to see Kai. He descended and stopped by the driver.

"Is this the place we spoke of?" he asked, his hazel eyes sober.

"Yeah, this 'ere is it. I'd thank you kindly for not mentionin' it to the others, though. Don't want them spooked, if ya' know what I mean." The driver looked worriedly at the other passengers as they scattered to set up their picnics.

"I won't. Thank you." The man turned from the driver and surveyed the meadow.

The man reminded Kai of someone, but he couldn't put a name to the face. He removed his hat to reveal dirty blonde hair slicked back and carefully placed the hat in the coach.

"But Professor Wallick," the driver said. "We found graves, but there's two missin'. Maybe they were carried off, but maybe they survived."

Professor Wallick whipped around to the driver. "Are you sure about this?"

"Yes, Professor," the driver said nervously. "The coach left that day before me. I know how many passengers he 'ad, and I was the first 'ere. Two are missing."

"Which two?" Professor Wallick demanded.

"Who knows?" The driver shrugged. "No one's been found."

Professor Wallick walked slowly to the mounds like this was a task he was dreading. Kai watched, and realized the mounds were actually graves. *Why did this all feel so familiar?* He spun in a slow circle. *What if things were a little different?* If the coach was overturned. If the bags were scattered through there. The Razors loomed in the distance. He gasped. This was the meadow where Eladar brought him, and he met Lizzy and Taryn for the first time.

Eladar had buried the people from the coach. One was Mischa, Taryn's tutor. Kai remembered how Taryn took a long time to say goodbye. But who was this man? Kai watched as he went from grave to grave, tenderly touching the top of the mounds. Professor Wallick? But Wallick was Taryn's last name.

Kai laughed. This was Taryn's father! He darted to Professor Wallick by one of the mounds. "Sir, Professor Wallick. Taryn's alive. He's not in there!"

Professor Wallick ignored him. Kai felt a tinge of annoyance. Just like Taryn. Too good to talk to someone beneath him, but still, with news of Taryn, Kai thought it wouldn't matter.

He tried again, this time louder. "Professor Wallick! I know Taryn, and I know he's okay. Well, he was, the last time I saw him."

The man moved to the next grave. Kai stared after him. *What is his problem?* He stalked over to the driver.

"Hey, I don't know what's wrong with him, but can you tell him that his son isn't dead?" Kai hoped that nothing had happened to Taryn since he last saw him. "And, can I catch a ride to Northbridge?"

The driver ambled to the horses to check the harness. Kai watched him go. "Hey! I'm talking to you!" he shouted after him. The driver never turned around.

They can't hear me! Kai stormed up to the driver and yelled in his face. No reaction. Kai waved his hand in the driver's face. He didn't even blink. *What is going on?* He marched back to Professor Wallick and tried the same thing. No response.

"There's no way to truly know," Professor Wallick whispered. "If you were still alive, you'd find a way to reach Northbridge for your precious magic. You had Mischa. He could have saved you. The search doesn't start until Northbridge. I will not believe you are dead unless I have proof."

"He's not dead!" Kai shouted.

"He can't hear or see you."

Kai turned to the voice, only to see the Seeker, Volundr, standing behind him. He drew his sword and stood waiting for an attack. He was not going to be pushed between any trees this time. He was not going back.

Volundr laughed but didn't draw his sword. "Frustrating, isn't it? You could tell him so much about Taryn. They might even give you a ride home. Only they can't hear you."

Kai yelled and attacked. As he swung the sword, Volundr smoothly drew his blade and blocked the attack. Kai's teeth were knocked together, and he jerked back.

"Losing strength, are you? It happens." Volundr read the word on Kai's blade. "Failure? Do you fail at everything since you carry such a reminder around?"

Kai looked at the blade. "It doesn't really say that," he snapped. "It used to say...used to say..." *What did it used to say?* He finished the sentence slowly. "...something else."

"I'm sure it did," the Seeker responded dryly. "Put your sword away. Unfortunately, I'm not here to kill you."

"What's happening to me? Why can't they see me?" Kai demanded.

Volundr grinned with malice. His teeth were rotten and yellow. "Maybe you're such a failure that they don't care to have anything to do with you."

Kai couldn't find a response in the haze of his rage, so he struck again. Volundr easily blocked it and smacked Kai on the thigh with his blade. Kai tried to block it, but he moved too slowly like his body didn't know how to respond. The sword felt heavy in his hands.

"You're weak," Volundr scoffed, his amber eyes bearing down on him. "The only way you were ever any good was because the Master let you win."

Kai shifted on his feet, suddenly nervous that the Seeker was right. "Adoyni wouldn't let anything happen to me."

Volundr burst out into a peal of laughter although it sounded more like a roar. "Adoyni! You think He'd do anything to help you now? You failed Him so badly that He doesn't want anything to do with you anymore."

Kai yelled, unable to control his anger. But he knew the Seeker was right. He was too weak to fight. He could barely stand. He glanced over to the coach where Professor Wallick was eating a piece of chicken. He'd find Professor Wallick later and tell him what happened to Taryn. He'd do it in Northbridge.

But he wasn't going to fight Volundr this time. He spun away from the Seeker and dashed to the trees. He'd run until Volundr was gone. He made it to the trees even though he could feel his aches as he ran.

A branch from a tree slapped him in the face. He felt the sting and the warm trickle of blood on his cheek. He didn't stop or slow. Over his gasps of air, he realized that the Seeker wasn't following him. He laughed. He was going to get home. He ducked under some branches and leaped over a log.

Volundr roared. It was a hideous noise, filled with malice. It seemed to thunder after him like a wave of the ocean that crashes over the beach. Kai darted forward, pushing himself faster. He stumbled on some bushes and fell to his knees.

He risked a glance back to the meadow. Volundr was standing in the center, ringed by the graves, watching Kai. The other people were peacefully packing up and getting back onto the coach. Only the black horses showed any sign of what was happening as they pranced in place.

Kai got to his feet and started to run again. The roar still lingered in the air as he bolted between the trees. He heard the Seeker snap his fingers like he was standing next to the monster and the roar died as Kai took a running leap across a fallen tree.

But instead of more woods ahead of him, his vision blurred and darkened. Kai stopped in confusion. He was alone in the hallway again. The meadow with the forest around it was gone. He blinked, unable to see, and glanced around as his eyesight returned. In the silence, the slow shuffle behind him sounded again.

He clenched his jaw in anger. "No!" He punched the wall and yelled in agony when his fist hit the stone wall. He sank to the floor. He was so close to Northbridge, and now he was stuck again. He put his head between his hands as despair washed over him.

But he couldn't stop hearing what Volundr had said about being a failure. The words echoed as he sat in the dim smoky corridor. *I'm a failure. How could Adoyni love a failure?*

CHAPTER FORTY-TWO

Relief

Taryn shifted on the sand and glanced down at Kai. He was mumbling, but then his words changed to a bloodcurdling scream tainted with evil that sounded like his very soul was being torn from his body. Taryn recoiled from Kai in terror.

Kai jumped out of bed like a wild animal escaping a trap. He paused when his bare feet hit the sand, his legs trembling from the unfamiliar use. His shrieking stopped, leaving the cave quiet with only the reminder of the agony he was suffering.

Lizzy and Rev stared at Kai like they didn't know if they should run. Aric slowly stood up and stretched a hand out to Kai in the same way a person would approach a wild horse.

Who does he think he is? Taryn jumped to his feet. His pulse raced as the muscles in his body tensed. Sure, Aric had experience with healing and used that book filled with secrets that he never shared. But that meant nothing.

Taryn survived a terrible journey with Kai. They had fought each other and enemies. Laying a hand on Kai's cold pale arm, he gently pulled Kai toward the bed.

"Kai," he said with a reassuring smile. "Great to see you up, but..."

He never got any further. Kai jerked like Taryn's hand was acid on his skin. He shook Taryn off and spun to face him. His face was gaunt and all the color seemed drained out of it. His hair, hanging in front of his face, was messy, and his eyes were dark. Kai regarded him for a second and then, with a speed faster than a snake, punched him in the face.

Taryn yelled as he covered his face with his hands. It felt like a load of books had fallen on his head. He heard Lizzy screaming Kai's name as Taryn dropped to the sand and prayed for the pain to stop.

He sensed Aric running toward Kai while Rev came up and knelt in front of him. "Let me see," she said and placed her hands on his.

"No," Taryn moaned, knowing he was more embarrassed than hurt. "I'm fine."

She didn't respond as she forced his hands down. Using her fingers, she spread his eyelids. He could see, but she was fuzzy and out of focus.

"Ow!" He pushed her hands away. "Aren't you supposed to be making me feel better?"

Rev patted his knee. "A good old-fashioned black eye. You'll be fine."

"That's what I thought before you hurt me more." He expected a response to his bad attitude, but she turned away from him. Maybe all patients were surly. Maybe she was used to being around Aric's sunny personality.

With all the commotion, Kai backed into the far wall at the back of the cave. He had a wild look in his eyes like he was trapped. As Aric got nearer, Kai started to tremble so much he could barely stand. His legs buckled, and he grabbed the wall for support. As his hands slipped from their grip, tremors shook his whole body.

"Help me," he whispered. "Get me out."

Aric grabbed Kai and supported him back to the bed. By the time they reached it, Kai had slipped back into unconsciousness. Aric carefully laid him down as Kai's shivers began to subside. Aric straightened Kai's shirt and began checking his bandages.

"What's this?" he asked. "Rev, when did you...?" He broke off.

Taryn caught his breath. *Did Aric find the crystal? Oh, please, Adoyni, let him miss it. It's the only thing that will save Kai!* Aric loosened the bandages.

"A crystal!" Aric exclaimed. "Where did this come from?" He held up the stone Taryn had carefully placed on Kai.

***

Kai sat on the stone floor with his head on his hands. He didn't think he could lift his arms if he wanted to. He was going to give up. There was no point of going forward or backwards. And why try escaping through the doors? He'd sit here until he died.

The burning over his heart eased and then disappeared completely. He lifted his head and pulled his shirt forward. The burn on his skin was fading as rapidly as it had come.

He took deep gulps of air, savoring the feel of the simple movement of breathing without pain. Maybe he could keep going. He got to his feet and used the wall as support as he made his way slowly down the hallway.

***

Aric rocked back onto his heels and studied the crystal in his fingers. "I know you wouldn't have anything to do with magic, Rev."

He glanced at Lizzy and Griff.

Lizzy looked more confused, but the young boy gazed at Aric with hero worship in his eyes. Both of them shook their heads.

"You did it!" He crossed to Taryn. "Of all the idiotic, stupid things to do!"

"You don't know what you're talking about!" Taryn's face grew hot. "Crystals help with healing! And you won't even consider it!"

"I won't because I know there's a price!" Aric yelled. "You keep your magic away from him. And everyone else. I ought to beat you for this stupidity."

Taryn snorted. "Like you could." Although deep inside, he was afraid that Aric could do what he threatened. "Give it back."

"No." Aric's response was final as he slipped the crystal into his pocket.

Taryn wanted to protest and demand the crystal back, but he knew Aric was right. He had seen the truth about magic when they purified the water.

But it was so hard to wait for Adoyni to do anything. It was to trust. He was used to finding a way to get what he wanted and trying anything until he was happy.

He had forgotten that he had put magic behind him and given Adoyni control of his life. He forgot about the chains that bound him that he had escaped from and the love he had entered into when he accepted Adoyni's gift of life.

He only hoped he hadn't hurt Kai in the process. He glanced at his friend on the blankets. Kai seemed to be breathing better.

He took a deep breath and prayed silently that Adoyni would forgive him.

"What in Adoyni's world is happening?" Lizzy jumped to her feet and stood in between them. "What's wrong with him?"

Silence filled the room as everyone avoided Lizzy's eyes. Taryn wasn't going to say. It had been Aric's idea not to mention it to Lizzy, so he could be the one to tell her everything.

The silence grew longer.

"Stop ignoring me! All of you!" Lizzy yelled. "I'm not going to quit asking until I know. He's my friend, too. You can't hide it from me."

Taryn saw desperation in her eyes. The words wouldn't come, though. It was too hard to even think about, much less say out loud.

As long as no one talked about it, he could believe that it wasn't really happening.

"Look at him, Lizzy," he finally said quietly. "You know what he's fighting."

She studied Kai. The pale white skin. The veins were starting to show in his arms. His eyes, now closed, dark instead of bright blue. Even the pupils seemed to have disappeared.

"You've seen tons of them," he continued. "You've..." His voice cracked.

How could he finish the sentence? By saying that she'd killed some of them? The sentence hung in the air.

Horror filled her face as it drained of all color. Her green eyes were wide as she avoided looking at the bed where Kai was.

"Are you saying that he's...?" She stopped. No one filled in the words for her, so she continued. "That he's turning into an...an Unwanted?"

And like that the word was out. It was real. Taryn winced, ran his hands over his face, and nodded. Tears stung his eyes as he blinked them away.

Silence filled the cave. After a few minutes, Taryn risked a glance at Lizzy. She was staring at nothing while tears streamed down her face.

"But how?" She asked. "We were together the whole time. What happened to him that didn't happen to us?"

Taryn shook his head. "All I can think is that we split up at the castle. Kai didn't want to. He thought we should stay together. And we didn't. He went into that tower above the river. If he swallowed any of the water before it was purified, where the poison was most concentrated, that might have been enough to infect him."

"We should've stayed with him," Lizzy's voice broke as she spoke. "Eladar told us to listen to him, and we didn't."

"We'll do whatever it takes to heal him," Taryn snapped.

"If that's what Adoyni wants," Aric broke in.

Taryn glared at him. "I don't care about what Adoyni wants. This is my friend, and I'll do whatever it takes, even magic, to help him."

"You won't use magic here," Aric commanded. "I won't allow it!"

"Then you better find a way to cure him because what you're doing isn't working," Taryn yelled back. "I'm not going to let him become a monster."

A flash of anger crossed Aric's face, but before he could respond, Lizzy jerked back to the conversation.

"What are we going to do when he...he...he's not him anymore?" Lizzy asked.

Aric shook his head slightly and shifted in his seat. "That's why I need to tell you the rest of my story so that you can help us figure out the puzzle.

The key to the mystery may be hidden in the tale, so I dare not skip anything."

Taryn realized that Aric avoided the question, but he left no room for anyone to jump in as he continued his story.

Lizzy gave him a long look filled with worry. What were Aric and Rev's secret plans if Kai turned into an Unwanted?

"Wait!" Griffen broke in. The young boy had kept quiet until now. His sea green eyes were worried. "When my Mom was alive, she said that she should pray for anything. We haven't once prayed for Kai. Can we at least try that?"

Aric nodded. "I think that's a good idea. Why don't you pray, Taryn?"

Me! I'm not qualified to pray. I don't know what words to say. Are there special words that trigger Adoyni's healing as the Goddess uses?

He remembered the simple words Kai had used when Lizzy was hurt, and Taryn got the feeling that Adoyni wouldn't care about what he said but would care more about the heart. He took a deep breath and closed his eyes.

"Adoyni, I don't know how to do this prayer thing, but could You please heal Kai? We don't want to watch him die."

Taryn heard Lizzy sniff back tears as he continued. "We don't know what to do to make him feel better, but I know You could heal him, like you healed Lizzy. Please?"

Taryn opened his eyes hoping to see Kai jump out of his blankets and start yelling about how they had to get going now like he used to.

But nothing happened. The prayer didn't work at all. He slumped against the wall of the cave while Aric began his story.

CHAPTER FORTY-THREE

Royal Rage

We ran at a breakneck speed for a while. I clung to the saddle and hoped that Wonder could see the road better than I could, for although the moon was bright, the trees cast long shadows across the track.

It crossed my mind to slow the horses to a safer speed, but there was a fire inside of me to escape as quickly as I could. The pace and the distance did nothing to shake the growing fear inside of me that something evil was taking over the royal castle and the kingdom.

Although we rode side by side on the narrow dirt road, we never talked. Brief patches of moonlight revealed a worried look on Rev's face. The wind blew her hair back, and I could see tear streaks down her cheeks. She never once looked at me. She leaned forward over Kaspar's neck urging him to go faster away from the castle.

After some time passed and Medora was far in the distance, I realized I was riding with the reins in my left hand. I never did anything with my left hand.

When I tried to transfer the reins to my right hand, my fingers barely opened. I gritted my teeth and forced them to move. As my fingers slowly curled around the leather straps, I cried out in pain and dropped my arm back to hang listlessly by my side. It throbbed, creating a headache as well as turning my stomach.

When we reached the next bridge, I pulled Wonder to a stop and slid to the ground. The horse dropped her head and snorted. I loosened the cinch a little with my left hand.

"I think we could take a break," I said. "Water the horses a bit. Let them rest." I didn't add that my arm needed a rest, too, but it did.

She led Kaspar downstream. When I joined her, she was sitting on the side of the road. Her knees were curled up close to her chin, and she had the prison dress pulled over them as she wrapped her arms around her legs. She didn't move as I sat down beside her, trying to move carefully so that I didn't jar my arm.

After some time, she stirred. "You didn't have to get me out of the dungeon. Thank you for taking that risk."

Surprised, I grinned at her. Was she being nice to me? This was a change!

"You wouldn't have any of my clothes, would you? Or shoes?" she asked.

I groaned. I hadn't thought she would need anything like clothes. Besides, I didn't even know where to go to find such things. "I...ah...I...You see..." I stammered.

"You don't." She summed up, her voice flat.

"But I have some of my stuff." I jumped to my feet and swayed as black spots from the agony in my arm sprang up. I shook my head to clear it and clumsily opened the saddle bags.

Pulling a shirt and some breeches out, I threw them to her. She smiled, although it didn't reach her eyes, and slipped into the woods. When she returned, she didn't sit down.

"Thanks for the clothes," she said. "We'll have to buy shoes when we get to a village."

"Ah," I stammered as realization hit me. "I didn't actually bring any coin. All I have to do is tell people who I am, and they'll give me whatever I want."

"And that will make it easy for Belial to track us," Reveka snapped. "We can't tell a soul. In fact, the less people we see, the better!"

"Well, maybe you should've been the one to pack! I guess I was too busy trying to figure out how to get you out of the dungeon to think of every little detail!" I yelled, but I realized she was right. That's what stung most of all.

Silence descended between the two of us for a short time, and then she changed the subject. "So where are we going? And why are you favoring your arm?"

I bristled at her questions. But as I looked at her in my clothes and traces of the dungeon still clinging to her, I couldn't bring myself to chastise her. I told her about my suspicions of Belial, my poisoned blade, the book I snatched from Belial's secret room, and my plan to bring Belial down. Dawn was breaking as I finished.

As I talked, she plucked a piece of grass and knotted it over and over, flicking it away to start *again. I told her everything, even my plan to contact Lord Fariel and rally support. When I finished, she sighed and rubbed her eyes.*

"That's the dumbest plan I've ever heard."

That wasn't the reaction I was expecting.

She ignored me as she ripped my plan to shreds. "First, you don't know where Lord Fariel is. His land borders my Dad's land, and I know he has at least four different houses. So, where do we go?"

She didn't wait for an answer before continuing. "Besides that, you don't really have any proof. So what if your sword is poisoned? Belial could say you did it to make him look bad. As for the note and book, there's no evidence that shows Belial wrote it or that he even had it. We have nothing. And someone who is playing around with magic, probably Belial, will be hunting us."

"What's with you and all this magic stuff? Surely you don't believe it's real?"

She ignored the question. "Let me see your arm," she commanded.

I was too worried and in too much pain to argue. It was a relief that someone else knew. I eased my shirt off my arm and watched as she unwrapped the bandages.

"I took care of a lot of wounds at Shiel," she said. "And we've been seeing a lot of weird stuff lately." Her nose winkled as the stench escaped. "Did you think to bring any medicine?"

I pointed to my saddle bags, and she quickly got it. I didn't dare look at the wound as my stomach was queasy. She cleaned it, causing shooting tremors down my arm, and poked at it a few minutes until I growled at her to stop.

"I've never seen anything like it. To me, it doesn't look like the disease that's sweeping across the country." She bandaged it up. "But what worries me is that it's spreading down your arm and up into your shoulder. It might take over your body eventually."

I was starting to wonder why I got her out of the dungeon. I held my groans back as I put my arm in my sleeve.

She ignored me. "Look, I've been thinking. That note says Belial was in Vesmir posing as a priest of Adoyni, right?"

I nodded as I tried to move my fingers. They lay at the end of my arm, lifeless and dead. They wouldn't even move. I pinched one and didn't feel a thing. The nausea in my stomach increased as I considered what life would be like with one arm.

Reveka didn't notice my distraction. "We'll go there and find someone who knows something bad he's done. While we do that, we'll ask around about Lord Fariel. One of the commoners will know. With real proof, we'll go to him and bring Belial down."

She stopped talking and waited like she expected me to break out in thunderous applause at her terrific plan.

Did it even occur to her that I couldn't move my arm? What was I thinking when I cut my arm with a sword I thought was poisoned? If only I could go back to that first day. I wouldn't get mad at Father, I wouldn't hurt Patrin, and everything would be normal.

Reveka shifted. "What about something to eat? I didn't get any dinner. We always eat after your Mother has finished, and they didn't serve anything in the dungeon."

"I don't think I packed any food. I figured we'd get some along the way." I spoke slowly and deliberately.

"Without money? How are we supposed to do that?" she demanded.

"I don't know. Whatever people do to get money. It's easy enough. Everyone I know has figured it out. The peasants are only poor because they're lazy," I responded in the same tone.

"What kind of idiot are you?" Reveka yelled and made the horses jumped. "You live in this perfect world where you never have to work, but can't you see that everyone has to work their fingers to the bone just to survive?"

I couldn't take it anymore. I yelled back at her, using all my anger and frustration that had built up over the last few weeks. "You will not call me an idiot! So I didn't have much time to plan for this trip, but at least you're out of the dungeon." I pulled myself up and used a line that Father loved to use. "You would do well to remember who I am."

"Who you are?" she mocked with a smile on her face. "A spoiled Prince who's never worked. A Prince who takes no interest in his future realm or the people in it. And, oh yeah, the best part of it all, thanks to my parents' wonderful planning, my future husband!"

Her smile was replaced by a look of fury. In the rising sun, her cheeks reddened and her eyes flashed with anger. She spun on her heel and stomped to Kaspar. He tensed as she tightened the cinch.

I jumped to my feet and took one step. Before I could even form words, black spots appeared in front of my eyes. I shook my head and tried to rub them away with my hand, but before I could get my hand to my face, everything went black.

CHAPTER FORTY-FOUR

Fresh Feathers

Aric stumbled, and before I could do anything, he fell flat on his face in the mud. I dropped Kaspar's reins and rushed to him.

When I turned him over onto his back, he groaned softly as the movement jolted his right arm, but he never opened his eyes.

"Aric?" I didn't know what to do. Would he accuse me of assaulting the Crown if I slapped his face to wake him up? Probably. Knowing him. But if we didn't get moving, Belial would catch up.

"Aric? Wake up. Come on. We've got to get going."

No response. I checked his breathing and heart rate. The heart beat seemed a bit fast, and his skin felt clammy, but everything else seemed fine.

Although I wasn't a healer, I'd worked with plenty of animals. I knew dying when I saw it, and Aric was flirting with it. He'd need some serious help if we were going to stop that poison.

"Aric. We've got to get going." I said a bit louder and gently slapped his face. I expected him to open his eyes and yell stuff about beating the Royal Prince, but there was nothing.

*I tied my hair back into a ponytail and wanted
to scream. Ever since I caught Aric trying to steal
Kaspar that morning, he'd wrecked my life. All I
wanted was to find some answers for the disease
that was sweeping through our province.*

*I felt bad about leading the Queen to think my
parents were dead. But it wasn't my fault that she
jumped to her conclusion.*

*I said they were gone, which was true. They left
our province to find a renowned healer for Mom
who was feeling worse every day. Dad left me in
charge of the province, which was something I had
been waiting for all my life.*

*It wasn't my fault that the Queen assumed that
gone meant dead. Maybe I should've corrected
her, but I didn't want to answer any questions
about who I really was. The moment they found
out I was engaged to Aric, they'd have me wrapped
up in lace and not let me go.*

*I looked back at Aric lying in the dirt. As soon
as this was over, I'd destroy all the agreements Dad
made with the King. There was no way I was going
to live my life with him. I got up and tightened up
the cinches on the horses.*

*When I returned, he was groaning and
moaning. His eyelids fluttered like he was trying to
wake up but couldn't.*

*"Are you awake?" I asked, as I realized what a
dumb question it was. "We've got to move."*

*He nodded slightly. His eyes were unfocused,
like he was still unconscious. He closed his eyes,
and I almost had a heart attack thinking he passed
out again.*

But he blinked and pushed himself up like it took all his energy to sit up. I pulled him to his feet. He leaned on me, about knocking me over, and we shuffled to the horses.

Aric climbed onto Wonder, using me as a climbing post. Wonder swayed, and for a minute, I was certain she was going to fall on us. Then Aric was on, breathing heavily and clutching the pommel. His skin was covered with a sheen of sweat as he stared blankly ahead.

As I got on Kaspar, I knew that Aric was far sicker than I thought. How were we going to make it to Vesmir? I had never felt so alone or helpless as when I took Wonder's reins and continued down the road we had chosen.

To make matters worse, dark storm clouds gathered over us, and cold rain began pelting me. Its icy drops found their way down my face all the way to my bare feet.

Within a few minutes, everything was soaked. Including me. It didn't take long for my feet to feel like they were frozen, and I kept wiggling my toes to make sure that they weren't solid ice yet.

I kept the horses at a walk, mostly because I was getting worried they'd slip in the deep mud and injure their legs. It seemed like we were getting nowhere. If we didn't hurry, Belial's soldiers were going to catch up to us.

My frustration grew into anger as I got colder. I glanced back at Aric and saw his warm boots. What kind of idiot doesn't bring food or money on a trip like this? And why hadn't he gotten any of my things, like my shoes?

A small part of me whispered that I was far better here - cold, hungry, wet – than in that dungeon. When the soldiers had pulled me from the Queen's chambers, I was furious.

But as we entered the prison, the rage quickly changed to terror at being helpless. When the cell door clanged shut, and I was trapped alone, I knew there was nothing I could do.

The memory was something I'd give anything to forget. I thought I was the type that never gave up, but in the darkness of the dungeon, I lost all will to fight. I crumpled under defeat and wept.

I wiggled my toes again. This was better, but not by much.

We plodded along for hours while I was lost in self-misery until Kaspar paused. I nudged him with my heels, but he ignored me with pricked ears.

As I urged him on a second time, he turned his head to look back the way we came and blew softly through his nose. I knew in a flash what he was trying to tell me.

"Come on, Wonder," I said. She followed as we slid off the road into some trees. I carefully threaded through them to avoid breaking off branches and got the horses out of sight.

There was no sound of anything coming up behind us. Maybe I still had time. Tying Wonder's reins to my saddle, I took a deep breath and slid off Kaspar.

The cold mud on my bare feet made me gasp from shock. I glanced down to see the brown sludge sliding between my toes and covering my feet. Glaring once more at Aric's boots, I tied Kaspar to a tree.

"Okay, you two," I said to the horses. "Quiet. You understand? No whinnying. Be quiet." I glanced up at Aric. "That includes you, too. No groaning or yelling."

I slipped back to the road. I needed to wipe out our tracks before anyone came along and saw them. But when I reached the road, I could hear the soft beat of hooves.

I groaned, knowing we had left a trail that a blind man could see. I crouched down, ignoring the mud and rain, and crawled closer to where the trees slightly parted.

Ten horses slowly trotted around a bend of the road toward me. The soldiers rode side-by-side in their full armor with long swords hanging off their belts.

The first rider on the left was carrying a banner. It was weighed down by the rain, but I saw enough of it to know it was Belial's symbol. I'd never hated a dragon as much as I did right then.

I crouched in the mud like a rabbit waiting to see if its predator catches its smell as they drew closer. The first four horses passed. I held my breath and willed my horses to stay quiet.

Remembering our tracks, I risked a glance to where we left the road. Our footprints were smoothed out. I couldn't even tell where we had slid down to the trees.

How had that happened? It hadn't rained enough for the water to smooth them down. Did someone else do it? I felt a surge of excitement as the horses passed by and continued down the road.

But my joy faded as I realized that Belial wouldn't send only ten men after us. This was the first patrol. I made my way back to the horses and wondered what we should do.

For the first time, I was hoping that Aric would be conscious enough to discuss whether we should stay on the road or risk getting lost traveling through the woods.

But when I made it back to the horses and Aric, I saw something that chilled me more than the cold rain. There was a set of hoof prints around Wonder. Someone had ridden a horse right up to Aric, stopped for a minute, and then circled to his other side.

I followed the trail for a few yards but came to a dead end. The tracks just stopped. The ground was soft and perfect for leaving tracks behind. But there were no tracks. It was like the horse flew away.

I snorted. As I whirled back around to Aric, a small black patch in the middle of the mud caught my eye. I bent down and picked up a black feather no longer than my finger.

I twirled it through the air. No bird would be dumb enough to fly in this weather. Where had it come from?

When I returned to Aric, I saw that he was in no condition to talk, although he mumbled something about being hot. I touched his hand and was shocked to feel his palm sweaty.

Not knowing what else to do, I got on Kaspar and headed to the road. As the day continued, we dodged more soldiers. Either Kaspar would alert me or I'd hear them.

One time we barely got off the road before they turned the corner. Twice I caught a glimpse of a black horse through the trees. Was that how Kaspar knew when the soldiers were coming? I found a few more feathers around the horses.

As darkness began to fall, I picked a meadow near the road and got Aric off Wonder. He could barely walk and cried out in pain every time his arm was touched. He lay down under a tree to get out of the rain. I put the horses under the trees and unsaddled them.

As I went through the bags Aric had packed, I felt like crying again. There was no tinder box, so there was no hope of a fire. There was no grain for the horses. No brush to clean the mud off them. No pick to clean their feet. No food. No blankets. What was he thinking?

I took his medical kit over to him and took the bandages off his wound. A stench of rotting flesh came out of the bandages. My hands were shaking so badly from the cold I could barely put on some ointment and re-bandage it.

The wound wasn't healing. It was spreading. The whiteness of his flesh was up to his shoulder, but I was certain the wound was a larger gaping hole. Suppressing shudders of revulsion, I settled closer to the horses and tried to sleep.

In the morning, it was still cold and raining. I did the only thing I knew to do. I saddled the horses, got Aric on Wonder, and kept going down the road. As we travelled closer to Albia, the flat land grew hilly and was dotted with trees.

As we turned the first corner, I almost kicked myself for stupidity. If I'd gone a little bit farther last night, we would've been out of the cold.

The trees gave way to a large meadow off the road. It was filled with large tents with smokestacks peeking out the tops. Warm campfires with pots bubbling on them were scattered in between them as children ran and played in the mud.

I kicked Kaspar. He lunged forward and trotted down the hill as I grinned. We were going to be okay.

CHAPTER FORTY-FIVE

Learn to Lie

Women streamed out of the tents as we came closer. The children stopped playing and stared at us. I was sure we were a sight. I still didn't have any boots, and everything was caked with mud. One lady, draped in a purple cloak, pushed her way through the crowd.

"Merry meet," she said.

I didn't know what to say. Merry meat? What was that? I hoped it was tasty, but I got the feeling that she wasn't talking about food.

"Hi," I replied. "I was hoping you all could help us. A...Arnall, my brother, isn't feeling well." My voice was shaky with the lies.

The women burst into action like a well-trained army. Several came forward, fussing about the mud on the horses and gear. I didn't even have time to protest as they took the reins from my hands.

"They'll be right outside, sweetie," one said. "Let us take care of the poor dears."

Two other women helped Aric down from Wonder. He groaned and his head rolled back like he was unconscious again.

"What's wrong with him, my dear?" the first
woman asked as she took my arm and led me with
Aric to a nearby tent.

"I don't know. There's a cut on his arm," I
stammered. I had to get better at lying really fast.
And I'd better figure out how much I was going to
tell them. "It keeps getting worse."

"Come out of the rain, and we'll see what we
can do." The woman pushed open the flap of the
tent to reveal a large room.

Partitions lined the back with a high bed
between them for privacy. The women carried Aric
to one of the beds and placed him on it. They
began cleaning the mud off him while taking off
his shirt. He moaned as they worked.

"Sit here." The woman commanded and
pointed to a chair close to the entrance. She called
out for warm water. "My name is Damiana."

"Are you the leader?" I asked as women bustled
around. Someone brought me some warm boots.
Another lady placed a large tub of hot water and a
thick towel in front of me.

"Wash up, and take the boots. We share what
we have no need of," Damiana smiled. "I don't
consider myself a leader, for we have no need of
titles, but if you need it explained that way, I guess
I would say that I'm the head." She took off her
cloak to reveal a purple dress underneath. Her
long brunette hair was braided down her back,
and her hazel eyes studied me intently.

A young girl with long blonde hair hanging
loose over her shoulders set a platter of food next
to me. The smell of chicken with garden herbs

drifted on the air. I quickly plunged my hands in the hot water, shivering at the abrupt temperature change, and washed my face.

"Are you sure?" I picked up one of the boots. "They're worth a fortune."

"Only peace and community are worth a fortune," Damiana laughed. "Take them as a gift!"

"Thank you!" I pushed my foot in one and found that it fit perfectly.

Damiana poured a large cup of hot tea for me. She slid it closer. "This is tea from a willow tree. It's bitter, but it will warm you as it takes away your pains."

I took a sip and choked. She laughed and motioned me to try it again. I took a small swallow and managed to get it down. Another woman came with a tray of the chicken I smelled with a large potato beside it.

"I imagine we look a little strange out here," Damiana continued as I wolfed down the food. "But we've found this is the best place for us to worship Zoria. We find freedom in the trees, and a closeness to Her impossible in the cities."

I choked again. I'd heard of these communities springing up. Groups of people living in the woods, communing with their Goddess. I wasn't the religious type, and I certainly didn't want to get wrapped up with a bunch of freaks. I'd had enough of that at the royal castle.

"Small sips help, my dear," Damiana said. Before she could say more, she was interrupted by one of the women tending to Aric.

"I'm sorry, Damiana," the older woman said. "But you really need to look at this. I'm afraid it's far worse than we're used to."

Damiana didn't look back as she hurried to Aric. I shoved my other foot in the boot and stuffed the bread in my mouth before following. When I got to the table, I saw Aric was lying on it with his shirt off. The bandages were gone. The wound on his arm oozed blood. But it was his skin that caught my eye.

The skin on his arm was an angry red. The red spread from his fingers all the way up to his shoulder. I gasped. I'd seen people die of a disease that turned the skin white, and then transparent, so that a person could see the veins. But this was different.

Damiana shook her head. "I don't know what it is, but it looks like some poison. That's the only thing I can think of to explain the rash like that."

Aric opened his eyes. "Where...where are we?"

I rushed to his side. "It's okay, Arnall. It's Mali, your sister. I'm right here and these ladies are going to help you get better." This lying thing was getting easier.

"Mali? That's not your...?" His blue eyes focused, and he realized what I was saying. "Oh."

"Removing the poison is very difficult," Damiana said. "It will take much of our skill."

My heart sank. She wanted me to offer them something as payment, but we didn't have anything, thanks to Aric's wonderful planning. "I...we...don't have much."

"Oh, we wouldn't take payment," Damiana said. "But it would help put the Goddess in the mood to heal if you donated something to Her. As one gives, so does the Goddess give."

I almost snorted. I knew what was happening. I'd give something to the Goddess, and Damiana would take it "Can you heal him?"

"Oh, no, I can't," Damiana said. She seemed surprised that I asked the question. "But I can guide the energy to provide a means for the Goddess to heal Arnall."

I glanced at Aric. His fingers on his good hand were curled up like he was in great pain. He was watching me and nodded slightly when I raised my eyebrows. Fine. If this was what he wanted, and if it worked, it would be worth it.

"What would you...I mean, what would be something the Goddess would like?" I asked.

"Hm, that is a good question, my dear, for She only approves of gifts that are worthy to her. It has to be something that you value. Gold coins are not something She is interested in."

That was good because we didn't have any coins. But I wasn't prepared for her next words.

"I don't have to tell you that this is a serious poison. Arnall will die if he doesn't get help. You are asking for a lot of the Goddess. The horse you rode up on would please Her."

Kaspar! Why did everyone want him? He was mine, and I wasn't giving him to the Crown Prince or to this woman! I shook my head. "No deal," I said, trying hard to hide my anger. "That's my horse. I won't let him go."

"Not even for the life of your brother?" Damiana gasped. "Not even for the privilege of knowing the Goddess is well-pleased with your gift?"

I was getting real tired of this woman and her games. I knew exactly who Kaspar was for. And it wasn't any goddess. I shook my head. "We have two horses." I saw Aric nod on the bed as I talked. "The other one is great. You...the Goddess...can have her."

I winced as I said it. If they accepted Wonder, we were down to one horse. We wouldn't get far with Kaspar, even with as good of a horse that he was. It would be harder to run from the soldiers. Someone would have to walk most of the time, and I knew it wouldn't be His Royal Highness. But what else could I do?

Damiana's face fell with disappointment, but there must have been something in my face that she knew not to argue with. She nodded her head. "The Goddess will be well pleased with the other horse, too. Do we have an agreement?"

I hated to do it. I hated to lose Wonder. She was a great horse, one I'd like to take home. I hated to be slowed down. I hated the thought of these women taking care of Wonder. I looked at Aric. He nodded, his blue eyes pleading me to stop the pain. Well, she was his horse after all. But still it rankled me.

"We have a deal," I said.

CHAPTER FORTY-SIX

Faulty Agreements

I shook hands with Damiana, although I hated to do it. Aric sighed deeply and closed his eyes as the women bustled around again. One woman took four white candles and placed them in the north, south, east, and west. Two others put a white blanket in the center of the candles while several helped Aric to his feet and got him to lay down on it. As I watched, I was filled with misgivings. I wanted to grab Aric and run out of here while we still could. But I didn't.

Damiana turned to me. "Stay quiet during the ceremony. And try to keep your thoughts positive. We can't have any negative energy here."

I nodded, but I didn't really know what she meant. I was positive all of this was crazy. I was positive I didn't want to leave Wonder. And I was positive Aric was continually wrecking my life. But I had a funny feeling that was not what she was talking about.

All but Damiana and two of the older women left. Damiana sat close to Aric and closed her eyes while the two other ladies lit the candles and joined her around his body. Aric glanced over at me before the ritual started. I couldn't tell if he was apprehensive or eager for healing.

They joined hands and began chanting quietly. I was too far away to hear, and honestly, I didn't want to. There was something about these women that I didn't like. I was probably being silly because they were caring and nice. My toes were warming in the boots, and my stomach was full.

But they still made me feel that something was wrong. Instead of feeling the calm and peace they seemed to convey, I felt prickly, edgy, and restless.

They continued their low chanting. The three women simultaneously stopped their prayer and sat holding hands with their eyes closed.

I struggled to keep from fidgeting. Was he healed? What were they doing? I tried to keep a smile, but it must have looked as forced as it felt.

Why were we wasting time on silence? The soldiers were looking for us, and they could find these people as easily as we did. I studied Aric, hoping to see a change even from my distance, but nothing happened. I clenched my jaw and forced myself to stay still.

Aric jerked violently. The ladies flinched away as he thrashed back and forth on the floor. One lady leaped to her feet and began extinguishing the candles with a snuffer while the other two tried to hold Aric down. But as they grabbed his arms, he started to yell.

I shot to him and knelt down on the floor. While they pinned his arms to the floor, his legs continued to kick. His eyes were still closed, but he was shrieking in pain.

"Make it stop!" he shrieked. "Make it stop!"

I glanced at the women. "Is this normal?"

They ignored me. Only one replied, "Look!" She pointed to Aric's chest.

The white on his arm was disappearing! He was getting better! I laughed with delight. Perhaps if we told the women that Aric was the Prince, they'd let us keep Wonder for future payments. Within the week, I could be home at Shiel.

But why was he in so much pain? He stopped yelling, but he still hadn't opened his eyes or relaxed yet. His body was taut like it was filled with pain. I looked back at his arm.

What was left of white skin was turning to a deep red. It stretched from his fingers up to his shoulder and started across his chest. The wound oozed pus that stank badly enough that I could smell it from where I was.

Damiana stared at Aric. "Ladies, go now!" The words were quiet, but I heard the authority in them. They left the tent without a word. Damiana waited until the flap was closed before she turned to me.

"You have brought negative energy into our camp," she accused.

I was getting real tired all this energy stuff. "What's happening to him? Is he healed?"

"No, he's not. We did our best, but the negative energy you brought in has affected his healing. In fact, it is strong enough to counteract the spell and has made him worse."

Damiana rose gracefully and gathered a few bandages. She returned to wrap up Aric's arm. "My only suggestion is that you find some way to purge the negativism in both your lives. Once you have done that, find another healer and see if the energies align correctly for you."

"You're saying you made him worse?" I snapped. It was hard to breathe now, like my lungs couldn't get enough air.

"I'm saying the negativism made him worse," Damiana said forcefully. "Attitudes like your present one of rising anger is exactly what blocked the positive energy from healing him. You must find the solution to your negative attitudes quickly. He doesn't have much time left."

"**My** negative attitudes? What about him?" I yelled. "Why are you assuming it's me? It's him you're healing. What about his state?"

"Your current state is a good indication of your spirit. You are filled with anger, contention, and self-pride. His condition is so weak he doesn't have the power to block the healing energies." She finished wrapping the wound and stood up to face me. "I cannot allow such strong negative energy in my camp. This is a place carefully cultivated to exclude anything that hinders us on our spiritual journey. My ladies will help you dress him and get your horse ready to go, but you must leave."

That was fine with me. They'd done nothing but make Aric worse and tick me off. I was only too happy to leave. But then I realized what she said.

"Wait," I called as she turned to go. "You said horse. You didn't heal him. You shouldn't keep Wonder. We'll take both horses with us."

Damiana gave me a sympathetic look that I wanted to slap right off her face. "Our deal wasn't conditional on healing. It surprised me that you

didn't ask for that. Most of our patients do.
However, our work was done, and you wouldn't
expect us to work for free, would you?"

Oh, no. I sure wouldn't. It probably would
mess up their precious energies. I glared at her,
unable to hide my loathing.

"That isn't fair," I argued.

"Yes, but regrettably, life isn't fair. It's just life."
She placed her hands on my shoulders. "Listen,
my dear, I shall give you some advice because I can
see you are in a bind. You can't change it, but you
can learn to accept it. Give up your anger and your
striving. Perhaps this happened so that you can
discover the true power of positive energy from
the Goddess."

She gave me a smile that I was sure was
supposed to warm my soul and give me a bucketful
of that precious positive energy, but I only felt the
burning urge to punch her out and haul Aric out
to the horses. Both of the horses. The only thing
that stopped me was that she was right. I hadn't
made the deal conditional on healing.

She glided to the entrance of the tent and
turned around again. "Keep the boots as my gift to
you. Perhaps they'll lead you to the truth." With
that, she was gone.

I started to take off a boot to chuck it at the
entrance but stopped when two other women
bustled in and began packing up Aric. I rubbed my
face and pulled back my hair. Without any words,
they packed us a small amount of food, dressed
Aric who was still mostly unconscious, and hustled
us out the door.

Kaspar stood waiting for us in the rain, freshly groomed. The women hoisted Aric up on him and put the bag on behind the saddle. I saw Wonder tied to a hitching post by the tent next to us. I walked to her and scratched her head.

"You can't come with us," I whispered. My eyes welled up with tears. "I'm so sorry. You're a good horse, and they'll take care of you. But I'll come back for you. I promise. I'll come and get you and take good care of you always. Hold on until I do, okay?"

Wonder put her head on my chest like she knew what I was saying and was sad. I petted her neck for a minute. I stepped back and kissed her nose. "I'll be back. Wait for me, okay?"

I walked away, not daring to look back. She blew softly through her nose as I gathered Kaspar's reins. I looked to the edge of the tents before she nickered once, loudly, as if reminding me that I was leaving her.

I stopped and glanced back. Wonder was straining at the end of her rope with her ears pricked in our direction. She stomped her foot and whinnied.

"Stay, girl," I said. I wanted to say that I'd be back. I really wanted to break our agreement, but there were too many women around, and I could see Damiana peering out of a tent at us. I vowed again that I'd rescue Wonder.

Aric moaned a little, jerking my thoughts back to the present. I gripped the reins tighter, put my head down to keep out of the rain, and walked away. Wonder whinnied again, but this time I kept going.

I led the way to the road and climbed the hill, dropping down to the other side without looking back. Aric groaned with every bump. But I didn't look at him. I didn't want him to see the tears streaming down my cheeks.

CHAPTER FORTY-SEVEN

Climbing Post

I walked blindly for a long time. All I could think about was Wonder's confused nicker, the fact that Aric was worse and was riding my horse. If he was awake, I knew he'd find the whole situation amusing. I couldn't believe he'd finally won and was sitting on Kaspar.

I hated the boots on my feet for their constant reminder of Damiana. I continued stomping through the mud, dodging soldiers, but once night came, I realized I couldn't make it much farther. I turned off the road and set up a small camp for the night. Aric groaned as I pulled him off Kaspar, opening his eyes only once.

I thought the boots would keep me warm, but the rain soaked everything, and I was frozen. I spent the night curled up with no sleep.

Getting Aric on Kaspar in the morning was almost impossible. He finally woke up enough to help a little. He groaned as I hoisted him up until he was able to swing a leg over. I knew my shoulder and my ribs were bruised from him kicking me.

I hadn't gone far when the trees opened up to a large clearing. Orchards grew throughout the open land. And in the center of it was a large

farmhouse with a barn beside it. I made my way
through the orchards in case any more soldiers
came down the road, but there was only silence.

When we reached the farmhouse, I tied Kaspar
to the post by the house and bounded to the front
door. Pounding loudly, I waited for a response, but
there was none, not even a farm dog barking. I
knocked louder and then pushed open the door
slowly.

"Hello?" I called. "Anyone home?"

No answer.

I paused. Where would they be? I walked in
farther and called again. But there was no
response. My boots were caked with mud, so I
slipped out of them and went into the living room.

There were odd heaps of clothing on the
couch and the large chair close to the fire. I
moved closer as my heart began to pound. There
was something wrong in this house.

As I got closer, I knew I was wrong. It wasn't
just clothes. There were two bodies. I screamed
and jumped back. Forcing myself to look, I saw an
older woman with hair that was slightly gray, lying
on the couch. Across the room, there was an older
man dead in his chair.

I bolted from the living room and into the hall.
What had happened to them? They looked exactly
like the people and animals dying on Dad's estate.
Was it the same disease? I was shivering. I didn't
know if it was from fright or from cold. I crept up
the staircase.

I slipped into their bedroom. Feeling like a
grave robber, I found boots in their closet. I

hesitated. I didn't really need them. But I wanted
nothing to do with Damiana, other than getting
Wonder back. I slipped the farm boots on my
frozen feet and decided they were much better.

I grabbed some extra blankets and stopped at a
small wooden chest sitting on the side of their bed.
Feeling rotten about what I was doing, I said a
short prayer to Adoyni and opened the lid.

Coin! There was good sized pile of gold coins
with a scepter on them in the box. My heart
dropped. It had been a little while since Belial
issued coins with a flame on them. But it was long
enough that the scepter coins had dropped in
value. I hated the Flames. None of our tenants
could afford to get them, and they were slowly
unable to pay for anything as the Flames became
more popular.

I grimaced and sifted through the pile of coins.
Even as scepters, there had to be enough to pay
for a healer for Aric. I emptied the gold coins into
my pocket.

"I'm not stealing," I said to the empty room.
"But you don't need it now, and we'll die if we
don't use it. I'm sorry."

And I truly was. But that didn't stop me from
raiding the kitchen of all the food while I stuffed
my face. I trotted out to Kaspar and grabbed the
pack. I crammed food, blankets, tinder box, and a
few rags for bandages. That left enough room for a
few supplies for Kaspar. I threw the pack on
Kaspar and ran to the barn. My fear had changed
to an urgency that we had to get going. Now.

I burst into the barn. Two milk cows and several pigs jumped at my appearance. Slowing my pace, I checked on them. They were out of food and water. Repressing a sigh, I trotted to the hay. I was taking their money and supplies. The least I could do was take care of their livestock.

The tack room, where I assumed the grain was, had a stack of fence posts and other random wood piled in front of the door.

I groaned. "Why do I always have to fix everything? The whole place is as neat as a thumbtack, but the one door I need to open has junk piled in front of it."

I looked at the milk cows for sympathy, but they flicked their ears, eager for a meal. "I'll get you some food, okay?" I said to them. "I don't have time to clean your stall although it needs it. Someone else will have to do that."

I trudged over to the pile of wood and began throwing the posts aside. The quiet of the farm descended on me. I'd spent my whole life helping Dad run the province. He wasn't one to rule from a distance.

We cleaned stalls, fed animals, broke ice in the ponds during the winter for them to drink. I was more comfortable in a barn or outside than in any room inside a house. I loved the solitude and the work.

But I couldn't stop thinking about the pile of wood. Everything from the house to the barn was neat. Why was there this mess in front of a door that they needed to open frequently? What made them throw a pile of wood right in the way like they were in a massive hurry?

The silence was eerie. I tried to shake it off and told myself it was my imagination getting away from me. I threw the last piece away. It would take a few minutes to get the animals some grain and hay. I'd fill my grain bag, and we'd be off. I wiped my hands on my pants and opened the door to the tack room.

Rows of harnesses hung on the wall. Grain barrels and stacks of hay lined the opposite wall. Pitchforks, shovels and hoes lined the back wall. I grinned. The place was exactly like I thought it would be.

A rustling started behind the hay. My heart began to beat faster as I caught a glimpse of a guy about my age leap from behind the hay. He was as white as snow. His clothes were ragged and torn. I barely noticed any of that.

My attention was on the hoe in his hands that he was swinging at me. He launched himself across the room with a menacing growl and swung again.

I leaped back as the hoe came at me with the speed of a cat. It brushed my face in a near miss. My feet teetered on the threshold of the doorway.

Caught off balance, I waved my arms frantically to grab the door jam, but I was too late as I fell onto my back. I landed with a crash as the man flung himself at me.

CHAPTER FORTY-EIGHT

Spooked Horse

I groaned as I hit the dirt. Air whooshed out of my lungs, and I hit my head hard on the wooden floor. I couldn't see, and my body refused to budge. I knew the man would be on me in a flash. In a panic, I threw myself to the left as he landed beside me.

I got to my knees and tried to crawl away quickly, but my limbs twisted and tangled under me. My right arm gave way as I put weight on it. I scrambled away. The man yelled in anger and grabbed one of my legs. He pulled as I screamed.

My left hand flew forward in my desperate attempt to escape. I didn't even know what he wanted. Did he want to eat me? Kill me? Obviously the dead couple had locked him in the tack room until I came along and opened it up. What an idiot I was!

My fingers scraped against one of the rakes in the pile I had so carelessly thrown aside. I felt myself slipping back as he yanked my leg. The strange thought passed through my mind that neither of us had said a word, and yet I was about to die.

The man managed to pull me back three inches in the dirt. I felt a rising panic. I knew I was going to die, but I didn't know why. I searched for the rake. Had I been pulled back too far? With my face on the ground, I swallowed in dirt and coughed as I couldn't breathe.

Splinters shot under my fingernails as I found it. I twisted to my back and pushed myself up against the man's body as hard as I could and grabbed it.

Shattering the silence, I yelled as I lurched to a sitting position and swung the rake with all my strength. It whipped through the air.

The man saw it coming and put up a pasty white arm to block the impact. The rake smashed into his arm and threw him off me. I scrambled through the dirt and got to my feet.

The man yelled, but it sounded like an animal roaring. Goosebumps trickled up and down my spine when I realized that his eyes were pure black. I took a small shaky step, hoping to circle him and make it to the door.

He sniffed the air and glanced around the barn. Smiling an evil grin, he grabbed a post and whipped it through the air. That would shatter anything I could use as a weapon. I didn't have the strength to fight him. I didn't think anyone did. I was going to lose.

"Easy now," I said reassuringly, like to a spooked horse. "Easy. I don't want to fight."

He stopped swinging the post and cocked his head like he was trying to understand me. One of the cows behind me stamped its foot, and the man jumped, startled by the noise.

With a snarl, he rushed me. I tried to dodge his attack and smack him away with my rake, but in my terror, I missed. He did not.

The post he was carrying struck my ribs. I yelled in pain and fell to the ground. He struck my legs with the same strength. I shrieked and pulled my legs up to my chest while I curled into a ball.

Over my screams, I heard the only sound he had made so far. He began to laugh. As he continued the evil sound, he kicked my feet away from my chest and put his almost naked foot on my throat.

A putrid smell flooded my senses as I grabbed his ankle and struggled to push it off. He only pressed harder until black spots appeared in my eyes. I stopped fighting to get some air. He continued to laugh as he pulled back to swing at my head.

I couldn't fight him with a stick. I screamed for him to stop. But he took his aim and began to swing. The barn was suddenly filled with a loud noise like the beating of a drum. The man looked behind him.

I caught a glimpse of a black horse coming into the barn so fast it seemed like it was flying. I thought I saw long black wings before I leaped backwards and tripped over the rake I'd dropped.

I fell into the dust and forgot about the fight. All I could see were long black wings attached to the most beautiful horse I'd ever seen. I was torn between awe and wanting to scream that I was right. I had seen a black horse outside Belial's

palace. Then I remembered that poor man who
was tied to the table and his warning.

"He's coming."

Was he talking about the horse like I originally
thought? There was no way I could fight both of
them.

Before I could scream for help, the black horse
lunged at the man. I back-crawled to the stall and
huddled in the dirt and straw, trying to breathe
and ignore the throbbing in my ribs.

The man swung the post at the horse. I knew it
was going to whack the horse in the head and
couldn't stop the scream that was meant as a
warning.

My scream died off as the post stopped five
inches from the horse's head like it had crashed
into an invisible wall. The man's arm vibrated from
the force. He dropped it and grabbed his hand in
pain.

The horse whinnied and reared up on its hind
legs. It struck out with one of its hooves. The man
threw up one of his arms, but it was too late. The
hoof slammed into his skull. Without a sound, he
dropped and lay still in the aisle of the barn.

I got to my feet, my legs shaking so badly I
didn't think they would hold. I leaned against the
stall and held on for balance.

Go, girl. A man's voice echoed in my head.
Take your grain and go to the Prince.

I obeyed without thinking. I grabbed a bag of
grain in the tack room and sprinted to Aric. I
threw it onto Kaspar, grabbed the reins, and began

jogging toward the road. When we reached the dirt track, I risked one backwards glance.

The farmhouse had reverted back into silence. The cow and pigs were wandering out of the barnyard into the pasture.

Get moving, girl! *The voice returned.* You don't have much time left. Go as fast as you can!

I looked back at the barn. Was it the horse talking to me? The black stallion was standing by the padlock gate.

He reared and broke into a run towards the woods. As he picked up speed, he spread large black wings and flew over the trees and out of sight.

CHAPTER FORTY-NINE

Muddy Bread

I jogged down the road until the house with the barn was out of sight. When I glanced back to see if the farm was gone, I noticed Aric was leaning to the side almost sliding off.

I stopped, but Kaspar snorted and shook his head in protest. He slowed but pranced in place like he knew the need to get out of that wretched place.

The words I heard lingered in my head.

You don't have much time left. Go as fast as you can!

Was it really the Archippos that spoke them? Was it tracking me? I shook my head as I soothed Kaspar. Dad had given him to me as a foal when I was twelve. I'd never forget the hours we spent working with him until he was ready to ride.

Since then, Kaspar was my closest friend. I knew his very thought and movement before he did, and he was certainly capable of reading my mind. Mom said it best. She said that we weren't horse and rider. We were a team.

But an Archippos! They existed. Or at least one did. I thought the stories were tales to amuse children or scare them into obeying Adoyni. But now I had seen something right out of the stories.

And if they existed, did that mean all the other things were real? Would Adoyni really work miracles like they said He did? What about the scarier creatures like Seekers?

There were too many questions, but I couldn't help wonder what it'd be like to ride a horse that you could talk to! And one that flew! I could get around the province so much faster.

I resolved to do my best to catch the black stallion the next time I saw him although I didn't know how I'd do that with those wings. There had to be a way, though, and I'd find it.

Aric was sliding off Kaspar. I pushed him back into the saddle and was shocked at how warm his arm was. He groaned loudly as he was moved into position, but his eyes were shut.

You don't have much time left. Go as fast as you can!

Was the horse talking about Aric? Was he running out of time before the poison took over his body? Or was the voice referring to Belial's soldiers patrolling the road?

I glanced back the way we had come, nervous again about the soldiers and other monsters that might be roaming around.

I grabbed a short section of rope from my saddle bags and began tying Aric into his saddle. We had to make some time, and I wanted to get as far away from that farm as we could before night fell. As I was finished tying the last knot, Aric jerked and opened his eyes.

"Stop it," he protested weakly when he saw the rope.

"I can't, Aric." I tried to explain. "You're sick. We've got to hurry, but you keep falling out of the saddle."

He let go of the rope and spoke with more force. "Hungry."

I repressed a sigh. Did he lose all ability to use complete sentences? But if he was hungry, maybe he was improving. I stifled my impatience and got some bread out of the pack.

"Here." I held out the bread. "This is all we have."

"Not hungry," he mumbled. His words were soft and hard to hear.

What in the world? He said he was. "You have to eat." I pushed the bread into his hand. "You have to keep your energy up."

His fingers tightened around the bread. He started to nibble on the bread. I sighed. As long as he ate, he'd be fine. I watched as he swallowed half of the slice. Then he paused.

"Want some water?" I asked.

He shook his head, his face even whiter. He leaned over Kaspar towards me and threw up all the bread he'd just eaten.

I screamed as I felt the warm glop slide down the side of my face. I brushed it off, feeling like I was going to copy him, and wiped my hands in the dirt, trying to hold back my furious words and keep the contents in my stomach down.

As I was going through convulsions to keep from throwing up, Aric continued to heave before he straightened up and dropped the uneaten bread in the mud.

The convulsions stopped, but I found a mud puddle and scrubbed my face as hard as I could before I thought about what had happened more and was unable to control my stomach. I led Kaspar as Aric closed his eyes and dropped into unconsciousness.

I knew he was sick, but I'd never been so furious in my entire life. Aric had ruined my plans to find a healer for my province, possibly allowing hundreds to die from the poison taking over our land. He'd gotten me entangled in some sort of political intrigue, and now I was stuck with him as he threw up all over me without even a thank you or an apology.

The rain started as the horses plodded down the road. I'd never felt so miserable, scared, and alone as at that moment.

Little did I know, things were going to get worse.

CHAPTER FIFTY

Face First

The next few days were agonizing. The rain never stopped. It kept us and everything we had continually drenched. Even with my farm boots, I was still frozen. I tried to use the tinderbox I got at the house, but if I was lucky enough to find something dry to burn, it was soaked by the time I was ready to light a fire. Soon I was too exhausted to even try.

Mud was everywhere. Everything we touched was covered with it. Soon everything was filthy, including the horses and gear. The only good thing was that we camouflaged well when we hid from the soldiers looking for us.

We constantly had to duck off the road and hide while patrols passed by. I lived in fear that Kaspar would whinny or Aric would call out while they were close, but so far, we were lucky. When I left to cover the tracks, I'd find the tracks already smoothed out, and Kaspar always stayed quiet.

I couldn't help but wonder if that flying horse was helping me out. Was he alerting Kaspar when soldiers were coming from behind so that I could get off the road? Was he keeping Aric and Kaspar calm while I spied on the soldiers?

I never got any answers. I saw hoof prints around when I returned and often I'd see them in the mornings, but I never caught another glimpse of him. Slowly the sight of him flying out of the meadow began to fade. Maybe I didn't really see that. Doubts grew until I'd see another black feather beside Kaspar and know what I'd seen.

Aric had an endless fever, either shivering from the cold or sweating, despite anything I did. Ever since he had thrown up, he refused food. I tried to force water down his throat during the day, but he normally rejected it. His eyes were glazed over like he was no longer seeing out of them.

When I woke up from my restless sleep, I couldn't bring myself to face another day like the one before. I shivered on the hard ground.

No one was going to help us. Most of the farms we had passed were deserted or burned to the ground. I'd only seen one farm with people, but Belial's soldiers were camped in the fields.

My body ached like I'd been doing days of hard labor in the fields. Aric had kicked me, punched me, and used me as a climbing post getting on and off Kaspar. I was sure I was covered with bruises, and I had blisters all over my feet from my boots.

I pushed myself up and ate the last of the beef I had. After saddling Kaspar, who was as weary and sick of the rain as I was, I tried to get Aric on him. But he had no strength. He tried. I'd give him that. He was stubborn. The first time his legs crumpled as he was halfway on. He collapsed into me as I stumbled and fell back from his weight.

"Get off me!" I yelled as I wiggled out from under him. Mud crept under my pant legs and into my boots. I felt bad when I saw that he couldn't get up. I pulled him to his feet. His eyes were open, but they held no expression.

The next time his arms gave out and he lost his balance. I was ready for him this time, and I threw all my weight against Kaspar.

He sidestepped in surprise, and Aric fell on his face in the mud. I ran to him and rolled him over. One arm had protected his face from the fall. He looked up at me.

"Get...me...on," he gasped between words.

This time his legs quit working before he started climbing on, and I thought we had pulled Kaspar over onto us. He gave us a dirty look. Aric finally used me to step on and made it up.

I knew from the way they stung that my shoulders were bleeding from his boots, but there were only a few bandages left, and I wanted to save them for Aric.

My tears mixed with the rain as we began down the road. I didn't understand what went wrong. I'd worked for years beside Dad, taking care of the estate, and everything went well. I had problem after problem, from horses in trouble during foaling to handling difficult people, and every problem was solved.

But lately, everything I did had failed. And now, the only Prince of the realm was dying in front of me, and I couldn't fix anything. I didn't know if I was crying because I was exhausted, frustrated, angry, or because I didn't know what to do anymore.

Although I hadn't seen the sun in days, I knew night was coming. The thought of spending another night like this made me want to burst into tears again, but I gripped Kaspar's reins until they bit into my hand to get my mind off crying.

I scanned the trees along the road to find a good spot to hide behind, but they had thinned out, and I didn't see anywhere thick enough. The darkness grew deeper as I began to panic.

Without trees to conceal us, the soldiers would find us without even trying. I jogged faster up the next hill, hoping to find a copse to rest in.

But when we got to the top of the hill, I saw something even better than trees. In the valley below us lay a small town.

Lights flickered from the windows as smoke rose from the chimneys. People were dashing from one building to the next, and there was a wave of laughter and voices as doors opened up. On the wind, the smell of smoke and food wafted on the air. A village!

It was the most beautiful sight I had ever seen.

CHAPTER FIFTY-ONE

Let Him Die

I held Kaspar back as I studied the village. Squinting through the rain, I didn't see any soldiers or banners in the streets. I sighed. We'd have to keep our heads down and hope for the best.

Kaspar acted like he knew that a night without rain and a full bucket of grain was in front of him as he pushed ahead of me down the hill.

For the first time, I was suddenly glad for the rain. I didn't want any more people seeing Aric's face than was necessary, and the rain gave us a good reason to keep our hoods up.

I glanced around to see just townspeople hustling to get out of the rain. We stopped in front of the only inn. Its name was Blue Rose, but the rose on the sign looked brown.

I rang the bell that was beside the side door. In a few seconds, the door popped open, and an older man peered out.

"Do you have any rooms?" I asked, impatient to get out of the rain and cold.

He glanced our way and shook his head. "I only have one left."

"We'll take it." I practiced lying again, hoping Adoyni understood. "He's my brother. We can share." I didn't dare say he was sick.

The innkeeper nodded. "Take the horses around back. My stable boy's back there."

"Thank you!" I called, but the door was already shut. Tugging on Aric's cloak, I finally got him to notice me. "You've got to get off."

He nodded but did nothing. I pulled on his good arm a few times before he responded. He basically fell off Kaspar and landed on me.

I took a step back from his weight, caught my balance, and helped him to his feet. I sat him down on the stairs out of the rain.

"Stay here," I ordered. "Don't take off your hood. I'll be right back."

I knew he was really sick because if I had tried to talk to him like that while we were still at the castle in Medora, he would've yelled at me how he was the crown prince.

But now, he nodded his head and sank down on the steps. I put our bags next to him and grabbed the coins I'd collected.

Taking Kaspar's reins, I trotted to the barn and grinned as the door opened. The stable boy was a large man with black hair and eyes. He was older than Dad! I hid my smile as he approached us.

"Take your horses?" he asked. His big outstretched hand was calloused.

The stable was large with two rows of stalls where well-groomed horses calmly chomped hay. Everything I saw was neat and orderly. Something about the smell of the grain and horses made me *homesick. All I wanted to do was run back. But I blinked back the tears and took five coins from the pouch.*

"Please take good care of him. He deserves it." I handed them to the man. "And our gear. Everything's so muddy." I felt really bad about landing all this work on him, but I barely had energy to take care of myself, much less Aric.

He beamed. "Don't you worry about a thing, m'lady. I'll clean him up and settle him down with some grain and hay. And I'll have your tack sparkling clean in no time. Go get warm and get some food."

I nodded. Even being in the stable was making my feet and face thaw. I choked down my relief and stumbled back through the rain to Aric. He leaned on me as we hobbled to the door.

A wave of heat from the giant fireplace in the common room caused my cheeks to sting. The room was full of people lounging by the fire, but I found an empty table and plopped Aric down. He groaned about his arm as his hood fell back.

I left him when I saw the innkeeper come in. Now that there was light, I could see his face. He was the spitting image of the stable boy, just older. They had to be brothers.

"Ten Flames will get you a room, supper, and breakfast," he said.

I nodded. "Sorry about the mess. It's horrible out there."

"I've given up trying to keep the mud out," he smiled slightly. It looked like he was tired. "Your

room is up the stairs, the second to the last on the right. Do you want to eat first?"

"Yes." There was no way I'd make it up those stairs twice with Aric. "Maybe some soup for...Ar...my brother, if you have any."

"He doesn't look too good, if I do say so," the innkeeper commented.

I looked back. Aric hadn't pulled his hood up. My heart dropped. If anyone in the room had seen him or the King, our race was over. I glanced around, but everyone seemed intent on their stories or food.

"It's the cold," I murmured and went back to the table.

"Put your hood up," I commanded. Aric didn't move. "Put it up, now!"

He sat there as still as a log. I reached to pull the hood up for him.

"Don't touch me!" he yelled. "You don't have the right! You know who I am!"

I jerked back. The entire room fell silent and stared at us. If they hadn't noticed him before, they noticed him now.

"I know who you are," I spat back. "You're my ungrateful, worthless brother who dragged me out on this stupid journey."

The room gaped at us for a minute longer until a younger man in the back started laughing. Soon the rest of the room joined him and then went back to what they were doing. I heaved a sigh of relief.

But when I looked around the room, I saw an old man staring at us. He was stretched out on one of the few stuffed chairs by the fire with a book in his gnarled hand. His dark piercing eyes were watching every move Aric made while his other hand was stroking his short white beard. I caught his eye, but he showed no sign of friendliness before he returned to study Aric.

Did he know? Aric looked like a shell of his former self. I could hardly tell under the dirt and grime that he was the prince. How would this man know? I tried to calm myself, but I couldn't help checking on him every few minutes.

The innkeeper brought a plate filled with hot roast beef and mashed potatoes bathed in a huge pool of gravy. On the side of the plate were a heaping pile of corn and two thick slices of bread.

I smelled it coming before I saw it, and my mouth was watering. He set it down in front of me, and I had my fork in hand before I realized there was a large bowl of stew in front of Aric. The smell of it seemed to make him sicker.

I put some stew on the spoon and offered it to Aric. He shook his head.

"Come on, Aric," I pleaded. I was getting to the point of begging him to eat if that's what it took. "You have to eat something."

"Don't want to," he yelled back.

The room quieted for a second again. I put down the spoon. What was happening? He had never responded this way before. He hadn't said a word for days. Now he was shouting? In the worst possible place? Why couldn't he make anything easy for me?

I glanced around to see if anyone was watching. No one was. To my surprise, the old man who had studied us so carefully was gone. His chair was empty. I tried to get Aric to eat again.

"I will not do anything I don't want to do," he said in the loudest tone he could muster. "You can't make me. I'm the..."

He was going to announce who he was to the whole room. I panicked and tried to cover his words with something. But before I could think of anything, another voice resounded out over Aric's words.

"Let's get some music going to block out the endless rain!"

I looked up to see a traveling musician leap on the stage. Cheers filled the room while the man with reddish blonde hair announced that his name was Jal Shahido and that he fully expected dancing to begin.

Without missing a beat, he started a rousing song about a woman. I saw Aric's lips moving, but even I couldn't hear any words from him.

I sighed and picked up my fork again. But before I could get anything to my mouth, a hand slammed down onto the table between Aric and me. The other hand gripped my shoulder tightly. I swung around to see the old man who had been staring at us.

He said in a tone only I could hear, and a tone that was harsher than anything I'd ever heard before. "You fool girl! You can't let HIM die!"

BURNING

*"You must not argue when your house
is burning down around you."*
~STRACHAN DALYEL

Jehun fled out of the Temple of All. There was
no way he was going to travel to Elba Isle and chat
with Seiten, the most vile and evil creature in Eltiria.
Belial spoke of it so lightly as if it was nothing. Jehun
almost laughed. He knew now that Belial had no
interest in doing anything about his pain. Belial just
wanted to use him like everyone else.

He fumed through the city of Northbridge,
ignoring the people and the flurry of activity that
surrounded the giant rip in the earth. He didn't care
anymore. The only thing he cared about was to get
rid of that constant agony.

He slowed down when he realized he was in the
country. To obey Belial's orders, he'd have to go
west, past the coastline and farther out into the
ocean.

But what if he disregarded Belial? What if he
headed east? Or deep down to the core where the
lava flowed like living water? But if he didn't obey,
Belial would never heal him.

Jehun burned with a white hot rage at being
trapped into something he dreaded doing and barely

noticed the houses and barns that shivered and
plunged to the ground from the quake he caused.
He shook in fury as he remembered the coldness of
Belial.

A farmhouse that sat on a barren stretch of land
trembled. Jehun watched as the house began to
break apart and then collapse.

He began to turn away from the wrecked house
when a young woman, hollowed-cheeked and dirty,
raced from the barn screaming at the top of her
voice. A man about her age dropped the plow in the
sterile field and sprinted to the wreckage.

"Hagen!" The woman screamed as loudly as she
could. She reached the house and began to rummage
through the ruins. "Hagen!"

The woman threw the boards aside as she
searched frantically. The man joined her, calling the
same name and digging through what was left of the
house.

Jehun watched, transfixed on the panicked
couple. The pain that echoed through their voices
was the same as he felt. He longed for them to find
Hagen, but as their voices grew hoarse and their
hands bloody, they found no one.

The woman stopped, sank to the ground, and
sobbed. The man dropped a load of broken timbers
and made his way to her as quickly as he could on
the uneven ground.

He took her by the shoulders and gave her a gentle shake. "We don't give up until we find him. Do you hear me? He could be still alive."

The woman wept as the man pulled her close in a tight embrace. "He should be crying," she stuttered through her tears. "He'd be frightened. But it's silent. He's...he's..."

"We don't know what he is yet," the man said sternly. "We keep looking. Come on. Help me."

Together they worked. They stopped every so often to call his name. But there was still no response. Jehun forgot his pain and misery and watched in horror.

His actions had caused their disaster. He didn't know who this Hagen was, but it was clear that Hagen was deeply loved. He'd never forgive himself if he didn't survive.

Jehun could see the woman's arms tremble from exertion. The man was covered with a shiny sheen of sweat, but they continued through the heat of the day. The woman looked like she was going to collapse from the hard work or from grief when she gave a strangled cry and pointed.

The man tore at the boards in a renewed wave of energy. He stopped and bent down, carefully pulling out of the debris a bundle wrapped in a blue blanket. He placed the bundle gently in the woman's arms.

The woman sobbed as tears flowed down her cheeks. "Hagen. Hagen, wake up." Her voice was soft but urgent.

The man leaned closely and peered into the blue blanket. All was still for what seemed like an eternity for Jehun. All of a sudden, the sweet but loud sound of a baby's cry filled the air. The parents both screamed with joy, their tears turning to laughter.

"He's okay!" The woman exclaimed as she peeled back the blankets and inspected every inch of Hagen. She held the baby tightly as he squirmed at the strange treatment.

The man laughed with joy and swept both of them up into a tight hug. Tears of joy streaked his face. "Thank you, Adoyni! Thank you! I don't care about this house or the crops in the field. We are safe and together! You are good!"

Jehun shared their happiness, finally feeling good about something. He left feeling torn between shame of what he had done and confusion of what the man had said.

The man, with ruined crops and now a ruined house, only praised Adoyni. Why hadn't the man cursed Adoyni, like Jehun had? Why wasn't he angry at Adoyni for all that he had lost? Then he realized the answer.

The man still had what he loved. He still had his little boy. If the man had lost his son, then he would have cursed Adoyni. Jehun fled the small farm. Adoyni had let Jehun be ripped in two, but he had allowed the little child to live. Why hadn't Adoyni healed him?

Jehun knew that Adoyni either didn't love him or care about him. If he went to Elba Isle, he had a chance of being healed, so he began his journey west.

CHAPTER FIFTY-TWO

Shuffling

As Kai tripped and stumbled down the hallway, the torches were dimmer. He coughed from the smoke when he stopped to catch his breath. Everything was getting worse.

He slammed his fist into the rock wall and yelped from the blow, but it only made him hotter with rage. The fury he felt was a fire that was growing uncontrollably with each passing moment. *At least things can't get worse.*

Then the torches went out.

The darkness was blacker than anything he'd ever experienced, and the thought of never having light again made it hard to breathe. He inhaled slowly and exhaled, hoping something would change.

When nothing did, he slumped to the ground with his back against the wall. He drew his sword and traced the word *Failure* that was etched into the blade.

That's what I am. I failed. I didn't purify the water. I'm sure Rhiana is dead by now. As for Mom and Dad, I'd bet anything they don't want me around to remind them how awful I am.

His fingers scraped against the floor, and a small stone loosened. He picked it up. Eladar once said that he was an unpolished gem. Kai blinked back tears as he thought of the winged horse.

If Eladar could see me now, he'd say that I'm as useful as this pebble, if he took the time to speak to me at all. I did such a bad job Lizzy and Taryn don't want anything to do with me. They left me down here alone and don't even care if I die or not.

He threw the stone as far away as he could. It bounced down the long hallway until it came to a stop. The complete silence was almost worse than the darkness.

He remembered Mom coming to him when he was little and had woken up from a nightmare. She sat beside his bed and smoothed down the covers.

"Adoyni will never leave you or forsake you, Kai." She shook a playful finger at him. "Rest assured, even when all the lights go out, Adoyni is still with you."

Kai blinked back the tears. "Even when all the lights go out," he repeated softly. "Are you still here, Adoyni? I'm doing everything wrong, and I don't even know where Taryn and Lizzy are. I'm supposed to lead them, but I failed them, too. I've failed everyone."

There was no answer, but it didn't seem so scary or lonely anymore. *Maybe someone is praying for me. What if there's something right around the corner? What if I almost made it?* He couldn't give up yet. Getting up was the hardest thing he had done. Everything in him longed to sit back down and give up.

Now he knew what Mom was trying to say that night. Sometimes it felt like Adoyni wasn't there. Right now he felt like he was completely alone, and that everyone, even Adoyni, had deserted him. But that was a lie.

Where Taryn or Lizzy were w, but he knew that they were fighting to get back to him. Taryn was probably complaining the whole time about the food or the endless walking. Lizzy was most likely either bossing him around or singing as she worked.

He couldn't feel Adoyni's presence, not like before when they were traveling to the castle that held the poison. Yet Adoyni was right beside him. Kai didn't have to feel Him.

He just had to take another step. And another one. And he had to keep doing that until he found Lizzy and Taryn or Adoyni.

Just take one step.

His whole body ached, but he shuffled a step forward. As he groped his way down the hallway, he repeated the words Mom told him. "Adoyni will never leave me or forsake me. Adoyni will never leave me or forsake me." His voice grew stronger with each step.

He'd barely gone a little bit when torches ahead of him started to splutter into small, weak flames, putting out more smoke than light.

He grinned. He couldn't see more than a few feet ahead, but the light gave him hope. He trotted around a couple of corners before he stopped to take his breath. That's when he heard it again.

The slow shuffling of feet was behind him. He turned to jog away from the sound, but then he paused. He was sick of running and not knowing. He could see who was following him. He waited while his heart began to race and his palms started to sweat.

A man shuffled around the corner. He was dressed in an old brown cloak that was torn and ripped. A rusty and clipped sword without a scabbard hung off his hip. The hood of the cloak fell over his face so that Kai couldn't see the features of the man. There was a red stain on the man's right leg like he'd been wounded.

Kai expected a reaction from the man, but he was disappointed. The man continued his slow shuffle toward Kai like he hadn't seen him. *Am I dead?* He resisted the urge to pinch himself as the man came closer.

Kai couldn't wait anymore. "Hey. Do you know where we are at?"

The man didn't respond. He didn't do anything but continue toward Kai.

"Where are you going? I mean..." Kai's words trailed off as the man stopped out of arm's reach.

Kai tried to see under the hood, but there was no way he could make out any of the features. The man snarled and drew his sword. He slashed at Kai in a wide fashion.

"What are you doing?" Kai yelled as he dodged out of the way and took a step backwards. "Are you blind? I'm standing right here."

The man didn't respond. He closed the gap again and swung in Kai's direction. He reluctantly drew his sword. The word *Failure* on the blade almost blinded him. *I am a failure. I didn't fix the water, and I sure didn't save Rhiana. Why did I even think I could?*

A movement out of the corner of his eye caught his attention and he leaped sideways. The man's blade barely missed his shoulder. Kai wanted to smack himself. *Getting lost in my thoughts and not paying attention to what's going on.*

The man attacked again. This time he moved smoothly without any of the slowness or shuffling from before. Kai blocked easily, but the force of the blow shocked Kai. The man didn't look like he'd have much strength, yet the strike was as strong as a young warrior.

The man pulled back. Kai watched him warily. Without warning, the man attacked again with the speed and strength of a horse's kick. Kai blocked the thrusts each time, feeling like he was fighting a losing battle.

Every time he managed to stop the man's blade, it was already descending somewhere else. Kai managed to escape being hit, but the blows rained down on him until he was soaked with sweat and his arm was shaking. He stepped back to get a moment to rest, but the man pressed forward and forced him to continue.

Kai growled in anger. He didn't care anymore. He waited until the man stopped attacking and struck with all his wrath. The blow slipped past the guard of his assailant and managed to reach the strange man's leg. The sword left behind a ribbon of blood on the man's leg.

The man roared with pain, but he didn't stop. Surging forward, he lunged at Kai and struck. His blade, although covered with rust, was sharp on the edges. That was about all Kai saw as he ducked to his left. He slammed into the wall and felt a sharp pain down his left side.

Irritated at the lack of space, he returned the attack and pushed the man back with a flurry of blows. The man fell back as he tried to protect himself until he managed to return the attack with one blow. The rusty blade slipped through Kai's defenses and hit him in the ribs.

As Kai pulled free from the blade, he yelled in pain and anger. Blood flowed down his side as he pressed his free hand against it. He sucked in air as shock radiated through his body. Before he could think, he swung his sword at the man's chest.

As the man moved to block it, Kai shifted the direction of his sword to stab into his stomach. It slipped past the man's guard and hit the target. The man dropped his sword and gripped his stomach. Without a sound, he dropped to the floor and lay still.

Kai watched as he caught his breath. As the rage subsided, horror replaced it. *What have I done? I killed someone, and I don't even know who!* Fear overwhelmed him as he approached the body slowly. The sound of shuffling returned. He stopped in confusion and looked down. His left leg refused to move and he could only drag it along.

All he wanted to do was to run away before someone caught him next to the body of the strange man, but he had to know who it was.

He tried to ignore the shuffling and forced himself to crouch beside the body. His hand shook as he lifted the hood and uncovered the face. He sprang to his feet and jumped back with a cry of terror.

The face was his.

CHAPTER FIFTY-THREE

Family Found

Rhiana smiled at her reflection in the mirror. She was dressed in her red riding dress, and her long brown hair was twisted into a braid that hung over her left shoulder.

She grinned as her green eyes twinkled with excitement. Today was the first time she was going to ride her new pony, Diamond, outside the arena.

Just having her own pony overwhelmed Rhiana with happiness, but when Nighthawk told her that she could name the mare as well, she knew exactly what she wanted to call the pony.

From the moment she first saw the beautiful delicate chestnut with a diamond shaped snippet of white, she knew they were going to be great friends.

She spun around from the mirror and plopped down on the window seat. She felt like a princess with the green rug that stretched across to a large stone fireplace and a bookcase filled with all her favorite stories. Her bed covered with soft purple and yellow blankets was big enough to fit three people.

From her high vantage point in the Temple of All, she could see the countryside leading up to the Razors. Although the grass was brown, the mountains were covered with snow, the white contrasting against the blue sky.

She would've liked to see Northbridge, but Nighthawk told her that a view of the city would only make her remember all the awful things that had happened to her.

Her eyes filled with tears. She didn't know where Mom and Dad were, and she hadn't seen Kai for a long time. She sniffed. She hadn't thought about them for days. Maybe even longer.

She barely remembered what Mom's voice sounded like and how Dad's arms felt. She missed supper when everyone gathered around the table, and the stories of the day went flying across the table loaded with fried chicken and brown gravy and biscuits and pumpkin pie.

They all talked at once, the stories becoming a tangled mess, leaving them in laughter as everyone got more and more confused.

A knock on the door made her blink away the tears. She raced to the door. Throwing it open, she saw Nighthawk in a forest green riding dress with her hair pulled up in a bun. She had a long gray garment in her arms.

Nighthawk laughed and swept her up into a big hug. "Not excited, are you?"

"I can't wait!" Rhiana squealed. "Don't forget you promised we could go outside the ring today. You aren't going to change your mind, are you?"

Nighthawk smiled. "I'm not changing my mind. You've proven you can ride Diamond wonderfully. But first, I bought you this." She shook out the garment and handed it to Rhiana.

Rhiana took it with a flash of pleasure. Nighthawk was often busy, but when she had time, she always remembered a gift. This time it was a long cloak made out of thick gray wool.

"I want you to wear it today," Nighthawk explained. "While we are around people, I want you to have the hood up, so no one sees your face. There are people who would hurt you."

Rhiana remembered her earlier sadness. "Have you heard anything from my family yet?"

"Not yet." She shook her head. "We sent messengers everywhere looking for Kai, but they haven't found anything. Maybe he doesn't want to be found or has forgotten about you."

"He wouldn't forget about me!" Rhiana retorted. But deep inside she wondered if it was true. He hadn't even said goodbye to her when he left.

Nighthawk sighed. "I can't figure it out. I even got Belial to forgive his debt for the death of Kedar if he came back." She reached into a pocket. "Oh, before I forget, it's time for your medicine."

Rhiana took the silver flask. She hadn't met Belial, but she had to thank the Chancellor for helping them try to find Kai. She examined the flask. "Do I have to drink this?"

"Yes, dear, it makes you feel better."

"I know." She sighed. "It's just that..." She didn't want to drink it but couldn't figure out why. Nighthawk kept watching her, so she took a small sip. "What about Mom?"

"Drink it all, Rhiana." Nighthawk's voice was sharp and stern.

Rhiana jumped. Nighthawk never spoke like that to her. *Why did she want me to drink this so much?* She drank the rest even though the taste was bitter, and she wanted to spit it out.

"That's better," Nighthawk said softer. "Now what was your question?"

"I..." Rhiana paused. She couldn't remember. There was something very important she wanted to talk to Nighthawk about, right before she drank her medicine, but it was hard to think.

Nighthawk's face grew sad. "Maybe you don't want to tell me because you don't love me. I was hoping that maybe you'd love me as much as I love you."

"Oh, Nighthawk!" Rhiana threw herself into Nighthawk's arms. "I didn't mean to hurt you! Of course I love you lots!" Tears started to rise again.

Nighthawk's smile transformed her sadness into joy. "I love you, too, Rhiana," she whispered. "Now how about that ride?"

Rhiana grinned, unhappiness forgotten, and put on her cloak. Pulling the hood up over her face, she followed Nighthawk to the stables for their ride. As she closed the door to her room, she wondered what had made her so sad a few minutes ago. With a shrug, she gave up trying to remember.

CHAPTER FIFTY-FOUR

Booked

Taryn glanced over at Lizzy as she sat straight like she had heard something vitally important. He quickly thought over what Rev was saying.

She was relating how they were in a minuscule village while Aric was sick. There was nothing of significance that he could see.

"Did you say that the musician's name was Jal Shahido?" Lizzy interrupted, gripping her blankets tightly.

Rev stopped in midstream with a confused look. "Yeah," she replied, nodding as she seemed to think back over her memories. "Yes. That was his name."

"That's my father!" Lizzy was clearly excited and thrilled.

Taryn understood her excitement. Lizzy's mother, Re-Veen, rarely made mention of her last name. He knew Lizzy adored her father even though he left their family years ago without any explanation.

Kind of like my Mom did, although Dad said she died. The thought surprised Taryn. He never imagined having anything in common with Lizzy.

"Jal Shahido! The musician! That's my Dad!" Lizzy repeated in the same excited tone. "How is he? What did he say? When was this?" Lizzy took a breath like she was nervous about the next one. "What did he say about me?"

Rev shook her head with an unhappy look. "When we last saw him, he was okay. We didn't really get to talk to him. I guess Jal and Treven, the old man who approached me at the inn, had been traveling together for a while."

Taryn felt a wave of sympathy for Lizzy. *Why did Nighthawk, I mean Mom, leave me? If Father was so horrible she couldn't bear to live with him, why wouldn't she take me with her? If Aric's right, is Mom wrong for teaching others how to use magic? Surely magic isn't all bad.*

"I think you must be mistaken," Taryn said loudly. They turned to him with perplexed looks as he broke into their conversation. He struggled to find an explanation for his words without spilling his conclusions about Mom. "Your story is implying that Nighthawk is in league with Belial and therefore is evil. I don't think that's true."

Aric shifted. "Oh, there's no doubt about it. That woman is evil. As much, if not more, than Belial. She's so deep in this goddess stuff that I don't think there's any coming back."

Taryn stomped down his anger. He couldn't reveal his suspicions that Nighthawk was his mother yet. Not until he had some sort of proof. But surely Mom wouldn't be like that.

"Did you see her do anything?" He demanded.

"No, but if you keep listening, you'll see that Jal did," Aric responded slowly.

"How do you know Jal was telling the truth? Maybe he was lying for some reason." Taryn leaped on the hope that Nighthawk wasn't bad like it seemed Aric was saying.

"Are you saying Dad is a liar?" Lizzy turned to Taryn with an angry flash in her green eyes.

"Do we know if he can be trusted?" Taryn responded without thinking.

"Oh, right!" Lizzy yelled back. "Because we're travelling musicians, right? Like you said outside Aldholt. That we aren't good enough for the niceties of society, so we must be lying all the time, too!"

"I didn't say that! Well, I did, but I didn't mean that, and I don't know." Taryn felt his face reddening as he stumbled with his words. "I just...maybe the soldiers were doing it and not Nighthawk." He groaned inside.

How can I ever tell her that it's not her Dad, but my Mom that I'm trying to understand?

"I saw her," Griffen said quietly. "Right before I came to Merrihaven. She came to my village with a bunch of soldiers." Griffen's sea-green eyes were filled with pain.

Taryn had forgotten the young boy sitting next to Aric. Griff had never once mentioned what happened to him, and there was an unspoken agreement to let him bring it up first.

The boy reminded him of someone. But who? From where? Was it Mischa? No, that wasn't right.

Mischa had brown eyes. But there was someone he knew who looked like the young boy.

"Our village was a bunch of people who had left the cities to band together to worship Adoyni in safety. We'd been there only a few months when she brought a troop of soldiers. They burned all the houses and killed everyone. She told them to. I heard because the soldier held me and my family as hostages. When they finished, she left." The words spilled quickly out like a dam that had finally broken. No one interrupted.

"They told me that if I climbed to the top of a tree and jumped, they wouldn't kill us. I did. They laughed when I was on the ground and pestered me about getting up and walking. I couldn't because of my broken legs. Then they killed Mom, Dad, and my brother. That's when Sadron, one of the Archippi, showed up and brought me here."

"I didn't know, Griff. I'm sorry." Aric turned to Taryn. "That's enough proof for me. Besides, if you've met her, you'd know she gives people the creeps."

Taryn had been considering punching Aric for his arrogant behavior, but it was now all he could do not to hit him after saying that about his mom.

Maybe she isn't my mom. He shook his head. *No. It's the only thing that makes sense. Mischa said that my mom is n...n... Why in the world did Lizzy interrupt him right before he died? Why didn't she realize what she was doing?*

Lizzy stopped glaring at Taryn and turned back to Aric. "You were sick and doing unusual things?

You were turning into an Unwanted, right? That's why you're able to help Kai?"

Rev put her hand on Lizzy's knee. "No. That's not it. You have to understand. No one, either on Eltiria or here, has healed someone from being an Unwanted. Many have tried. But once the disease starts, there is no known cure. The Archippi believe that it has to do with the soul being torn from the body."

Aric continued the conversation. "When the disease that makes people become Unwanteds first started, some Archippi were allowed to go to Eltiria and bring back a few who were sick. Eladar was one of them. The best healers, both human and Archippi, worked relentlessly for a cure. None was discovered."

Rev jumped into the conversation. Aric shot her a look like he didn't appreciate her interrupting him. "The Archippi fear the disease so much that if they'd known Kai was infected with the disease when you came, you would've never been allowed to come. That's why we had to escape from their care. We were afraid of what they would do to him."

Aric nodded. "Even if we are successful in finding a cure, I suspect it will take them a long time to trust Kai, thinking the disease is lurking somewhere until he weakens again."

"You aren't even trained healers. What makes you think you can succeed where so many others have failed?" Lizzy asked.

"We have Treven's journal," Rev said.

"What about the book you took from Belial?" Taryn asked. "What happened to that?"

"We'd tell you if you'd stop asking so many questions," Aric snapped at Taryn, his patience clearly gone. "But it's gone."

"You lost it?" Taryn couldn't believe his ears. "That probably had the key to curing Kai in it. Why didn't you keep it?"

"I tried!" Aric yelled. "But now I'm glad it's gone!"

"Why would you say that? Do you really want Kai to die?" Taryn roared back.

"Because it was filled with ways to do magic. There's no way I'd let you have it." Aric crossed his arms with a cold expression on his face.

"Why not?" Taryn demanded. He felt his face growing red with anger.

"I'll say it again." Aric's voice began to rise. "We are NOT doing magic here."

"I'll do whatever it takes to cure Kai!" Taryn yelled back.

Aric took a deep breath and exhaled slowly like he was trying to regain control. He flipped through the pages so they could see inside. "We have this."

Lizzy saw passages crossed out with large words beside them. "Doesn't look like the person who wrote it knew much with all that stuff crossed out."

"That shows he was trying to learn what no one else was!" Rev glared at Lizzy.

Aric gave Rev a dirty look. "The science of healing is a strange science. Someone cures a stomach ache with a carrot. Then carrots are considered the new miracle treatment. Everything is treated with carrots. But no one stops to think that the carrot was eaten with a glass of milk and that maybe milk is better for a stomach ache."

"That's a bit trite, but it works as an example," Rev continued, glowering back at Aric. "This is his life's work to find the truth about what was taught and to find a real workable cure for every ailment. He spent decades on this, despite being mocked as crazy and futile."

Lizzy took a deep breath. "If anyone could help Kai, it sounds like this man would know what to do. What does it say about Unwanteds?"

Rev's face fell. "Nothing helpful. He mentions a woman named Iseabail had the disease, but all he says about the cure is useless." She nodded to Aric. "Show them."

Aric flipped through the book and held up a page. He tapped the words on the right side in the middle of the page. Taryn leaned closer to read the sloppily written words.

Back to the beginning!

"That's why it's so important that I tell you everything from the beginning." Aric snapped the book shut. "Perhaps you can help us figure out what Treven was talking about."

"Can't you ask him?" Taryn asked. He was leaning forward with his elbows on his knees peering at the journal.

Aric snapped the book shut. "That's the next part of the story."

CHAPTER FIFTY-FIVE

A Love Affair

The din of the music of Jal Shahido and the sound of feet dancing on the wooden floor of the inn faded to the background.

I sank back into my chair, too shocked by the old man to notice anything around us. His words pounded in my brain so loudly I couldn't hear Jal singing anymore. All I saw was the old man glaring at me.

Whoever this man was, he knew Aric was the Prince. Would he betray us? He didn't pay me any attention as he put his arm over Aric's shoulders. Aric was acting as meek as a lamb.

I grabbed our saddle bags. I wasn't about to leave my dinner behind, so I took the plate and reached for Aric's bowl.

"Leave his food but bring yours," the old man growled. "That's not what he needs. And lead the way to your room."

I obeyed before I knew what I was doing. I slipped through the room, avoiding the dancers, and climbed the stairs. The old man followed behind me, half-carrying Aric.

I led the way down the poorly-lit hallway and opened the door to the second room on the right.

Inside was a sparsely furnished room with a bed, a small table beside it, and one chair.

The man lowered Aric onto the bed. "Get some candles so we can see. Quickly. He doesn't have much time left."

Whirling away, I found some candles in a box at the beginning of the hallway. I lit them and trotted back to the room. The old man was gone.

Aric lay on the bed, tossing and turning, like he couldn't get comfortable. There was a loud bang behind me. I spun around to see the man had returned. He carried a small satchel and a worn book.

"Put the candles on the table." He didn't look at me as he hustled to the bed. "And then eat. You need your strength, too, and I don't want to take care of both of you."

I held back my anger. I was dying to know who he was and what he was planning to do, but I knew from his manner he'd ignore my questions or tell me to be quiet.

As much as I wanted to disobey him or question him, I couldn't resist the chance to eat. I sat in the chair, shoveling the food in my mouth while I watched the old man.

The man began taking off Aric's boots and cloak and stripping him of his wet clothes. "So what is it? A love affair, but you're not good enough for the royal father and mother?"

I bristled at his comment. Why was his first assumption romance? "Marry him? Never!" I said around a mouthful of potatoes. "And I'm good enough for all of them."

The man stopped working for a second and shot me a look, but I couldn't tell from his green eyes if he doubted me or found my remark amusing.

"It's his left arm." I swallowed. "He cut himself with a sword that was poisoned."

"Although he needs no introduction, who are you?" the man asked.

I hesitated. Do I lie and give him a fake name? Or do I tell the truth? I was sick of lies and deception after being in the castle for so long.

"Reveka, but you can call me Rev," I said, deciding not to share my last name.

He noticed the lack of the last name, but he didn't ask for more information. "My name is Treven."

"Are you...a healer?" It seemed like the dumbest question, but I had to know if he was qualified to help Aric, and he didn't look like a healer with his beard and unkempt clothes.

"I was. A long time ago." Treven regarded the dressing over the wound. "Now I'm a seeker for solutions."

Sounded kooky to me, but I nodded as a bite of bread and butter slid down my throat. I realized that was my last bite. I thought about licking the plate and getting more, but I didn't want to leave Aric with a stranger.

"Did you wrap this?" Treven asked.

I nodded, not really paying attention, since I was still considering how to get more food.

"Good job," he said. "You have talent."

As he began to take the bandages off, Aric started to thrash around. He swung at Treven, and Treven barely ducked in time.

"Come hold him down," he ordered.

I did as he said and watched as the bandages changed from brown mud to crimson red blood. When the bandages were gone, and the wound lay open, I gasped.

When I first saw it, it was a cut about two inches long and barely wider than a hair. Now it was tripled in size and as wide as two of my fingers. The skin around it looked angry and irritated. The red burn spread down his whole arm and up to his neck.

Treven looked grim. "That's what I was afraid of. I can't cure this poison."

"What do you mean? Who can?" My heart dropped at his words. I didn't really like Aric. But I didn't want to see him in pain either, much less die.

"No one. Not even the finest physicians that he could afford." Treven reached for his satchel. "I've seen this poison before. It eats its way to the heart and kills there. I've tried everything to stop it, but nothing works. It's highly difficult to make, works slowly, but it's extremely efficient. How long has he been infected?"

"What are we going to do? Can't you help?" I couldn't stop the wave of panic from spilling into my voice as I ignored his question.

"We're going to bandage him up and send him back to the royal castle before he dies." Treven *refused to meet my eyes. "If we can make it in time."*

"We can't do that!" I yelled. "We just came from there! You don't understand. The king is sick. He's dying, too."

Treven began wrapping the wound. "I know. They need to say goodbye and plan for whoever will take over the throne. The Prince is closer to death than the King. He's going to die quickly, Rev. There's nothing we can do about it."

I was too shocked to comprehend what he was saying. We couldn't go back, and Belial would be king if both Aric and his father died right now. Why did Aric have to go and make everything so much harder?

Before I knew what to say, footsteps came thudding down the hallway and stopped outside. There was a knocking with great urgency on our door. I realized with a start that the music had stopped, and there was a faint sound of screaming.

Treven flung the door open. Jal Shahido, the musician from downstairs, was standing in the hallway. "There's a woman here with a bunch of soldiers! They stopped at Lethia's house. You know, the white one on the edge of the village. The woman asked where the Prince was. They didn't know, so the soldiers slit their throats and set the house on fire."

Jal continued. "You've got to get out of here. She said she's going to burn every house to the ground until she finds the Prince. You've got to run."

CHAPTER FIFTY-SIX

Not Over

"Rev, get your stuff!" Treven turned back into the room. "Jal, I'll need your help getting the Prince to the stables."

"Are you helping us?" I cried. "Why would you do that?"

Treven stopped packing up his supplies. "I don't know what trouble you two got into, but I know Nighthawk Nephesus, and if she wants you, then I'll do everything in my power to make sure she doesn't get you. Now hurry!"

I followed as Jal and Treven carried Aric down the back stairs of the inn to the stables. But when the cold rain hit my face, I jerked back to what was happening.

I was going to spend yet another night out in the rain, mud, and cold because of Aric. If he wasn't dying, I'd punch him. I plodded through the mud to the stables.

The warmth of the stable stung my cheeks as I ducked into the stables and shook the rain off my cloak. Kaspar blew a welcome from the closest stall. Aric moaned as Jal and Treven laid him on a pile of hay bales.

Without a word, we worked quickly. Jal and Treven brought out a covered wagon. I got Kaspar

*out and saddled him. I was relieved to see that the
stable boy had done his job as well as I would have.
Everything was clean and dry.*

*Treven hooked up a small white horse to the
wagon and helped Jal carry Aric into the back of
the wagon. I peeked in to see a long bed on the
side, with jars and books lining the other.*

*Treven covered up Aric with a blanket and
jumped out. "We won't be able to go fast. Snowball
is tough, but she can't take the fast speeds. You
lead the way."*

I nodded.

*Treven leaped to the seat of the wagon and
slapped the reins on Snowball's back. "Pray for a
miracle. That's our only hope now."*

*Jal slid the doors open. He lifted a hand as the
wagon passed him. "Safe travels, my friend."*

*"You, too," Treven called back over the creak
of the wagon. "Tell the others that I'll return soon.
And tell Mischa that he still owes me a game of
chess! I'll pray you find your way back to your
daughter and son again."*

*I nodded in gratitude as I rode by, but from my
vantage point on top of Kaspar's back, I could see
flames leaping through the air. The smell of
burning wood and straw hit me as a scream
echoed down the quiet street.*

*I trotted ahead of the wagon and opened the
gate that led to a small lane behind the inn.
Standing up in my stirrups, I saw Nighthawk in the
light of the flames standing among a group of
soldiers. She turned toward a house and waved her
hands high in the air.*

Flames shot up in the house and began to lick the straw roof. I wanted to charge Kaspar at her to make her stop, but our only hope, which wasn't much at all, was to run. I leaned down and opened the gate for Treven.

The wagon creaked over every bump. I winced at every noise. If anyone turned and saw us, we would be caught. Treven glanced at me as he drove by, his face taut.

I called softly to him. "Are you sure you want to come with us? Why risk your life?"

Treven glanced at the fires and turned back to me. "Because I don't believe in giving up without a fight. It's not over until it's over." He slapped the reins a bit harder on Snowball's back as she slowly trotted into the lane.

I shut the gate and followed behind until the track opened wide enough for me to pass. Treven's words echoed in my head. It's not over until it's over. But the words didn't encourage me as the cold rain hit my face and mud splattered over me. Even if we escaped, Aric was going to die.

"Please, Adoyni, protect the rest of the village," I breathed. "Help me find a way to cure Aric. I can't do this on my own anymore."

Like most children, I grew up believing in Adoyni. But, in recent years, I never bothered with any thought of Him. I was too busy taking care of things. Besides, I didn't really need him. But tonight I needed Him. I only hoped He could do something about this mess because I sure couldn't.

CHAPTER FIFTY-SEVEN

If Only

The lane led out of town. Northwest of us was Albia and Vesmir. Southeast lay the royal castle in Medora. I trotted Kaspar to where Treven had stopped Snowball. He was huddled in his cloak and had one hand tucked inside his sleeve for warmth.

"Which way?" he asked. "Go to the King or continue on your flight?"

I tried to keep Kaspar still as he pranced. "Before we go any farther, I want you to know this is not a love thing. We know that Belial and Nighthawk are doing something bad, perhaps even trying to take over the throne. We're trying to find proof to take to the King."

"Is that not proof enough?" Treven said dryly as he gestured toward the village.

I turned Kaspar around so that I could see the town again. It looked like the fire was spreading despite the men's efforts to stop it. The sight made me sick. What kind of person kills innocent people to get what they want?

"That way." I pointed to the northwest and hardened my heart to the destruction behind me. "To Vesmir."

I kicked Kaspar harder than I needed to. He jumped under me. I felt bad for being rough and soothed him. I heard Treven slap the reins and the wagon creak as Snowball started again in her slow trot.

I wanted to run back and stop Nighthawk. I wanted to do anything to save those people. They weren't my responsibility like the tenants on Dad's land, but I had brought this evil to them. If only Aric hadn't cut himself with his dumb sword.

Most of my problems started with "If only Aric hadn't..." If only Aric hadn't left the castle that night long ago. If only he hadn't tried to steal my horse. If only he hadn't made me dance with him. If only he hadn't forced me to sneak into Belial's house. If only he hadn't dragged me out on this wild attempt to find some way to force Belial out of the royal castle.

But my heart lurched and tears stung my eyes when I realized that soon I'd be saying, "If only Aric hadn't died." Why were we even running? Whether it's at Nighthawk's hand or because of the poison doesn't really matter. What if I went back, gave Aric to Nighthawk, and saved some people? Then I'd be done. I could go home and worry about my own problems.

The thought was tantalizing. Tears trickled down my cheeks. I was so tired, so worried. I wanted it to be all over. This wasn't my problem, and I didn't know how to handle people trying to overturn the government. My place was on Dad's lands. This was too big.

The trickle of tears turned into a stream that mixed with the cold rain on my face. I didn't want Aric to die. I didn't like him, but that didn't mean I wanted to see him die. "Oh, Adoyni, what are we going to do?" I whispered.

Be strong, daughter. A man's voice rang out in my head. Adoyni sees your troubles.

I sniffed, suddenly alert. It was the same voice I had heard when I saw the black horse in the barn. The horse with wings. Was its rider around? I glanced past the hood of my cloak to peer into the night, but I couldn't see anything.

It was strange, but the words helped. I didn't feel like crying anymore. The thoughts about going back to Nighthawk seemed stupid. Did I really think that she would let me go? There was no way either Belial or Nighthawk would allow anyone who knew the truth to live.

I led the way down the small dirt road for hours. The darkness never lightened, and the rain never let up.

A sharp whistle pierced the sound of the rain and the plop of Kaspar's feet in the mud. I whipped around to peer behind me. The hope that there was an Archippos behind me and a tall warrior on its back ready to set everything right flared in me.

Snowball stood in the middle of the road. Her head was low as she panted and snorted. Treven was climbing into the wagon. He glanced back at me and waved at me to return. I started to shout out that we needed to keep going, but he was already in the wagon. What in all blazes was he doing?

I kicked Kaspar in the ribs a bit too hard, and he lunged forward, knocking me off balance. I pulled him in with an apology and trotted to the back of the wagon.

As I got closer, I heard groaning. I brought Kaspar up to the back of the wagon and pulled the flaps to see inside. Treven was bent over Aric.

Treven glanced up, his face grim. "He doesn't have long as long as I thought. Maybe an hour."

I winced. "What do you suggest? What can we do?"

"Rev, we can't do anything." Treven sat back on his heels. "We wait."

"For what?" I cried. "What are we waiting for?"

"His death." Treven rubbed his hand over his eyes.

I dropped the flap in anger and spun Kaspar away from the wagon. Sit and do nothing? I sat in the rain, getting more chilled by the second, and seethed about everything.

Kaspar shifted, eager to get out of the rain or to get moving. I pulled myself back to the moment. It would do no good to sit on the road where the soldiers could easily find us.

I spotted a small copse of trees up ahead. I grabbed Snowball's reins and started for the grove. Treven's head popped out of the wagon.

When I felt like we were far enough off the road, I jumped off and trotted back to the road to wipe out our tracks. I knew in the back of my mind that nothing I was doing would heal Aric, but it felt better to do something.

I chopped a branch off a tree on the far side from the road so that the soldiers wouldn't notice a freshly cut limb. After I wiped away most of our tracks going off the road, I could only hope that the rain would wash away the tracks on the road.

It was going to look rather obvious that the wagon didn't go any farther, but it wouldn't matter when they caught up to us. To Aric, at least.

I stood in the downpour with the branch in my hand and didn't even try to stop the tears. I'd never been in a situation that I couldn't fix.

I thought I was so smart and capable, and everything had fallen apart. Because of my failures, the whole kingdom was going to be destroyed.

"Adoyni, help us," I prayed. "I can't do this on my own. I can't fix anything. Everything I do gets worse. I've seen an Archippos from the old stories, and I know now that You can work miracles. We need a miracle. Heal Aric and keep us from being caught by Nighthawk. Please. I want to go home. I know now that I need Your help. I need You."

As I prayed, an image of being together with everyone by the lake came to me. Ayala was making us laugh. Mom was healthy. Dad didn't have the cares of a province being destroyed by sickness. The memory made me cry harder.

"Please, Adoyni. Don't let Aric die. Don't let Belial win." I sank to my knees in the mud and repeated the words until the sobs drowned them.

CHAPTER FIFTY-EIGHT

Awfully Rude

It felt like an eternity that I sat there and sobbed. My hood fell back, but I barely felt the cold rain as it trickled down my face. I heard footsteps behind me and the thought occurred that it could be one of Nighthawk's soldiers.

I didn't care. If they wanted to seize me and drag me back to her, I wouldn't fight. I was too exhausted to struggle anymore.

A hand squeezed my shoulder. I forced myself to stop crying. I wasn't going to fight, but they weren't going to get see me cry. I raised my head and prepared to be hauled to my feet.

"Rev," Treven said gently. "I'm sorry. I truly am. But it's time to say your goodbyes. He doesn't have long."

I closed my eyes and wondered briefly if I'd rather be pulled away by the soldiers than being there when Aric left this world.

What am I going to tell the King and Queen? What will happen when Belial becomes the king? Treven released my shoulder and helped me stand.

"Is there nothing we can do for him?" My voice broke.

Treven shook his head sadly, his eyes serious and full of pain. "I've seen this poison before. There's no cure."

I nodded and looked away before tears fell again. I followed Treven back to the wagon, not even bothering to hide our tracks. What did it matter anymore?

Once he was gone, all of our hopes were gone. I didn't even bother to wipe away the tears that flowed again as I trudged through the mud to see Aric one last time. Would he be conscious? What would I say?

It didn't seem right to say that it was nice to know him when we had fought the whole time. But still, he was dying. I had to say something nice. It was fun? Thanks for the dance? I tripped as I began to blubber again.

Treven broke through the trees and after taking one step into the meadow, he stopped. I didn't notice he had come to a standstill until I ran into him.

"What in the world?" Treven exclaimed.

I peered around him. There was the black Archippos again, but this time it was standing by the back of the wagon! Its head was stuck inside like it was looking at Aric.

"Is it hurting him?" Treven whispered.

I shivered. I'd grown up with tales about Archippi. Everyone had. They normally were good. And yet the stories all agreed with one thing. Archippi had powers. Supposedly, they could do about anything.

*One thing was similar in all the stories. No one
ever knew what the Archippi were going to do. A
bolt of fear shot through me. I pushed Treven
aside and strode forward, tears forgotten.*

*"Hey!" I shouted. "What are you doing? Leave
him alone!"*

*There was a slight shake of the wings, but no
response.*

*"I said leave him alone!" I yelled loudly. The
Archippos was not responding. I glanced around
for something to throw.*

*I still had the branch in my hand, so I hurled it
at the wagon. The limb flew through the air and
banged against the side of the wagon with a loud
clatter. The black horse startled briefly and
stomped its front hoof.*

When you ask for help, it's awfully rude to
chuck things at it when it arrives. *My head was
filled with a man's voice.* Instead, you could be
grateful or stretch yourself to be a little happy.

*My jaw dropped in surprise, and I turned to
Treven. "Who said that?"*

*The horse withdrew his head from the wagon
and shook it.* If you're done throwing stuff, you
can call me Thalion.

*"You're the one. You're the horse that saved
me in the barn!" The words spilled out of my
mouth as I studied him closer.*

*Thalion had a finely shaped head with a strong
neck, and his forelock and mane were thick and
long. I hated to admit it, but he was far more
beautiful than Kaspar was. I'd never tell Kaspar
that, though. All thoughts of catching him seemed*

foolish, although I'd give almost anything to ride him.

Yes, I am. I've been watching you two for a while now. If I had known how badly Prince Aric was back at that farm, I would have healed him then. But I thought that was a sickness that would heal in time, and there were other pressing events needing my attention.

"What's more important than the life of the Crown Prince?" I blurted out. I knew I was being rude, but I was reeling from grief and the sudden appearance of a fabled creature.

Events that do not concern you. However, I am certain that Belial is trying to seize the throne, but I have no proof for my leader. *Thalion shook his black mane.* You must fly before Nighthawk catches up with you. Lord Fariel is a friend of mine. Run to him in Zolari. Together you should be able to defeat the evil.

My relief gave way to frustration. Why was I supposed to do this? My participation ended when Aric was with Fariel. Then I'd go home and return to my own problems. I certainly didn't want to get caught up in whatever defeat the evil meant.

"Can't you do that? You could get to Fariel much faster," I suggested.

I could. But I've been in Eltiria for far too long, and my shields are weak from healing Aric of this poison. If I remain longer, I may not have the strength to return to Merrihaven.

"Can you heal this disease that is sweeping the land?" Treven broke in, eager for an answer. "The one that people are saying is making Unwanteds?"

That I cannot do. Adoyni has not shown us a way to cure that disease yet.

My heart sank. That was the same disease that was sweeping through Dad's province and killing many of our people. There had to be a way to cure it. But then I realized what the Archippos had said about leaving. I didn't know this Thalion or what his intentions were, but I kind of liked having him around. "What about us?"

You have a head start on Nighthawk and the soldiers, but you have to run. Don't slow down, don't stop. Not until you get to Fariel's castle.

"Snowball won't be able to keep up, not with the wagon," I protested, trying to find a way to keep Thalion with us.

I gave the horses an extra burst of energy. She won't win any races, but she'll keep up. *Thalion's voice held a tone of warmth when speaking of the horse pulling the wagon, but it changed to a stern warning.* But only if you do not tarry. I was able to smooth out your tracks and mislead them, but they'll soon be after you.

I tried to suppress the chill of fear, but I couldn't.

"What about Aric?" Treven suddenly asked.

In my fascination of the Archippos, I had forgotten that Treven was beside me. I realized with a wince that I had also completely forgotten about Aric. It wasn't so nice to be reminded.

He is waking up now. *Thalion cocked an ear back at the wagon, and then his ears pivoted forward.* Run fast. You don't have much time. I will return when I can.

Before we could say another thing, Thalion reared and took off faster than I'd ever seen a horse run. His large black wings spread out and his hooves left the ground. We watched as he cleared the trees and faded in the distance.

I heard Aric's voice from the wagon.

"Reveka? What's happening? If whoever owns this wagon kidnapped me, the King will hunt you down and take your head off. Reveka? Are you there?"

I groaned. Aric was awake.

CHAPTER FIFTY-NINE

Dirty Old Wagon

I should've been happy when I woke up, but the first thing I noticed was that my mouth tasted horrible, like I'd been eating garbage. To make matters worse, I was in a dirty old wagon that I'd never seen before. I had no idea what day it was or where I was.

It bothered me that I didn't even know where Reveka was. Had she left me to go back to her family? I thought of the harsh things I'd said to her and how she'd been thrown in the dungeon for no real cause.

I knew if I were her, I'd be gone. I'd leave me at the first chance I got. Reveka made it very clear she didn't like me. And why should she?

I hadn't been a real friend to her. I didn't even know anything about her. And now that she was gone, I wanted a chance to be a better friend to her.

Groaning, I sat up and smacked my head on a shelf that was over the bed. I yelled and flopped back down on the bed. I craned my neck and saw a row of jars filled with different plants.

Across the wagon was a series of larger shelves. They were filled with massive books with loose papers stuffed through them. Jars of meat and vegetables were next to the books. I sat up carefully, feeling the blood rush to my head, and got to my feet.

My left leg refused to work as my head spun, and I crashed to the floor. As I yelled in surprise, the flaps at the back of the wagon flew open, and an old man I'd never seen before rushed to my side.

"Take it easy," he ordered in a strict tone. "You've been down for a long time. You can't expect to leap out of bed so quickly."

I tried protesting as he pulled me back into bed and poured me a glass of juice. I glared at it. "Who are you?" I asked. I couldn't keep the suspicion out of my voice. "Where's Reveka?"

"Reveka? Oh, you mean Rev." The man shoved the glass in my hand.

"So you know her?" I took a small sip. "I thought she'd abandoned me."

"Then you don't know your friends!" The old man snapped. "She hauled you through the worst rainstorm we've seen in years, managing to hide you from a host of soldiers. She kept you warm and let you rest while she went hungry, cold and sleepless. She's been at your side day and night when it was cold, uncomfortable, and frightening. She hasn't had a full night's sleep for days! I have a lot of good friends, but very few who'd do what she did for you."

I lowered my glass and stared at the old man. No one ever talked to me that way. I started to complain, but he interrupted me again.

"Oh, yes. I know exactly who you are, Prince." His voice dropped on the last word and then regained strength. "I know everyone's treated you with kid gloves. But you don't treat your friends like that, and you don't yell at people for speaking the truth!"

I was speechless. Unlike Father's scolding tone, these words cut right to my heart and made me truly regret my actions. I was torn between admitting he was right and my old habit of regaling him for the way he spoke to me. But a movement caught my eyes.

Reveka stood in the rain outside the wagon. She wore a cloak that I didn't recognize. Her face was streaked with mud, and her eyes were red like she'd been crying. I didn't know what had been happening, but she looked exhausted.

He was right. I had no idea what she'd done for me. I suddenly was very uncomfortable. "Reveka, I...uh..." I stammered. I didn't know what to say, and the words weren't coming out right. "I...well... you probably saved my life...uh...thank you."

It wasn't the grandest of speeches, but it was the first time in a long while that I could remember expressing any sort of gratitude. I felt my face getting hot.

Reveka shifted on her feet like she wanted a fight instead of this. Her face flushed instantly, and she looked like she wanted to disappear. "You're welcome," she smiled slightly. "I'm glad to see you feeling..."

"Who are you?" I asked the old man. I was interrupting, but I'd missed out on so much.

"Treven," he responded and motioned me to drink some juice.

"Look, Aric," Reveka broke in. "We've got to get moving. Thalion said..."

"You must be some healer," I said over her. "We have the best physicians in Medora, but they can't heal this. Patrin has the same thing. How long has it been since we left?"

"It's been five days since we left, and he didn't do anything," Reveka answered. "It was that Archippos."

I broke out in a laugh which made me feel tired. "What have you been reading? Some old tale? This is serious."

"Five days?" Treven broke in with surprise. "This poison is slow. It can take up to months to kill, maybe even longer if the victim is healthy. Have you been infected for long?"

I shook my head. "No. Not long at all."

"It was that Damiana woman," Rev said angrily. "We ran into some women who claimed magic would heal him. They were one of those clans that worship Zoria. They took one of our horses as payment but made him worse."

"You sold Wonder?" I gasped. "She wasn't even yours!"

"You nodded like you wanted me to do it!" Rev snapped back.

"Easy." Treven held up his hands. "It's done and not important right now. But that explains it. I've never seen magic work for all the claims that people whisper about, but I have cleaned up *plenty of messes that it made. Something rotten makes whatever it touches worse."*

"Magic?" I spat out. "It made me sicker?"

"It made you almost die!" Treven said. "There was a black Archippos here. Said his name was Thalion. I was telling Rev that it was time to say her goodbyes to you. Then he appeared and healed you."

"We need to go." Rev glanced at Treven. "We don't have much time."

"Where are we? Where are we going?" I didn't like not knowing what was going on.

Rev flipped the reins over Kaspar's neck. "Zolari. To Lord Fariel."

"Fariel? You said we should go to Vesmir instead," I protested. "Why do you think you have the right to change plans without asking me first?"

"Ask you?" Reveka's voice rose with her anger. "Maybe I should've asked you if it was okay to find you food and then have you throw up all over my face. I've been doing all the work here and dragging your sick, royal butt around! Don't try to tell me I have to ask you for permission!"

"Vesmir?" Treven questioned. "Why would you two decide to go there? We must get moving. Rev, you stay close this time. Both of you have some explaining to do."

There was something in his tone that made us obey him. Reveka pulled up her hood and leaped onto Kaspar. She led the way out of the trees back to the road at a trot. The white pony that pulled the wagon followed close behind at a speed I was surprised at. I settled back on the bed with my head close to the wagon seat as Reveka drew up and rode beside Treven.

Treven glanced back at me. "Whatever you are playing at, people have been killed because of your actions. My life is at risk by being with you. It's time for you to fill me in with what you are doing."

I sighed. "Fine."

It was an odd conversation since I couldn't see either of them. But in a strange way, it helped. When I told about injuring Patrin and some of the other stupid things I had done, I didn't have to see the condemnation in their eyes.

When I finished, I twisted around in the bed to see Treven's back. He was nodding like he was processing the information.

"Why Vesmir?" he asked.

"We know Belial was there. We know he was already worshipping the Goddess at that time. If we can find one person to testify something bad about him, maybe we can prove he is evil and up to no good." I shifted on the bed. I was weaker than I wanted to admit, even to myself.

"Why are you so interested in Vesmir?" Rev asked Treven.

Treven didn't answer for a long time. I heard him clear his throat as if he was going to speak, but Reveka interrupted in a stressed tone.

"Get off the road! Someone's coming!"

Chapter Sixty

Instant Chef

Rev pointed frantically at some trees ahead. "Get behind those!" she commanded as she whipped Kaspar to the closest tree.

I sat up, blinking away the black spots that appeared in my eyes, and peered out the back of the wagon to watch her.

Treven drove the wagon into the trees and stopped. "Get down, Prince. We may be able to cover for you if they don't see you."

I dropped the flap and sat back on the bed. Beside me was my sword. I picked it up and regarded it. Could I even defend myself if I had to? Straton had clearly shown me that I wasn't that good with the blade, and now I was weaker than ever.

I waited as the rain pounded on the canvas above my head. To distract myself from going crazy with the agony of not knowing what was happening, I studied the books on the shelves.

Most of them were worn with much use, but the last one on the right was especially tattered. Papers were shoved into it haphazardly.

I stood up carefully and pulled it from the others. As I flipped through it, I saw each page had a heading of some disease or ailment. On the page were scribbled possible causes and cures.

Often times, they would be circles with a different ink declaring, "WRONG!" Sometimes the words were scratched out entirely. Lines with arrows were drawn to other pages and notes. It was a mess.

Treven shifted on his seat, and I hastily shoved the book back on the shelf. I dropped onto the bed, exhausted from my brief exercise. What would I do if I needed to fight?

There was a sound like many people talking at once. I couldn't make it out but could hear men calling out above the noise. I held my breath as the din came closer and slowly moved on. The stillness fell back down and only the questions in my head kept pounding.

"Farmers moving cows," Treven stated. "You can look out now if you want."

I looked out over the seat. Reveka was on Kaspar, leading the way back to the road. Treven glanced at me before he snapped the reins, and Snowball resumed her fast trot.

The rest of the day progressed the same way. It felt like we had barely started down the road when one of us would hear something, and we'd dart into the woods.

Each time we hid, I took down the old book and read some to take my mind off what was happening. It was interesting to see what Treven had found would work.

When the sun was lower than the trees in the west, Rev scouted ahead and found a camping spot. We pulled in while she wiped away our tracks.

The rain had let up enough that I could get out of the wagon. I started to climb out, but my legs gave way, and I basically fell out of the wagon. Reveka dropped her saddlebags to support me.

"Thanks, Rev," I said quickly. She grinned slightly as she went back to her work.

I didn't want to admit it, but between the fright and impatience, I was exhausted. Far more than I'd ever been in my whole life.

Father was right. I did have it easy. They began taking care of the horses and setting up camp. As I tried to help, Treven motioned to the ground.

"Sit and rest," he said. "We'll take care of it until you regain your full strength."

I dropped onto a canvas sack Rev had placed on the ground. It felt strange to want to help. I was always content with letting others do the work, but now I felt like they had already done so much for me that I wanted to return the favor. It was odd.

Rev deposited a small load of wood in front of me. "Dry oak. Won't make much smoke. We can warm up some food and then put it out." Without waiting for an answer, she left to take the harness off Snowball.

Treven was in the wagon banging around where I couldn't see him. He climbed out with his arms full of blankets and a basket. He dropped a basket by me as he continued to spread out the blankets on the canvas.

I opened the basket to see a tinder box and some jars of food. I grinned. Here was something I could do without taxing myself too much. I gathered the wood into a pile and lit a fire.

There was a surge of satisfaction when I heard the soft popping of the fire. Rummaging through the supplies Treven placed beside me, I found a pot.

Opening the jars that looked like stew, I poured the contents into the pot. The fire had grown to a respectable size, so I placed the pot over the flames. That was when I started to laugh. Rev regarded me with a confused look.

I winked at her. "This may come as a surprise to you, but this is the first time I've ever cooked. I didn't know it was this easy."

Rev rolled her eyes. "If you think that's cooking, you have been spoiled." But her grin took the sting out of her words.

We settled down to our meager food. After we had eaten our fill, Treven cleaned up the dishes while Rev put out the fire.

"Why are you so interested in Vesmir?" Rev asked.

Treven looked off into the night. "I don't know where Belial came from. He came to Vesmir as a replacement for a priest of Adoyni's who had passed away. He promised to improve all our problems, for weren't Adoyni's children supposed to be free from sickness, poverty and every other problem?"

I saw a far off look on his face. His expression was blank, like telling us this information was

painful, too painful to allow any thought of
sadness in, or it might overtake him completely.

"For a while, sickness suddenly went away. One
family with bad land prospered. People streamed
to him for healing, prayer, and to listen to him.
Vesmir was my home. When he was there, I was a
healer with my wife and young son. I often helped
Belial. My wife cooked dinners for him so he'd
have more time for spiritual tasks. My son followed
him like a puppy dog." Treven ran a hand over his
face. "There were seven families that helped him.
We supported him in whatever he needed."

I broke in. "Are they still there? Would they
testify about him if we went there?"

Treven winced and said nothing.

After a long pause, Rev leaned forward with an
expression on her face like she didn't really want
to ask the next question. "Treven, what happened
to them? To your wife and son?"

Treven took a ragged breath and blinked
quickly like he was holding back tears.

"They're all dead. He killed all of them."

Chapter Sixty-One

Lies and Assumptions

Treven kept talking, not noticing our shock and dismay over his last sentence. Once the story had started, he wasn't going to stop until he was finished.

"Belial decided we could be more effective if we lived in the same place. He picked the largest farm and encouraged us to sell all we had and join him. To my great disappointment, a plague hit a nearby town, and I was the only healer in the area."

Treven stopped for a minute, regarding the blackened wood where the fire had been. I heard an owl hoot in the distance and wondered if Nighthawk was camped somewhere along a road, waiting for the daylight to haul us back to Medora and Belial.

"I left. Soon I was up to my neck in vomiting, diarrhea and stomach aches. I'd seen this disease before and knew that it was due to contaminated water. Between treating the patients and trying to stop their dehydration, I worked with the town to clean their water to prevent the disease. I was gone for over two months."

Rev leaned forward. "What happened when you returned to Vesmir?"

Treven sighed. "Every one of our group was deathly sick. I returned to find my wife and my son in bed. I couldn't figure out what was wrong. They were weak, writhing with pain, delirious, and pale. Sometimes they knew who I was, but most times they fought anything I tried to do for them with a viciousness of a hurt wild animal. Around their necks hung a small crystal. A few of the older people died."

"That's the same thing," Rev interrupted. "We lost fifty people. There was nothing we could do. Mom was looking like she had it. Dad took her south to see if healers there could do anything for her. I was in charge of the estate, but when more died, I knew I had to either catch up with Father or find someone who knew how to cure this sickness."

"Wait a minute," I joined in. "You told my parents that your parents were dead. That's why Mother took you in. She thought you were an orphan. You lied to them." The last sentence came out a harsh accusation. I shifted as I remembered all the times I'd lied to them.

"I did not," Rev grinned. "I said they were gone. And that's true. They are gone from our estate. The Queen assumed that gone meant dead."

I opened my mouth to protest but realized that she was right. I snorted. "Clever," I drawled. "What happened, Treven?"

He stared moodily into the fire. When he continued, it was with the same detachment. "Now I've heard people call them Unwanteds. Belial helped me move them into the temple building so I could watch over all the families and mine as well. A woman named Nighthawk joined him at that time. I didn't sleep or eat for days. I battled for their lives for three weeks. Then they started to die. Some left quietly. Some went screaming like they were being tortured. My son was one of the first. I was with him when he closed his eyes for the last time. I didn't even know he was gone for a few minutes."

He stopped as his voice broke and then continued. "My wife was the last. The last thing she said was "Help." Her face changed, and she snarled at me before she took her last breath. I fell sick with exhaustion and grief at that point. When I recovered, I learned Belial had taken all the bodies and money and disappeared. I packed up the wagon and left. I have journeyed this world to find a cure."

"Have you found it?" Rev breathed eagerly.

He stared into the fire for a few minutes. "There is one woman, Iseabail. She's one of us that have gathered together for protection from those that persecute anyone who follows Adoyni. Jal is there. Another one of my friends, Mischa, helped us settle there before he was set on another task. But, I digress. Iseabail came many years ago, but recently came down with the disease. She's better now, yet I don't know if it's something I did or if Adoyni intervened."

"You have to come with us and tell your story to Father," I ordered. "This story of Belial is what we were searching for."

"Then we find the cure and end this sickness Belial has loosed on the world," Rev added.

As we settled down for the night, I had to grin even though Treven's story made me feel bad for him. We were close to the end, and everything was going to turn out okay. In a few days, we'd be back at the castle, and life would return to the way it was supposed to be. I drifted off to sleep with thoughts of what I would do to set all the wrongs right.

Chapter Sixty-Two

Stand Down

The next morning I woke up feeling like I hadn't slept a wink. My whole body ached from sleeping on the hard ground.

I tried not to be surly when Rev handed me a hard piece of bread and a cold piece of beef for breakfast, but I knew I wasn't holding back my bad temper very well.

At least the sun was peeking over the trees and the clouds looked to be breaking apart. I was sick of rain and mud. I fingered my sword as I walked to the wagon.

Even if the slightest cut could evidently kill a person, I knew I wasn't ready to be part of a fight. However, it was the only protection we had. I strapped it around my waist unwillingly.

Rev was taking her saddle to Kaspar. I considered telling her that I wanted to ride him, but I decided that wouldn't go over very well. Besides, I didn't know if I had the strength to handle him. My legs still felt weak.

"We can't hide the wagon." Rev flopped her saddle onto Kaspar's back. He blew air out his nose like the weight was heavy. Rev patted the

horse's neck as she continued. "They'll be on us before long, and it takes a lot of trees to hide it."

"Maybe we don't have to hide it," I spoke up. "They're looking for me and probably you, not some old man in a wagon."

Treven glared at me when I mentioned his age.

I grinned an apology. "If you stay on the road, they may question you a bit, but they're not looking for you. And the wagon would cover our tracks."

"You really believe that?" Rev questioned. "You didn't see what they did to those villagers! Why wouldn't they question Treven and then kill him for the fun of it?"

"They had reason to believe the villagers knew something about us. They probably thought they were hiding us." The thought of them harming Treven bothered me, but I really did think he'd be fine. "They wouldn't think that of someone on the road, especially a road that we may or may not have gone down."

"There's a risk," Treven agreed. "But I think the Prince is right. I won't leave the wagon, and we can't hide it properly at a minute's notice."

"We'll stay close in case they find out we are together. We're not completely helpless, you know." I motioned to my sword on my hip. "It might be better if we're together."

We moved out quickly without much talking. My crankiness transformed into impatience as I settled beside Treven on the wagon seat. I was sick of the journey. I wanted to see Belial ousted, Father and Patrin healthy, and Mother happy.

Rev trailed behind the wagon. At times, she disappeared as she stopped to cover our tracks. We'd left the main road when the morning was half gone and now were on a small track that Treven knew circled Albia and would lead us to Zolari.

Treven filled in the hours by talking about the little village he belonged to. Most of the people had settled there because it was too dangerous to worship Adoyni openly.

It was yet another reminder of how much Belial had changed the realm under Father's nose. It was one more thing I had to fix.

I was ready to be done for the day. My energy was more depleted than I had thought. I twisted in my seat to check on Rev only to see Kaspar bolting to the wagon. Her hair was in a tangled mess as she pulled him to a stop.

"Soldiers. Coming down our road." She took a deep breath. "Coming fast, too."

I was not going to be hauled back to the castle again. I glanced back. "We run. Then we hide if we have to."

Snowball broke into a run. Rev kept with the wagon and drew Kaspar up alongside me.

I glanced over. "How many?" I shouted.

The wrinkle between her eyebrows deepened. "Maybe four. Like a scouting party."

My whole body screamed with the jolts and bumps. I didn't know how long I'd be able to bear it. I tried to ignore the agony, determined to do whatever it took to escape.

"We can't go long like this," Rev yelled back. "Snowball can't..."

I didn't hear the rest of the words over the noise of the wagon, but I knew what she was trying to say. Snowball wouldn't be able to pull the wagon at this speed for long before falling down dead.

Treven must've agreed because he slowed the white mare down to a walk. Her flanks were heaving and dripping with sweat.

"I want to see the soldiers," I said. "Treven, keep going at whatever speed you think is fast enough, and we'll catch up. If they get too close, we'll hide and find you later. Just remember our story."

Treven nodded, his face white. "Be careful. I've seen Belial's soldiers in action before. They don't play around."

Rev motioned for me to climb on behind her. I started to argue, but I saw the look on her face and scrambled on behind her. We spun back down the road to a crest of a hill and dismounted. She hunched down as we peered over the edge.

"Look! They're almost to us!" I exclaimed.

She followed my finger to the base of the hill. Through the gaps in the trees, I saw three soldiers trotting side by side. The one in the front on the left carried a banner. The sun glinted on their armor as the wind gently blew to reveal a dragon on the standard.

"Let's erase some of our tracks and then go through the woods back to Treven," Rev ordered. "If we stay hidden, maybe they'll pass on by."

I wanted to protest, but it was a good plan. Getting back on Kaspar took more strength than I thought it would. I hoped it wouldn't take long to weave through the trees and catch up with Treven. Rev zigzagged through the forest, staying out of sight of the road.

Every so often, she'd pull Kasper up, swing her leg over his neck and drop to the ground to wipe away our tracks. After a while, she slowed Kaspar down to a walk and motioned me to be silent.

Using the brush as cover, she guided us back to the road. My heart started to pound as we didn't see Treven or the wagon. Were we too late? I wanted to kick myself for suggesting that we go back to look and allowing Rev to take us through the forest.

A flash of blue caught my eye. The wagon! I tugged on Rev's sleeve. She shot me a warning look to be quiet, but I grinned at her. As far as I saw, everything was fine. I slid off while she threw the reins over a branch.

But as we approached the road where the wagon was, I heard angry voices. Rev hunched over and glided through the trees silently. I did my best to copy her, despite the small twigs that snapped under my feet. She hesitated and gave me a dirty look again.

Rev dropped to her knees and gestured for me to come closer. I crawled up and peeked through the pine needles that were hiding us from the road. I gasped forward when I saw the wagon.

The back door was open, and broken bottles of medicine and bandages were thrown onto the road. Rev grabbed my arm and held me back. Slowly, she pointed to the side of the wagon.

The three knights surrounded Treven. His clothes were disheveled like he'd been pulled from the wagon. There was a fresh bruise below his eye, and he was holding his stomach. One of the soldiers shoved him against the wagon and grabbed his shirt under his chin.

"We know you were with them." The man shook Treven. "Now tell us where they are."

Treven took a shaky breath and slowly shook his head. The knight backslapped him across the face.

A small trickle of blood flowed from his lip, but he didn't say a word. The knight pushed him against the wagon hard and spun him around.

One of the soldiers hung back. "Captain Mabon, he's an old man. Maybe we should..."

"Maybe you should shut up," Captain Mabon snapped.

Treven pushed himself off the wagon and lurched toward the mess on the road. Mabon grabbed him again, twirling him around, and punched him in the nose.

Treven screamed and grabbed his face, but I saw blood pouring from his nose. He wiped the blood on his sleeve and slowly straightened.

Mabon stepped back and drew his sword. "I'll ask one more time. Then it will really start to hurt. Where are Prince Aric and the girl?"

Treven straightened carefully and put a hand on the wagon for balance. His hand shook as he wiped the sweat from his brow. "Fine. I'll tell you."

Rev's hand tightened on my arm. I gripped my sword. If he gave us up now, we'd barely have time to make it to Kaspar.

Treven continued. "He's in disguise. So you couldn't find him." His breath came in gasps. "He's right there." He pointed at Snowball.

Mabon snarled and his sword flashed. Treven ducked but cried out as he gripped his left arm. Blood oozed between his fingers as Mabon pulled back and struck again.

I drew my sword as quietly as I could and shook Rev's hand off my arm. I heard her protest softly but ignored it. Mabon was going to kill Treven. I was not going to watch that happen.

I crept through the woods. Leaves crunched under my feet, but the knight closest to me didn't notice. He was intently watching Captain Mabon.

Treven managed to dodge the last strike, but I knew he didn't have long. They weren't asking any more questions.

I hesitated at the edge of the trees. I watched the knight who was waiting for orders. Could I take all three of them? Father was always saying that I wasn't good enough. Straton certainly proved that I wasn't that proficient with the sword.

Were they right? I gripped the hilt tighter. I couldn't think about what I was going to do, or I'd never find the guts to start.

I heard Rev gasp as I stepped out from behind the trees. I ignored her and said in my most authoritative voice,

"I command you to leave him alone and stand down.

SKIRMISHES

"The real fight will come tomorrow.
This is only a skirmish that we lost."
~FODOR GWYDION

Jehun traveled through the countryside, ignoring his mission to speak with Seiten on Elba Isle. Obeying Belial wasn't something he really wanted to do, but there didn't seem to be another course of action. One thing he wasn't going to tell Belial about was his new obsession to find followers of Adoyni's where he might get some answers to his questions.

He knew where the temples were. He was there when they were built, but to his surprise, most of them were gone. Piles of rubble replaced the buildings of splendor. In other places, blackened grass and trees were the only signs of where the buildings had been.

He paused in the clearing of one of the temples that used to be a magnificent structure. What had happened? Like all the others before, it hadn't decayed over time. It was demolished. He could see charred wood. In a few places, rounded boulders like a trebuchet used were scattered around the wreckage.

Someone was systematically destroying the places of worship. But why? Who hated Adoyni enough to actively demolish His places? He searched for the priests that served in the houses of Adoyni. Maybe one of them would tell him what happened. But not one priest was found. As he explored the land further, he found unmarked graves close to where the temples once stood.

Jehun needed no further proof that someone was trying to wipe all traces of Adoyni from Eltiria. Even if the temples and priests were destroyed, Jehun knew there were some people out there who still believed in Adoyni like the young couple whose house he had accidently collapsed.

He searched diligently for them. And he found them scattered across the countryside. Some were hiding in caves, fearful for their lives. Others gathered in small villages, seeking refuge together.

He watched as a woman, who lost her home and her three children, refused to curse Adoyni and continued to praise Him. One man with five children lost his leg in a farming accident. Despite the pain of healing and agony of having no means to provide for his family, he never turned his back on Adoyni.

Jehun pulled away from the people and retreated deep inside himself. At the first point of pain, he had cursed Adoyni and turned his back on Him. But all that seemed to do was to create more pain.

A voice called to him and jolted him out of his thoughts. He pushed it away, knowing it was Belial summoning him. The compulsion grew stronger until Jehun finally heeded the voice.

"Where are you?" Belial snapped. "Are you there? Have you talked with Seiten?"

Jehun trembled and explained that he was close to Zolari.

"Zolari? What is taking you so long? You should've been halfway to Elba Isle by now!" Belial's voice was sharp. "Have you felt any of those three people I mentioned to you?"

Jehun was relieved that they hadn't returned. He didn't want to lie to Belial when he was in this mood.

Belial snorted with scorn. "None? Good. They must still be hiding with the Archippi. It won't be too long until the king dies, and then it won't matter where he is anymore. If any of those people return, you let me know the instant their feet hit the ground. Now get to Seiten quickly. If you tarry longer, I'll forget about taking your pain away."

Jehun listened to Belial with distaste. Never before had he heard Belial speak with so much hate, but now it seemed to ooze off him like oil came out of the ground. Had Belial always been like this?

Jehun wondered if he had made a poor choice of leaving Adoyni. But as he listened to Belial rant against those people with the Archippi and what he would do if they dared return, a shot of pain returned, and Jehun gasped.

But through his throbbing agony, he realized that Belial used a different voice than normal. Usually Belial's voice was higher and smoother. But today it was rough and low. Jehun had heard it before.

It was Belial who had commanded the rift in Northbridge. Jehun groaned as the pain washed over him. He had sworn his allegiance to the one who had caused him all this great agony.

He had no choice. To get rid of this pain, he must do what Belial wanted, then he could stop serving Belial and take care of himself.

He left the followers of Adoyni behind and traveled through Zolari and far west through the ocean to the small isle of Elba.

Meanwhile, lava grew into large lakes just under the surface of the earth.

CHAPTER SIXTY-THREE

Tangled Chain

Kai stumbled through the dim corridor for hours. He couldn't catch his breath anymore, and the only sound he heard was shuffling. Every time he stopped, the sight of his face on the dead body spurred him on, even though being only able to limp along made him want to scream in anger.

He knew what happened. He killed himself. But just the good parts of him. Everything he did that was good, anything honorable, was gone.

All that was left was a ruined, broken heap. There was nothing to redeem himself. Like his sword said. *Failure.* That was him. He was a failure.

He turned the corner and blinked at the brightness of a giant golden door surrounded by many torches. It was so dazzling he could barely look at it. He crept toward it.

Although his heart leaped with an unfamiliar feeling of hope, it was quickly dashed. The gold handle was locked shut by a gold chain linked to a ring embedded in the rock wall. There was no key.

He turned over the rocks that were beside the door, hoping the key was underneath one. Finding nothing, he groaned in frustration. He picked up one of the bigger rocks and threw it at the door.

It didn't even make a dent. He studied it closely. Surely the rock he chucked should've done something to the door. *Is it protected by magic?* He slumped against the opposite wall. Wouldn't it be ironic to die right here? Failing at everything, even escape.

He chuckled, but the laughter contained no mirth and seemed to echo in the empty hall. He stopped as soon as he heard the hollow noise and leaned back with his eyes closed as he nursed his grief and pain.

All he wanted was to go home. To see Mom. To eat her food. But it had to be when Shona was still alive. He wanted life to be the way it was before, when the biggest problem they had was how to pay the rent.

He smiled. *Perhaps the biggest problem was how to sneak down those stupid creaky stairs at night.* They'd given him away far too many times and woken Mom up to chase him back to bed. But the few nights he succeeded, he had wandered Northbridge. Since he could let himself in with the key, no one ever knew that he'd been gone.

The key! Kai's eyes popped open. *Mom always kept an extra key above the door in case we needed to get in! Surely it couldn't be that easy!*

He peered above the golden door and let out a hoot of triumph when he saw a rock ledge in the shadows along the top. He jumped to reach the top of the ledge. His fingers jammed against loose rocks, but halfway down the shelf, he felt cold metal just out of his grasp. He dropped to the ground and then launched off the closest rock and grabbed the ledge with one hand. Dangling in the air, and ignoring the sharp pain, he reached as far back as he could and seized the key.

He dropped to the ground, missed his feet, and landed on his back. The fall forced the air out of his lungs. He rolled to his side, gasping for breath, and prayed that the aches would stop. In his hand, he clutched the key.

As soon as he could, he rolled to his knees and used the wall to stand up. His knees were weaker than he remembered, and his breath came in short gasps. For some strange reason, the hallway felt like it was a hot summer day, and he was covered with sweat. He got to his feet slowly as his head spun. *Am I getting sick or sick of here?*

He shuffled to the door and tried to ignore the memory of his face staring up at him, dead on the stone floor of the hallway. And now all he had left was this broken, deteriorating body. *Did I kill the best part of me? Is there anything good left?*

He unconsciously fiddled with the cold chain as he paused. This corridor was bad. What was on the other side of the door? It might be something even worse. He snorted to himself. *What could be worse than this?* He put the key in the lock before he hesitated again and snapped it open.

The chain tangled around itself as he tried to pull it free. He growled with impatience as it spun loose. He tore the chain from the door, and in a frenzy like a starving animal, he flung the door open and raced into the sunlight.

CHAPTER SIXTY-FOUR

Rejuvenation

Kai burst through the door and blinked as the sunlight blinded him. He was in a large room with walls made out of whitish gray stone. The wall across the room was lined with large revealing rolling hills covered with trees and mountains reaching to the sky.

He stared at the mountains. He'd seen them before. He traced the line that met the sky, knowing each dip and curve. He'd studied half of the mountain range before he knew where he was. *The Razors!*

He dashed to the glass and gazed out at a long valley. Far below him was River Shammah. Nestled along each side of the river was Northbridge. He hit the glass with his fist in delight. He could barely make out the long circle that was the racing track and the barns of Shalock Stables. Home!

Somewhere down there was Rhiana, and Mom and Dad. He'd find them and get them to safety, some place where Rhiana could get medical help, and then he'd find Belial and deal with him. Maybe the king would be so grateful that he'd bestow Kai with great fortune, taking away all of their problems. Now all he had to do was find a stairway down!

Kai spun on his heel to find a door to lead him out of the room. A table covered with old books and parchments was in the center of the room. A man was sitting behind the table inside a pentacle of white, blue, and purple candles. His dark hair was slicked back and he wore no shirt. Kai saw a nub on his shoulder where the arm ended like it had been chopped off, but the skin was healed. There was something familiar about him.

The man was chanting with his eyes closed and his body was bent forward slightly, concentration utterly commanding his attention. Kai felt a chill in the air. He wanted out. Something felt very wrong.

Quietly, Kai sneaked to a wooden door on the other side of the golden one he came through, but as he approached it, he glanced back and saw the man's face.

It was Belial! The chanting continued, and Kai watched, transfixed on the sight. The nub, the arm that was cut off, was moving. The chanting grew louder and louder as the end of the arm slowly started to grow. Kai stared as the nub grew down to the elbow. He saw the elbow form and the flesh continue to push farther until there was the shape of a wrist.

Belial's chants were almost a shout as the arm seemed to slow in its growth. Sweat trickled down his face as he continued his spell. Kai knew he should leave. But he couldn't leave and not know what happened.

The arm surged forward as if an invisible wall had been holding it back and it suddenly had broken through. A hand formed, then fingers. Kai gawked in amazement as nails grew on the end of the fingers and the arm was complete.

Belial slumped forward and gasped for air like a runner at the end of a race. He rested on his left arm, panting, and then pulled himself up. With a grin, he ran his left hand down his new right arm. He waved the fingers one at a time. As each one responded, Belial started to laugh.

"Nothing is out of my limit," he said with a ring of triumph as he stood. "Not even the power to create." He laughed louder, full of victory. He turned to Kai with a wicked smile. "Think you had an advantage when I had only one arm?" He shouted out the last words. "Thanks to you, I'm more powerful than I was before."

Kai jumped back and seized his sword.

Belial laughed, clearly amused by his reaction. "Relax. Did you think you solved some great puzzle of the maze? Once there, you are trapped until you succumb to the disease. There is no escape. I brought you here on purpose so that we could have a little chat about your future."

"My future?" Kai snarled. "Let's talk about yours! I predict you dying by my sword in a few seconds. I chopped off one arm. I'll get your head this time."

The only response Belial made was to wave his arm to the right. Kai's body rose in the air and flew to the far side of the room. Kai caught a glimpse of

Northbridge out the window before he smashed
into the glass.

The force of the blow made his wounds pound,
and he yelled as Belial dropped him into a heap
on one of the rugs. He forced himself to get to his
feet although all he wanted to do was rest. His legs
trembled as he glared at Belial.

"Adoyni always requires a price," Belial stated
calmly as he sat back down in the chair. "You
followed Him, and now you are paying. Notice
He's not around to rescue you? He allowed you to
drink the poison in the tower. It was enough to kill
you almost instantly. But you were stubborn
enough not to die and that gave me a chance to
get a foothold into your life. Soon you'll be
completely under my control, and the Archippi
will be destroyed!"

"What are you talking about? What have you
done with Lizzy and Taryn? Where's my family?"
Kai thought about pulling his sword, but he didn't
know if he could even hold it.

"I guess I can humor you a little," Belial smiled
graciously, but Kai saw the evil behind it. "I assume
Taryn and Lizzy are in Merrihaven with the horrid
Archippi. You're there, too. I can imagine them
working night and day trying to cure you!" Belial
laughed.

Kai shook his head, confused. "I don't
understand. How can I be there when I'm here?"

"You're not really here," Belial grinned. "Your
mind is, and it needs a body to feel comfortable.
Your body is in Merrihaven."

"You're lying. This is another trick," Kai protested.

Belial slammed his hand down on the armrests of the chair and yelled. "Never accuse me of lying!" He started again in a calmer tone. "Years ago, I risked a journey to Elba Isle. I'd worshipped the Goddess long enough to know that she's another path to Seiten. I was tired of trying to find Seiten through that path, so I hired a ship and forced the sailors to go there."

He grinned wickedly. "It cost a much higher price than I thought, but I made it. I actually found the Isle and talked with him. I swore allegiance to him and promised to use his secrets to eventually free him. He told me things. Secrets to control the mind. Secrets to make objects do what I want. Poisons far more lethal than I'd already used."

"You went to Elba Isle?" Kai asked in disbelief. "Everyone knows that's impossible. It's so far out at sea only the Archippi can reach it."

"Everyone is wrong!" Belial yelled and jumped to his feet. "I killed every sailor, but we made it! On the way back, I lost the ship, but through the arts Seiten taught me, I was able to reach shore. I used my knowledge to create an army of Unwanteds. It took more time than I thought because there are two types of people. The first kind gives up and dies. The second kind is like you. In the Hallway, they let the dark into their souls until there is no turning back."

Kai remembered the rage that coursed through him as he killed Bowen and Yorath. He shivered.

Could my decisions allow Belial to use his evil magic through me? Oh, Adoyni, I've forgotten how You can heal and rescue me, and I set out to fix everything myself. Please, please don't let Belial use me for his wicked plans.

Belial paced to the window and stood with his back to Kai. "As I watched you, I was a bit worried. For if you chose the right door, you might've escaped. Your body would've died. But your spirit would've found its way to Adoyni's court. But you walked right by it."

Kai was confused. "What do you mean my spirit? What are you talking about?"

"Haven't you figured it out yet?" Belial looked surprised. "This disease is not physical like everyone thinks. It's spiritual. It separates the soul from the body and throws the soul into the stone corridor you came out. I know how to enter the hallway with the body and soul intact, and I can transport myself anywhere, even Merrihaven."

"That's impossible," Kai protested weakly.

"Is it?" Belial laughed. "As your body weakens, your spirit is growing stronger. As you let the rage in, your soul becomes mine. And once the King dies, I'll obtain the throne. My armies wait for my command to wipe out all followers of Adoyni. Then Eltiria will be mine. In a few minutes, the disease will take over your body, and I'll use you to slaughter the Archippi. And your precious little family? Your mother is working off your debt in my mines, but Rhiana has been quite a delight, although she has warmed up to Nighthawk more than me."

Kai sank to the floor and held his head. Belial wasn't lying. Even if he was miraculously healed, he'd be in Merrihaven and unable to stop Belial. His family was destroyed. And it was all his fault. His sword was right. He was a failure.

All he could hear was the sound of Belial's triumphant cackle. He could no longer hold back his tears as he silently pleaded to Adoyni for help.

378

CHAPTER SIXTY-FIVE

Prisoners

Lizzy stretched and glanced at Kai. Tears were streaming down his cheeks. The sight of him crying broke her heart. *What is he thinking or feeling? Is he in pain?* She leaned over and wiped them from his cheeks as Aric noticed what she was doing and stopped telling his story.

Adoyni, help us now! We can't do anything for Kai, and something's very wrong! Although everyone was watching her, no one said a word. She sat on her bed and fought back her own tears. She was so tired.

"Maybe we could get one of the Archippi to take Kai to Treven." She was unable to keep still anymore. "Maybe he's found the answer by now."

Rev shifted in her seat and avoided anyone's eyes. "Even if we could, the Archippi wouldn't agree to that since we..." She stopped and cleared her throat. "Since we..."

"Since we're not allowed to leave," Taryn filled in with an angry tone. His words were harsh and loud as he turned to Aric. "Tell her. Tell her how we're prisoners."

"Prisoners?" Lizzy said, shocked. "The Archippi are our friends! How could you say that? Look at all Eladar did for us. He died for us!" Her voice rose as her shock grew into fury.

"Eladar, yes!" Taryn responded. "But he said to be careful of the Archippi. And we weren't. We blindly hopped on the first ones that came along, and now we're stuck."

Aric interrupted Taryn. "What Taryn is saying is that there is an order laid down by my great-grandfather, Amhar. He ordered the Archippi away from Eltiria until a king calls them back. Eladar was one of the few who broke this rule, knowing that evil is gaining a foothold faster than we imagined."

Aric paused and rubbed his eyes. "Eladar was great friends with Faelon, their leader, but they disagreed on one thing. Eladar believed they should break the king's order and return. He gathered a few Archippi who believed the same thing. With his death, the others have scattered, scared of banishment or death. No one will break this rule. Until my father allows Archippi to enter Eltiria, we wait with the rest of them."

"But he'll never call them back!" Lizzy's voice took on an edge of panic as she understood Taryn's anger. "He's almost dead. And then Belial will take the crown, and we'll be stuck here until...until..." The enormity of the situation hit her. She continued in almost a whisper. "...until we die."

"And no matter what anyone says, they never change their minds," Taryn snapped. "Not that I had a chance to talk to them about it before Rev and Aric whisked us off to this island."

Aric held up his hands. "We have to be grateful for what they've done for us. I mean, not only did they allow us to stay in Merrihaven, they let us have a chance at healing Kai."

"Let us have a chance?" Lizzy repeated but didn't try to keep the skepticism out of her voice. "What else would they have done? Kill him?"

Silence filled the room. No one spoke for a long time. Lizzy gripped her blankets tighter and glanced over at Taryn. His face was filled with shock.

Aric shifted in his chair and started to speak. Looking at Rev in what seemed like a plea for help, he stopped and fell silent again.

"You've got to be kidding," Taryn said softly. His eyes sparked with anger and his face grew red. "So that's what you've been keeping from us."

"You can't blame them," Aric defended quickly in a sharp tone. "No one knows how the disease spreads. What if it infected all of Merrihaven?"

"What are you talking about?" Lizzy demanded.

Rev still refused to meet anyone's eyes or say anything. She rubbed her fingers across her eyes and stared at the floor.

Taryn waited a space of a heartbeat and leaped to his feet. He leaned over Kai's bed, gesturing at Aric. "If you harm one hair on Kai, I'll kill you myself."

The realization of what was happening dawned on Lizzy. "You're saying that the Archippi wanted to kill Kai right away."

"Not right away," Rev spoke quickly. "But once it became clear what was wrong with him, they did."

"What if you can't heal him?" Lizzy followed quickly. "What will they want to do then?"

"We're ordered to...to..." Rev swallowed and shook her head.

"To kill him." Aric said harshly as if the words made him sick. "We can try. But if nothing works, then there is no choice. We don't know how it spreads. We don't even know if Archippi can get it. Either way, they aren't going to risk having the disease spread in their sanctuary, even if Kai is one of the descendants of the Slayers."

"You'll have to fight your way through me before you touch him," Taryn warned.

Lizzy glanced at Taryn. At one time, she would have laughed at his threats, but not anymore. She had seen him kill Unwanteds with his axe and even bring down a Seeker.

Aric raised his eyebrows in amusement and anger. "You do know that a threat to the Crown Prince is considered treason and is punishable by death, right? Even a threat you have no hope in completing?"

Taryn yelled, "You can't have it both ways! You tell people not to call you a Prince, but the minute something doesn't go your way, you scramble onto your throne again! And don't you dare forget what I've done. I've killed a Seeker. Have you even used that sword you wear all the time, or is it for show?"

"Who do you think you are?" Aric leaped to his feet. "Speaking to me that way..."

"Enough!" Lizzy screamed. "Both of you stop it and sit down! This isn't helping."

The two of them glared at each other across Kai's body where he lay as still as death. For a moment, Lizzy thought they were going to start fighting, but their fists unclenched. Taryn plopped down in the sand close to Kai.

"The only way out of this is to cure him," Lizzy continued in a softer tone. "Once we do that, then we'll figure out how to get back to Eltiria. One problem at a time. Back to the beginning. What was Treven talking about?" She turned to Aric. "What happened to you next? Finish your story. Quickly!"

CHAPTER SIXTY-SIX

Roughed Up

The men spun as I stood on the road with my sword drawn and commanded Belial's soldiers to leave Treven alone. Only Mabon remained where he was, his sword outstretched, pointing at Treven.

"Prince Aric, I assume," he said casually. He had a long nose that reminded me of a weasel. His thinning red hair was combed over a bald spot and his green eyes held only scorn for me.

"I am he," I declared loudly, hoping my confident tone would scare them off. "And I order you to leave this man alone."

"Ah, too bad for you that I take my orders only from Chancellor Belial," Mabon sneered. He glanced at Treven. "Guess we don't need him anymore."

I saw the blade flash in the sunlight, and Treven screamed in agony. When Mabon pulled back, Treven's left side was red with blood. Treven fell to his knees, clutching his side and gasping for air.

Mabon placed the sword under Treven's chin and forced him to look up. "Do you want to live?"

Treven coughed and crawled closer to the wagon as if it could protect him.

"I might let you live," Mabon sneered. "If you beg for your life."

I couldn't hold back anymore. With a roar, I flew at Mabon with my sword ready to strike. One of the knights watching spun while drawing his sword. I could feel his disdain for me in the way he loosely held his blade.

I smacked it away, and it clattered to the ground. The other knight leaped from the wagon with his weapon out and was rushing toward us on my right.

I yelled and plunged my blade into the knight who hadn't retrieved his sword. He gasped as the blade pierced his heart. I pulled it free in time to meet the attack of the other soldier's blade. The first man crumbled to the ground as I weaved back to block the next thrusts.

Out of the corner of my eye, I saw the first man sink to the ground and stop moving. I barely heard Rev's scream as she emerged from the trees or the clash of blades against each other. I scarcely even noticed the attacks as I backed up and blocked.

I had killed.

Whether my strike was true or not, the poison on my blade took every chance of survival away. That soldier, who was obeying Belial's orders, was now dead because of me.

I had killed.

My stomach twisted. The urge to throw up grew inside of me. My hands started to shake as I stepped farther down the road. The man attacking me sliced at my face, and I dodged it at the last second. What would happen if I stopped fighting?

Treven was still on the ground with Mabon standing over him. Rev was frozen on the side of the road, her face white as she watched me. Mabon would kill Treven and take both of us to Belial. I'd be stripped of all proof before we even got close to Medora, and Father wouldn't listen. Belial would win.

That wasn't something I was going to let happen. And as much as I didn't want to kill, I wasn't going to stand there and let someone be murdered.

I ducked under the man's blade and swung underneath his arm. He jumped back, surprised at my attack. I grinned without any mirth and closed the distance between us.

Taking the offensive, I rained blows down on him as quickly as I could, hoping to catch him unprepared.

He scrambled to get away, but I kept pressing him back. My whole body ached from the effort, and my mind screamed that it was wrong to kill. But I focused on what the soldier was going to do next. He quickly blocked one of my thrusts, spun, and struck low.

I jumped in the air, only to land while he drove his blade straight at my heart. I pushed it aside with my sword, but I heard the fabric tear. When I glanced down, I saw a cut in the shirt.

I stared at the slice close to my heart, shocked at how close my own death had come. The soldier laughed maliciously and slashed at my face. I stepped back but tripped over my feet in dumb terror. As I dodged, I stumbled and fell onto the dirt, sitting with my feet in front of me.

My sword dropped out of my hand and clattered to a stop a few feet away. The soldier stopped with his sword a few inches from my face. All I could do was stare at the silver blade.

Mabon chuckled with his sword pointing at Treven's heart. "Well, the little prince came to rescue you and got caught himself."

Rev cried out and started toward me.

"Hold, girl!" Mabon ordered, his voice sharp like a whip. "One more step and the old man dies."

Rev hesitated. "Please, let us go," she pleaded. "We're not doing anything wrong."

Mabon ignored her. "Rough him up a bit, Trynt. Belial ordered alive, but he didn't say anything about a few bruises. Let him know the price of murdering a good soldier. Then come finish the old man."

The soldier nodded. I saw the blade flash and pulled back, but the flat of the blade caught me across the cheek. I yelled as I brought up my arms as defense.

The soldier growled and kicked me hard in the stomach. I gasped for air as he whacked me on the head again. And as the world started to go black, I heard Rev screaming.

CHAPTER SIXTY-SEVEN

Homeless Bandit

The blackness began to cover everything I saw. I felt myself slowly falling to the ground. Rev's scream increased, and I fought the darkness that threatened to overcome me.

Trynt was walking back to Mabon and Treven. Rev was still motionlessness in the middle of the road, obviously torn between me and Treven.

I glanced to my right. My sword was only a foot away. I watched Trynt while I reached for it. My hand grasped dirt and small rocks until I felt the cool of the hilt. I seized it and leaped to my feet.

"Leave him alone!" I shouted at Mabon.

Trynt turned, his sword hanging loosely in his hand. He jumped back and brought his blade up, but I'd had enough of this fight.

I slashed at him, ducked to thrust, and brought the sword around to catch him under his arm. The air went out of him as he dropped to the ground.

I refused to think about him or what I had done as I rushed across the road to Mabon.

"You're mighty good at beating up someone twice as old as you. How good are you, really?" I sneered.

"Better than you, Prince." Mabon made my royal title sound like an insult. "Don't get over confident. You're fighting for real now."

I laughed. "A real warrior wouldn't harm someone like Treven."

"Is that what your daddy taught you, little king?" Mabon scoffed. "Is he a warrior? He can't even keep his crown!"

I yelled and attacked. Mabon effortlessly blocked my wildly swinging sword. I let him think I was attacking out of pure rage, made careless through my anger.

I wanted him to grow confident and press me down the road. I needed to draw him away from Treven and Rev to give her the chance to tend to Treven.

Mabon fell for my plan. He took the offensive, blocking my wide swings easily, and pushed me down the road.

He was quick, much more so than I had thought he'd be. My arm was already tired. But stopping Mabon's vicious blows made it shake, and my fingers cramped as they struggled to grip the hilt.

Father was right. I wasn't ready. One practice session a day was nothing compared to a real fight. A duel didn't have the panic of trying to stay alive, the dirty tricks of the opponent, or the fear for people you loved.

Through Mabon's swinging blade, I saw that my plan was working. When we had moved away from them, Rev ran to Treven and laid him on the ground. I saw her get some bandages and cut his

shirt off. A sense of relief came over me as I
dodged another blow.

A searing pain shot through my right arm. I
instinctively grabbed it with my left hand as I
quickly backed out of Mabon's range. I could feel
warm liquid on my fingers. When I pulled my
hand away, I saw blood on it.

"Oh, the little prince bleeds." Mabon paused in
his attack. "Ever seen yours before? Or have you
always made other men bleed for you? I'd wager
all my coins this is your first time in a real fight. It's
not hard to win when your opponent knows he has
to let you win." He spat in the dirt.

I growled as the blood trickled down my arm. I
wasn't sure if I could strike with any force with that
arm, but his words stung more than the wound.
Patrin hadn't let me win. Had he? I fought back
the growing doubt. But Father's words kept
coming back to me.

Mabon grinned as he watched me. A fresh wave
of rage flooded me as I saw his triumph. There was
an eager cruelty in his green eyes. He was enjoying
watching my pain. He wanted to pound me into
the dirt, beat me up and haul me to Belial. He'd
brag for years about how he'd defeated the prince.

I shifted my grip on my sword and tried not to
wince at the pain as I took my stance and waited
for his attack.

He grinned maliciously. "Want more, little
prince? You could give up."

I ignored him. I was done talking. He shrugged
and leaped forward, his blade quicker than I could
see. I refused to step away.

Instead, I leaned to the left to evade his attack and blocked. His eyebrows rose as I didn't give ground, and I saw a hesitation in his movements.

I seized his uncertainty and attacked for the first time. My arm pounded in agony. I aimed high, but he easily stopped my blade. I fought back a cry of pain as our swords met in the air with a shriek of metal on metal. I disengaged my blade and swung low.

Mabon danced out of my reach, closer to the wagon. I pulled back. The danger of him using Rev or Treven as a hostage was too easy. I only hoped that he was enraged enough not to think of that. I had to keep him distracted.

"Maybe you're not man enough to defeat a Prince," I taunted. "You've grown soft attacking old men and little boys."

Mabon took the bait. He yelled, Rev and Treven forgotten, and lunged at me. Now his strikes were wild and unplanned. I fought through the pain and dodged easily.

That was when he made his first mistake. He left an opening. Striking high, he left his right side vulnerable. I swung with all I had.

There was a sound of blades scraping together. My blade cleared and shot under his arm. Mabon gasped, the breath rattling in his throat, and dropped his sword.

I pulled my sword back, sickened by the amount of blood that flowed from him and the look of death on his face. He grasped the wound as he stumbled back. Without a word, he sank to the ground, still trying to breathe.

I forced myself to watch, although everything inside of me was crying to turn away. This would be my punishment. I deserved to see what I had done so that I'd never want to do it again.

The urge to stop his bleeding was overwhelming. The cold, detached part of me knew that even if I did, he'd die a slow death from the poison either way.

Watching Mabon take his last breath was the worst thing I had ever experienced. I'd never seen death before, but knowing that it came from my own hand made the feeling worse. The fact that Mabon was a bully didn't comfort me.

I stepped away only after Mabon drew his last breath. My arm trembled from exertion and pain. The wound on my arm bled profusely, trickling to the hilt of my sword. I stumbled to the wagon, hoping for some rest and care.

Rev stood up from tending to Treven and took in the sight. The wagon's contents were chucked aimlessly across the whole road. The other men lay dead, scattered among the mess. There were puddles of blood from them and Treven.

Her face was white while she held up bloody bandages. She turned to me, her dark eyes wide and frightened. "What have you done?" she breathed. "You killed them all."

I could've taken her yelling at me. I could've taken her beating me up with accusations and berating me for doing something stupid. But the contempt and horror in her voice disarmed me in a way that the three soldiers couldn't.

I paused on the side of the road and heaved. My stomach refused to hold food any longer. After it was empty, I turned to Rev. She ignored me as she examined the closest man.

"They're all dead," she said as she blinked back tears. "You didn't have to kill them."

"I didn't...I mean...I..." I couldn't speak anymore. I collapsed to the ground, my knees unable to hold me up a minute longer. I hid my eyes in my left hand and tried to hold back the tears that threatened to fall.

Rev huffed at me and swung back to Treven. He softly groaned as she finished wrapping his wounds. I sat in the dirt of the road, surrounded by the mess and dead bodies, trembling from shock and pain, and wondered who I had become.

Had I traded being a Prince to being some homeless bandit who killed others to get what he wanted?

CHAPTER SIXTY-EIGHT

Too Far for Friends

"We've got to get moving," Rev ordered a bit later, her words emotionless. "And you've got to help."

I jumped back to the present. I didn't know how long I had sat there, lost in my bleak thoughts. I nodded, knowing she was right.

When I stood up, I found that the injury on my arm was even worse now. I thought about asking Rev for help, but she was gathering anything that might still be useful from the road.

The look on her face told me that she didn't want to have anything to do with me. Her coldness pierced my heart more than I ever thought it could. I'd taken her friendship for granted, and now that it was gone, I realized how much it meant to me.

I picked up a roll of bandages and stripped off my shirt. When I'd cleaned the blood out, I could see the cut went across my whole arm from side to side. I examined it for a minute, but as I pried at it, the pain took away my breath. I quickly wrapped it up and slipped my shirt back on.

I helped Rev clean up what was salvageable. She never once looked at me. Even as we helped

Treven into the bed in the back of the wagon, she made sure we never touched.

As we lowered Treven into the bed, I noticed how white his face was. As soon as he was settled, Rev stormed out of the wagon. I hesitated.

"Are you all right?" I asked, thinking that was the dumbest question ever.

He nodded slowly. "Just in pain."

"Thanks for what you did." I awkwardly patted his shoulder.

"You saved my life." Treven took my hand and squeezed it. "Killing was a terrible price, but those men would've killed us. Don't agonize over what you did."

I swallowed and winced. "I didn't know what else to do. I think Rev hates me now."

"Death affects everyone differently." Treven spoke slowly like it took a great effort to form the words. "Give her time. She'll come around. Others will be looking for those three. The time for hiding is gone. It's time for running."

He was right. When they didn't return, more soldiers would be sent. It wouldn't take much for them to piece together what had happened. We had to get to safety. But as I stepped down from the wagon, I didn't know where safety was.

"Adoyni," I breathed quietly so Rev wouldn't hear. "I need help. I don't have anywhere to go, and there's no one to help me. I haven't ever cared about the people I was supposed to protect, but if You help me now, I promise I'll do everything I can to set things right for them. I can't do this on my own."Knowing Adoyni was in control, I sighed and smiled slightly.

"Like what you see?" Rev asked, her voice dripping with scorn.

I shook myself. "That's not what I was smiling at," I said quickly. "It was..."

"Never mind." She pushed a shovel in my hand. "Time to get your hands dirty, prince."

"Rev," I broke in. "I didn't want to kill them, but they were going to kill Treven and probably you, too. And who knows what Belial was planning. I had to."

She refused to look at me. "I don't want to talk about it. Let's dig the graves off the road where they'll be harder to find. Come on."

It dawned on me why there was a shovel in my hand. I paused. She took small steps and glanced back at me. I cleared my throat. "We can't bury them, Rev. We've got to get moving. More will be coming."

Her jaw dropped, and I saw a flash of anger as she finally looked at me. "You've got to be kidding! You want to leave them lying here? That's barbaric!"

"We can move them off the road."I shifted the shovel to my left hand as my arm began to throb from its weight. "But we've got to go. Now."

"Of all the...the..." Rev stuttered. Then her anger turned to a full blaze. "Who do you think you are? You think you can take what you want, even someone's life. But that's not true."

"I know I haven't been who I should've been," I yelled back. "And maybe if I was more of that kind *of person, this never would've happened. But I can't change the past, and the only way to fix everything that's gone wrong is to get away from the other soldiers. I can't do that if I'm digging graves."*

Rev didn't look convinced. There was a moment of silence as she regarded me. "Can we at least get them off the road?"

I nodded, and we began to move the bodies. My arm ached from the heavy weight of them as we carried them into the brush. I groaned as we lifted the last one.

Rev gave me a sharp look. "Maybe you'll remember that pain next time you want to play soldier."

I lost it. I was sick with worry about Treven, combined with the pain in my arm and dealing with her hostile attitude. "I didn't want to kill them. It made me sick, and I never want to do it again, but I'm not going to apologize for defending Treven and you."

Rev stepped back as my voice rose to a shout. "You never apologize about anything!" She spun around and stalked off, leaving me speechless.

I looked back at the road. Even with the bodies gone, a blind person could see what happened. Garbage and blood were littered all over the road, and our footprints told the tale of the fights. We didn't have time to clean it up.

Rev stopped in the middle of the road. Her tone was sharp. "Let's go. Maybe they'll stop and bury the...the men. I don't suppose you know how to drive a wagon, do you?"

I shook my head. I rode in carriages, but it wasn't proper for the Crown Prince to drive. She huffed and climbed to the wagon seat. I hesitated. Would she attack me if I sat beside her? Or would it tick her off more to have me ride Kaspar?

She noticed my indecision. "Oh, ride him for once and get it over with. I know you're dying to. Just take care of him."

I nodded. I would treat him like precious dining china to avoid more wrath from her. As I mounted, Kaspar snorted and pranced a little but quickly settled down. Snowball glanced back at Rev with one ear to the rear like she was put out that Treven wasn't driving.

Rev ignored the white mare as she picked up the reins and slapped them gently on Snowball's back. The horse started forward, hesitantly at first, and then settled down to her slow pace.

I rode beside the wagon at first. It felt better to be close to someone, even if we weren't talking, than to be alone with my thoughts. I couldn't see or hear Treven, but every so often, Rev checked on him over her shoulder.

The farther we went, the more I wished she would at least look at me. I knew I wasn't what I should have been. I should have been the type of prince that served my people, instead of taking.

I should have done a lot of things differently.

Would Rev forgive me if I apologized, or had things gone too far for that?

CHAPTER SIXTY-NINE

Looking Back

I couldn't bring myself to apologize to Rev. I was too scared that she'd spurn my attempts at trying to fix our problems or laugh at me. We plodded along for what seemed like days, but I knew from the sun's position that not much time passed.

I found myself continually resisting the urge to get Snowball to move faster. My impatience grew so much it overtook the throbbing in my arm.

"I'm going to go back for a minute," I finally broke the silence. "To see if anyone's following or not."

Rev nodded. Although she looked pretty calm, her long hair was messed up, there was still dirt and blood on her face, and her eyes held a deep sadness. "Be careful. Don't be seen."

"I won't." I whirled Kaspar around and cantered back the way we had come. Once we turned the corner, I let him run as fast he could. The wind seemed to push all my dark thoughts away as we ate up the ground. After a few minutes, I remembered Rev's caution and pulled him down to a walk.

If I recalled correctly, there was a small cliff ahead that would overlook the road we were on. After a few minutes, the trees parted, and I saw the road far below me. I got off Kaspar and crept to the edge of the cliff.

The countryside lay below like a map. I scanned the area where I thought we'd hidden the bodies. I could see a group of people milling around, hustling back and forth. I caught sight of bright copper hair. Nighthawk had arrived.

My heart sank. They were not that far behind us, but I tried to reassure myself that maybe burying the bodies would slow them down, and we could get some distance between them. Maybe we'd make it to Lord Fariel before any more people caught up with us.

Soldiers were stirring around with their horses fidgeting at the smell of death. It looked unorganized, unlike the normal behavior of soldiers. It looked like they were waiting for something rather than taking any action.

On the side of the road, there was a flash of light as blinding as lightning. The soldiers turned away and shielded their eyes, but Nighthawk strode toward it quickly. From the light, a large golden door materialized. It opened, and I saw an expansive mountain range behind it.

A man stepped out, dressed in a black cloak and carrying a long staff. It was black like his cloak, but I caught the sparkle of a crystal at the top of it.

Belial. He was here.

My heart began to race. All I could think about was hiding or running far away from him. It was irrational. I should have been glad to confront him out here away from the royal castle, away from others, but I didn't want to face him at all.

Nighthawk and Belial held a huddled conference, and Nighthawk seemed to be doing most of the talking. When she stopped, Belial spoke briefly and then snapped his fingers. A soldier who was standing close by with a large black horse stepped forward and gave Belial the reins.

Belial mounted swiftly and pulled up his hood on the cloak as Nighthawk shook her head and spoke again. I could see Belial laugh. He said one more thing and spurred the horse forward. It was clear what had happened.

Belial was coming after us alone, and she didn't want him to. But he thought us so little of a threat that he laughed at her warning.

My apprehension boiled into anger. Who did he think he was? He thought of me as a spoiled prince, but I was a warrior. Didn't he know what I had done to his soldiers?

I peered down to watch his progress toward me. Belial seemed to sense my gaze, for after a moment, he stopped the horse. He lowered his hood and stared up to me.

I leaped back but instantly felt foolish for thinking that he'd be able to see me. Fighting my fears, I crept back to the edge and peeked over again.

Belial was staring right at me. I froze, knowing from Cedric's stories that movement only caught attention, and there was no possible way he could pick me out of the rocks, brush and trees around. I forced myself to breathe and calm down to think better.

Then he slowly raised his arm and pointed straight at me. I gasped. He knew! But it was impossible. After a long time, he dropped his arm and spurred his horse. It leapt into a run up the hill.

I bolted back to Kaspar and grabbed the reins. They tangled in my hurry. I growled as I untwisted them and jumped on the horse's back.

As I raced back to Rev, all I could think about was Belial pointing right at me. He had found me. All my attempts had failed.

"Oh, Adoyni, why won't You help me?" I groaned as I pushed Kaspar faster.

CHAPTER SEVENTY

Set Things Right

I pushed Kaspar hard back to Rev, not bothering to worry about whether I was running him too hard or not. Kasper's long legs caught up to the wagon quickly, and I pulled him to a sudden halt beside Rev.

The bay horse dropped his head and breathed deeply. I felt suddenly bad for the sweat I could see on his neck. Rev glanced over, surprised at my quick return.

"It's Belial." I said before she could lecture me about Kaspar. "He's right behind us."

She sucked in her breath in surprise. "Was he alone?"

I scanned the road for a place to hide. The plateau we were on was flat and bare. Small bushes dotted the landscape, but there were no trees to conceal the wagon.

"There's nowhere to hide." I knew I was panicking, but I couldn't control it. "What are we going to do? He's going to find us!"

Rev gave the sword at my hip a scornful glance. "You were fine with those other men. Why not do to Belial what you did to them?"

"You don't understand," I snapped. "He's not just one man. And if he fights, he's not going to use a sword. I don't think he even carries a sword. He'll fight a different way, and I can't do anything against that!"

"What in Adoyni's earth are you talking about?" Rev's face was a mixture of confusion and disgust. "How else would he fight?"

"He'll use..." I hesitated. It sounded weird even to me. I swallowed and started again. "He'll use magic. I've seen it."

Rev's face grew white and she clutched Snowball's reins tighter. "It will be fine." But there was no conviction in her words. "We'll hurry and hopefully get to some trees before he gets here." She slapped Snowball's back with the reins until the white pony broke into a fast trot.

I didn't say anything as I watched the road behind us, but I knew Belial was coming fast. We didn't have time to find a place to hide. Maybe he wanted to talk. But I knew that wasn't the case.

We made it a short ways when I turned back to study the road behind me. It stretched straight behind us for a long while. As I watched, Belial rounded the corner. Seeing us, the horse sped up faster, like a hound to its prey. I swallowed at the comparison.

"He's seen us," I informed Rev.

She pulled Snowball down to a walk. Running was futile now. "What are we going to do?" The scorn and disdain was gone from her voice. Fear replaced it.

"I don't know," I admitted. "But I'll think of something."

Her look of skepticism irritated me.

"I'm still the Crown Prince," I said defensively. "Even if the present company seems to forget that fact."

Rev smiled weakly. "I'm afraid he forgets that fact, too." She pointed back at Belial, who was growing larger by the second.

I winced. I didn't need that reminder right now. "How's Treven?"

"I checked on him after you left." She shook her head. "His breathing is shallow, and his bandages were soaked with blood. We'll have to change them soon if he doesn't..." Her voice broke, and she didn't finish her sentence.

I shuddered. Through my fear and anger, I was sorry Rev got mixed up in this. It wasn't fair to put her in this situation when she was already worried about her mother and their estate. It was time for me to start setting things right.

"We'll deal with whatever Belial wants and then stop for the night," I decided. "All the swaying and bumping in the wagon can't be good for Treven. We know enough to stop the bleeding. Everything will be okay." I tried to put conviction into my words, but I failed brilliantly.

Rev nodded. I was saddened to see that the usual fury she possessed was missing. She was tired of running, tired of struggling. In place of anger, there was worry and fear in her expression. She looked like she was trying to believe what I had said but couldn't do it.

Glancing back, I saw that Belial had gained on us. It would only take a few minutes for him to catch us. I pointed ahead to a small meadow on the side of the road. "Let's stop there. We'll see what he wants. Maybe we could camp there for the night and take care of Treven."

She nodded again and pulled Snowball to a stop in the middle of the meadow. The white horse snorted through her nose and began eating the grass at her feet.

I debated for a few seconds about staying on Kaspar but finally decided that it didn't matter. I wasn't going to abandon Rev or Treven.

I slipped off, scratched Kaspar's neck, and threw his reins over the front wheel of the wagon. There was enough time to check on Treven.

It was dim inside the wagon, but there was enough light to see that his skin was a deathly white while the bandages were dark red. His skin was cool and clammy to the touch. As I felt his forehead, his eyes flickered open.

"Take it easy," I whispered. "We're taking a break for a few minutes to rest the horses." There was no need to worry him about Belial. "Keep resting."

He nodded and closed his eyes. I knew Belial was getting close and didn't want Rev to have to confront him alone, but it broke my heart to leave Treven in that shape.

As I tried to convince myself that Treven would be okay for a few minutes and that I could deal with Belial, the doubts that I didn't show Rev pushed any confidence I had aside.

These were problems that were too great for me to handle. I wished that Father was here. He'd know what to do to keep everyone safe. I should've paid attention to him when he tried to teach me how to rule.

I jumped to the ground and caught a glimpse of Rev. The sight of her gave me some hope. I wasn't alone. Maybe together we could actually pull this off.

Belial slowed his horse to a walk when he approached the meadow. He wore no weapon, other than the long black staff that he carried. I saw the white crystal entwined in the staff like it had grown around the gem.

He stopped a few yards away from the wagon and regarded the pair of us without speaking for a minute. Then he leaped from his horse and came closer.

"Nice work with the soldiers. I assume that it was you, Prince Aric, who killed them." Belial's words dripped with acid.

I was stunned by the raw hatred in his words and gripped the hilt of my sword. Rev kept quiet beside me.

"I sent them to see what you'd do, but I didn't really think you had it in you to actually kill them," Belial continued. "It seems like even kittens have claws."

I thought about drawing my sword. He surely wasn't here to talk. But I hesitated, waiting to see what he wanted.

"By now, you should realize I can track you and your family anywhere with very simple, how should

I say this, techniques. I thought your father would be the difficult one, but you certainly have caused the most trouble. No matter, though. I think this works better. The rebellious Prince runs away. The King sickens. On his death bed, broken from sorrow over his son, he does the only thing he can think of. He appoints his loyal Chancellor as king."

"You wouldn't." I couldn't keep the words back. "You vile..."

Belial laughed and turned to Rev. "Unfortunately for you, girl, you decided to leave that dungeon cell. I would have let you out at some point. But you chose to go with the Prince. I can't have anyone around that knows what happened to him, so you must die, too."

"You can't kill us," Rev protested, although she didn't sound too convincing.

Belial chuckled, clearly enjoying this moment. "Both of you are going to disappear forever. Then I will take over Eltiria. It's a shame you won't see the new era I shall begin."

"You'll not take the throne! Not while I have anything to say about it!" I yelled and pulled my sword.

Before it was clear of the scabbard, Belial swung his staff at my head. I saw a flash of wood before it smashed against my temple and threw me to the ground. I lay in the grass, groaning. Rev screamed from what seemed to be far away.

Belial stood over me with his staff poised. "You won't have any say about anything in a few minutes."

And then he struck again.

CHAPTER SEVENTY-ONE

Pinned

I curled up into a ball as Belial stood over me and beat me with his long staff. All I could do was endure his attack. The hatred behind his blows shocked me as I yelped from the pain. I prayed for him to stop, for a chance to breathe, and then at one miraculous moment, he did.

I gulped air and rolled away from his feet. As I did, Rev screamed again, and I saw her run toward Belial. I pushed off the ground to stand up, not wanting her to get hurt.

But my arms and legs didn't work. I pressed harder although it was futile. I couldn't move. In a panic, I tried to roll farther away. That failed, too.

I was pinned to the ground by an invisible force, made to watch Rev take on Belial alone. I roared in frustration. Belial never even glanced at me. When she was close, he held up his staff like it was shield in front of him. Rev stopped like she had run into a wall, and then her body lifted off the ground.

Belial smirked at Rev dangling in the air. I struggled to break whatever held me, but nothing worked.

"What did you think you were going to do, little girl?" he sneered. "Protect your dear little Prince?"

"I'll tear your eyes out," Rev threatened. Although she struggled to break free, she was as trapped as I was.

"You have courage," Belial's voice changed from scorn to thoughtfulness. "Swear allegiance to me, and I'll spare your life." His words were silky. "I am a good Master to those that serve me."

Rev paused like she was considering what he proposed. She glanced at me in the dust. I desperately tried to shake my head, but I was paralyzed.

"You will do great things and have power," Belial continued, jerking Rev's attention back to him. "And your family and estate? I'll give you the ability to heal your Mother and give the cure to the disease for anyone who lives on your Father's estate. A few simple words and all your problems will be over."

Rev hung in the air, now alive with hope. I wanted to shout out a warning not to believe Belial and struggled again against the unseen bonds that held me, growing angrier when my tongue didn't work.

"What...what about him?" Rev nodded to me, lying in the dirt.

Triumph filled Belial's face. "The monarchy is dead. All of Eltiria is calling out for a new era. Wouldn't you rather be on the winning side?"

Rev's feet reached for the ground as she considered his words. I knew that she was almost convinced. I stared at her, trying to communicate with my eyes that he was a liar, but she barely glanced at me.

"And my family?" She asked in a whisper.

"They will be under my protection," he promised. He stepped closer, within arm's reach away of her. "Swear allegiance and all will be well."

Rev hesitated again, weighing his words. Her eyes barely flickered my way as she dangled in the air. "All will be well," she repeated slowly. Then she took a deep breath. "Except for the fact that we'll be serving an evil, heartless tyrant who'd wreck the world to gain something for himself." She pulled back her arm and punched him hard in the face.

I wanted to cheer as Belial jerked back, taking the full force on his cheek. He stumbled and yelled in anger. Then he swung his staff through the air.

Rev whipped through the air back toward the wagon. She crashed into the wooden frame and crumpled to the ground, landing with her left arm twisted strangely under her.

I yelled in anger and pushed against my bonds. To my surprise, I shot to my feet. Belial's hold on me had vanished during his assault on Rev. I didn't give him time to bind me again as I launched myself at him.

CHAPTER SEVENTY-TWO

Pummeling

Belial didn't see me as he watched Rev fly through the air and smash into the wagon. I crashed into him with my full weight. Belial staggered and fell to his knees before tumbling into the dirt. I let myself go with him, letting him take the brunt of the plunge. I heard him grunt as the air went out of him.

Grinning with triumph, I got to my knees over his body and pummeled him with my fists as hard as I could. Through my rage, I didn't even bother aiming for weak spots as Patrin always taught. I was too intent on driving Belial into the dust and being done with him.

Belial yelled and struggled as I beat him. I felt a wave of victory sweep over me, and I almost laughed when I thought how scared I had been of him. Defeating him was much easier than I had ever thought. My hands ached from the impact, and my leg throbbed from the fall. I pulled back and punched him hard in the kidneys.

He shouted out a word that I couldn't make out as an invisible hand slammed into my stomach. I fought for my breath as I bent over. Belial shook me off as he got to his feet and kicked me into the dirt. I collapsed onto the ground, struggling for air.

Belial dusted himself off, keeping his staff tight as he stood over me. I swallowed a gulp of air and desperately breathed deeper for more. Belial placed his foot on my leg, right where Mabon's sword had cut it deeply. I twisted to try to shake off his foot, but he pressed harder. I screamed as the pain grew.

"After all the headaches you put me through, I like to hear you scream." Belial smiled coldly.

I wanted to stop yelling, but I couldn't. The pain in my leg shot up and down through my whole body. I barely heard his words over my agony.

He pressed harder. "You never grasped who I am, thinking you could play your little games with me. You have no idea what I've done or who I am. I have conferred with Seiten, who has given me more power than you could ever conceive."

All I wanted was for the pain to stop. I thrashed with my free leg and arms, frantic to ease the pain. Belial watched me with a sneer on his face and then reached down and took the book I had stolen from him out of my pocket. Then he pushed harder on my wound as he put the book in his cloak.

"This book wouldn't have done you much good, even if you had tried to use it. I hope you realize by now that I will win," Belial jeered. "I will kill you and that worthless girl, and then I'll kill your father. I may let your mother live, depending on how receptive she is to my reign. But if I decide to let her live, she'll live serving me, her master."

I wanted to yell at him. I wanted to fight back. I wanted to pound his face in the dust. All I could do was lie there in torment and listen to his bragging. I struggled but to no avail. His foot pressing hard on my wound tied me down more securely than his invisible bonds had.

Through the dots of darkness that threatened to take over, I saw Belial's head jerk forward. A stone then smashed into his shoulder. The agony in my leg eased as he fought to catch his balance.

In the reprieve, I turned my head to see Rev sitting on the ground with a pile of stones beside her, throwing them at Belial with her right hand while her left arm hung awkwardly by her side.

Belial stepped away from me as another rock hit him in the legs. I grinned, despite the throbbing, remembering the force behind those pinecones she had chucked at me.

Rev continued to pelt him. Belial moved away from me as he tried to protect his head from the large rocks being heaved at him.

She chose a large one and threw it with as much strength as she had. It flew gracefully through the air. He didn't see it coming with his arms over his eyes. It dropped toward the earth and smashed into his head. He stumbled once and dropped to the ground.

Rev leaped to her feet, stumbled away from the wagon, and lurched to where my sword was lying in the grass. She hefted the blade and threw it awkwardly at me. "Kill him," she ordered as she threw the blade to me.

"I thought you didn't want me to kill anyone." I protested as the blade fell close to my hand. I gripped the hilt and felt instantly better. "You can't keep changing your mind."

She hesitated and glanced at Belial, who was sitting on the ground. "Just one more," she said.

I wasn't sure if I could get up. Pushing myself up to my knees, I used my sword as a cane and weakly got to my feet. My good leg trembled as blood ran down my left leg.

Belial pushed himself up with a great effort. "You are persistent. Not that it will do you any good." He reached down and picked up the largest rock by his feet. "Let's see how persistent you are with the girl gone."

Before I could react, he hurled the rock back at Rev with more force than the strongest of men. It whipped through the air faster than I could see. Rev's head flew back as it smashed into her forehead. She didn't say a word or make a sound.

She sank to the ground and didn't move.

CHAPTER SEVENTY-THREE

Crushed

"Rev!" I limped over to her as quickly as I could. Her hair had come loose and covered her face. As I approached, I couldn't even tell if she was breathing or not. I prayed over and over for her not to be dead. "Rev!"

I was almost to her when a searing pain ripped through my back and spread throughout my whole body. I screamed as I fought to maintain my balance on my one good leg, but it shook like it was a dead leaf barely hanging onto the tree in a strong wind.

I tightened my grip on the hilt, and I felt it digging into my palm. But those things were distant, happening far away to someone else. All that I was aware of was the intense pain that took over every thought and sense. All I could hope for was that it would stop.

It finally did. I remained standing, my scream continuing as the pain slowly faded and my limbs stopped shaking. I spotted a large boulder close to me. Was that what had hit me? Gasping deeply to fight back the pain, I turned away from Rev's lifeless body to face Belial.

He stood with his staff in his hand like a scepter. His black robes were spotted with dust from Rev's stones, but not a hair was out of place. He wore a slight smile that held only malice, and his dark eyes were cold.

"If we're going to throw things, I thought I'd join in the fun," he scoffed.

A box shifted in the wagon and launched itself at me with tremendous force and speed. I barely dodged it. Belial laughed as a pot from inside the wagon quickly flew at me.

I whirled and struck it aside with my sword. It clanged as it hit my blade and bounced at Belial. He growled as more contents of the wagon began to pelt me. Books, blankets, jars of food and more came at me faster than I could dodge.

I yelled as the rain of Treven's stuff bombarded me. I blocked my head with my arms, but a small chest smashed into my shoulder and threw me to the ground. I crawled away from the wagon, trying to escape the torrent. Then, without warning, it ended.

Belial was panting like he had exerted himself. I grabbed my sword and pushed myself to my feet. The ground around me was littered by all of Treven's supplies and goods. Years of gathering herbs and medicine were wasted. Jars of food carefully canned and preserved for the future smashed for no good reason.

Seeing Treven's ruined items, knowing he was dying, filled me with a kind of fury that I'd never imagined. My whole body ached in ways I'd never known, but I forced myself to ignore it. I had to get to Belial and stop him. Then I'd rest.

I stumbled toward him. "Run out of things to throw? Maybe now you'll have to fight."

"There's one thing left, Prince," he said scornfully. "Too bad the girl is in the way. I don't think she'll survive."

He raised his staff and pointed at the wagon. The far wheels on the right creaked like they were moving. I blinked. Surely I was seeing things. The wheels on the left inched up slightly.

He was going to tip over the wagon! I gasped. He had the power to move something so heavy! I watched, strangely fascinated, as the wagon began to sway back and forth. Was he going to actually tip it over? As the wheels on each side cleared more air, I realized that he was.

Rev was still lying on the ground unconscious. I gasped as the wheels on our side rocked high enough that I could've crawled under them. It was going to fall over and land on Rev. I dashed to pull her to safety.

The wagon swayed closer to me when I reached Rev. I had to get her out of here before it crashed down on top of us. I knelt down beside her and glanced up. The wagon was teetering on the rims of the wheels. A small breath of wind, and it would be on us.

I grabbed Rev's arms and pulled. She was heavier than I imagined. Despite my efforts, she only moved a couple of inches. I yelled as I jerked her again. The wagon was swaying back to the other side.

I silently prayed for it to fall that way as I tugged Rev. Fall that way! I didn't know how far I'd have to go, but I knew I wasn't even close to being out of its range.

The far wheels landed on the ground with a loud clatter. I saw the canvas continue to rock away from us. I had a little time before it swayed our direction again.

I tugged on Rev's lifeless body, worried that I may hurt her by pulling on her, but I didn't know what else I could do. Her head flopped forward and bobbed with each of my yanks.

The wagon settled on its wheels again on its way back to us. I heaved on Rev harder and made it a few more inches.

Belial said a word I didn't catch, and the wagon started to fall toward me.

It didn't stop.

CHAPTER SEVENTY-FOUR

Defeat

Before the wagon could fall on us, I jerked Rev as hard as I could, tripping over my feet as I struggled to get out of the way. The wagon wavered on the rim of two wheels for a breath before smashing to the ground.

I saw it coming and gave Rev one last heave. As I fell, I pulled her up and over me. The dust flew up in the air in a giant cloud as the wagon hit. Over the thud, I heard a whinny of pain coming from Snowball, but I couldn't do anything about her yet.

I shoved Rev off, relieved to see that we had managed to escape being crushed by the wagon, if only by inches.

Rev tumbled to the ground limply. I couldn't take the time to check on her as I swung to my feet, for I realized that Treven was in even greater danger. Belial looked surprised as he tumbled out of the wagon and rolled clear. I couldn't tell if he still lived or not.

Belial strode over to him and used one of his feet to turn him on his back. Treven rolled over, his hand flying wide and limp. I saw blood soaking the front of his shirt.

Belial regarded him for a minute and then
recognition hit him. "I remember him!" He poked
him with the toe of his boot. "He's the healer from
Vesmir that escaped. I thought the grief of what
happened to his family killed him." He laughed
shortly. "How strange you two would meet." He
snorted. "How strange that after all these years, I'd
get to kill him."

"You're not going to kill him," I panted. "I
won't let you!"

I flew at him with my sword, ready to strike. He
stepped away from Treven and waited for me to
come. As I swung high at him, he spoke softly, and
his staff glowed hot. Red lightning sparked from
his hand to the crystal as he blocked my attack.

When the staff met my blade, the red lightning
ran down the blade and up my arm. The force of
the bolt shook the sword out of my hand as I
shrieked with the resounding pain spreading from
my arm to my feet. It filled my head and echoed
through my skull. It continued down through my
heart, causing it to beat irregularly.

As it flowed down my legs, it made my wound
shriek with pain. I shook with the impact and fell
to the ground, curling up in a ball, tossing and
turning, unable to stop yelling.

When I thought I couldn't take another second
before the anguish gained complete control and
my heart exploded, the red lightning disappeared.
I lay in the dust, gasping for air, disgusted by my
groveling, but there was nothing I could do. I
couldn't fight lightning.

Despair filled my heart when I thought of Rev lying helplessly in the dirt. Was she dead? What would Belial do to her once he was finished with me? What would happen to Treven? I had lost. I gulped back the sobs and thought of my parents.

I was so sorry that I was not the kind of son and prince I should've been. I should've listened when they tried to teach me. I should've told them every day that I loved them. But now it was too late.

"This is how you wanted it, isn't it? You as the hero, bringing me to your daddy for punishment? Think you suffered at my hand earlier? Now the spoiled prince will see what suffering really is." Belial chuckled as he moved between me and the wagon.

My heart lurched as I thought of Treven unable to protect himself. I forced myself to my knees and reclaimed my sword. Although it was as useless against magic as a piece of ribbon in a sword fight, I felt better with it in my hand.

If I could get to Belial without touching his staff, then maybe I had a chance. With an effort that took all of my strength, I stood up, barely able to ignore the throbbing in my leg as the blood streaked down to my ankle. I barely had the strength to hold my sword, much less raise it.

"Your schemes will fail." My voice shook, but I took a deep breath and continued. "Adoyni will not let you succeed. He'll cause others to rise up against you. Kill me if you want, but you will be torn down and brought to justice." I took a tentative step forward.

Belial burst out laughing. As abruptly as his laughter began, it ended. His voice was hard. "Believe what you want, Prince. No matter what you think, Adoyni has lost His power, and this world will be mine to control."

My wounded leg threatened to collapse under me, but I made it through one more step.

"My reign will wipe out all mention of Adoyni's name. I will be a god-king who reigns with a hard fist. The whole world will bow to me and serve my command," Belial gloated.

I hardly heard what he was saying. Walking took all the strength and concentration I had. I was sweating so badly that I was terrified I'd drop my sword. My leg almost collapsed every time I put any weight on it. The rest of my body ached.

I prayed that I'd have the strength for one good hard swing at Belial. One good hit was all I needed. Even if I died, at least Belial would be dead, too.

Five steps away. A small burst of hope flowed through me, giving me extra strength. I stumbled forward.

Belial watched me. "But first I will kill you. And then I'll kill your friends."

Lightning flew out of the staff again. It was faster than before and struck me hard in the chest. Some part of Patrin's training must have been embedded in my mind as my arm instinctively blocked the staff.

The lightning trickled down my blade again and jarred my teeth, but this time some of it bounced off the steel and flew through the air back at Belial.

It missed him. I didn't have time to respond. Disappointment flooded me like a large dam breaking. I collapsed to the ground as he held the staff on my chest. The lightning licked its way through my mind.

I heard myself screaming as I grasped as the dirt and grass in a desperate attempt to get away from it. Over the sound of my voice, I heard laughter from Belial.

Images flashed through my mind. Father laughing as he gave me my sword. Mother reading books to me. Patrin leading out my first pony. Rev throwing pine cones at me. I fought an irrational desire to laugh as the memories of good times came and went. But as they disappeared, the agony that took their places felt worse than before.

My body arched with the force of the attack, and I shrieked even louder. I knew this was the end. The thought brought a wave of relief through me. Belial couldn't hurt me anymore once I was dead. It would be over in a few seconds. I'd be free of the pain.

All I could do was pray. The words circled in my head because my lips couldn't move. "Adoyni, please help us. I know I was wrong to act how I did. I'm sorry I didn't see Your way and chose my own. My heart was rotting away, and I didn't know it. Please help me save Treven and Rev. Please help me kill Belial and stop the evil he's heaping on this land. Even if it means I die. Please help us!"

Behind Belial, I saw the wagon had caught on fire. Smoke billowed high in the air around Treven's body. Somewhere behind me, Rev lay, unconscious, blissfully unaware that we had lost.

My screams grew louder, yet over the sound of my voice, I heard a loud thudding of air. All I could think of was that Belial had summoned a giant bird to carry away our bodies.

The air around me stirred and dust flew into my face. I felt the air pulsating around me in strong beats. Then all grew quiet. The lightning continued to surge through my body as a new panic seared my brain.

What was Belial going to do to me next before he killed me?

CHAPTER SEVENTY-FIVE

Chosen Sacrifice

Through the torment that racked my body, I saw a large black horse standing between me and the wagon. Perhaps my brain was making things up from childhood stories to escape the agony, for this horse had large wings that looked strong and capable of lifting it into the air.

A flying horse. An Archippos. I recalled the stories that I had read when I was young. Archippi were the agents of Adoyni, banished to Merrihaven by one of my ancestors until called back, and there was one alive in front of me.

Rev was right. She had seen a black horse with wings. I glanced at her still lying where she had fallen. There was no sign of whether she lived or not. Would I ever get the chance to tell her that she was right?

The pain increased, driving all thoughts away. I yelled louder as my entire body filled with lightning. My body contorted unwillingly as I thrashed around, frantically trying to escape.

Dark spots grew over my eyes as I began to slip into unconsciousness. A part of me screamed to fight the blackness and stay awake, but there was a

*larger side that welcomed the darkness as a deep
sea of respite from the pain.*

*As I rolled in the dirt and grass, I saw the horse
stamp its right foot. The air shimmered for a few
seconds and snapped into place again. Belial's staff
crackled with the lightning, but the Archippos had
created an invisible shield around me that the
bolts couldn't break through.*

*Belial leaped back and snarled at the horse. I
sat up and stared up at the large black horse. It
shook its wavy mane with a welcoming nicker.*

The shield will block the lightning, Prince Aric.
*A strong man's voice reverberated through my
head.* But not for long. We must flee.

*"What are you? I mean, who are you?" My voice
shook like I hadn't used it for a long time.*

My name's Thalion. *There was a strain in the
voice in my head. However the Archippos had
created the shield, it was causing him a great
effort.* Now get to your feet.

*I instantly obeyed without thinking about it. I
didn't even care about his motives. He was a way to
escape Belial. But as I put pressure on my left leg,
it crumpled underneath me. I fell to my knees
before I could stop myself.*

*I grabbed my sword. Using it as a cane, I was
able to push myself to my feet. As I rose, I found
that although the lightning no longer reached me,
my entire body was still aching from the abuse. I
could hardly move, and it felt like I had no
strength left.*

As I hobbled toward Rev, Belial snarled and shot another bolt of lightning at us. The shield deflected it once again.

"Filthy Archippos," Belial yelled. "I'm surprised you had the nerve to finally show your face. Hiding in the shadows seems more your style."

I paused to see the effect Belial's words would have on Thalion.

The horse twitched one of his finely sculpted black ears. Get Reveka on my back.

I had a strange feeling that only I could hear those words, but before I could say anything, Thalion diverted his attention to Belial. You won't win. Whatever schemes you have, they will fail.

As I stumbled around Thalion, I realized that he was one of the biggest horses I had ever seen. He was also one of the most beautiful with his finely chiseled head, strong neck, wide chest and broad back. The wings added a sense of exotic beauty to him. What would it be like to ride him?

"That's what you believe," Belial snapped. "But no one has had power such as mine."

To prove his point, rocks under his feet flew into the air and launched themselves at the shield that now surrounded Thalion and me.

I found it hard not to duck until I reached Rev. I shoved my sword through my belt and fell to my knees, ignoring the protests throughout my body, and gently rolled her over to her back.

I brushed away her hair from her face, terrified by the strange paleness that had replaced her tan. I felt her throat for a pulse and was relieved to feel a faint beat. But her eyes didn't open.

"Rev?" I asked, tempted to shake her awake. "Rev? Can you hear me?"

Now that I was closer, I could see a slight movement of her chest, telling me that she still breathed. But the relief I felt quickly disappeared as I examined her head. The rock had hit her in the forehead, leaving a deep gash that gushed blood. It soaked her hair and dripped down her cheek. I quickly tore my shirt and wrapped it around her head. She didn't even groan as I pulled it tight.

Hurry, Prince. Thalion pranced sideways as rocks began to overcome the shield and fly toward him. As I watched, a boulder cleared the shield and struck him in the side. He whinnied in pain as he fought to maintain the shield.

I glanced at Belial as he summoned more objects to fling at us. Behind him, the fire on the wagon canvas had overtaken the roof. Its hungry flames began to work its way to the wood. My heart sank for Treven because he'd be engulfed in the fire. I had to find a way to get to the wagon.

But how? And even if I reached Treven, could Thalion take three of us? Someone would have to be sacrificed, but the price was a life. Who was willing to do that?

It was then that I knew exactly what I had to do.

CHAPTER SEVENTY-SIX

Avenged

The meadow was a horrible nightmare. Treven's body was lying close to the overturned wagon that was burning. Belial stood in the middle of Treven's things, throwing anything he could see at Thalion with magical forces.

I looked over at the large Archippos and was surprised to see the streaks of sweat on his chest and flanks. Holding a shield that large must have been costing him greatly.

I swallowed, knowing what I had to do. Belial wanted me above all else. He'd let the others go to get me.

I clumsily got to my feet and tugged on Rev's body. I didn't have the strength to lift her fully but was able to half carry, half drag, her to Thalion. He saw my struggle and met me half way.

Bending a front leg, he partially bowed to give me more of a chance to lift her on his back. I heard more rocks pelting his body as he waited for me to get her leg over him. Once she was set, I stabilized her as he rose.

Belial, enraged at our potential escape, swung his staff to the wagon. I held my breath in fear for Treven. But instead, using his staff, Belial created a fire ball from the flames licking at the wood. The ball rolled away from the wagon, growing in size and heat. Belial laughed cruelly as he suspended it in midair, admiring it. With wicked aim, he launched it straight at Thalion.

Thalion reared and leaped to the side as the shield disappeared. Rev slumped and almost fell off as the fire ball hit Thalion in the chest. The fire latched onto his mane and forelock as smoke filled the air. I heard a twinge of fear in his whinny.

I rushed to him and beat out the flames with my hands. I felt the burn, but ignored it, as I suffocated the fire. But before it was out, Belial sent another fire ball spinning our way. I grabbed Rev as Thalion dodged it.

The jolt must have wakened Rev, for I saw her eyes flicker.

"What...what's happening?" she asked faintly.

"Rev!" I seized my opportunity before she passed out again or died. Words poured out without hesitation. "I'm sorry! I shouldn't have ever tried to steal Kaspar. I was wrong. I was wrong about so much stuff. I treated you horribly. I've treated everyone horribly. I wasn't the type of Prince Adoyni wants me to be. But if we get out of this, I promise I'll be better. I know now that I should serve others and look out for their good. I didn't want to kill those soldiers, but I didn't want you or Treven to die. I'm so sorry. Can we be friends? Please, please forgive me!"

Rev clung at my hand to stay on. "I forgive you! I do! And I'd be honored to be your friend." There was warmth behind her voice, even though *it was weak. She patted my hand gently.* "I'm sorry, too, Aric."

Thalion pranced to the left. *As sweet as this is, can we go now? His voice sounded both irritated and amused.*

"Hang on!" I commanded Rev. *I realized that I'd never apologized to anyone before. I'd said the words, but only as a way to get out of trouble or because Father told me to. I was surprised to feel good.* "I'm getting Treven."

Thalion reared and let out a huge breath of air. Belial stumbled back like a fist had struck him in the chest. He crashed into the wagon, his head close to the fire, before he shook himself and stepped away from the flames.

Get on! There's no time! *Thalion commanded.* I can't protect you two and fight him at the same time!

The black Archippos was right. We were divided, something that Patrin and Cedric always warned about. "I'll get on only if we go to Treven before we leave."

Fine! But get on now! *Thalion ordered.*

I could still work out my plan with Thalion's agreement. Once we got to Treven, I would get him on Thalion and send them off to safety. I knew now that my responsibility as Crown Prince wasn't about sitting in banquets or attending ceremonies.

My place was in between the citizens of Eltiria and anyone who tried to hurt them. We couldn't all get on Thalion, and I was not leaving either Treven or Rev behind with Belial to torture or

murder them. I was putting myself in the place I
always should have been - between evil and safety.
Even if it cost me my life.

I placed my hands on his back and tried to
vault on as I had on the royal horses for years, but
my arms gave out as I placed all my weight on
them. Belial threw fire balls at us in quick
succession.

Thalion evaded them as well as he could
without dropping Rev off his back. But he took the
full force of several. I slapped out the flames on
Rev's leg and tried to get on Thalion again to no
avail.

"Go!" I ordered. "Get her to safety!"

"No!" Rev's voice gained some strength. "Get
on!"

Without you, the monarchy fails. *Thalion
danced to the left and threw another air blast at
Belial. Belial fell against the wagon.* I can't leave
without you.

"And I won't leave without Treven!" I yelled
and followed Thalion, frantically trying, but
failing, to get the strength to leap on him.

If only he'd stand still for a minute, but that
would mean that he would be assaulted by fire and
rocks while I mounted. If those rocks hit me while
I was flying through the air, they would probably
knock me off before I could get settled. We were
trapped. Besides, there was still Treven to rescue.

As I squinted through the smoke, I saw a flash
of metal behind Belial. The flames had burnt away
the fabric and wooden poles that held the canvas
of the wagon in place.

Treven was creeping up behind Belial with a metal bar in his hands like he was ready to swing. I had no idea how he'd had the strength to move, but I could see blood flowing from his wound.

Treven paused and glanced my way. As our eyes met over the flames and smoke, he smiled. Although his face was pale, there was a look of true happiness and peace on his face. Then he shifted his gaze to Belial, the smile quickly fading from his face.

Before I could cry out for him to stop, he swung with all the strength he had left. Belial never even saw it coming. The metal bar arched through the air and smashed into the back of Belial's head. I heard Rev yell behind me.

Belial bent over from the unexpected hit and stumbled away from the wagon, clutching his chest. Treven tightened his grip and prepared to swing again. I lurched forward to the wagon, determined to save Treven.

I hadn't even made it halfway across the meadow when Belial gathered himself. Reaching into his cloak, he pulled out an ornate knife and launched himself at Treven.

Treven didn't struggle as Belial rushed him. At a moment that I thought was too late, he swung. A loud thud filled the air as the metal bar smashed into Belial's head. Belial froze in midair for the briefest of moments and then slumped to the ground.

I ran to Treven, determined to snatch him up and haul him to Thalion, but then I saw the knife buried deep in Treven's heart. Treven dropped the bar and stared at the knife in his chest like he couldn't comprehend what had happened. He wrapped his hands around the hilt but didn't bother to try to pull it out.

He looked at me, his eyes more distant than ever. "My journal. In my pocket. Take it. It has the answer for the disease. The beginning. Don't forget the beginning. My family is avenged," he whispered. Then his eyes went blank, and he dropped to the ground beside Belial.

I yelled and fell down beside him. But even before I rolled his body over, I knew it was too late. He was dead.

"No, Treven." I shook his shoulders. "I was going to die for you. That was my job!"

Prince Aric. Thalion's voice filled my head. We must go now. While we have the chance. In this, we honor Treven's sacrifice.

I wanted to scream at the Archippos. I wanted to argue. But he was right. I turned away from Treven before I stopped.

"Come on!" Rev called. "Belial's waking."

At my feet, Belial was stirring, coming back to consciousness. We had only a few seconds. I searched Treven's pockets, blinking back the tears that began to flow freely. My hand closed on the worn leather, and I stuffed it in my pocket.

I paused before I left Treven's side, even though I heard Belial stirring. I closed his sightless eyes. "Thank you. I'll never forget what you did."

The words sounded empty, not enough, for such a great sacrifice. But they were sincere. I finally complied with Thalion's insistent urgings

and limped over to him. He was standing beside a large boulder. Rev clung weakly to his mane.

Belial got to his knees and started crawling to his staff as I raced past him to Thalion. The horse whinnied as I climbed clumsily onto his back and wrapped my arms around Rev.

I turned back to Belial. "I'll never forget what you have done to my family and to Treven. You will die for all the pain and death you have inflicted upon the citizens of Eltiria. I'll hunt you down myself!"

"Run, little prince," Belial spat back. "And don't come back."

He reached for his staff as Thalion's giant wings began to beat. For a horrible moment, I didn't think Thalion had enough strength left to fly. But as Belial pushed himself up to his feet and swung his staff, Thalion broke into a run, faster and faster until his wings lifted us into the air, and Belial faded to a small dot in the distance.

CONVERGING

"I hope to one day have a reunion with myself."
~STRACHAN DALYEL

Jehun lingered on the edges of Elba Isle. It was an eerie choice by the Archippi who had imprisoned Seiten there. The entire land mass was black from hardened lava.

Heat radiated from it so that the air looked like it was shimmering, alive, and angry. There wasn't one bit of green, not one living thing, among the heaps and piles of molten rock.

He could sense more than see the walls the Archippi had built to keep Seiten on the island. They were almost invisible, but when he stared closely, he could tell where they were.

Placed offshore by a good distance, the waves crashed into the walls with a force that would have destroyed any manmade structures. The walls reached up to the sky, and he lost sight of them in the glaring sun.

How had Belial managed to breach them and speak to Seiten? And then get out? The questions gave Jehun a chill despite the hot air. Belial had more power than Jehun realized.

Jehun remembered the ancient books Belial studied. Was there a gate or door referenced in those

books that Belial found? What else had he found in all those ancient books and parchments that were forgotten by everyone else?

Jehun considered going back without completing his assignment. But what would Belial do to him if he returned without the information? He shuddered.

That thought was almost more frightening than what he was asked to do. He slipped under the walls, deep down in the hidden layers of earth, and crept forward.

As he approached the island, a growing sense of evil permeated everything. It seeped into the water, the air, the rocks that lay deep in the ground. Would it attach to him and leave him as corrupted as Seiten himself?

"Come closer."

The words were deep but rich with warmth and invitation. Jehun froze. He was close enough to see who had spoken. He searched for a form, a shape, on that hardened lava, but there was nothing.

"Ah, Jehun!" Seiten continued. "It's been a long time. I must admit that I'm a bit surprised that you are the one Belial sent. I thought you were with Adoyni."

Jehun didn't know what to say. Should he tell how Adoyni had let him be torn in two? Should he mention that Adoyni seemed to love others more than him? Or that Belial had trapped him and was forcing him into doing things he didn't want to, like talking to Seiten right now?

"It's okay," Seiten crooned. "I understand. I once thought that Adoyni loved me, too. I know what you are going through."

Jehun remembered the stories that told of Seiten being one of Adoyni's chief servants until he rebelled. Suddenly he wondered why Seiten had decided to leave. Jehun searched for a form on the land but saw nothing.

"That is a story for a different time." Seiten responded as if he knew what Jehun was thinking. He returned to his smooth tone. "And now you are here for Belial. Let me guess. He found that I have armies still hidden, waiting for a word to raise them." He paused as if sensing Jehun's reaction.

A chuckle filled the air, and Seiten continued. "I see I'm right." The laughter cut off, and the voice was now sharp and bitter. "I knew Belial was resourceful when he showed up, and I wondered how long it would be until he found out about them."

The voice roared. "My armies! I saved fifty thousand! I hid them where only I can find them. For me to use when I got out of this prison! Not to give away to the first power hungry sorcerer who waltzes in here!"

Jehun could make out a shadow on the far side of the island. He peered through the bright sunlight and could make out the shape of a tall man. The form flickered away each time he was able to focus on it.

"Right after I hid the army, before the Archippi managed to overcome me, one of those infuriating Sentinels found out that I had managed to conceal it. But they haven't been smart enough to find it, even after all these years, and my agents have been very successful in convincing everyone to believe the Sentinels are brainwashed." Seiten laughed. "Imagine their surprise when my army that's right underneath everyone's feet springs up. I'll use the army to enslave them. I've been waiting for hundreds of years for my freedom!"

Jehun racked his brain for where an army that big could be hiding and why he didn't know about it. It chilled him to think of something that vile and that large in his soil.

A man shaped into view. He was tall with blonde hair, but in the blinding sun, Jehun couldn't see his eyes or make out much of his face. The stories told of Seiten's power and that the prison blocked him of his use of magic.

Jehun began to worry what would happen if Seiten became too angry. But it made Jehun furious, too. He was tired of being used. Both Belial and Adoyni were always telling him what to do. He was fed up with being ordered around without ever having the chance to do what he wanted. And he was sick of being powerless to do anything about it.

Seiten continued. "Belial's smart. I'll give him that much. If I don't tell him where the army is, he won't get me out of here. I know, because I'm the king of betrayal, that if I tell him where it is, he'll get greedy with power. He won't risk losing all his control. He'll take my army. Use them to wipe out the Archippi and then renege on his promise to free me!"

Jehun waited, afraid to say anything, fuming in his weakness. What could he do so that he was no longer helpless? But even more importantly, what would it be like if he could do anything he wanted? Jehun backed up as the voice grew stronger in anger.

"Don't go!" Seiten snapped. "I have no choice. I will tell Belial what he wants. But only what he wants. He'll be back asking for my help in little time. I guarantee it! Let him use up his energy getting rid of the Archippi."

Jehun listened carefully as Seiten revealed where his army was hidden and the commands needed to control them. As he fled the island with the information Belial wanted, an idea grew in his mind. He wondered if Seiten had placed it in him, but, no, surely this was his very own scheme.

As it became more tangible, he stopped worrying about where it had come from and started laying out plans of his own this time.

CHAPTER SEVENTY-SEVEN

More Toxin

Kai realized that Belial wasn't even paying him attention. *Am I so little of a threat that he isn't even concerned I'm in the same room as he is?* He thought about getting up and rushing Belial with his sword. He'd chop him down and flee out into the streets to find Rhiana, Mom and Dad.

His fingers wrapped around the hilt of his sword, but then he remembered Belial's words that his family was destroyed and soon he would be Belial's slave as well. He let go of the sword and slumped back to the floor.

The golden door opened, and Nighthawk whisked in. She was wearing a green dress with a gold key hanging off her belt. Her long copper red hair was loose like she was in a hurry.

"Belial, how'd it work?" She gasped at the sight of Belial's new arm. "You did it! It worked!" She glanced at Kai. "And he's here already."

"Here and in the process of changing. It won't be long." Belial grinned at Kai like he was a trained animal doing something special. Kai shoved down the hate that rose with Belial's smile. Belial turned back to Nighthawk. "Even my newly-acquired fiancée in Albia is playing into my hands nicely. Soon the Archippi will be annihilated by my new servant, the king will give me the throne, and Seiten will give me his army. Eltiria will be mine."

"How is your sweet fiancée?" Nighthawk asked in a mocking tone.

"You know, at first, I thought it was a petty sort of revenge, but I'm starting to be very fond of her. She's beautiful and will make a good queen, as long as she keeps her opinions to herself. That's something we'll soon have to start working on."

Nighthawk nodded like she didn't really care. "And then we can repair the rift at Northbridge. I know the Goddess is hurting because of that."

Belial laughed. "I see no point in putting out that much energy for the Goddess. It's not like you really believe she exists."

Nighthawk seized the key on her belt, fiddling with it nervously. "Are you testing me? Of course she exists. She's the Goddess of Eltiria and any pain in Her creation causes Her pain, too. The Goddess has been suffering since you tore Northbridge apart."

"Oh, come on," Belial scoffed. "Surely you haven't been deceived like the commoners. You know as well as I do that the Goddess is a lie, and that lie has made a few of us, like yourself, very rich. Don't give me that righteous indignation routine."

"It is you who are deluded." Nighthawk's face grew white as she stood in front of Belial's desk. Her whole body seemed to tremble with anger. "I believe in the Goddess. I have since I was young. I dedicated myself to her at the age of twelve. I chose to never have a husband or a child, so that I could be used more effectively by Her."

Belial scoffed. "A great sacrifice for nothing. Find yourself a man and have a child."

"Say what you will," Nighthawk replied, her face livid. "You serve Seiten. I serve the Goddess. Both are real. They are partners against the delusion of Adoyni, as we are. And as her servant, I chose to forgo children."

Kai listened closely. If they started to really fight, perhaps he had a chance. If he were to die, it'd be worth it if Belial died with him. *Would Lizzy and Taryn rescue Rhiana and Mom?*

"I've seen Seiten," Belial laughed with a bit of an edge to it. "I know things you do not know. The Goddess Zoria is another name for Seiten. She was made up to distract people from Adoyni. A trick, I might add, which has worked well, as you are proof. Go get yourself a husband and have a child before you are too old. Seiten doesn't care what you do."

Nighthawk gripped her staff until her knuckles turned white. "You'll regret your mocking words. With Zoria's help, I will find a way to stop your despicable plans of ruining the earth."

"Enough!" Belial slammed his hand down on the table. "I will not argue with someone intent on ignoring the truth! Did you bring her like I asked?"

Nighthawk looked like she was still going to argue. Her face turned red as she seemed to struggle to control herself. She stalked back to the door and opened it.

"Come in," she said a bit more gently. "The Chancellor will talk with you now."

Kai caught a glimpse of red skirts and nut brown hair on a small girl as Nighthawk led the way back into the room. Belial smirked at him like he was waiting for a response.

Nighthawk moved so that Kai had full view of the girl. Rhiana was standing in front of him, not looking at him, but gazing adoringly at Belial with her hand in Nighthawk's. He yelled as loud as he could. It tore his heart apart to seeing her staring up at Belial with awe.

Rhiana either didn't or couldn't see him. Maybe Belial was blocking her from noticing. Maybe since he was a spirit, she wasn't able to. He didn't know. And he didn't care.

"Rhiana! Rhiana! I'm here! Rhiana! Look at me!" He shouted as loudly as he could.

Rhiana never even turned his way. He continued to yell until he was almost hoarse as she curtsied awkwardly to Belial.

"I'm so happy to meet you," Rhiana beamed up to Belial. "Nighthawk told me that you are the one who knew where I was and sent her to rescue me."

"Of course, my dear." Belial moved from behind the table and knelt down. "And my only payment is a hug!"

Kai roared again as Rhiana threw herself in his arms with a giggle. "Don't you dare touch her! Don't touch her! Rhiana! Stop now!"

But Rhiana didn't seem to hear him. She squeezed Belial tight and when Nighthawk held out her hand, she returned to the woman. Her cheeks were flushed, but Kai saw that she was dressed in fine clothes and had plenty to eat. She no longer looked sick, even though her eyes looked glassy. *Why doesn't she look at me?*

He struggled forward. If she couldn't see or hear him, maybe she could feel him. He inched across the floor, dragging his hurt leg behind him. Belial's eyes flickered his way, and he snapped his fingers behind his back.

Kai slammed into an invisible wall. His fingers jammed as he knocked against it. He yelled in frustration and rolled to the left. But no matter which way he went, he was blocked. And no matter how loud he yelled, Rhiana never looked his way.

"I understand you want to dedicate yourself to the Goddess," Belial grinned at Rhiana.

"I do!" Rhiana exclaimed. "I want to help other people like Nighthawk did. I want to be just like her."

Nighthawk laughed. "Well, let's hope you're better than me. But I'll do what I can to show you the way."

"You will not!" Kai yelled. "She's not yours! She's my sister! You leave her out of this!"

"We'll have your dedication ceremony soon. I promise. It will be a glorious day!" Belial said, smiling broadly. "Unfortunately, I must first do a few things."

"Oh, I understand that you have important work to do. Thank you, Chancellor Belial, for everything you've done," Rhiana exclaimed with joy. "I can't wait!"

Nighthawk led her away as Kai beat against the invisible wall and pleaded for her to bring Rhiana back. He threatened Belial with everything he could think of as he hacked at the wall with his sword. He yelled and screamed at Rhiana to come back.

When Rhiana reached the door, she pulled back from Nighthawk and paused. Like she was in a trance, she turned back to the room and stared at Kai. He stopped thrashing at the wall and called her name again.

She smiled slightly as if she heard him but wasn't sure where he was or who he was. He called her name again, and she took a step to him.

"It's Kai, your brother! I love you so much, and I'm coming to get you! Don't give up on me, and don't do anything until I get to you! Do you hear me? I love you! I'm coming!"

Rhiana grinned, her face lighting up with gladness, and her eyes lost the glassy look. She took another step closer to Kai. He fell to his knees and pushed against the wall. She approached slowly with a look on her face like she was trying to understand what she was seeing.

"Can you see me? Rhiana, I'm right here! I'm sorry I left. I'm trying to get back to you. I'll get to you soon. Hang on until I do! I'm right here. Hang on to your memories!"

"Rhiana!" Nighthawk's voice was sharp.

Rhiana froze in place, still staring right at Kai.

"I'm right here. Right here!" Kai shouted.

The glassy look returned to her face. She shook her head like she was clearing it and then turned away. Nighthawk held out her hand until Rhiana joined her.

Belial spoke softly as the door was closing. "More toxin, Nighthawk."

Nighthawk glanced over her shoulder and nodded as she took out a silver flask. Then the door closed, and Rhiana was gone. Kai slumped to the floor and wept.

Belial stood over him with a look of triumph. "Look at how white your skin is. And your eyes, they're almost black. It won't be long now." Belial pushed Kai onto his back with his foot.

Kai rolled away. "I won't do it. I won't kill the Archippi." It was the only resistance he could muster.

"Oh, yes, you will," Belial sneered. "And if they manage to kill you first, I'll use the hidden doorways of the world that I've found to get to Merrihaven and hunt the Archippi down with my armies. But having you kill those horses will be so much more fun."

Kill me. Kill me. Kai pleaded in his brain to Lizzy and Taryn. *Before it's too late. Let me die.*

CHAPTER SEVENTY-EIGHT

A Distant Rumble

Lizzy shifted on her bed. Aric's story was over. They now knew everything that he did. Could they solve Treven's riddle and cure Kai? He wouldn't have given up on them. She wasn't about to stop trying.

Back to the beginning? She remembered when she first met Kai and he threatened to burn her guitar. Later when they had to leave it behind, he seemed to understand how much the instrument meant to her. No. She wasn't giving up. She'd keep fighting for him.

That's what friends did. They helped each other. When everyone else left, when everyone else thought you were crazy, when everyone else gave up. Friends weren't just for the good times when you laughed until you cried and when the world was perfect. Friends were also for the times when everything was wrong. Friends stood and fought battles at your side.

"What happened next?" She asked.

Rev jumped in. "I don't remember much of the ride up here until I saw the rocks and dirt of the islands. But as Thalion flew higher, I saw the top soil, and then the fields filled with lush green grass and flowers of every kind. Then I saw the mountains, the waterfalls, and the meadows lush with vegetation."

Aric took up the story. "Thalion took us to the island of Rapha where most of the healers live and study. That's the same place where you arrived. As we got better, we began helping them out with different ailments. Some they couldn't cure, but we could, thanks to Treven's book. For some reason, we never told them about it, but it helped us out a time or two."

Rev gestured to the worn journal next to Aric. "We're read that and re-read it. All Treven says is what we've told you. Back to the beginning. That may be the answer to the disease, but we can't figure it out. We've tried every method, every remedy, in there. Nothing worked. We're out of options."

"Let me try," Taryn said. It was not a request, only a command. "Maybe I can find the answer."

"You're not a healer," Aric scoffed. "How would you know it when you saw it? It's a waste of time."

Taryn's face flushed with anger as he snapped out his words. "I may not be a healer, but my father was pushing me into choosing between a career as a physician or a lawyer. I've probably taken more courses than you in the medical field. Give me the journal."

"It wouldn't hurt to have him look it over." Rev supported Taryn. "It's worth a shot."

"It might not hurt," Aric conceded. "But every minute we delay and hang on for change, it gets harder to think about what we agreed to do. I

know you're thinking that I'm cold-hearted and
that I don't care for Kai. But this is tearing me
apart. I never dreamed we couldn't cure him. The
longer it goes, the more I don't think I can bring
myself to do it."

All the anger seemed to drain out of Aric as he
slumped back against the cave wall, not looking at
anyone during his confession. Lizzy felt a sudden
urge to make him smile while relieving some of
the horrible burden he'd been carrying since they
arrived. No wonder he looked tired. But even with
the wave of sympathy, she knew she'd stand with
Taryn if either Aric or Rev tried to hurt Kai.

"Give me the book," Taryn ordered again. "The
only way we were able to purify the water was by
not giving up. And having faith in Adoyni." He
nodded toward the book in the sand by Kai. "It
says in my book that anything is possible if we ask
Adoyni. And there's all these stories about people
being cured from all kinds of diseases, even being
raised from the dead. I believe Adoyni can heal
him."

Aric nodded as he carefully passed the journal
to Taryn. Lizzy could tell by the way he held it that
the journal was precious to him. "Don't damage
it," Aric warned. "It's all we've got left of Treven."

Taryn took the book as carefully as Aric had
given it to him. "Go and rest." His anger was gone
now that he had the book. "I'll keep an eye on Kai
while I read."

Rev and Aric nodded, relieved that the burden
was off them for a little while. Lizzy noticed for the
first time that Rev and Aric were exhausted. They

had dark circles under their eyes and their shoulders drooped. She watched as they stumbled out of the cave and down to the tents.

Griff wandered around outside the cave, looking lost without anything to do. Taryn flipped through the journal quickly, like someone getting his bearings.

"You, too, Lizzy," he said without looking at her. "You look exhausted. And once Kai gets better, he'll be tearing down the mountains to get off these islands and back to Eltiria. Sleep while you can. Besides, with these two hair-brains talking about giving up on Kai, we'll need to watch him in case they get any stupid ideas in their heads."

Lizzy sank down on her pillow and closed her eyes without protest. As sleep overcame her, she couldn't stop thinking about what they'd do if they didn't find a way to cure Kai.

Her dreams were filled with Kai, his skin white and eyes black, trying to kill them.

***

Kai heard a distant rumble of voices in his head. He shrank back from Belial and tried to listen closer. Through a haze of blackness and pain, he recognized Lizzy and Taryn's voices. The other two people were vaguely familiar, but he didn't know why.

He struggled to wake up or to move. But the darkness covered his eyes and trapped him so that he couldn't even squirm. The more he fought, the more the shadows seemed to grow.

Taryn was speaking. Kai strained to hear, but all he caught was the words *give up*. Kai tried to scream that he was alert and alive.

He wanted to yell at them to keep trying to help him. He needed them to know that he was fighting to return to them.

But he couldn't. All he could do was to sink into the pain and the darkness – going deeper and deeper until all light and hope disappeared.

CHAPTER SEVENTY-NINE

The Beginning

Taryn stared out the entrance to the cave for a long time after the others had fallen asleep. The journal sat heavy in his hands, but he couldn't bring himself to read it yet. He'd watched Aric study it and wanted to try to decipher the clues for days. Instead, he'd been forced to wait, reading only the wordless book they had found in the altar in that strange meadow so long ago.

I have to stop calling it the wordless book. He smiled. Once they had reached Merrihaven, every word was there. *And start calling it something more like the mysterious book.* There was no reason for the change that he could find.

Taryn set the journal carefully beside his book and quietly paced to the entrance of the cave and back. Now that Aric was being honest with them about what was wrong with Kai, there was even more pressure to cure him.

But what if he couldn't? What if his hopes were just hopes? Was Kai doomed to die? Or, even worse, was he doomed to live as an Unwanted?

Taking a deep breath, he collapsed beside Kai's blankets. Kai never moved. He took the journal and turned it over in his hands a few times. *What if old Treven hid some message in the binding?*

He ran his hands over the cover and inspected the insides of the cover. There didn't seem to be any break or bumps, but still the work could have been carefully done.

What would Aric do if I cut the cover into pieces? Taryn snorted. Aric would probably order his head cut off and expect some servant to leap from nowhere to do it. Setting the thought of the cover aside for the time being, Taryn opened the journal and began reading.

Unlike most journals, this one had notes scribbled all over the pages. Sometimes lines and arrows were drawn to point to other pages. Notes were at times connected, but they were mostly random. Typically, they never explained a thing.

"Poison Ivy" was followed with "Honey!!!!!" But there was no explanation. Was honey to help with the itching, or was it to prevent the rash? Or, even more discouraging, remained the thought that maybe he had helped someone with poison ivy, and they had paid him in honey. There was no way of telling.

Taryn struggled through the journal. It was laborious reading. It was difficult to make out what the sloppy handwriting said and then work out how it applied to the diseases mentioned. The snores from Lizzy irritated him illogically. Everyone needed sleep, but now he felt abandoned when he was trying to solve the problem.

He scanned the end of the journal. Blank pages were all that were left. He slammed the journal shut, heedless of Aric's warning, and slumped against the cave wall. Nothing but four words. *Back to the beginning.*

He reviewed Aric's story from the beginning, but there wasn't anything about the disease. It was mostly of the slow takeover by Belial and the gradual introduction of magic in the life of the royal castle.

He shook his head. Aric was wrong. He was too conceited to think of anything else but himself. The beginning Treven was referring to didn't have to do with the Prince. Treven didn't even know Aric when he had written those words.

No, it had to do with another beginning, but which one? When Belial had introduced the poison into the water? Belial's exposure to Seiten?

Taryn groaned. Everything had a start. It was impossible to nail down one beginning. *Back to the beginning.*

The beginning of *what?* Maybe it wasn't a what. Maybe it was a *who.* He ran through the list of great physicians and their careers, but there was nothing that he could relate to the disease.

Kai twitched and moaned in his unconscious dreams. *What is he going through? Is he even aware of what was happening to him?* If he didn't figure out what beginning Treven was talking about soon, Kai wouldn't make it out alive.

Was it the beginning when all life started? The professors taught in the universities that once the world was formed, then organisms began. Small creatures with basic functions came out of the ocean and adapted to land.

Countless years passed before simple animals evolved. Then came the fish, plants, reptiles, and mammals. The first humans were seen with the mammals, slowly changing into what they were today.

Others thought differently, but such radical thoughts of Adoyni creating the world was dangerous to speak about. The book Taryn had found in that altar so long ago told the story of Creation, but Taryn knew that people who still believed that were shunned by the academic world and many others. They slowly disappeared into small hidden villages in forgotten corners of Eltiria to escape persecution.

Anyone who had any education knew that first the land took shape. Water evolved. Then tiny organisms came out of the sea.

Water! Taryn sat up with a jerk. It all started for water, both the evolution and the disease. Maybe Treven was giving a clue that the cure to the disease was with water.

Taryn got to his feet and paced the cave, wishing for the libraries filled with resources that he had in Albia. Even an hour would give him more information than he needed. How could the cure and the disease both be in the water? He dropped down beside Kai again in despair. If he had all the resources of the libraries of Albia and all the time in the world, he'd solve it. But he had a day. Maybe even less.

***

Lizzy woke with a pounding headache and a sense of impending doom. Something bad was going to happen. She knew. Just as she had known the bags of salt were buried in the sand. Just as she knew that it was dangerous to enter Aldholt so long ago.

Rubbing her head, she slowly sat up and re-oriented herself. Kai was as white as the sheets pulled up to his chin. He twitched and muttered to himself, but she couldn't catch what he was trying to say. Beads of sweat were on his forehead, and his hair was wet.

From what she knew about the disease, he would grow quieter and quieter until it looked like he had died. Then, after a few hours, the change would be complete. He would wake up. His skin would be completely white. His eyes completely dark. And only Kai's body would remain.

Surely Adoyni wouldn't let Kai die this way after he'd done so much for Eltiria. *What glory would his death bring to Adoyni? What purpose?* But as little as she knew about the disease, she knew it was winning.

Taryn was slumped beside Kai. But when she checked on him, her frustration turned to anger. He was sitting with his head on his hand. Treven's journal lay open on the sand in front of him. His eyes were closed like he was sleeping.

Sleeping! Taryn had pestered Aric for days to read the journal. Kai was quickly approaching death. Northbridge was ripped apart by a giant earthquake, they had no idea of the safety of their families, and he chose to nap after he had bragged that he could find the answers. She leaped out of bed and ignored the rush of blood to her head.

"What are you doing?" She yelled. "Why in Adoyni's world would you be sleeping? I thought you said you'd find the answer."

Taryn jumped and sat straight up. Sand spilled over the journal, and he grabbed it to shake the sand off it. The pages crumpled as he waved it in the air before he realized what he had done. He smoothed the pages and glared at her.

"Nice," he shot back sarcastically. "Now when your precious prince Aric yells at me about ruining his book, I suppose you won't mention that you were the one that made me do it."

"I made you?" she snapped. "If you weren't sleeping on the job, it never would've dropped. Weren't you supposed to *read* it? Holding it to your stomach isn't going to help Kai one bit."

"Reading it isn't going to help him one bit, either," Taryn responded louder. "For your information, *Mother*, I did read it, although I don't know why I'm being accountable to you. I read it all. There's nothing in it. Aric and Rev were right. Treven locked the answer for the disease in a riddle no one but him could unlock."

"So then you decide to take a nap?" Lizzy fumed. "Knowing that Kai's life is doomed, you could still drift off to sleep like it was nothing! What kind of friend are you?"

"I wasn't sleeping," Taryn yelled. "I was thinking! Something you should try sometime, instead of accusing people falsely!"

"Yeah, right." Lizzy briefly wondered if he was telling the truth, but she was far too livid to back down now. "It looked a lot like sleeping to me. What deep thoughts were you thinking about?"

"Sand." Taryn snapped. He closed the journal and dropped it gently beside Kai's bed. He picked up a handful of the golden sand and let it run through his fingers.

"Sand?" Lizzy asked with amazement. Taryn didn't acknowledge she had spoken or elaborate on his comment further. His silence only fueled her rage. "You might as well have been sleeping then!" She dropped onto her blankets. "I thought you cared about Kai. I thought you were his friend!"

"I am his friend!" Taryn yelled. "What got into you? Why don't you try to help instead of sitting there yelling at me all the time?"

Lizzy glared at him, unable to quickly think of a biting retort. She hadn't really tried to help Kai at all. She had spent more time taking care of herself. Words swirled in her head, but nothing came out. Before she could think of anything to say, she heard the sound of footsteps at the entrance of the cave.

"Think they fought all the time as they purified the water?" Rev whispered.

Lizzy whirled around, horrified that they had seen her and Taryn fighting. Sure enough, Rev and Aric were standing in the entrance with shocked expressions on their faces. Rev's hair was tangled and Aric's stood straight up. Lizzy's face grew hotter by the second. Griff peered around them to see what was happening.

"Probably not." Aric responded without a smile. "They never would've gotten anywhere if they had."

"We fought the whole time," Taryn answered without turning to Rev. "Ask Lizzy about raspberry juice."

Lizzy's jaw dropped in shock. *How dare he bring that up in front of them?* She turned back to him. "That was all your fault! You still haven't apologized for dousing me with it!"

Taryn laughed. "It was barely a drop, and I apologized when Kai made me."

"Ha." Lizzy scoffed. "That wasn't an apology, and you know it."

"I'm lost," Rev broke in. "You're arguing over sand and raspberry juice?"

"Yes, we are." Taryn began pacing. "Because *someone* doesn't understand that sometimes the answer to the problem isn't right in front of your face, and you have *think* to find the answer. But that's not good enough for her."

Lizzy wished she could beat him over the head with the journal. She might have if Aric and Rev weren't watching. "You were sleeping," she said in a softer tone. "You said you were thinking of sand to cover for your nap."

"The journal says to go back to the beginning," Taryn countered. He stalked to the journal and flipped through it to the middle. "Look! But it doesn't make any sense to be *your* beginning, Aric. Why would it? Treven would know about your birth, but there's no way he'd know of Belial taking over the kingdom like he is. Why would Treven relate a cure back to the Crown Prince? "

He handed the journal back to Aric and kept talking like he was a professor lecturing a class. "The scope of possible beginnings to cover is almost impossible. There are only several that I can note that might have significance to our situation. They are when Belial chose to deny Adoyni and worship Seiten, when Belial actively began practicing magic, when Belial met with Seiten, or when Belial started to take over the kingdom."

Taryn clasped his hands behind his back and paced the cave. Lizzy briefly wondered if this was what Taryn's Dad was like when he taught.

"However, Treven wasn't around Belial at any of those times. He wouldn't have had any knowledge of those events enough to decipher the cure or leave a clue. So that brings me back to sand. The only beginning we all share is when we were created, when the first creatures crawled out of the ocean onto the sand. That's why I was thinking of sand!" He spun on his heel and pointed at Lizzy to emphasize his defense.

"When you interrupted me, I was trying to figure out what sand has to do with the disease." Taryn took a breath before continuing.

"Because while I may have found which beginning Treven was talking about, I have no idea of how sand would cure this disease. Without that, Kai still dies."

CHAPTER EIGHTY

Time's Up

Lizzy knew she should probably apologize to Taryn, but the words stuck in her throat. No one said anything for a long time. *Why doesn't Adoyni do something?*

Always before, whenever they were stuck, they got help. There was Alyn when they were trapped in the canyon. There was the oasis when they were out of water in the desert. There were bags of salt when they needed the cure for the water.

But now they were alone. *Is it because we did something wrong? Maybe we weren't supposed to get on those Archippi and come here.*

But to let Kai die was too great a consequence for any mistake. Maybe even Adoyni couldn't heal this disease.

Aric laughed. "Well, wouldn't that be amusing that the cure was lying under our feet, and we didn't know it? Of all the places we could've chosen to camp! Maybe Adoyni has a sense of humor, after all. So what do we know of sand?"

Aric kept asking even when no one responded. "Come on. We've got to try. Can you think of sand being used for anything?"

"Yeah, to make bricks." Taryn rubbed his hands over his face.

"Sandy soil is good for crops like peaches," Rev jumped in. "Some people use it for telling time."

Lizzy shook her head angrily. "Time, bricks, peaches. What does that have to do with a disease? Are we supposed to feed him peaches?"

Rev shot her a glance like Lizzy had said something important. "Most things that Treven suggested were taken orally. Like eating mint leaves when you had a stomach ache. What if the cure is to eat sand?"

"That's nasty." Lizzy wrinkled her nose.

"Come on," Taryn protested. "I personally know the physicians in Albia that have studied this disease since it started. They've worked non-stop to find a cure. A disease this bad has to require a complex remedy. Do you really believe swallowing a little sand would do anything?"

"It doesn't matter what I believe," Rev stated firmly. "It only matters what works."

"It's not going to work," Taryn said in a tone that said he was not going to budge on this.

Aric left without a word. Rev and Lizzy sat in silence as Taryn returned to his pacing. Lizzy watched him but didn't have anything to say. *What do I know about sand?*

There was the sand her mother put in her facial soaps to soften her skin. There was the thick deep sand at the beach, and the dry, black sand she had walked through with Kai and Taryn in Seiten's Anvil. *But what did that have to do with healing?*

Aric returned with a cup and scooped a bit of sand in it. He added some water and stirred the brown, murky water with a spoon.

Lizzy stared at the cup with disgust. Aric couldn't really mean to force that down Kai's throat. If it were her, she'd throw it back up in seconds.

Rev must have been thinking the same thing. "Are you sure that's such a good idea?"

"Got a better one?" Aric retorted and then he sighed. "I have no other ideas. And at this point, what's the harm?"

Rev finally joined him by Kai's bed. She held Kai's head as Aric began pouring the dirty liquid down his throat. Lizzy winced and gagged as she watched.

Kai fought them at first by trying to jerk his head free. Unable to do that, he coughed and gagged as the water trickled down his throat.

When the cup was empty, Lizzy thought more had gotten on his pillows and face than down his throat. Rev wiped him clean as Aric changed the blankets around him.

"Now we wait." Aric sat close to Kai's bed.

They all gathered close to watch the changes, but after a few minutes, when nothing happened, Taryn leaped to his feet and began pacing.

"It's not working," he exclaimed. "Why didn't Treven give more explanation?"

"Because he never dreamed we would come along and drag him into a fight with Belial," Rev snapped.

No one had anything to say to that. Lizzy knew that everyone was thinking one thing but couldn't say it. *Is it time to admit defeat?*

Kai's shallow breathing filled the cave, a quiet reminder that his life was slowly draining away. *I never thought I'd watch him die.* Lizzy tried to think about sand. *What could Treven have meant?*

A deep beating echoed through the stone walls. It grew louder until Lizzy recognized the sound of large wings in the air. She looked up expectantly. *Maybe the Archippi would have an idea about sand as the cure!*

Rev was clearly frightened. "What are they doing here? They promised they wouldn't come unless it was something bad. And what if they ask about Kai? We can't lie."

His face drained of all color. "We can't tell the truth, either. We have to stall."

"But how?" Rev questioned.

A black Archippos landed by the tents. Lizzy followed the others outside and down the hill. For some strange reason, she felt nervous, although she didn't know why. Aric smiled as he approached the black stallion.

"Greetings, Thalion," Aric said with obvious relief. "It's about time. What's the news?"

The tall stallion snorted softly and sidestepped like he was nervous. He was almost as big as a draft horse with long hair falling over his hooves. His thick mane looked like it had been braided and set loose with wavy curls. Lizzy couldn't see one spot of white on him.

Greetings, Prince Aric. I can only stay here a few minutes. I haven't been able to get away before this. Faelon, our leader, is coming in the morning. How is the human doing?

"As you can see, Lizzy woke this morning." Aric waved his hand in Lizzy's direction. "But Kai is still asleep."

Thalion shook his head. His mane, unsettled from the wind of flying, re-arranged to the same side of his neck. *Is the disease cured?*

"Not completely." Aric shifted. "We are closer to finding a cure."

Lizzy almost snorted. *Yeah, next we're baking Kai a sand cake.* She held her emotions in check, though, in fear of what the orders would be if they were honest about the lack of progress.

After our recent disobedience of rescuing the three humans which led to the death of Eladar, Archos Faelon has ordered there be no more loosening of the rules. Archippi stay here until the king calls them back or risk full banishment. Any permanent eviction means death for us. As you know, if we do not return to Merrihaven, we will weaken and die quickly. Faelon is so grief stricken from the loss of Eladar that he won't permit the human to live.

Lizzy suppressed her irritation as Thalion used the term human. *He has a name!* She tried to keep her thoughts and emotions deep where he wouldn't hear them, but she didn't think she succeeded all that well.

Archos Faelon is coming shortly, and if he finds that there has been no improvement, he will command you to fulfill your promise by killing the human and end the threat the disease poses to the security and welfare of Merrihaven.

Lizzy glared at Thalion, unable to hold back her emotions. The black spoke in a flat tone as if Kai wasn't a human, but rather a thing that could be murdered without thought or care. *Let this Archos Faelon come. He'll find that it takes more than an order to kill someone I love!*

Aric didn't show any emotion at Thalion's words. His face was smoother and calmer than she'd ever seen. "He'll be fine. Thanks for the warning."

Do not give up hope. Adoyni is in control. Thalion spread his wings. *Trust that He will finish His good work in all of us.* He reared and leaped into the air as his wings took him upwards.

Within seconds, he was gone from sight. Lizzy longed to fly away from all her problems as easily as he had.

Aric strode to a nearby boulder and perched on it to regard them with a serious expression. "I guess that's it. We have until the morning. I mean, Kai has until the morning. If Faelon comes here and sees him as he is now, it will be death for him."

"I don't care what that flying nag or any of the others say," Taryn burst out. "I'm not letting anyone touch him!"

"That sounds great." Aric ran his hands through his hair. "But even if I refuse to fulfill my promise, they can take any action they want. With the skills Adoyni gave the Archippi, I really don't think they even have to touch him."

Lizzy remembered ways Eladar had killed the Unwanteds when they were attacked. Very few of his methods involved actually touching the creatures. She shuddered when she thought of those techniques being used on one of her friends.

Aric gazed out over the meadow. "If I do it, I can give him something that will cause him to slip into sleep, and he won't feel any pain."

"You can't really be considering that," Rev spoke sharply. "We took oaths saying that we'd never intentionally harm anymore. How could you even think about killing someone who you've sworn to heal? Someone who needs our help?"

"Because I can't help him!" Aric's voice cracked with desperation as he swung around to Rev. "Because I can't convince myself that letting him live is not harming him. Because all of us have tried, and there is no cure. We've done all anyone can do. We even prayed for Adoyni to cure him, but nothing's happened. Now time has run out. Does Adoyni really want us to sit here and watch him turn into a monster? Watch him pollute all of Merrihaven?"

No one had any answers for him. After several minutes of silence, he continued. "Twenty-four hours. That's all we've got left to save Kai."

CHAPTER EIGHTY-ONE

No Change

Taryn paced the cave and watched Kai sleep. Aric entered and knelt down to fill a large bucket full of sand.

"Treven didn't say how much to give," Aric said to no one in particular. "Maybe we gave too little."

He heaped a huge amount of sand in the cup and poured a little bit of water in it. The golden color turned into a dark sludge as he stirred. "Start thinking of other ways we could use it if this doesn't work. Right now no idea is a bad idea."

Taryn kept his mouth shut. *It's not going to work. It's too simple. What was Treven trying to say? Back to the beginning? Why didn't he write down the answer?*

Rev helped Aric pour the sludge down Kai's throat again. Kai choked and coughed most of it up. Taryn winced as he thought about how it must taste. *Poor guy. He's dying, and we're shoveling sand down his throat. I wonder what he'd want for his last meal.* Taryn grimaced at his thoughts, but no matter how he tried to ignore them, they lingered.

They watched Kai for a moment, but there were no changes. Taryn plopped to the ground *Of course I had to be right.*

"Mother used to wash her face with special sand that was supposed to keep wrinkles away." Lizzy piped up. "She'd cake it on and wait until it dried to wash it off. I tried it once when she wasn't looking, and it made my skin real soft."

The girls mixed up some more and smeared it over Kai's face. Taryn would have laughed if it wasn't so horrible. It dried, and they washed it off.

Again they waited. No change. They tried everything. Aric remembered that some people claimed toxins came out of the feet. They tried the sand on his feet.

No change.

Rev suggested a warm compress made of sand on his chest. She warmed up some water and put it in a rag. They waited until it cooled on his chest.

No change.

Aric went back to the swallowing idea and force-fed Kai three heaping spoonfuls of sand.

No change.

Lizzy and Rev dumped it on Kai's face, chest, and feet. The blankets where Kai lay were now brown with sand that had fallen on them. Kai was in no better shape with sand dribbled, dropped, and poured over his body. *If he wakes up now, he's going to be angry.*

No change.

The sun sank toward the horizon as time ran out. Kai was never moved, his breathing becoming even shallower, his skin whiter. He didn't have

much time from either the Archippi or the
disease.

They ran out of ideas as the afternoon began to
wane. Lizzy was the first to give up. She sank down
on her bed, hid her face from them, and began to
quietly cry.

It wasn't too long before Aric stormed out to
the ledge of the cave and slumped on the ground.
Rev continued fussing but gave up and flopped
onto the closest blanket.

Taryn paced for a while as the same thoughts
tumbled through his head, repeating over and
over. With a sigh of frustration, he dropped beside
Kai's bed and watched as his friend struggled to
breathe.

No one slept. No one talked. No one figured
out what Treven meant.

Back to the beginning.

**

Kai knew he was losing. It didn't take much to
figure that out, but he hadn't admitted it to
himself until now.

He thought back to Eladar with a sense of
shame. Eladar believed in him. He once said that
Kai was an unpolished gem and that he was
supposed to lead Lizzy and Taryn.

Kai almost snorted at the memory. He couldn't
even find the others, much less lead them. He still
couldn't remember what happened at the castle in

the canyon. *Did we purify the water, or did I fail at that too? Maybe Lizzy and Taryn found a way.*

Taryn and Lizzy! He hadn't thought about them in a long time. What had Belial said? Something about them in Merrihaven looking for the cure to the disease that was trying to overtake him. They hadn't left him.

Better yet, he hadn't left them. It was this horrible disease that made him feel like he was abandoned, but in reality, he was sure Taryn and Lizzy were slaving away, trying to help him.

He stifled a laugh as excitement built. If there was anyone he'd want to fight for him, it was Lizzy and Taryn. He couldn't help them or tell them anything, but he could do one thing.

Leading didn't always meaning storming into battle. Sometimes all it meant was doing the very best thing, doing what Adoyni put in front of you to do, when nothing made sense. Even if he never saw Taryn or Lizzy again, he was going to be the kind of leader they would be proud of.

He glanced at Belial, who was sitting at his desk with his back to Kai. *Could I still fight?* Kai slowly and quietly began to draw his sword out of the scabbard.

CHAPTER EIGHTY-TWO

Big Cure

Taryn groaned and rubbed his hands over his face as the sun crept into the cave. He had a feeling that he knew the cure for Kai, but it wouldn't come. He watched the sun as it began to rise over the mountains. Time had run out. The Archippi would be here any minute.

Sand. Why did that sound so familiar and yet so wrong? He stretched on his blankets as his hand hit the wordless book they had found in the meadow.

He picked up it and smoothed down the pages. *Odd that all the words are visible up here.* Kai forgotten, he wondered where the book had come from and who had made it. Even the Archippi he had showed it to didn't know anything about it.

He flipped through the pages to make sure they were straight. The book told amazing stories about the creation of Eltiria, the miracles and ways Adoyni had worked throughout the ages, and the story of Lesu giving His life for redemption. Some of the stories were so odd that he wondered if they were true.

There were references to being a Son of Adoyni, but he didn't understand how he could be one. Some of the tales were familiar. He'd heard most of them from his mother when he was little and some from Mischa, his tutor who had died. However, reading them with his newly-found faith was different.

Lizzy sat up from her blankets and groaned when she saw the sun. "Taryn, we've got to do something!"

Taryn nodded. "I know, but I don't know what to do."

Lizzy crawled over to the other side of Kai and curled up beside him. "Remember what he said about his family? We have to tell them how he never forgot them." Her voice broke. "I'll never forget swimming in that oasis on the other side of the Anvil. I think that's one of my favorite memories. It was fun."

Taryn didn't know what to say. He nodded again, feeling like a fool, but not trusting his voice.

Lizzy continued. "He's so dirty. We should clean him up before...before..."

Taryn nodded again but stopped. "What did you say?"

"I said he's covered with dirt!" Lizzy snapped, her green eyes flashed from sorrow to anger. "We should clean him up. Weren't you listening?"

"He's covered with dirt," Taryn repeated slowly. Something was in there. Something that fit far better than what he previously had thought. "He's covered with dirt..."

Without warning, Taryn felt like his mind was a puzzle dumped onto the ground and miraculously every piece fell into place. *The beginning!* It was so simple a child could figure it out. But was he right?

He reached around and found the mysterious book they found. His fingers fumbled as he flipped to the beginning of the book. The pages flipped too fast, and he knew he had passed it. He willed his fingers to be steady as he turned two pages back and found the word.

He laughed and repeated, "He's covered with dirt!" He reached across Kai and grabbed her in an awkward hug.

She pushed him away. "What are you doing?"

He pointed to the word.

Dirt.

"Lizzy, of all people, you stumbled on it! Who would have thought?" Taryn laughed again.

"Stumbled on what?" Lizzy questioned.

Taryn ignored her. "ARIC!" he bellowed.

The reactions from his yell were instantaneous. Rev jumped like she had forgotten anyone else was around. Aric didn't even hesitate. He catapulted himself off the large boulder he was sitting on outside the cave and didn't stop until he reached Kai's bed. He quickly felt Kai's forehead and checked his breathing.

Finding nothing changed, he turned his anger to Taryn. "What in Adoyni's world are you yelling for?"

Taryn matched his tone and waved the wordless book to him. "I know how to fix Kai!"

Aric slumped down on Lizzy's blanket. She flushed and pulled back to give him more room as he talked. "Taryn, we've tried everything. Whatever

Treven was trying didn't work, or we just don't have enough information."

"That's right!" Taryn said excitedly. "We didn't have enough information...with Treven's journal. That's why we needed this one!"

"Is that the one we found in the meadow?" Lizzy asked, puzzled. When Taryn nodded, she continued. "Why would that help us now? And how would Treven have known about it?"

"Would you say that Treven was a follower of Adoyni?" Taryn ignored her questions. "And not someone who said they did, but someone who lived it and knew the stories."

"Of course." Rev joined them and stood at the foot of Kai's bed. "We didn't talk about it much, but I know he was."

"Back to the beginning!" Taryn jabbed the mysterious book. "I was all caught up on what is taught in the universities today. They say how evolution made us from simple little creatures into humans. But, that's not what Adoyni says, according to this. This tells a different creation story. How were humans created?"

"Adoyni did it," Aric replied. "What's the point?"

"But how?" Taryn repeated.

"Hawaa was made out of Akamu's rib," Rev contributed.

"And before that, Adoyni created Akamu," Lizzy added, thinking hard. She was as unfamiliar with the stories as Taryn had been. "But how was he made?"

"Adoyni formed him out of the dirt of the earth and breathed on him to give him life," Aric said in a dull tone. "What does this have to do with anything?"

"Dirt!" Taryn exclaimed. "Adoyni took some dust, breathed on it, and poof, there was life! This disease takes everything that is human away from our bodies. It takes away our souls and turns us into shells without Adoyni's gift of life!"

He groaned in frustration as he watched their faces. They weren't getting it! *Why can't they see?* The sun rose higher as he tried to calm himself and explain it better.

"Adoyni made the whole body from dirt and then breathed life into it. We need to use what Adoyni used." He grabbed a handful of sand and flung it into the air. "Sand is rocks. It's dead. Nothing grows in it. No life can live in it. What we need to do is submerge him in dirt, where life can begin. We need to get him to the point where Adoyni breathed life because that life is being torn out of him. Kai needs a mud bath!"

Silence filled the cave. Taryn waited for them to jump into action at his sudden revelation. Instead, Aric burst out laughing and didn't stop.

"That's it?" He gasped between the bursts of laughter. "That's your big cure?"

"Wait a moment!" Taryn's joy at finding the cure turned into anger. "You said no idea was a bad one. In fact, my idea is even more valid because of this." He held up the book again.

"Yeah, maybe we should..." Lizzy never finished her thought as the familiar deep beat of wings in the air grew louder. She stopped talking as her expression filled with horror. "That's them, isn't it?"

Taryn could barely hear her over the noise. He looked up in time to see a large grey Archippi lowering himself to the ground. Behind him, two more Archippi flew past the cave and landed in the meadow below them. The grey Archippi shook his mane into place and pawed once.

Faelon had come. Kai's time was gone.

***

Kai pulled the sword free and balanced it in his hand. The word *Failure* made him want to wait until the disease took over his body, but he turned the blade so he only saw the edge.

Maybe he was a failure. That didn't matter anymore. He believed Adoyni loved him, whether he had purified the water or not.

Adoyni, maybe I failed in the past. I may have lost any chance of saving my family, and perhaps Lizzy and Taryn will die because of what I dragged them into. But help me kill Belial so that no one else suffers.

I know I'll probably die, but maybe my past failures don't matter. Maybe I can forget all that and still do some good with Your help. I don't care if I live anymore. Help me do something good for those I love.

He didn't have much time. Using the window behind him, he pushed himself to his feet. He leaned against the glass and tried to catch his breath. He was far weaker than he thought he was, but he wasn't giving up until Belial was dead.

He took a step forward and prepared to strike.

CHAPTER EIGHTY-THREE

Deathbed

Aric wanted to hide when he saw Faelon. It wasn't that the gray Archippos was uncaring or unkind. He was fairly nice and someone that Aric wouldn't mind talking to about leadership and life. But he was aloof and sometimes cold in his decisions, and the sight of Faelon meant that their time was up for helping Kai.

He rose wearily to his feet and slowly made his way down to the meadow. He felt like he was going to his death sentence. The others shuffled behind him without saying a word.

Aric paused before approaching the winged horses, gathered himself, and stepped closer while blinking in the glare of the rising sun. Two chestnut Archippi stood quietly behind Faelon.

"Greetings, Faelon." His words lacked all emotion. *How are we going to do this?* He couldn't even believe that they had come to this point. He was so sure he could cure Kai.

Morning, Prince Aric and other humans. The deep voice rumbled loudly in Aric's head. *Lizzy, although we haven't met yet, I am pleased to see you recovered.*

"Thank you, sir." Lizzy said respectfully yet coldly. Aric knew she was holding back her fears for Kai.

Before we discuss the sick human, I must pass some news to you, Prince Aric. I only received it a little while ago, and I thought I should be the one to inform you.

Aric braced himself as a cold fear rushed through him. *Oh, Adoyni, please let my parents be okay.* He shifted his feet before he realized what he was doing and made himself stand still.

We have found out that your Father the King is very sick. He is lingering at death's door. Our sources have told us that he will die in a short time.

Aric felt like his head was spinning. He closed his eyes and felt a hand on his arm. Opening them, he saw Lizzy with a concerned look holding his arm. He tried to smile but forgot how. "He...he was sick when I left." His voice broke.

Faelon tossed his head. *Our reports say he is on his deathbed and has begun preparations for what will happen to the kingdom once he is gone. A great search for you has swept across the land now. He offered a large reward for information of you.*

Aric wanted to collapse, but there was nowhere to sit other than the ground. *If he dies, I'll never get to tell him why I left or what he means to me.* He fought back the tears, determined not to cry in front of the others.

Someone put their hand on his shoulder. He didn't know or care who it was, but he fought back the urge to yell at their stupidity to think that one hand was going to make him feel better. He focused on Faelon as if glaring at him would drive away the grief.

You know the law. I cannot send you back. The words from Faelon were final.

"Why not?" Lizzy exclaimed, clearly angry. "Eladar broke the rules to save the world from poison. If Aric doesn't go back, Eltiria will be ruled by Belial! Is that what you want?"

Faelon lowered his head. *I don't want Belial to be king, either. I can only imagine the horror and suffering he would unleash on the people. But the Archippi were given a rule, and until Adoyni or the king changes it, I cannot break it. Adoyni will work in His perfect way. He sets up rulers and takes them down. All we can do is pray and trust Adoyni.*

Even Lizzy didn't have a response to that.

Aric knew he was right. Adoyni had all of life under His control, knew what Belial was doing, and loved all of Eltiria. But it seemed so wrong that Adoyni would let his father die without giving him a chance to say goodbye. It seemed wrong that Adoyni let evil rule while the good suffered. What kind of love was that?

There is also the other matter we need to discuss, Faelon continued. *I'm assuming since he is not among you, the other human is still fighting the disease.*

Rev cleared her throat. "He is fighting it, sir. All he needs is more time."

We have already given him time enough to overcome it. There's been more than sufficient time for you to find a cure in that journal. Faelon's voice came across without any emotion. *Time has run out.*

"But we know what will cure him!" Taryn moved to stand between Aric and Faelon. "We discovered it minutes ago! At least give us a chance to try!"

Faelon hesitated.

Taryn seized his chance. "There were so many things to try. We didn't know exactly how the cure was to be applied. Minutes before you arrived, we stumbled upon the answer. It will work. I know it will work. Please let us try."

"Just because you lost your friend doesn't mean we have to lose ours," Lizzy burst out. She continued in a softer tone. "Please, he's our friend."

Faelon snorted softly as he shook his head. *I will return to my home. Upon my return, I will send six Archippi to bring you back. I'm sending six in the hopes that you are right. When they arrive, the human needs to be cured or put out of his misery. This is all the time I can give you.*

Taryn whirled around and raced back up to the cave without saying another word. Lizzy gasped a quick thank you and trotted after him with Rev and Griff.

Aric watched them go without moving. It wouldn't work. Nothing else had worked. And he was forced to sit helplessly by as his father died and his mother was subjected to some unknown fate.

"Please let me go back." He pleaded once more to Faelon. "At least long enough to see him before he...he...dies."

Pray, Prince. Faelon spread his wings. *Pray and trust. That is all we can do now.* With a blast of wind, he leaped into the sky and was gone before Aric could respond.

Aric stayed where he was and watched Faelon until he was a small dot in the sky. *How long will Father live? How long until I have to end a life instead of save one?*

With a weary shove, he pushed himself up, wondering if his legs would hold him. They did. But he felt weak all over and tired. He shuffled to the cave.

The others were in a blur of motion. Lizzy and Rev were wrestling a giant tub closer to Kai while Taryn and Griff were racing from the nearest stream with buckets of dirt. They dropped the buckets close to Kai's bed and then raced off for more.

Once Lizzy and Rev were satisfied at the position of the tub, they joined Kai and Griff by packing up jugs of water and throwing them in the tub.

Aric collapsed on Lizzy's blankets next to Kai and wished that they would stop. He was sick of hopes being raised only to find them smashed down again.

"It's not going to work," he stated simply when Taryn was there. "You're wasting your energy. Spend time with him before it's too late."

"I'm not...giving up...on him," Taryn panted. He took a deep breath. "It will work. It has to." With that, he dashed out again.

Lizzy and Rev ignored Aric as they began mixing the dirt with water.

"Let's leave it pretty thick," Rev suggested. "If Taryn is right about the dirt, I think we shouldn't water it down with..." She paused and grinned slightly. "Well, with water."

Lizzy nodded as mud splashed on her face. "Do you think it will work?"

Rev shrugged, and the grin disappeared off her face. "I don't know. But it's worth a try. Besides, it's better than doing nothing."

"It won't work," Aric broke in. He saw Lizzy and regretted the pain he was causing her, but she'd thank him later. "There's no way to beat this. Treven didn't ever cure anyone of it as far as we know. Maybe that note was an idea he had. Why don't you sit with Kai before it's too late? I'd love to spend a few minutes with Father before he dies."

Lizzy looked like she was going to cry, and he hated himself for making her feel that way, but he couldn't stop.

Rev picked up the long stick she was stirring the mud with and turned away from Aric. "Lizzy, I think we'll need more water when Taryn and Griff come back. Why don't you fill the buckets one more time?"

Lizzy jerked like she had forgotten anyone else was in the room. With a nod, she picked up the buckets and left. The second she was gone, Rev whirled back around and stormed up to Aric.

"What do you think you're doing? I'm sorry about your Father, and I'm even sorrier we're stuck here! But that doesn't mean you can bring everyone down, too!" Rev stomped back to the tub of mud and began stirring it with a frenzy. "This may or may not work, but at least we haven't given up. If you want to give up, then do it quietly and keep your mouth shut."

Aric remembered a time when he would have gotten angry at Rev for speaking to him that way. But now her words did nothing. He had no energy to respond, no strength left to get respond.

He gulped back the tears as he thought of Father. He left to save Father and the kingdom, and he had failed. He sat on Lizzy's bed, wanting the others to ignore any tears they might see.

Rev paused and watched him for a minute. He didn't dare look at her. She moved towards him.

"Aric," she said softly. "I'm sorry."

He shook his head. He didn't want sympathy, for he wouldn't be able to hold it together if they showed any kind of compassion. He didn't want to talk about it. He wanted to be alone.

Thankfully, Taryn and Griff flew in again with buckets heaped with dirt in each hand. They didn't notice the silence or lack of activity as they dumped the buckets into the tub.

"That should do it," Taryn nodded. He quickly put down the empty buckets beside the tub. "Maybe a little more water."

"Lizzy went to get some." Rev turned to the tub. "We didn't want to make it too runny."

Lizzy appeared with two pails of water and dumped them in with the dirt. It looked like she'd been crying, but her face was now dry. She didn't say anything.

Taryn took the stick from Rev and stirred. "Anyone think of anything else to do?"

Aric wasn't included in the question. It was like they had a silent agreement to leave him alone. A part of him felt awful about giving up. He should have been the one to try every idea, but a large part of him didn't care. It hurt too badly to fail.

Taryn waited a minute, but no one said anything. He cleared his throat. "Okay, then. Let's get Kai into the tub."

CHAPTER EIGHTY-FOUR

A Stick and A Sword

Kai felt like his legs were going to collapse as he pushed away from the window and took another step closer to Belial. His arm shook so hard that the sword was waving like a branch in a strong wind. He took a shallow breath and shuffled forward.

Belial still hadn't noticed him. *Please, Adoyni, please. Let me kill him so it's all over.* He was only three steps away from striking. He gripped the hilt harder, trying to still his arms enough to make an efficient strike.

He pulled back the blade and hobbled forward. Taking a deep breath, he let out a yell as he swung at Belial's neck.

Belial leaped from his chair and pulled out a staff that was sitting hidden underneath his desk. He jumped sideways, away from Kai's reach. His face was taut with rage.

"Die!" he yelled at Kai. "Get it over with! I'm sick of waiting for you to give up! You're nothing. When you die, everyone will be glad because you're such a failure!"

His weapon's a staff? What could a stick do against a sword? Kai smiled. "Maybe I have failed at everything. Maybe all my friends will be glad when I die, but I'll kill you."

"You are too weak. You can barely hold your sword." Belial backed away from Kai. "Besides, all I have to do is wait you out. It'll be any second now, and you will be mine."

"NO! I WON'T LET YOU TAKE ME!"

Kai rushed Belial although it felt like he was moving in slow motion. Belial blocked the first strike and backed away, circling around his desk. Kai stumbled, caught himself on the corner of the desk, and followed him.

"You want to fight?" Belial mocked. "The exertion will probably only make you change faster. Come on, stable boy. Show me what you've got. Maybe I'll tell your Mom how you begged for mercy."

Kai yelled, unable to form words. He caught up with Belial and struck low. He knew that he was barely moving and longed for the speed that he had when he fought the Seeker. *Why isn't Adoyni helping?* "This time I'll cut your head off!"

He closed the gap and attacked Belial with all the strength he had left. The hilt twisted in his sweaty hand, but it flew past Belial's block and the flat of the blade struck him in the thigh.

Belial yelped with surprise and jumped back. His foot caught on a corner of a rug that had flipped up. He fell through the air and landed on his back.

Kai rushed at Belial's prone form on the floor. Belial's eyes were closed and he didn't move. Kai used the desk as a crutch until he reached the end, then he lurched forward, his feet tripping over each other in his exhaustion.

His sword blade fell down toward Belial's neck. At the last possible second, Belial's eyes snapped open and his staff flew up to block the blade. Kai yelled in anger as Belial easily stopped the strike and pushed him back.

Belial rolled away and flipped up to his feet. He spoke a word that Kai couldn't hear. The staff transformed into a whip with long strips of leather hanging from the handle. Glass and sharp objects were woven into each strand. Belial snapped the whip off to the side. The room filled with the sound of popping.

Kai held his ground, unsure of what to do. *Alyn only showed me how to fight another person with one blade. How do I fight nine things at once?* Belial snapped the strands again.

Kai charged. He had no strategy. Perhaps he could survive the whip and manage to take Belial down. It only mattered if Belial died. He feinted left and quickly changed his thrust to the right. But before he got close, Belial smoothly adjusted and cracked the whip.

The long strands wrapped around Kai's leg before he could react. He yelled as the glass cut deep through his breeches and into his skin. When he glanced down, he saw large stripes of blood where the whip had been.

Why didn't Adoyni do anything? He tried to force himself to move lightning fast like when he dueled Alyn, but it never happened. He was fighting alone. Adoyni had left him to deal with

Belial on his own, and yet he knew that he didn't
have the strength even when he was at his best. He
was completely alone.

Kai backed up until he ran into the table. He
used it for support as Belial struck with the whip
again and again. He flayed widely with the sword,
hoping to at least defend himself.

The strands of the whip tangled around his
right arm and cut deeply in his flesh. He yanked
free, leaving trails of blood where his shirt was cut
away, and twisted. His sword flew through the air
and clattered to the floor as he tried to block his
body with his other arm.

The whipping stopped as a new torture began.
It felt like flames were climbing up his right leg
although he couldn't see any fire. He slammed
back onto the table and yelled in agony as it began
to take over his whole body. *What was Belial doing
now? Am I becoming an Unwanted now?* There
was no answer as he continued to writhe in pain.

***

Taryn stood beside Kai's bed and looked down
at his friend. Kai's body was wasting away. The
white skin looked gaunt and pinched like he was
starving, even though Taryn knew they had given
him broth. Already the veins were starting to show
in his hands and arms. Kai twitched and moaned
in his restless sleep.

Taryn wanted to think of Faelon as mean and cold, but it wouldn't be much longer until the disease took over and Kai was no more. Taryn hesitated, though, despite his urgency to throw Kai into his mud bath. *Something's missing. There's something else that we need.*

It came to Taryn in a flash. "Prayer!" He pointed to Lizzy. "That's what Kai and I did in the desert when you needed healing. We need to pray first."

They nodded in agreement and closed their eyes. He cleared his throat. *Am I supposed to do it? I don't know the right words.* But everything he had read in the wordless book spoke of faith before healing. It wasn't the words. It was faith.

He cleared his throat again and shut his eyes, wishing that he didn't feel like a complete idiot. "Uh, Adoyni, You probably know already that Kai is really sick with this dumb disease." He paused. *Since Adoyni is God, He knows everything. Why am I telling Him this and wasting time?* He tried to focus on the task of praying. "We think we know what You want us to do to help heal him, but we can't do it without You. You are the one that has to heal Him. Please help him come back to us."

Lizzy sniffed.

Taryn cleared his throat and tried to think of something else to say. "Thank You for all you have done already. Amen."

Taryn waited a minute and watched the pale skin on Kai's right arm. *Maybe it will turn. Maybe Adoyni will heal him right now.* But there was no change. He glanced at the girls. "Ready?"

They nodded. He took Kai's right arm and leg as they split the weight between them. As they lifted Kai from the bed, his eyes snapped open.

"NO! I WON'T LET YOU TAKE ME!"

In pure shock, they dropped Kai halfway back onto the bed. His eyes remained open, but he stared into blank space and didn't seem to see them. Taryn felt a jolt of terror when he saw that Kai's eyes, normally blue, were as black as night.

"What was that about?" Lizzy asked quietly. "He hasn't said anything for a long time."

"I don't know," Taryn said shortly. "But we're taking him to the tub. No matter what he says. Remember he doesn't know what he's doing or saying. Get him in it."

They started again. Kai remained quiet this time, but as they shuffled closer to the tub, he struggled. He twisted and turned so violently that Lizzy dropped his left arm. Kai used his freedom and began beating Taryn.

Taryn tried to avoid the blows, but he couldn't move much without losing his hold. Kai's fist slammed into his jaw and his head snapped back. "Get...a hold...of...him!" Taryn ordered between blows to his face and chest.

Griff leaped from where he was waiting with a bucket beside the tub and helped Lizzy grab Kai's arm. Together they held on tightly as they started to inch their way to the tub. Kai thrashed harder in his rage.

Taryn's arms began to burn as they crossed the room to the tub. He wanted to set Kai down on the floor and rest, but after the violent attack from one arm, he didn't think they'd be able to control him again.

As they reached the tub, Kai's struggling intensified. To make matters worse, Kai screamed as loudly as he could. Sometimes Taryn could catch a word or two, but it was mostly gibberish. They inched around the tub so Kai was above the mud.

"Get him in!" Taryn yelled. He lost hold of Kai's leg and it plopped in the mud.

"NO!" Kai's scream returned. The word was a roar of pure pain. "IT BURNS!"

"Get him out! Quickly!" Rev ordered. "It's not working."

Taryn felt his heart drop as he attempted to recover the hold he had on Kai's leg. Rev was right. Kai was too violent, too strong, for the mud to be working. He grabbed Kai's pants and began to pull it out of the mud.

"Wait!" Aric yelled over Kai. He leapt from the bed and ran to them. "Put him back in!"

"It's hurting him!" Lizzy shouted back.

"Nothing else has done anything to him. Something about that mud hurts him. Perhaps it's working!" Aric grabbed Kai's shoulders. "Put him in! Now!"

They dropped Kai in the mud tub. Mud splattered over them as Kai frantically tried to escape the tub. Aric gripped Kai's shoulders tightly and pressed down. Kai continued to resist and yell as Aric was hit in the face with a glob of mud.

"Grab hold and get ready to push him into the mud," Aric said loudly. "All at once. So he's completely submersed. Ready? One, two." He paused and looked at Kai. "And three."

*** *

Kai collapsed to the floor and thrashed violently in the effort to find relief from the pain. Nothing worked as the burning continued up from his legs to his abdomen and then up to his chest. He could barely breathe between the shrieks that were coming from his mouth.

Through his anguish, he noticed that Belial had stepped back and watched as if confused. Kai knew that he wasn't on fire although it felt like it. Were they burning his body in Merrihaven?

He wanted the pain to stop. He wanted this to be all over and have one moment of happiness. He was sick of the dark, the pain, and the loneliness.

Loneliness. Mom talked about loneliness when they first moved into Northbridge after Dad's accident. He had lost all his friends in the move, but that wasn't a surprise. Even if they had stayed where they were, no one would talk to them since Dad wasn't a jockey anymore.

He left for his first day of work at the track certain that he would catch up with his friends, but they stared at him and walked by without a word. He came home that first day depressed and lonely.

Mom saw it when no one else did. As he helped her clean up dinner, she paused with her hands in the soapy water.

"You know what one of my favorite promises from Adoyni is?"

He didn't bother to respond as he handed her the last of the dirty plates.

"Do not fear, for I am with you; do not be dismayed, for I am your God. I will strengthen you and help you; I will uphold you with my righteous right hand."

Kai thought about those words as he lay on the stone floor with Belial watching him. Adoyni was with him. He didn't need to fear or despair. In every part of the hallway, Adoyni was there, giving strength to continue and hope to take one more step. It was so black that it didn't feel like it, but Adoyni was still beside him. Perhaps the disease was the only way to get him close enough to Belial to kill him.

Help me not to give into the blackness, Adoyni. Help me know what you want me to do and give me the strength to do it. He thought about praying for Lizzy, Taryn, and his family, but he figured he could ask Adoyni face to face to protect them in a few minutes.

He spoke the words softly. "Do not fear, for I am with you. I will strengthen you and help you." *Oh, I need your strength and help now!*

As he repeated the words Mom taught him, the pain eased enough that he felt like he could get to his feet. His legs shook, but he found he could stand.

"Do not be dismayed, for I am your God. I will uphold you with my righteous right hand." *Uphold me, Adoyni, because I can barely stand.*

Belial hadn't moved in the time it took him to get back onto his feet. He studied Kai intently, waiting patiently for Kai to get to his feet. The leer on his face radiated victory, like he thought the battle was over and Kai was soon going to be his slave.

I don't think so. Not if I have a say to any of this. Knowing Adoyni was with him gave him the ability to take a step forward. He was going to kill Belial. Then he could die without any regrets, knowing that Adoyni had taken him on this torturous journey for a reason.

He glanced around him. His sword was too far away to get with the way his legs were shaking. There was nothing else he could use as a weapon. Without pausing, he threw himself at Belial with only his bare hands.

Belial leaped backwards, surprise and worry showing on his face. He tripped over his long cloak, stumbled, and fell on his back. His head made a loud cracking sound as it slammed into the stone floor. He didn't move.

Kai lurched to a stop. Belial had pulled this trick once before. He searched for anything that would be a weapon. The whip was flung on the other side of Belial. He disregarded it and grabbed one of the massive books sprawled on the table. *Please, Adoyni, let me kill him.*

He hobbled up to Belial who lay completely still. A small pool of blood was gathering underneath Belial's hair. He watched, strangely fascinated at the reminder that Belial bled like other people. He seemed so cold and superior.

The book was weighing him down as he struggled to hold it in both hands. He stood at Belial's head. *What was I thinking? A book isn't going to kill him.* He snarled and swung the book at Belial to knock him out.

The bulky book almost dropped out of his hands as it flew through the air. He let it slam into Belial's face, feeling nothing but cold indifference. The book smashed onto Belial's nose and slid to the floor.

"Guess books are good for something," Kai said, but the words were hard to form and get out of his mouth. "Taryn was right."

He watched blood dribble out of Belial's nose and wished he could've told Taryn that he had finally found books useful. *I wonder if he'd laugh or get mad at me. Probably mad that I didn't respect some precious old papers.* He snorted although he didn't feel like laughing.

The burning grew stronger as it reached his chest. There wasn't much time left. He limped to his sword, half expecting Belial to leap to his feet and attack with more sorcery. But Belial never stirred.

Bending over to retrieve his sword caused more agony than he expected, but he reached the hilt and shuffled to Belial. As he got closer, he started laughing even though the burning was over his whole body. He was going to do it! *Thank you, Adoyni! Now my family will be safe.* He drew the sword back and swung. He wished Belial's eyes would open so he'd know that Kai was the one to kill him.

But as the blade was falling to Belial's throat, the fire stopped burning his flesh and made its way inside. He felt it lick its way through his mouth, spread through his brain, travel down his throat, and consume every part of him.

He fell to the floor, convulsing, every part of him shaking and quaking. He couldn't stop the shrieks that sounded like they belonged to an animal being tortured. He saw Belial get to his feet, but there was nothing Kai could do.

He had failed again. He lost his chance of killing Belial. He didn't care anymore. All he wanted was for the pain to stop.

Belial didn't even bother to collect his whip as he approached Kai and watched with a big smile on his bloody face. He waited until there was a break between the screams and spoke.

"And so you become mine."

CHAPTER EIGHT-FIVE

Turning

Aric pressed down hard on Kai's shoulders, holding him deep in the tub. He was up to his elbows in the mud. Glancing up, he saw Rev, Lizzy and Taryn were pushing Kai deep down in the tub as well.

But how long does he need to stay under? Did Kai actually hear me when I told him to take a deep breath? What if we drown him in mud?

As if Kai could hear his thoughts, he stopped fighting and went limp. He let up on the pressure, but Kai didn't respond.

"He's dead." Rev pulled her hands out of the mud. "I knew we shouldn't have done that. He was yelling like we were killing him."

Her voice was getting angrier by the second as she turned to Aric. "What have you done?"

"What have *I* done?" Aric yelled back. "This wasn't even my idea!"

"Pull him out!" Lizzy broke in, her voice loud and harsh. "Maybe it's not too late."

Aric hastily found Kai's shirt in the mud and heaved his head out of the tub. As Kai's head surfaced, it fell forward at an awkward angle. Rev leaned forward and put her hand under his nose.

"He's not breathing!" she panicked.

Taryn groaned in frustration. "We held him under too long! Of all the idiotic, stupid things to do! We killed him!"

He smacked Kai's back in frustration as if to prove his point.

***

Kai noticed the room going black as he squirmed on the carpet. Belial knelt down beside him.

"The last thing you'll see as a human is my face. Your precious Mom will die a slow and horrible death in my mines. Rhiana is my little pet, and Shona is my slave. Your Dad?" Belail started laughing before he continued.

"Who really cares about that helpless cripple? He'll starve to death as he begs on the streets. And you will be the death of the Archippi. You haven't failed at all. You've done exactly what I wanted you to do."

Kai tried to yell his protests to Belial, but he could no longer form words. The burning slowly faded away as the room grew blacker. The last thing he saw was Belial's sneer.

He couldn't fight it anymore, and he stopped struggling as he was overcome.

***

Aric hit Kai's back, only to see him fall forward. He grabbed Kai's shirt and pulled him upright again. All the frustration he suppressed inside erupted. He smacked Kai on the back as hard as he could. Lizzy shrieked in protest.

Kai jerked forward with the blow, and glob of mud slid out of his mouth. The cave fell silent as they watched him for any sign of life. Then Kai shuddered and took a shallow breath.

"Is he...did he...?" Lizzy began but didn't finish.

Everyone knew what she was going to ask, but no one wanted to answer.

Aric felt the smallest gleam of hope begin although he refused to give it any credence yet. He was too ready to believe the worst and give up on miracles.

Kai breathed again, a deep ragged breath that seemed to catch and stop as it slid down his nose and into his lungs.

"Ow!" Taryn yelled. Everyone else jumped. He shook his hand free from Kai's grip and held it with his left hand. "He was gripping my hand really tight."

Kai took another deep breath like a swimmer preparing for a long distance under water. "Die, you worthless piece of garbage!" He yelled although his voice was weak and scratchy.

"Kai!" Lizzy's voice held a note of reprimand.

Before anyone could say anything else, Kai opened his eyes and began thrashing in the mud. "Where is it?" He was shouting. "Where'd it go? Where am I?"

With strength he shouldn't have had, he pushed himself out of the tub and stood panting beside it. Aric leapt back with his hand on his sword.

Why didn't I think Kai might lose his mind? If he becomes violent with this disease, we have little to control him or defend ourselves with!

Aric slowly began to back up to the packs of supplies and tried to catch the others' eyes to warn them to stay away. They were transfixed on Kai as he continued yelling.

"Where is my sword?" He demanded loudly. "What did you do with it now? Where's Belial? Don't tell me that he's gone. I had him. I had him!"

Rev held up a hand in an effort to calm him. "It's right here. We'll get it for you. Calm down."

"Don't you dare give him that," Aric ordered. "You don't know what he'd do with it."

He could read surprise, confusion and even anger in their faces. His own irritation grew. *Are they questioning me?*

They were so eager to heal Kai, but now that he was, would they ignore him and do anything Kai said? But he was the Prince. He shifted on his feet.

Lizzy said their weapons were gifts from a Sentinel. Were the three of them really related to the Slayers?

If so, what did that mean for the crown which had to be worn by a descendant of a Slayer as commanded by Adoyni?

He hid the horrible thoughts in his head and forced a grin. "Let's make sure he's really him before we give him a sword."

He hoped everything was going to be okay, but he was still concerned. He could feel the crystal he had taken from Taryn in his pocket, a burning reminder of Belial and his magic. He wanted to destroy it.

What he wanted even more was to get back to Eltiria, take care of his father, and begin to live as a Prince of Adoyni should. But it already felt like it was too late and he had missed his chance to help his people.

***

Lizzy couldn't understand Aric. Why wasn't he happy? They had done it! They had found the key to curing the disease that plagued Eltiria. For her, this was better than purifying the water. And most importantly, Kai was cured.

But she could tell by the tightening around Aric's blue eyes and the guarded expression on his face that he wasn't happy.

"His eyes," Rev broke in. "Look at his eyes."

Lizzy turned back to Kai and realized Rev was right. Kai's face was caked with drying mud, but his eyes were a brilliant blue, like when she first met Kai in the meadow with Eladar so long ago. The small ray of hope burst into full gleam as bright as the sun.

She whipped around and opened the large pack that held the weapons Alyn had given them. Pulling out Kai's scabbard, she ignored Aric's protests and returned to push the blade in his hands.

Kai seized the hilt with trembling hands. His knuckles showed white through the mud. He took another deep breath before drawing the sword.

"Please, Adoyni, let this be over," he whispered.

Kai slowly pulled the blade from the scabbard like he didn't really want to draw it. He waited until it was completely free before looking down. It was almost like he was dreading what he might see.

When he finally glanced at it, he heaved a big sigh. "Is it over? Can it really be over?" He started to laugh although the mirth had more panic than amusement to it. "It says *Surrender!* Look! Surrender!" He stopped and turned to Taryn. "What chore did Lizzy make you do after Eladar left?"

Taryn blinked, obviously confused by Kai's question. "I didn't...wait. She made me load and unload Minnie every day, when I could've been doing something more valuable with my time, like studying."

"You needed to learn how to take care of yourself, you idiot!" Lizzy felt her cheeks grow hot with the memory of the old argument. "You couldn't even light a fire!"

Kai held up his hand to stop Lizzy's tirade. "And what was Taryn's favorite meal?"

"He didn't like anything." Lizzy was confused. "He complained about everything." She grinned. "Oh, I know what you mean. Squirrel! Squirrel was definitely his favorite meal!"

She laughed, too happy to contain her joy anymore. Kai was better, and the disease was cured!

When they returned to Eltiria, she wasn't going to waste her time trying to make Mother love her. She was going to help every single person she met get cured from that horrible disease.

It was time to stop focusing on the negative and start letting Adoyni use her to make the world better.

Kai dropped his sword. It clattered to the ground unheeded as Kai let out a groan. "Then you *are* real! Why in all the blazing barns did you bring me back right then? Couldn't you have waited a few more seconds? You ruined everything!"

***

Taryn couldn't believe what Kai said. *Blazing barns? And here he is, thinking about himself again. Doesn't he care what we've done? Does he even realize how we struggled to keep him alive?*

Taryn broke the silence. "What are you talking about?"

"I was in Northbridge with Belial." Kai answered Taryn. "I was fighting him. A couple more seconds, and I would've killed him. But then you all decided to heal me right at that moment and ruined it all."

"I don't know who you think you are, but I've fought Belial, and I don't think you could defeat him," Aric argued.

Kai looked him up and down. "Maybe you don't know how to fight very well."

Lizzy gasped. "Kai, this is Prince Aric."

"The lost Prince!" Kai grinned. "Well, it looks like you have been found, Your Highness. How are we getting back to Eltiria?"

"We're stuck until the King calls us back." Taryn spoke up.

"Only he's about to die and Belial is about to take the throne, so that will never happen," Lizzy said quietly.

Out of the corner of his eye, Taryn caught Aric shifting like he was going to say something. He had that same guarded expression on his face like he did when the Archippi came back with their news of his father.

Kai rubbed his hand over his eyes, spreading the dirt around. His blue eyes started to twinkle with mischief. He wiped all the mud from his shirt onto his hand.

Before Lizzy could react, he grabbed her arm and smeared the muck over her face. She screamed and pushed him away, but instead of retaliating, she flung bits of mud in Taryn's direction.

Kai burst out laughing and gathered Lizzy in a bear hug. Lizzy pushed him away with mild protests that he was smearing mud all over her. He turned to Taryn and punched him in the shoulder. Taryn winced. Kai chuckled and gave him a one-armed hug.

"It is good to see you guys. I didn't think I'd ever see you again." His laughter vanished. "But it's not over. What's he going to do to my family now? We've got to get back right away!"

Taryn tried wiping off the sludge Kai left behind. "We won't be going anywhere." He knew his voice held a trace of bitterness.

Kai glanced at the others in the room. "Who are you? More lost royalty?"

The girl with the hair shook her head with a beautiful smile. "I'm Reveka Turow, daughter of Melchior Turow, Lord of Shiel, but you can call me Rev. This is Griffen. It's awfully good to see you on your feet, but I am sorry about the mud." Rev flushed slightly.

Kai winked at her. "I'd shake your hand, but I don't think you want to get muddier. Let's get clean before we head to Eltiria."

"What was happening to you?" Taryn had to ask.

Kai shook his head. "I don't know. Belial said that my soul was being torn from my body."

"Is that possible?" Lizzy looked horrified.

"I don't know," Kai sighed. "But whatever it was, that was the worst thing I've ever gone through. I plan to find out when we get back."

"We won't be going back," Aric answered in a low tone. "The Archippi won't take us."

"Ridiculous!" Kai responded quickly with a confident shake of his head. "Belial is going to destroy all of Eltiria. Besides that, he's holding my family hostage. Surely you don't want that to happen!"

"Of course I don't want that to happen!" Aric yelled. "But I don't see what we can do about it. They refuse to do anything to help us. I don't know what else to do!"

Kai flexed his hands, and Taryn caught a glimpse of them shaking before Kai shoved them into his pockets.

What did that disease do to him? Is he not completely better?

Now that Taryn was watching for it, he saw Kai's face and voice were hard, like he'd been through a blacksmith's anvil.

But what had he been shaped into?

Taryn knew he should be celebrating. Kai was cured of the terrible plague on Eltiria. Father would be so proud his son was the one to find the cure of the disease.

But he had to get back and find Nighthawk. Surely she wasn't evil like everyone kept saying. He had to hear from her that she was his mother. And he had to know the reasons for what she had done.

While he longed to know more about being a Son of Adoyni, he really needed to get some answers from Mom.

But as he watched Kai, he felt a deep sense of misgiving.

Was he completely cured?

***

Kai's knees shook as he forced himself to stand up. He wanted to rest, but he wouldn't let himself. Even though he was worn out, he wasn't going to stop until Belial was dead. He worried about the hate that sprung up when he thought of Belial and the other dark emotions roiling through him. But he was more worried about his family. He'd stop at nothing to save them.

He tried to think, but it was so hard. His head was foggy, and he felt like he couldn't discern what was real or not. It didn't help to have Rev sitting there. He hadn't ever met any girl that was so pretty. *Was she repulsed by the fact he had almost become an Unwanted?* By her friendly smile, she didn't seem to be horrified by what he had been through.

It didn't make anything easier having Aric glaring at him, either. But he didn't care. Kai wasn't going to wait around for him to do something because he was the Prince. His family was down there, being corrupted by Belial, and he was going to go rescue them before they were hurt anymore.

Kai tried to hide his shaking hands in his pockets, but he had a feeling that everyone noticed. He repeated the words in his head again.

So do not fear, for I am with you; do not be dismayed, for I am your God. I will strengthen you

*and help you; I will uphold you with my righteous
right hand.*

Adoyni's plan was not for him to kill Belial, but
there had to be a reason for his suffering.

He glanced at his sword on the ground with
the word *Surrender* written on it. He picked it up
and wished that he had managed to kill Belial.
And yet, Adoyni had a plan. He would wait for
Adoyni's perfect timing.

With the cold steel in his hands, he promised
himself that he'd make Belial pay for every pain he
had inflicted, and he'd free Rhiana from the
enchantment Nighthawk had used to enslave her.
He was no longer a weak stable boy. He was
Adoyni's warrior. It was time to fight.

At least they were together again. Whether he
was their leader or Aric, he knew that being with
friends was better than fighting alone. If he had
almost killed Belial on his own, then together with
Taryn and Lizzy, they might have a chance.

He breathed a prayer of thanksgiving to Adoyni
that he had made the right choice to continue
through the darkness and that his friends had
never given up on him. Belial had taken a lot away,
but he didn't have the power to take away
friendship.

"Eladar told us to stand firm. I say it's time to
fight." He slid his sword into its scabbard
vehemently. "Get ready to go. I know what will
change their minds."

REDIRECTION

---

*'Many are the plans in a man's heart,
but it is the Lord's purpose that prevails."*
~Proverbs 19:21

Jehun fled Elba Isle, hoping that sheer speed would blow away the wickedness that clung to him. He'd never been so happy to leave a place. As the distance widened, his panic and fright ebbed. He slowed until he was barely moving

He realized with a shock that he knew more than even Belial did. He knew where Seiten's army was. The Sentinels believed the army existed, but even after years of searching, they had never found it. Now they were considered deluded. Close-minded. Even foolish.

But Jehun knew that they were right. Seiten had been clever. He'd been extremely cunning in his choice. Knowing where the army was, he could now feel their vile intentions oozing out of them like water that always finds a crack to drip through solid rock. The earth around the army was corrupted and poisoned, but it was so subtle that no one, not even Jehun himself, had questioned it.

Belial knew the army existed, or at least he hoped it did. But he had made one critical mistake. He lied to Jehun and then sent him on a mission to retrieve something he desperately needed to overwhelm the Archippi and any humans that still followed Adoyni.

Jehun knew the lava of the inner core was overflowing and leaking faster than Jehun had ever let it go. But he chose to ignore that. There were more important things to take care of right now.

He knew what Belial needed. And he knew exactly what he was going to do with it.

TO BE CONTINUED

Want to Know What Happens Next?

Go to www.vickivlucas.com and sign up for the newsletter. I will let you know when new releases are out, information on contests, and much more.

You Can Help!

If you loved the book, I would really appreciate a short review on Amazon or Goodreads.

Your help in spreading the word is gratefully appreciated. Reviews make a huge difference to helping new readers find the series.

PRONUNCIATION GUIDE

People

Kai: k-eye. Sounds like *bye*.
Shona: SHOW-na
Rhiana: RE-an-a
Rica: RE-ka
Lizzy: Li-zee. Sounds like *dizzy*.
Zoria: zor-I-a
Belial: bee-LIE-al
Taryn: TEAR-n
Mischa: MISH-ka
Nighthawk Nephesus: Nef-e-sus
Timo: Tea-mo
Tadd Teschner: Tad Tesh-ner
Eladar: EL-a-dar
Alyn: AL-an
Lesu: LEE-sue
Aric: A-ric. Sounds like Eric.
Patrin: PA-trin
Griffen: GRIFF-en
Fariel: FAIR-e-el
Straton: Strat-on
Cedrik: CE-drik
Reveka: RE-va-ka. Sounds like Rebeka.

Places

Eltiria: el-TEAR-e-a
Albia: AL-be-a
Shalock Stables: Sha-lock
Shiel: she-ll. Like *shield* without the d.

Beings

Adoyni: add-DA-nigh
Seiten: see-TEN
Foehn: föhn. Sounds like *phone.*
Jehun: JAY-hoon
Kedar: Ka-dar
Thalion: tha-le-on
Faelon: Fay-lon

Other

Archippos: arc-HE-pus
Archippi: arc-HE-pi
Norsaq: NOR-sack

A NOTE FROM VICKI

This book would not have been completed without the help of many people like my editors, my amazing cover designer, and my Mom who taught me almost everything I know.

However, it was my husband who contributed the most. He encouraged me, never hesitated to tell me if an idea needed more thought, watched our daughter so that I could write, stopped talking when I got "hit" with a great thought and rushed off to capture it, lived with dirty dishes, meals uncooked, and laundry stacked high. He has edited, analyzed ideas, judged covers, managed my business, helped sell, and carried way too many heavy boxes filled with books. I could never have completed Rancid without him.

There is one more person I must thank – You! Thank you for reading Toxic and wanting the sequel so much that you kept pestering me about it. "Is it done yet?" is music to a writer's ear. Thank you for giving me a try. Thank you for coming along on the ride. Thank you for the gifts to inspire me. Thank you!

Finally, thank you to God, Who has given me much more than I deserve –forgiveness, love, a wonderful family, and so much more. I pray my words bring glory to You.

Enjoy the ride,
Vicki V. Lucas

ABOUT VICKI V. LUCAS

www.vickivlucas.com

vickivlucas@gmail.com

I have always struggled with the question "What are you going to be when you grow up?" I received my Bachelor's in Psychology with no desire to counsel people. I switched to Teaching English as a Second Language and obtained my Masters from Seattle Pacific University.

Teaching at universities and community colleges gave me eleven years of remarkable coworkers and unforgettable friends from many different countries. However, the distant mountains called, and I settled in Montana with my husband and my daughter. I have begun to write the stories I heard on the wind.

I love to hear what you have to say. Please visit my webpage to read my blog or send me an email. But if I don't respond very soon, just remember that I may be off in the lonely mountains.

Other Places:

FaceBook:
https://www.facebook.com/pages/Vicki-V-Lucas/296644940383708?ref=hl

Amazon:
http://www.amazon.com/Vicki-V.-Lucas/e/B006X7117U/ref=sr_ntt_srch_lnk_1?qid=1379971952&sr=8-1